Arskane watched with w————————————————————————
hey moved among. "Mountains—man made—that is what
ve see here. But why did the Old Ones love to huddle
ogether in such a fashion? Did they fear their own magic?
Vell, they died of it in the end, poor Old Ones."

Fors kicked at a loose stone. "They had such
nowledge—we are groping in the dark for only crumbs
f what they knew—"

"But they did not use all their learning for good!"
rskane indicated the ruins. "This city came out of their
rains and then was also destroyed by them. They built
nly to tear down again."

Fors' head snapped around. He had caught a whisper
f sound, a faint pattering. And had he, or had he not,
een the loathsome outline of a bloated rat body slipping
ito a shattered window? There were sounds among the
tones almost as if some thing—or things—were following
hem.

Lura's ears were flat to her skull, her eyes only battle
its. The big cat stood staring back along the track they
ad come, the tip of her tail quivering. Then the mare
wung up her head and gave a wild cry. Fors saw the dart
a the gaping wound which had torn open her throat.

"In—" Arskane's hand about his wrist jerked him into
cavern opening in the front of the highest tower. They
aused at the top of a ramp which led down into murky
hadows. Arskane pointed to the floor. Beaten in the dust
nd dried mud was a regular path of footprints—made by
eet too narrow—clawed feet! Lura backed away from that
ighway spitting and snarling.

So—they had not escaped but come straight into the
tronghold of the enemy! And it did not need the cry of
iumph from without, coming in shrill inhuman exultation,
o confirm that . . .

BAEN BOOKS by ANDRE NORTON

DARKNESS AND DAWN

ANDRE NORTON

DARKNESS AND DAWN

This is a work of fiction. All the characters and events portrayed in this book are fictional, and any resemblance to real people or incidents is purely coincidental.

A Baen Books Omnibus

Baen Publishing Enterprises
P.O. Box 1403
Riverdale, NY 10471
www.baen.com

ISBN: 0-7434-8831-8

Cover art by Bob Eggleton

First paperback printing, June 2004

Library of Congress Cataloging-in-Publication Number 2002038393

Distributed by Simon & Schuster
1230 Avenue of the Americas
New York, NY 10020

Production by Windhaven Press, Auburn, NH
Printed in the United States of America

CONTENTS

DAYBREAK—2250 A.D.

1

A Thief By Night

A night mist which was almost fog-thick still wrapped most of the Eyrie in a cottony curtain. Beads of moisture gathered on the watcher's bare arms and hide jerkin. He licked the wetness from his lips. But he made no move toward shelter, just as he had not during any of the long black hours behind him.

Hot anger had brought him up on this broken rock point above the village of his tribe. And something which was very close to real heartbreak kept him there. He propped a pointed chin—strong, cleft and stubborn—on the palm of a grimy hand and tried to pick out the buildings which made straight angles in the mist below.

Right before him, of course, was the Star Hall. And as he studied its rough stone walls, his lips drew tight in what was almost a noiseless snarl. To be one of the Star Men, honored by all the tribe, consecrated to the gathering and treasuring of knowledge, to the breaking

3

of new trails and the exploration of lost lands—he, Fors of the Puma Clan, had never dreamed of any other life. Up until the hour of the Council Fire last night he had kept on hoping that he would be given the right to enter the Hall. But he had been a child and a fool to so hope when all the signs had read just the opposite. For five years he had been passed over at the choosing of youths as if he did not exist. Why then should his merits suddenly become diamond-bright on the sixth occasion?

Only—his head dropped and his teeth clenched. Only—this was the last year—the very last year for him. Next year he would be over the age limit allowed a novice. When he was passed over last night—

Maybe—if his father had come back from that last exploring venture—If he himself didn't bear the stigma so plainly—His fingers clutched the thick hair on his head, tugging painfully as if he would have it all out by the roots. His hair was the worst! They might have forgotten about his night sight and too-keen hearing. He could have concealed those as soon as he learned how wrong it was to be different. But he could not hide the color of his close-cropped hair. And that had damned him from the day his father had brought him here. Other men had brown or black, or, at the worst, sun-bleached yellow, covering their heads. He had silver white, which showed to all men that he was a mutant, different from the rest of his clan. Mutant! Mutant!

For more than two hundred years—ever since the black days of chaos following the Great Blow-up, the nuclear war—that cry had been enough to condemn without trial. Fear caused it, the strong, instinctive fear of the whole race for anyone cursed with a different physique or unusual powers.

Ugly tales were told of what had happened to the mutants, those unfortunates born in the first year after

the Blow-up. Some tribes had taken drastic steps in
those days to see that the strain of human—or almost
human—lineage be kept pure.

Here in the Eyrie, far apart from the infection of
the bombed sectors, mutation had been almost
unknown. But he, Fors, had Plains' blood—tainted,
unclean—and, since he could remember at all, he had
never been allowed to put that fact from him.

While his father had lived it had not been so bad.
The other children had yelled at him and there had
been fights. But somehow, his father's confidence in
him had made even that seem natural. And in the
evenings, when they had shut out the rest of the Eyrie,
there had been long hours of learning to read and
write, to map and observe, the lore of the high trails
and the low. Even among the Star Men his father had
been a master instructor. And never had it appeared
doubtful to Langdon that his only son Fors would
follow him into the Star Hall.

So even after his father had failed to return from
a trip to the lowlands, Fors had been confident of the
future. He had made his weapons, the long bow now
lying beside him, the short stabbing sword, the hunting
knife—all with his own hands according to the Law.
He had learned the trails and had found Lura, his great
hunting cat—thus fulfilling all the conditions for the
Choosing. For five years he had come to the Fire each
season, with diminishing hope to be sure, and each time
to be ignored as if he did not exist. And now he was
too old to try again.

Tomorrow—no, today—he would have to lay aside
his weapons and obey the dictates of the Council. Their
verdict would be that he live on sufferance—which was
probably all a mutant could expect—as a worker in one
of the cave-sheltered Hydro farms.

No more schooling, no fifteen or twenty years of

roving the lowlands, with further honored years to look forward to as an instructor and guardian of knowledge—a Star Man, explorer of the wilderness existing in the land where the Great Blow-up had made a world hostile to man. He would have no part in tracing the old cities where forgotten knowledge might be discovered and brought back to the Eyrie, in mapping roads and trails, helping to bring light out of darkness. He couldn't surrender that dream to the will of the Council!

A low questioning sound came out of the dark and absently he answered with an assenting thought. A shadow detached itself from a jumble of rocks and crept on velvet feet, soft belly fur dragging on the moss, to him. Then a furred shoulder almost as wide as his own nudged against him and he dropped a hand to scratch behind pricked ears. Lura was impatient. All the wild scents of the woods were rich in her widened nostrils and she wanted to be on the trail. His hand on her head was a restraint she half resented.

Lura loved freedom. What service she gave was of her own choosing, after the manner of her kind. He had been so proud two years ago when the most beautifully marked kitten of Kanda's last litter had shown such a preference for his company. One day Jarl himself—the Star Captain—had commented on it. How that had raised Fors' hopes—but nothing had come of the incident, only Lura herself. He rubbed his hot cheek against the furry head raised to his. She made again the little questioning sound deep in her throat. She knew his unhappiness.

There was no sign of sunrise. Instead black clouds were gathering above the bald top of the Big Knob. It would be a stormy day and those below would keep within shelter. The moisture of the mist had become a drizzle and Lura was manifestly angry at his stubbornness in not going indoors. But if he went into any building of the Eyrie now it would be in surrender—a surrender to the loss of the life he had been born to lead, a surrender to all the whispers, the badge of shameful failure, to the stigma of being mutant—not as other men. And he could not do that— he couldn't!

If Langdon had stood before the Council last night—

Langdon! He could remember his father so vividly, the tall strong body, the high-held head with its bright, restless, seeking eyes above a tight mouth and sharp jaw. Only—Langdon's hair had been safely dark. It was from his unknown Plainswoman mother that Fors had that too-fair hair which branded him as one apart.

Langdon's shoulder bag with its star badge hung now in the treasure room of the Star Hall. It had been found with his battered body on the site of his last battle. A fight with the Beast Things seldom ended in victory for the mountaineers.

He had been on the track of a lost city when he had been killed. Not a "blue city," still forbidden to men if they wished to live, but a safe place without radiation which could be looted for the advantage of the Eyrie. For the hundredth time Fors wondered if his father's theory concerning the tattered bit of map was true—if a safe city did lie somewhere to the north on the edge of a great lake, ready and waiting for the man lucky and reckless enough to search it out.

"Ready and waiting—" Fors repeated the words aloud. Then his hand closed almost viciously on Lura's fur. She growled warningly at his roughness, but he did not hear her.

Why—the answer had been before him all along! Perhaps five years ago he could not have tried it— perhaps this eternal waiting and disappointment had been for the best after all. Because now he was ready—

he knew it! His strength and the ability to use it, his knowledge and his wits were all ready.

No light yet showed below. The clouds were prolonging the night. But his time of grace was short, he would have to move fast! The bow, the filled quiver, the sword, were hidden between two rocks. Lura crawled in beside them to wait, his unspoken suggestion agreeing with her own desires.

Fors crept down the twisted trail to the Eyrie and made for the back of the Star Hall. The bunks of the Star Men on duty were all in the forepart of the house; the storage room was almost directly before him. And luck was favoring him as it never had before, for the heavy shutter was not bolted or even completely closed as his exploring fingers discovered. After all—no one had ever dreamed of invading the Star Hall unasked.

Moving as noiselessly as Lura he swung over the high sill and stood breathing in a light flutter. To the ordinary man of the Eyrie the room would have been almost pitch dark. But, for once, Fors' mutant night sight was an aid. He could see the long table and the benches without difficulty, make out the line of pouches hanging on the far wall. These were his goal. His hand closed unerringly on one he had helped to pack many times. But when he lifted it from its hook he detached the gleaming bit of metal pinned to its strap.

To his father's papers and belongings he might prove some shadowy claim. But to that Star he had no right. His lips twisted in a bitter grimace as he laid the badge down on the edge of the long table before clambering back into the grayness of the outer world.

Now that the pouch swung from his shoulder he went openly to the storage house and selected a light blanket, a hunter's canteen and a bag of traveler's corn kept in readiness there. Then, reclaiming his weapons and the impatient Lura, he started off—not toward the narrow mountain valleys where all of his hunting had been done, but down toward the forbidden plains. A chill born of excitement rather than the bite of the rising wind roughened his skin, but his step was sure and confident as he hunted out the path blazed by Langdon more than ten years before, a path which was not watched by any station of the outpost guards.

Many times around the evening fires had the men of the Eyrie discussed the plains below and the strange world which had felt the force of the Great Blow-up and been turned into an alien, poisonous trap for any human not knowing its ways. Why, in the past twenty years even the Star Men had mapped only four cities, and one of them was "blue" and so forbidden.

They knew the traditions of the old times. But, Langdon had always insisted even while he was repeating the stories to Fors, they could not judge how much of this information had been warped and distorted by time. How could they be sure that they were of the same race as those who had lived before the Blow-up? The radiation sickness, which had cut the number of survivors in the Eyrie to less than half two years after the war, might well have altered the future generations. Surely the misshapen Beast Things must once have had a human origin—or had they? Men were playing with the very stuff of life before the Blow-up. And the Beast Things clung to the old cities where the worst mutations had occurred.

The men of the Eyrie had records to prove that their forefathers had been a small band of technicians and scientists engaged in some secret research, cut off from a world which disappeared so quickly. But there were the Plainsmen of the wide grasslands, also free from the taint of the beast, who had survived and now roamed with their herds.

And there might be others.

Who had started the nuclear war was unknown. Fors had once seen an old book containing jotted fragments of messages which had come out of the air through machines during a single horrible day. And these broken messages only babbled of the death of a world.

But that was all the men of the mountains knew of the last war. And while they fought ceaselessly to keep alive the old skills and learning there was so much, so very much, they no longer understood. They had old maps with pink and green, blue and yellow patches all carefully marked. But the pink and green, blue and yellow areas had had no defense against fire and death from the air and so had ceased to be. Only now could men, venturing out from their pockets of safety into the unknown, bring back bits of knowledge which they might piece together into history.

Somewhere, within a mile or so of the trail he had chosen, Fors knew that there was a section of pre-Blow-up road. And that might be followed by the cautious for about a day's journey north. He had seen and handled the various trophies brought back by his father and his father's comrades, but he had never actually traveled the old roads or sniffed the air of the lowlands for himself. His pace quickened to a lope and he did not even feel the steady pour of the rain which streamed across his body plastering even his blanket to him. Lura protested with every leap she made to keep pace with him, but she did not go back. The excitement which drew him on at such an unwary speed had spread to the always sensitive mind of the great cat who made her way through the underbrush with sinuous ease.

The old road was almost a disappointment when he stumbled out upon it. Once it must have had a smooth surface, but time, disuse, and the spreading greedy force of wild vegetation had seamed and broken it. Nevertheless it was a marvel to be examined closely by one who had never seen such footing before. Men had ridden on it once encased in machines. Fors knew that, he had seen pictures of such machines, but their fashioning was now a mystery. The men of the Eyrie knew facts about them, painfully dug out of the old books brought back from city lootings, but the materials and fuels for their production were now beyond hope of obtaining.

Lura did not like the roadway. She tried it with a cautious paw, sniffed at the upturned edge of a block, and went back to firm ground. But Fors stepped out on it boldly, walking the path of the Old Ones even when it would have been easier to take to the bush. It gave him an odd feeling of power to tread so. This stuff beneath his hide boots had been fashioned by those of his race who had been wiser and stronger and more learned. It was up to those of his breed to regain that lost wisdom.

"Ho, Lura!"

The cat paused at his exultant call and swung the dark brown mask of her face toward him. Then she meowed plaintively, conveying the thought that she was being greatly misused by this excursion into the dampness of an exceedingly unpleasant day.

She was beautiful indeed. Fors' feeling of good will and happiness grew within him as he watched her. Since he had left the last step of the mountain trail he had felt a curious sense of freedom and for the first time in his life he did not care about the color of his hair or feel that he must be inferior to the others of his clan. He had all his father had taught him well in mind, and in the pouch swinging at his side, his father's greatest secret. He had a long bow no other youth of his age could string, a bow of his own making. His sword was sharp and balanced to suit his hand alone. There was all the lower world before him and the best of companions to match his steps.

Lura licked at her wet fur and Fors caught a flash of—was it her thoughts or just emotion? None of the Eyrie dwellers had ever been able to decide how the great cats were able to communicate with the men they chose to honor with their company. Once there had been dogs to run with man—Fors had read of them. But the strange radiation sickness had been fatal to the dogs of the Eyrie and their breed had died out forever.

Because of that same plague the cats had changed. Small domestic animals of untamable independence had produced larger offspring with even quicker minds and greater strength. Mating with wild felines from the tainted plains had established the new mutation. The creature which now rubbed against Fors was the size of a mountain lion of pre-Blow-up days, but her thick fur was of a deep shade of cream, darkening on head, legs, and tail to a chocolate brown—after the coloring set by a Siamese ancestor first brought into the mountains by the wife of a research engineer. Her eyes were the deep sapphire blue of a true gem, but her claws were cruelly sharp and she was a master hunter.

That taste possessed her now as she drew Fors' attention to a patch of moist ground where the slot of a deer was deep marked. The trail was fresh—even as he studied it a bit of sand tumbled from the top into the hollow of the mark. Deer meat was good and he had few supplies. It might be worth turning aside. He need not speak to Lura—she knew his decision and was off on the trail at once. He padded after her with the noiseless woods walk he had learned so long before that he could not remember the lessons.

The trail led off at a right angle from the remains of the old road, across the tumbled line of a wall where old bricks protruded at crazy points from heaped earth and brush. Water from leaves and branches doused both hunters, gluing Fors' homespun leggings to his legs and squeezing into his boots.

He was puzzled. By the signs, the deer had been fleeing for its life and yet whatever menaced it had left no trace. But Fors was not afraid. He had never met any living thing, man or animal, which could stand against the force of his steel-tipped arrows or which he would have hesitated to face, short sword in hand.

Between the men of the mountains and the roving Plainsmen there was a truce. The Star Men often lived for periods of time in the skin-walled tents of the herders, exchanging knowledge of far places with those eternal wanderers. And his father had taken a wife among the outlanders. Of course, there was war to the death between the human kind and the Beast Things which skulked in the city ruins. But the latter had never been known to venture far from their dank, evil-smelling burrows in the shattered buildings, and certainly one need not fear meeting with them in this sort of open country! So he followed the trail with a certain reckless disregard.

The trail ended suddenly on the lip of a small gully. Some ten feet or so below, a stream—swollen by the rain—frothed around green-grown rocks. Lura was on her belly, pulling her body forward along the rim of the ravine. Fors dropped down and inched behind a bush. He knew better than to interfere with her skillful approach.

When the tip of her brown tail quivered he watched for a trembling of Lura's flat flanks which would signalize her spring. But instead the tail suddenly bristled and the shoulders hunched as if to put a brake upon muscles already tensed. He caught her message of bewilderment, of disgust and, yes, of fear.

He knew that he had better eyesight than almost all of the Eyrie men, that had been proved many times. But what had stopped Lura in her tracks was gone. True, upstream a bush still swayed as if something had just pushed past it. But the sound of the water covered any noise and although he strained—there was nothing to see.

Lura's ears lay flat against her skull and her eyes were slits of blazing rage. But beneath the rage Fors grasped another emotion—almost fear. The big cat had come across something strange and therefore suspect. Aroused by her message Fors lowered himself over the edge of the gully. Lura made no attempt to stop him. Whatever had troubled her was gone, but he was determined to see what traces it might have left in its passing.

The greenish stones of the river bank were sleek and slippery with spray, and twice he had to catch hurriedly at bushes to keep from falling into the stream. He got to his hands and knees to move across one rock and then he was at the edge of the bush which had fluttered.

A red pool, sticky but already being diluted by the rain and the spray, filled a clay hollow. He tasted it with the aid of a finger. Blood. Probably that of the deer they had been following.

Then, just beyond, he saw the spoor of the hunter that had brought it down. It was stamped boldly into the clay, deeply as if the creature that made it had balanced for a moment under a weight, perhaps the body of the deer. And it was too clear to mistake the outline—the print of a naked foot.

No man of the Eyrie, no Plainsman had left that track! It was narrow and the same width from heel to toe—as if the thing which had left it was completely flat-footed. The toes were much too long and skeleton-thin. Beyond their tips were indentations of—not nails—but what must be real claws!

Fors' skin crawled. It was unhealthy—that was the word which came into his mind as he stared at the track. He was glad—and then ashamed of that same gladness—that he had not seen the hunter in person.

Lura pushed past him. She tasted the blood with a dainty tongue and then lapped it once or twice before she came on to inspect his find. Again flattened ears and wrinkled, snarling lips gave voice to her opinion of the vanished hunter. Fors strung his bow for action. For the first time the chill of the day struck him. He shivered as a flood of water spouted at him over the rocks.

With more caution they went back up the slope. Lura showed no inclination to follow any trail the unknown hunter might have left and Fors did not suggest it to her. This wild world was Lura's real home and more than once the life of a Star Man had depended upon the instincts of his hunting cat. If Lura saw no reason to risk her skin downriver, he would abide by her choice.

They came back to the road. But now Fors used hunting craft and the trail-covering tricks which normally one kept only for the environs of a ruined city—those haunted places where death still lay in wait to strike down the unwary. It had stopped raining but the clouds did not lift.

Toward noon he brought down a fat bird Lura flushed out of a tangle of brush and they shared the raw flesh of the fowl equally.

It was close to dusk, shadows falling early because of the storm, when they came out upon a hill above the dead village the old road served.

2

Into the Midst of Yesterday

Even in the pre-Blow-up days when it had been lived in, the town must have been neither large nor impressive. But to Fors, who had never before seen any buildings but those of the Eyrie, it was utterly strange and even a bit frightening. The wild vegetation had made its claim and moldering houses were now only lumps under the greenery. One water-worn pier at the edge of the river which divided the town marked a bridge long since fallen away.

Fors hesitated on the heights above for several long minutes. There was a forbidding quality in that tangled wilderness below, a sort of moldy rankness rising on the evening wind from the hollow which cupped the ruins. Wind, storm and wild animals had had their way there too long.

On the road to one side was a heap of rusted metal which he thought must be the remains of a car such as the men of the old days had used for transportation. Even then it must have been an old one. Because just before the Blow-up they had perfected another type, with an entirely different propulsion system and non-metallic bodies. Sometimes Star Men had found those almost intact. He skirted the wreckage and, keeping to the thread of battered road, went down into the town.

Lura trotted beside him, her head high as she tested each passing breeze for scent. Quail took flight into the tall grass and somewhere a cock pheasant called. Twice the scut of a rabbit showed white and clear against the green.

There were flowers in that tangle, defending themselves with hooked thorns, the twining stems which bore them looped and relooped into barriers he could not crash through. And all at once the setting sun broke between cloud lines to bring their scarlet petals into angry life. Insects chirped in the grass. The storm was over.

The travelers pushed through into an open space bordered on all sides by crumbling mounds of buildings. From somewhere came the sound of water and Fors beat a path through the rank shrubbery to where a trickle of stream fed a man-made basin.

In the lowlands water must always be suspect—he knew that. But the clear stream before him was much more appetizing than the musty stuff which had sloshed all day in the canteen at his belt. Lura lapped it unafraid, shaking her head to free her whiskers from stray drops. So he dared to cup up a palmful and sip it gingerly.

The pool lay directly before a freak formation of rocks which might have once been heaped up to form a cave. And the mat of leaves which had collected inside there was dry. He crept in. Surely there would be no danger in camping here. One never slept in any of the old houses, of course. There was no way of telling whether the ghosts of ancient disease still lingered in their rottenness. Men had died from that carelessness. But here—in among the leaves he saw white bones. Some other hunter—a four-footed one—had already dined.

Fors kicked out the refuse and went prospecting for wood not too sodden to burn. There were places in and among the clustered rocks where winds had piled branches and he returned to the cave with one, then two, and finally three armloads, which he piled within reaching distance.

Out in the plains fire could be an enemy as well as a friend. A carelessly tended blaze in the wide grasslands might start one of the oceans of flame which would run for miles driving all living things before it. And in an enemy's country it was instant betrayal. So even when he had his small circle of sticks in place Fors hesitated, flint and steel in hand. There was the mysterious hunter—what if he were lurking now in the maze of the ruined town?

Yet both he and Lura were chilled and soaked by the rain. To sleep cold might mean illness to come. And, while he could stomach raw meat when he had to, he relished it broiled much more. In the end it was the thought of the meat which won over his caution, but even when a thread of flame arose from the center of his wheel of sticks, his hand still hovered ready to put it out. Then Lura came up to watch the flames and he knew that she would not be so at her ease if any danger threatened. Lura's eyes and nose were both infinitely better than his own.

Later, simply by freezing into a hunter's immobility by the pool, he was able to knock over three rabbits. Giving Lura two, he skinned and broiled the third. The setting sun was red and by the old signs he could hope for a clear day tomorrow. He licked his fingers, dabbled them in the water, and wiped them on a tuft of grass. Then for the first time that day he opened the pouch he had stolen before the dawn.

He knew what was inside, but this was the first time in years that he held in his hand again the sheaf of brittle old papers and read the words which had been carefully traced across them in his father's small, even script. Yes—he was humming a broken little tune—it *was* here, the scrap of map his father had treasured so—the one which showed the city to the north, a city which his father had hoped was safe and yet large enough to yield rich loot for the Eyrie.

But it was not easy to read his father's cryptic notes. Langdon had made them for his own use and Fors could only guess at the meaning of such directions as "snake river to the west of barrens," "Northeast of the wide forest" and all the rest. Landmarks on the old maps were now gone, or else so altered by time that a man might pass a turning point and never know it. As Fors frowned over the scrap which had led his father to his death he began to realize a little of the enormity of the task before him. Why, he didn't even know all the safe trails which had been blazed by the Star Men through the years, except by hearsay. And if he became lost—

His fingers tightened around the roll of precious papers. Lost in the lowlands! To wander off the trails—!

Silky fur pressed against him and a round head butted his ribs. Lura had caught that sudden nip of fear and was answering it in her own way. Fors' lungs filled slowly. The humid air of the lowlands lacked the keen bite of the mountain winds. But he was free and he was a man. To return to the Eyrie was to acknowledge defeat. What if he did lose himself down here? There was a whole wide land to make his own! Why, he could go on and on across it until he reached the salt sea which tradition said lay at the rim of the world. This whole land was his for the exploring!

He delved deeper into the bag on his knee. Besides the notes and the torn map he found the compass he had hoped would be there, a small wooden case containing pencils, a package of bandages and wound salve, two small surgical knives, and a roughly fashioned notebook—the daily record of a Star Man. But to his vast disappointment the entries there were merely a record of distances. On impulse he set down on one of the blank pages an account of his own day's travel, trying to make a drawing of the strange footprint. Then he repacked the pouch.

Lura stretched out on the leaf bed and he flopped down beside her, pulling the blanket over them both. It was twilight now. He pushed the sticks in toward the center of the fire so that the unburnt ends would be consumed. The soft rumble of the cat's purr as she washed her paws, biting at the spaces between her claws, made his eyes heavy. He flung an arm over her back and she favored him with a lick of her tongue. The rasp of it across his skin was the last thing he clearly remembered.

There were birds in the morning, a whole flock of them, and they did not approve of Lura. Their scolding cries brought Fors awake. He rubbed his eyes and looked out groggily at a gray world. Lura sat in the mouth of the cave, paying no attention to the chorus over her head. She yawned and looked back at Fors with some impatience.

He dragged himself out to join her and pulled off his roughly dried clothes before bathing in the pool. It was cold enough to set him sputtering and Lura withdrew to a safe distance. The birds flew away in a black flock. Fors dressed, lacing up his sleeveless jerkin and fastening his boots and belt with extra care.

A more experienced explorer would not have wasted time on the forgotten town. Long ago any useful loot it might have once contained had either been taken away or had moldered into rubbish. But it was the first dead place Fors had seen and he could not leave it without some examination. He followed the road around the square. Only one building still stood unharmed enough to allow entrance. Its stone walls were rank with ivy and moss, its empty windows blind. He shuffled through the dried leaves and grass which masked the broad flight of steps leading to its wide door.

There was the whir of disturbed grasshoppers in the leaves, as a wasp sang past. Lura pawed at something which lay just within the doorway. It rolled away into the dusk of the interior and they followed. Fors stopped to trace with an inquiring finger the letters on a bronze plate.

"First National Bank of Glentown."

He read the words aloud and they echoed hollowly down the long room, through the empty cage-like booths along the wall.

"First National Bank," he repeated. What was a bank? He had only a vague idea—some sort of a storage place. And this dead town must be Glentown— or once it had been Glentown.

Lura had found again her round toy and was batting it along the cracked flooring. It skidded to strike the base of one of the cages just in front of Fors. Round eyeholes stared up at him accusingly from a half-crushed skull. He stooped and picked it up to set it on the stone shelf. Dust arose in a thick puff. A pile of coins spun and jingled in all directions, their metallic tinkle clear.

There were lots of the coins here, all along the
shelves behind the cage fronts. He scooped up handfuls
and sent them rolling to amuse Lura. But they had no
value. A piece of good, rust-proof steel would be worth
the taking—not these. The darkness of the place began
to oppress him and no matter which way he turned
he thought he could feel the gaze of that empty skull.
He left, calling Lura to follow.

There was a dankness in the heart of this town,
the air here had the faint corruption of ancient
decay, mixed with the fresher scent of rotting wood
and moldering vegetation. He wrinkled his nose
against it and pushed on down a choked street,
climbing over piles of rubble, heading toward the
river. That stream had to be crossed some way if
he were to travel straight to the goal his father had
mapped. It would be easy for him to swim the thick
brownish water, although it was still roily from the
storm, but he knew that Lura would not willingly
venture in. He was certainly not going to leave her
behind.

Fors struck out east along the bank above the flood.
A raft of some sort would be the answer, but he would
have to get away from the ruins before he could find
trees. And he chafed at the loss of time.

There was a sun today, climbing up, striking specks
of light from the water. By turning his head he could
still see the foothills and, behind them, the bluish
heights down which he had come twenty-four hours
before. But he glanced back only once, his attention
was all for the river now.

Half an hour later he came across a find which saved
him hours of back-breaking labor. A sharp break in the
bank outlined a narrow cove where the river rose
during the spring freshets. Now it was half choked with
drift, from big logs to delicate, sunbleached twigs he

could snap between his fingers. He had only to pick and choose.

By the end of the morning he had a raft, crude and certainly not intended for a long voyage, but it should serve to float them across. Lura had her objections to the foolishness of trusting to such a crazy woven platform. But, when Fors refused to stay safely ashore, she pulled herself aboard it, one cautious paw testing each step before she put her full weight upon it. And in the exact middle she squatted down with a sigh as Fors leaned hard on his pole and pushed off.

The weird craft showed a tendency to spin around which he had to work against. And once his pole caught in a mud bank below and he was almost jerked off into the flood. But as the salty sweat stung across his lips and burned in his blistered palms he could see that the current, though taking them downstream, was slowly nudging them toward the opposite bank.

Sun rays reflected by the water made them both warm and thirsty, and Lura gave small whines of self-pity all the rest of the hour. Still, she grew accustomed enough to the new mode of travel to sit up and watch keen-eyed when a fish rose to snap at a fly. Once they slipped past a mass of decayed wreckage which must have been the remains of a boat, and twice swept between abutments of long-vanished bridges. This had been a thickly settled territory before the Blow-up. Fors tried to imagine what it had looked like when the towns had been lived in, the roads had been busy with traffic, when there had been boats on the river—

Since the current was taking them in the general direction of the route eastward he did not struggle too quickly to reach the other side. But when a portion of their shaky raft suddenly broke off and started a separate voyage of its own, he realized that such carelessness might mean trouble and he worked with the pole to break the grip of the current and reach the shore. There were bluffs along the river, cutting off easy access to the level lands behind them and he watched anxiously for a cove or sandbank which would give them a fair landing.

He had to be satisfied with a very shallow notch where a landslide had brought down a section of the bank containing two trees which now formed a partial barrier out from the shore. The raft, after much back-breaking labor on his part, caught against these, shivered against the pull of the water, and held. Lura did not wait, but was gone in a single leap to the solid footing of the tree trunks. Fors grabbed up his belongings and followed, none too soon, as the raft split and whirled around, shaking into pieces which the river carried on.

A hard scramble up the greasy clay of the bank brought them into open country once more. Grass grew tall, bushes spread in dusty blotches across the land tamed by centuries of the plow and the reaper.

Lura let him know that it had been too long since their last meal and she intended to do something about supplies. She set off across the faint boundaries of the old fields with grim purpose in every line of her graceful feline body. Grouse scuttled from underfoot and there were rabbits everywhere, but she disdained to notice such small game. She pushed on, with Fors half a field behind her, toward a slope which was crowned with a thick growth of trees.

Halfway up she paused, the tip of her tail quivered, the pink rosette of her tongue showed briefly between her teeth. Then she was gone again, fading away into the tall grass as silently and effortlessly as the breeze might pass. Fors stepped back into the shade of the nearest tree. This was Lura's hunt and he must leave it to her.

He looked out over the waving grass. It seemed to be some form of stunted grain, not yet quite ripe, for it had a seed head forming. The sky was blue with small white clouds drifting across it as if the storm winds had never torn them, although at his feet lay a branch splintered and broken by yesterday's wind.

A hoarse bellowing brought him out of his half dream, bow in hand. It was followed by the spitting squall which was Lura's war cry. Fors began to run up the slope toward the sound. But hunter's caution kept him to such shelter as the field afforded so he did not burst rashly out onto the scene of the combat.

Lura *had* tackled big game! He caught the sun flash on her tawny fur as she leaped away from an inert red-brown body just in time to escape the charge of a larger beast. A wild cow! And Lura had killed her calf!

Fors' arrow was already in the air. The cow bellowed again and tossed her wickedly horned head. She made a shambling run to the body of her calf, snorting in red rage. Then crimson froth puffed from her wide nostrils and she stumbled to her knees and fell on her side. Lura's round head shot up above a stand of thick grass and she moved out to the side of her prey. Fors came from the trees where he had taken cover. He would have echoed Lura's rasping purr had it been in his power. That arrow had gone straight and true to the mark he had set it.

It was a pity to have to waste all that meat. Enough to keep three Eyrie families for a week lay there. He prodded the cow with a regretful toe before starting to butcher the calf.

He could, of course, try to jerk the meat. But he was unsure of the right method and he could not carry it with him anyway. So he contented himself with preparing what he could for the next few days while Lura, after feasting, slept under a bush, rousing now and then to snap at the gathering flies.

They made camp that night a field or two beyond the kill, in the corner of an old wall. Piles of fallen stone turned it into a position which could be defended if the need arose. But neither slept well. The fresh meat they had left behind drew night rovers. There was a scream or two which must have come from Lura's wild relatives and she growled in answer. Then in the early dawn there was a baying cry which Fors was unable to identify, woods learned as he was. But Lura went wild when she heard it, spitting in sheer hate, her fur rising stiff along her backbone.

It was early when Fors started on, striking across the open fields in the line set by his compass. Today he made no effort to keep cover or practice caution. He could see no menace in these waste fields. Why had there been all the talk back in the Eyrie about the danger in the lowlands? Of course, one did keep away from the "blue" patches where radiation still meant death even after all these years. And the Beast Things were always to be dreaded—had not Langdon died in their attack? But as far as the Star Men had been able to discover those nightmare creatures kept to the old cities and were not to be feared in the open. Surely these fields must be as safe for man as the mountain forests which encircled the Eyrie.

He took an easy curve and came out suddenly on a sight which brought him up—blinking. Here was a road—but such a road! The broken concrete was four times as wide as any he had seen—it had really been two roads running side by side with a stretch of earth between them, two wide roads running smoothly from one horizon to another.

But not two hundred yards from where he stood gaping, the road was choked with a tangle of rusting metal. A barrier of broken machines filled it from ditch to ditch. Fors approached it slowly. There was something about that monstrous wall which was forbidding—even though he knew that it had stood so for perhaps three hundred years. Black crickets jumped out of the weeds before him and a mouse flashed across a stretch of clear stone.

He rounded the jumble of wrecked machines. They must have been traveling along the road in a line when death had struck mysteriously, struck so that some of the machines had rammed others or wavered off to pile up in wild wreckage. Others stood solitary as if the dying driver had been able to bring them to a safe halt before he succumbed. Fors tried to pick out the outlines and associate what he saw with the ancient pictures. That—that was certainly a "tank," one of the moving fortresses of the Old Ones. Its gun still pointed defiantly to the sky. Two, four, five more he counted, and then gave up.

The column of machines stretched out in its forgotten disaster for almost a mile. Fors brushed along beside it in the waist-high weeds which bordered the road. He had an odd distaste for approaching the dead machines more closely, no desire to touch any of the bits of rusted metal. Here and there he saw one of the alternative-powered vehicles, seeming almost intact. But they were dead too. All of it was dead, in a horrible way. He experienced a vague feeling of contamination from just walking beside the wreckage.

There were guns on the moving forts, guns which still swung ready, and there had been men, hundreds of men. He could see their white bones mixed with the rust and the debris driven in by years of wind and storm. Guns and men—where had they been going when the end came? And what was the end? There were none of the craters he had been told were to be found where bombs had fallen—just smashed machines and men, as if death had come as a mist or a wind.

Guns and men on the march—maybe to repel invaders. The book of air-borne messages treasured in the Eyrie had spoken once or twice of invaders coming from the sky—enemies who had struck with paralyzing swiftness. But something must have happened in turn to that enemy—or else why had the invaders not made the land their own? Probably the answer to that question would never be known.

Fors reached the end of the blasted column. But he kept on walking along the clean earth until he topped a rise and could no longer sight the end of a wasted war. Then he dared once more to walk the road of the Old Ones.

·*3

The Dark Hunter

About half a mile farther on the shadow of a woodland swallowed up the road. Fors' heart lifted when he saw it. These open fields were strange to a mountain-born man but he felt at home in a thick coat of trees such as the one before him now.

He was trying to remember the points on the big map which hung on the wall of the Star House, the map to which was added a tiny mark at the return of each roving explorer. This northern route crossed the wedge end of a portion of territory held loosely by Plainsmen. And the Plainsmen had horses—useless in the mountains and so untamed by his people—but very needful in this country of straight distances. To have a horse at his service now—

The cool of the woods lapped him in and he was at home at once, as was Lura. They padded on, their feet making but the faintest whisper of sound. It was a scent

carried by a tiny puff of breeze which brought them up—
Wood smoke!

Fors' thought met Lura's and agreed. She stood
for a long moment, testing the air with her keener
nostrils, and then she turned aside, pushing between
two birches. Fors scraped after her. The guiding puff
of wind was gone, but he could smell something
else. They were approaching a body of water—not
running water or the sound of its passing would be
heard.

There was a break in the foliage ahead. He saw Lura
flatten herself out on a rock surface which was almost
the same color as her own creamy hide, flatten and
creep. And he hunkered down to follow her example,
the gritty stone biting knees and hands as he wormed
out beside her.

They were belly down on a spur of rock which
overhung the surface of a woods-hemmed lake. Not
far beyond a thread of stream trickled away and he
could spot two islands, the nearest joined to the mainland by a series of stepping stones. On the shores of
this islet crouched someone very busy over a cooking
fire.

The stranger was no mountaineer, that was certain.
In the first place his wide-shouldered, muscular bronze
body was bare to the waist and at least three shades
darker in skin tint than the most deeply tanned of the
Eyrie men. The hair on his round skull was black and
tightly curled. He had strongly marked features with
a wide-lipped mouth and flat cheekbones, his large dark
eyes set far apart. His only clothing was a sort of
breechclout kilt held in place by a wide belt from which
hung the tassel-ornamented scabbard of a knife. The
knife itself, close to eighteen inches of blue steel,
flashed in his hand as he energetically cleaned a fresh-
caught fish.

Stuck upright in the ground close to his shoulder were three short-shafted spears, a blanket of coarse reddish wool draped over the point of one. Smoke rose from the fire laid on a flat stone, but there was no indication as to whether the stranger had merely halted for a meal or had been camping on the islet.

As he worked the fisherman sang—a low, monotonous chant, which, as he listened to it, affected Fors queerly, sending an odd shiver up his backbone. This was no Plainsman either. And Fors was just as sure that he was not spying on one of the Beast Things. The few mountaineer men who had survived a meeting with *them* had painted a far different picture—they were never to be associated with peaceful fishing and an intelligent, pleasant face.

This dark-skinned newcomer was of a different breed. Fors rested his chin on his folded arms and tried to deduce from the evidence this stranger's background—as was the duty of an explorer.

The lack of clothing, now—that meant that he was accustomed to a warmer climate. Such an outfit could only be worn here before fall closed in. He had those spears and—yes—that was a bow lying with its quiver beyond. But it was much shorter than the one Fors carried and did not appear to be made of wood but from some dark substance which reflected light from the sun.

He must come from a land where his race was all-powerful and had nothing to fear for he camped in the open and sang while he cooked as if he did not care if he attracted attention. And yet he did this on an island, more easily defended from attack than the shore itself.

Just then the fisherman impaled the cleaned fish on a sharpened twig and set it to broil while he got to his feet and hurled a baited line back into the water.

Fors blinked. The man on the island must tower a good four or five inches over the tallest of the Eyrie men and his thatch of upstanding hair could not account for more than two inches of that difference. As he stood there, still humming, his hands skillfully adjusted the fishing line, he presented a picture of strength and power which would daunt even a Beast Thing.

The odor of the fish carried. Lura made a faint slurruping sound as it reached them. Fors hesitated. Should he hail the dark-skinned hunter, make the peace sign, and try to establish friendly relations or—

That question was decided for him. A shout tore the serene silence of the lake. The dark hunter moved—so fast that Fors was left gasping. Spears, blanket, bow—and the broiled fish—vanished with their owner. A bush quivered and then was still. The fire burned—on a deserted pebbled beach.

A second shout bore down wind, reinforced by a trampling crash, and down to the edge of the lake trotted a band of horses, mares mostly, each with a small foal running at her side. Urging them on were two riders, bent nearly flat on the backs of their mounts to escape the low sweeping branches of the trees. They herded the mares to water and waited for them to drink.

Fors almost forgot the dark hunter. Horses! He had seen pictures of them. But living horses! The age-old longing of his race—to possess one of those for his own—made a strange ache in his thigh muscles, as if he were already mounted upon one of the sleek backs.

One of the horse guards dismounted and was rubbing down the legs of his animal with handfuls of grass pulled up from the bank. *He* was undoubtedly a Plainsman. His sleeveless jerkin laced across the chest was almost twin to the one Fors wore. But his leggings were of hide and polished by hours of riding. He wore his hair shoulder length as the sign of free birth and it was held out of his eyes by a broad band on which was painted the sign of his family clan and tribe. The long lance which was the terrible weapon of the horsemen hung in its loops at his saddle and in addition he wore at his belt the curved, slashing sword which was the badge of his nation.

For the second time Fors wondered whether he should make overtures. But that, too, was quickly answered. Out of the trees came a second pair of riders, both older men. One was a chief or sub chieftain of the Plainsmen, for the metal badge in his headband had caught the sun. But the other—

Fors' body jerked as if an arrow had thudded home between his shoulder blades. And Lura, catching his dismay, voiced one of her noiseless snarls.

That was Jarl! But Jarl was the Star Captain—now exempt from travel in the lowlands. He had not been exploring for two years or more. It was his duty to remain at the Eyrie and portion out the tasks of other Star Men. But there he was, riding knee to knee with the Plainsman chief as if he were any apprentice rover. What had brought Jarl down to the lowlands against all rule and custom?

Fors winced—there was an answer to that. Never before had the sanctuary of the Star House been violated. His crime must have brought Jarl out of the hills. And if he, Fors, were captured—what would be the penalty for such a theft? He had no idea but his imagination could supply quite a few—all of them drastic. In the meantime he could only remain where he was and pray that he would not be detected before the herders moved.

Luckily most of the horses had drunk their fill and were turning away from the lake. Fors watched them longingly. With one of them to lend four feet and save his two, he could be well beyond Jarl's reach before the Star Captain knew of his presence. He had too great an opinion of Jarl's skill not to believe that the man from the Eyrie could cross his trail within a day or so.

The second herder urged the last mares away from the water while his companion mounted. But Jarl and the chief still sat talking and looking out idly across the lake. Fors silently endured the bites of flies which seemed to have accompanied the horses, but Lura growled again softly. She wanted to leave, knowing full well that if she did not want her trail followed it would not be. Fors could not hope for such results himself, so he hesitated until the cat's impatience or some change in the air current changed their luck as it carried Lura's scent down to the peaceful herd.

Within seconds there was wild confusion. Mares squealed, wild-eyed with fright for their foals, tramping up the bank and bursting between the riders—dashing ahead to get away from that dangerous place. The Plainsmen had been caught off guard. One was borne along with the rush, fighting to regain mastery of his own mount—the other could only ride after the rout.

Lance in hand the chief went after them. But Jarl remained where he was for a long moment, searching the shoreline of the lake with narrowed eyes. Fors flattened against the rock, sending a stern warning to Lura to do likewise. Fortunately Jarl was on the opposite side of the water and the Star Captain could not match the keen sight of his quarry. But how much protection that offered he had no means of telling.

Hardly daring to draw the shallowest of breaths, cat and boy inched back. Jarl stayed, alert, watching. Then came the thunder of hoofs, just as Fors' boots struck earth. He was off at his best woods' pace, heading north, away from the camp which must lie somewhere on the other side of the lake. He wanted a horse, needed a horse, but not enough that he dared brave Jarl to get one. Fors had a very hearty respect for the abilities of the Star Captain.

As he sped away he wondered what the hunter on the island had done and whether he, too, was now putting some miles between himself and the Plains camp.

At least *he* had that broiled fish to take with him. Fors munched a handful of parched corn from his emergency rations as he trotted along and some shreds of dried meat, giving the rest to Lura who downed it in a single gulp. Half-ripe berries snatched from bushes as he passed were sauce of a sort. But there still remained a feeling of emptiness in his middle which grew with the lengthening shadows of the afternoon.

They had used the feeder stream of the lake as a guide, but the thinning of the trees around them now and the appearance of open patches suggested that the end of the wood was close. Fors paused and tried to plan. He was at home in the forest country and knew how to conceal his trail there. On the other hand, in the open, out in the once cultivated fields, one would make better time and be able to cover a good many miles before the daylight failed entirely. The hunters of the plains—if human—were mounted men and any pursuit would be easily seen. And there were plenty of scattered clumps of trees and running tongues of brush to give him shelter in a pinch. He decided to venture out.

A brown animal with a black mask about its eyes surveyed him critically from a pile of rocks but was gone in a flash when Lura's head came out of a tall stand of grass. That was the only living thing they saw until they skirted the rotting timbers of a farmhouse, missing a tumble into its half-exposed cellar only by chance.

A sound answered Fors' yelp and his hand swept to the hilt of his sword. He skidded around, bare steel out. An ugly naked pink snout, still smeared with earth and slime, protruded from a tangle of brush, and the wicked tusks below it caught and held the light. Fors hurled pouch and bow from him and half crouched, waiting for that most dangerous of all rushes, the attack of a wild boar.

It came with all the deadly ferocity he had expected, the tusks slashing for his legs. He struck, but the creature dodged so that, though a red and dripping line leaped out along its head and shoulder, it was not sent kicking. It grunted loudly, and there came answers. Fors' mouth dried—he was facing a whole pack of swine!

Behind him was a pile of the collapsed timbers which had once been the wall of a small building, but they were pulpy with rot and they dipped dangerously toward the cellar. If he jumped for them he might well crash through.

From the bushes came a squall of rage and pain. The boar tossed its tusked head and blew foam. Its eyes in the black-and-white spotted face were red and evil. Another squeal came from the herd, this time followed by an answering snarl. Fors loosed a thankful breath.

Lura was keeping the herd occupied. Under her ripping claws the younger and weaker ones would certainly break and scatter. But not this old leader. It was wily and there were scars and bare patches enough on the hide to mark it victor in other battles. It had always won before so it was confident now. And—the charge came again!

Fors leaped to the left, slashing down as he moved out of danger. That stroke cut across the grinning devil's mask of the boar, chopping off an ear and shearing the sight out of one red eye. It shook its head, sending a spray of blood flying, and squealed in rage and pain. Under the prod of pain it lost its cunning, wishing now only to tusk and trample the dancing figure before it—to root the life of the enemy away—

As Fors saw the heavy shoulders tense he took a step backward, groping for firm footing on which to maneuver. And in so doing he nearly lost the fight. His heel caught and was held as if a trap had snapped on it. He was still trying to pull loose as the boar charged for the third time.

And that pull unbalanced him so that he fell forward almost on top of the mad creature. There was a red dagger of pain across his leg and a foul stench filled his nostrils. He stabbed wildly. Then his steel struck bone and slip deep beneath the mangy hide. Blood fountained over both of them, then the sword was wrenched from Fors' blood-slippery hand as the boar pulled away. It staggered out into the full sunlight and fell heavily, the hilt of the sword protruding behind its powerful shoulder. Fors rocked back and forth, his face twisted with pain as his fingers tried to rip the cloth away from a nasty, freely bleeding slash down the outside of his left thigh.

Lura emerged from the bushes. There were unpleasant stains on her usually fastidiously kept coat and she moved with an air of general satisfaction. As she passed the boar she snarled and gave the body a raking clout with one front paw.

Fors worked his heel free from the rotten board which had clamped it and crawled toward the Star pouch. He needed water now—but Lura would sniff that out for him. The worst would be going lame for

a while. He would be lucky if he did not have to stay
where he was for a day or two.

Lura did find water, a spring a little beyond the
farmhouse. And he crawled to it painfully. With dry
twigs he kindled a fire and set a tiny pan of the clear
water to boil. Now he was ready for the worst—boar's
tusks were notoriously dirty and deadly.

Setting his teeth he cut and tore away the cloth of
his leggings until the skin around the still oozing slash
was bare. Into the bubbling water he dropped a minute
portion of the wound salve from the Star pouch. The
secret of that salve belonged to the Healer of the tribe
and the Captain of the Star Men alone. It was wisdom
from the old days which had saved many lives. A
wound anointed with it did not rot.

Fors let the water cool until he could just bear
it and then poured more than half of it into that
ragged tear in skin and muscle. His fingers were
shaking when he thrust them into the water left in
the pan, holding them there for a minute before
tearing open the packet of the bandage. With an end
of the soft material he washed and dabbed delicately
along the cut. Then he smeared some of the
unheated paste across it and bound a pad tightly
over it. The bleeding had almost stopped, but the
wound was like a band of stinging fire from hip
socket to ankle bone. His eyes grew misty as he
worked, following the instructions which had been
drilled into him since his first hunting trip.

At last he could put out the fire and lie quietly. Lura
stretched out beside him and put a velvet-gloved paw
on his arm. She purred soothingly, once or twice
drawing her rough tongue across his flesh in her
favorite caress. The burning in his leg eased, or else
he was growing accustomed to the torment. He stared
into the sky. Pink and gold streamed across it in wide

swaths. It must be close to sundown. He would have to have shelter. But it was a struggle to move and his leg had stiffened so that even when he got up and clutched at bushes to pull himself along he made slow progress.

Lura went down the slope and he stumbled after her, glad that only tall grass covered most of it. She headed for the farmyard, but he did not call her back. Lura was hunting shelter for them both and she would find it, if any such existed.

She did bring him to the best housing they had had since they had left the Eyrie, a stone-walled, single-roomed building. He had no idea for what purpose it had been built. But there was only one door, no windows, and part of the roof was still in place. It could be easily defended and it was shelter.

Already small scavengers were busy about the bodies of the pigs. And with the dark the scent of blood would draw more formidable flesh eaters. He had not forgotten the quarrels over the bodies of the cow and calf. So Fors pushed loose stones into a barrier about his door and decided upon a fire. The walls would hide it from all but birds flying overhead.

He ate sparingly of dried corn. Lura jumped the barrier and went hunting on her own, questing through the twilight. But Fors nursed his point of fire and stared out into the gathering darkness. Fireflies made dancing sparks under the straggling limbs of ancient orchard trees. He watched them as he drank from the water in his canteen. The pain in his leg was now a steady throb which arose into his head and settled in his temples—beat—beat—beat—

Then Fors suddenly realized that that steady rhythm was not born of pain and fever. There was an actual sound, hanging on the night air, low and carrying well. The measured note bore no resemblance to any natural noise he had heard before. Only, something in it suggested the odd crooning song of the fisherman. If something not unlike the same series of notes was being tapped out on the head of a drum now—

Fors jerked upright. Bow and sword were within reach of his hand. The night, which was never as dark for him as it was for others, was peaceful and empty—save for that distant signal. Then it stopped, abruptly, almost in mid-note, with a suggestion of finality. He guessed that he would not hear it again. But what could it mean?

Sound carried well in these lowlands—even if listeners did not have his keenness of ear. A message sent by such a drum might carry safely across miles.

His fingernails dug into the flesh of his palms. There was a trace of sound again—coming from the far south—a disturbance in the air so faint it might only be born of his imagination.

But he did not believe that. The drummer was receiving an answer. Under his breath Fors counted off seconds—five, ten, fifteen, and then again silence. He tried to sort out his impressions of the fisherman—and again came to the same conclusion. He was not native to these lowlands, which meant that he was probably a scout, an explorer from the south. Who or what was now moving up into these lands?

·∗∗∗ **4**

Four Legs Are Better Than Two

Even before dawn it began to rain, a steady, straight downpour which would last for hours. Fors' wound was stiff and he had trouble crawling back into the corner of the hut where the broken roof still afforded some protection. Lura rolled against him and the warmth of her furry body was a comfort. But Fors was unable to drop back into the restless, dream-broken sleep which had held him most of the night.

It was the thought of the day's travel still before him which plagued him. To walk far would reopen the gash and he thought that he had a touch of fever. Yet he had to have food and better shelter. And that drumming— Being disabled he wanted to get out of the near vicinity of the drummer—fast.

As soon as it was light enough for him to distinguish a black line on white paper he got out his scrap of map, trying to guess his present position—if it were on that fragment at all. There were tiny red figures printed

between certain points—the measured miles of the Old
Ones who kept to the roads. By his reckoning he might
yet be at least three days' journey from the city—if,
of course, he was now where he believed himself to
be. Three days' journey for a strong and tireless
traveler, not for a crippled limper. If he had a horse
now—

But the memory of Jarl with the horse herders put
that thought out of his mind. If he went to the Plains
camp and tried to trade, the Star Captain would hear
of it. And for a novice to steal a mount out of one of
the well-guarded herds was almost impossible even if
he were able-bodied. But he could not banish his
wish—even by repeating this argument of stern
commonsense.

Lura went out hunting. She would bring back her
kill. Fors pulled himself up, clenching his teeth against
the pain that such movement gave his whole left side.
He had to have some sort of crutch or cane if he
wanted to keep going. There was part of a sapling
among the wood within reach. It appeared almost
straight, so he hacked it down with his knife and
trimmed off the branches. With this aid he could get
around, and the more he moved the more the
stiffness seemed to loosen. When Lura returned with
a plump bronze-feathered turkey in her jaws, he was
in a better frame of mind and ready to eat breakfast.

But the pace at which they started was not a
speedy one. Fors hissed between set teeth when now
and again his weight shifted too heavily on the left
leg. He turned instinctively into what once had been
the lane tying the farmstead to the road, and
brushed between the encroaching bushes, leaning
heavily on his cane.

Rain made sticky mud of every patch of open ground
and he was afraid of slipping and falling. Lura kept up

a steady low whine of complaint against the weather and the slowness of their travel. But she did not go off on her own as she might have done had he been himself. And Fors talked to her constantly.

The lane came to the road and he turned into that since it went in the direction he wished. Soil had drifted across the concrete and made mud patches which gave root to spiked plants; but, even with that, it was better footing for an almost one-legged man than the wet ground. Lura scouted ahead, weaving in and out of the bushes and tall grass along the side of the old thoroughfare. She tested the wind for alien scents, now and then shaking head or paws vigorously to rid them of clinging raindrops.

All at once she bounded out of the brush to Fors, pushing against him with her body, forcing him gently back toward the ditch which ran nearby. He caught the urgency of her warning and scrambled to cover with all the speed he could muster. As he lay against the greasy red clay bank with his palms spread flat, he felt the pounding long before he heard the hoofs which caused it. Then the herd came into sight, trotting at an easy pace down the old road. For a moment or two Fors searched for the herders and then he realized that none of the horses wore the patches of bright paint which distinguished ownership among the Plainsmen. They must be wild. There were several mares with foals, a snorting stallion bearing the scars of battle on his shoulder, and some yearlings running free.

But there was one mare who had no foal. Her rough, ungroomed coat was a very dark red, her burr-matted tail and mane black. Now and again she dropped to the back, stopping to snatch a mouthful of herbage, a trick which at last earned her a sharp nip from the stallion. She squealed, lashed out with ready hoofs, and then ran swiftly, breaking ahead of the rest of the band.

Fors watched her go with regret. If he had had his two feet under him she might have been a possible capture. But no use thinking of that.

Then the herd rounded a curve and was out of sight. Fors took a moment's breather before he pulled himself back on the road. Lura was there before him, kneading her front paws on a mat of grass, staring after the vanished horses. To her mind there was no difference between one of those foals and the calf she had pulled down. Both were meat and meant to be eaten. It was in her mind to trail along behind such a wealth of food. Fors did not argue with her. He still thought of the mare who ran free and followed her own will.

They came up again with the herd before the hour was past. The road made a sudden dip into a valley which was almost cup-shaped. At the bottom rich grass grew tall and there the herd grazed, the watchful stallion standing guard halfway up the rise.

But what caught Fors' eyes was the shell of a building which stood almost directly below. Fire had eaten out its interior so that only the crumbling brick of the outer walls remained. He studied it carefully and then tried to identify the horses beyond.

The mare was apart from the herd, grazing close to the building. Fors wet his lips with his tongue tip. There was just a chance—a very wild chance—

It would depend largely upon Lura's co-operation. And that had never failed him yet. He turned to the great cat and tried to form a mind picture of what must be done. Slowly he thought out each point. Twice he went through it and then Lura crouched and withdrew into the grass.

Fors wiped sweat and rain from his forehead and started crawling in turn, edging down into a maze of fallen bricks. They could never do it if the wind was not just right. But fortune was favoring to that extent.

He swung himself up on a ledge above the widest gap in the broken wall and unwound from his waist the light tough cord all mountain men carried. The weighted noose at the end was in his hand. Good, the rain had not affected it. Now—!

He whistled, the clear call of one of the Eyrie country birds. And he knew, rather than saw, that Lura was in position and ready to move. If the wind would only hold—!

Suddenly the mare tossed up her head, snorted, and stared suspiciously at a clump of bushes. At the same time the stallion reared and thundered forth a fierce challenge. But he was almost the full length of the valley away, and he stopped to send the rest of his harem out of danger before he came to the mare. She wanted to follow but plainly the hidden menace now lay between her and freedom. She whirled on two feet and pounded back in the direction of the ruin where Fors waited. Twice she tried to go with her mates and both times she was sent back on the opposite course.

Fors coiled his rope. He had only to wait and trust to Lura's skill. But the seconds that he was forced to do that were very long. At last the mare, her eyes white-rimmed with terror, burst through the gap in the masonry. Fors cast and as quickly snubbed the rope about a girder of rusting steel protruding from the brickwork. The heart of the metal was still sound enough to hold, even against the frantic plunges of the terrified horse. The scream of the aroused stallion, thundering down to the rescue, shook Fors. He did not know much about horses but he could imagine that there was danger now.

But the stallion never reached the ruin. Out of the bushes, directly at his head, leaped Lura, leaped and raked with cruel claws. The stallion reared, trumpeting like a mad thing, slashing out with teeth and hoofs.

But Lura was only a flash of light fur covering steel springs and she was never there when the stallion struck. Twice more she got home with a wicked, slashing paw, before the horse gave up the battle and fled back down the valley, following the herd. The mare cried after him. He turned, but Lura was there, and her snarled warning sent him on again dripping blood.

Fors leaned back weakly against a pile of rubble. He had the mare all right, a rope about her neck, a rope which would hold her in spite of all her plunges and kicks. But here was no gentled mount already broken to ride. And how was he, with a bad leg, to conquer the fear-maddened animal?

He made the rope fast, looking ruefully at the burns on his hands. Just now he could not get near her. Might be well to let her become used to captivity for an hour or so—to try to win her—But would she ever lose her fear of Lura? That was another problem to be solved. Only—it must be done, he could not go on in this one-legged way. He certainly was not going to beg shelter from the Plains camp and so fall into Jarl's hands. He believed that he could make his own way in the lowlands—now was the time to prove that!

After a time the mare ceased to fight for freedom and stood with drooping head, nervous shudders running along her sweat-encrusted limbs and flanks. Fors stayed where he was but now he began to talk to her, using the same crooning tone with which he called Lura. Then he ventured to limp a few steps closer. Her head went up and she snorted. But he continued to talk to her, making an even monotone of his voice. At last he was close enough to touch her rough coat and as he did so he almost jumped. Still faintly sketched on the hide was a dab or two of fading paint! Then this was a Plainsman's mount from one of the tame herds. Fors gulped weakly. Such luck was a little uncanny. Now, seeing that, he dared to stroke her nose. She shivered under his touch and then she whinnied almost inquiringly. He patted her shoulder and then she nudged him playfully with her nose. Fors laughed, tugging at the ragged forelock which bobbed between her eyes.

"So now you remember, old lady? Good girl, good girl!"

There remained the problem of Lura and that must be solved as quickly as possible. He unfastened the rope and pulled gently. The mare came after him willingly enough, picking her way daintily through the piles of fallen brick.

Why hadn't she scented the cat on his clothes? Unless the rain had dampened it—But she had shown no fright at his handling.

He whistled the bird call for the second time, after he had snubbed the mare's lead rope around a small tree. The answer to his summons came from down valley. Apparently Lura was following the herd. Fors stood talking to his captive as he waited. At last he ventured to rub down her flanks with tufts of grass. Then he felt her start and tremble and he turned.

Lura sat in the open, her tail curled neatly over her forepaws. She yawned, her red tongue pointing up and out, her eyes slitted, as if she had very little interest in the mare which her hunting companion chose to fondle so stupidly.

The mare jerked back to the full length of the rope, her eyes showing white. Lura took no notice of the open terror. The mare reared and gave a shrill scream. Fors tried to urge Lura back. But the big cat paced in a circle about the captive, eyeing her speculatively from all angles. The mare dropped back on four feet and shook her head, turning to keep her attention ever upon the cat. It seemed as if she were now puzzled when the attack she had expected had not come.

Maybe some message passed between the animals then. Fors never knew. But when Lura finished her inspection, she turned away indifferently and the mare stopped trembling. However, it was more than an hour before Fors improvised a bridle from the rope and a saddle pad from his blanket. He climbed upon the bricks and managed to throw his good leg over the mare's back.

She had been well trained by the Plainsman who had owned her and her pace was so even that Fors, awkward and inexperienced at riding as he was, could keep his seat. He headed her back on the road which had brought him to the valley and they came up into the rolling fields once more.

In spite of the nagging ache of the wound Fors knew a surge of exultation and happiness. He had won safely out of the Eyrie, after plundering the Star House. He had dared the lowlands, had spent one night in the heart of a dead town, had crossed a river through his own skill. He had spied successfully at the woods lake, faced the savage boar from which even the best of the mountain hunters sometimes fled, and now he had a horse under him. His weapons were to hand and the road open before him.

Judged unfit for the Star, cast aside by the Council was he? His even teeth gleamed in a grin which bore some likeness to Lura's hunting snarl. Well, they would see—see that Langdon's son, White Hair the Mutant—was as good as their best! He would prove that to the whole Eyrie.

Lura drifted back and the mare side-stepped as if she were still none too pleased to have the big cat venture so close. Fors jolted out of his daydreams, paid heed to his surroundings.

There were piles of rubble scattered through the brush, skeletons of old buildings, and, all at once, the mare's unshod hoofs raised a different sort of noise. She was picking her way across pavements in which were set long straight lines of rusted tracks. Fors pulled her up. Ahead the ruins were closer together and grew larger. A town—maybe even a small city.

There was something about these ruins which made him uneasy. The farms which had been recaptured by wild vegetation had none of this eerie strangeness about them. He knew again the faint sickness, neither of body nor spirit, which had gripped him on the road when he had traveled beside the wrecked convoy. Now he wiped one hand through the mare's coarse mane as if he would like to rub away an unpleasant smear. And yet he had touched nothing in this place. There was an evil miasma which arose mistlike even through the steady drizzle of rain.

Mist—there was real mist, too! Ahead he saw coils of dirty white drifting in, wreathing the tangled bulk of rotting wood and tumbled brick and stone. A fog was gathering, thicker than the mountain ones he had known, thick and somehow frightening. His fingers left the horse hair and flipped against his sore leg. The stab of pain which followed made him cry out. This fog would put an end to travel for the day as far as he was concerned. Now he needed a safe place to hole up in where he could light a fire and prepare another treatment for his wound. And he wanted to be out of the rain for the night.

He did not like the ruins, but now they might hold what he needed and it was wiser to penetrate farther into them. But he held the mare to a slow walk and it was well that he did. For soon a break in the pavement opened before them—a gaping black hole rimmed with jagged teeth of broken concrete. They made a detour, edging as far from the crumbling lip as the ruins would allow. Fors began to regret leaving the stone hut on the farm. His constant pain he could no longer ignore. Perhaps it would have been better to have rested for a day or two back there. But if he had done that he would not now be riding the mare! He whistled softly and watched her ears point up in answer. No, it was worth even the grinding in his flesh to have such a mount.

Twice more the pavement was broken by great holes, the last being so large that it had the dimensions of a small crater. As Fors rode slowly around it he crossed a strip of muddy, but hard-beaten earth which came up out of its shadowed maw. It had the appearance of a well-worn and much-used path. Lura sniffed at it and snarled, her back fur roughened, and she spat with a violent hissing sound. Whatever made that path she counted an enemy.

Any creature which Lura, who would tackle a wild cow, a herd of roving swine, or a stallion, so designated was not one which Fors cared to meet in his present crippled state. He loosened rein and urged the mare to a brisker pace.

Some distance beyond the crater they came to a small hill on which stood a building of white stone, and it still possessed a roof. The slope of the hill was clear of all save a few low bushes and from the building Fors guessed one could have an almost unhampered view of the surrounding territory. He decided quickly in its favor.

It was a disappointment to discover that the roof covered only a part and that the center was open to the storm—being a small amphitheater in which rows of wide seats went down to a square platform.

However, there were small rooms around the outer rim, under the roof, and in one of these he made camp. He tied the mare to one of the pillars forming the aisle to the amphitheater and contented her with grass pulled from the hill and some of his parched corn which she relished. She could have been hobbled and left to graze but the memory of that worn path by the crater kept him from doing that.

Rain had collected in broken squares of the pavement and Lura drank eagerly from one such pool while the mare sucked noisily at another. From the drift of wind-driven branches caught among the pillars Fors built a fire, placed behind a wall so that it could not be observed from below. Water boiled in his pan and he went through the ordeal of redressing the gash in his leg. The salve was working, for the flesh was sore and stiff but it was clean and without infection, and the edges were already closing, though undoubtedly he would be scarred for the rest of his life.

Lura made no move to go hunting, although she must have been hungry. In fact, since she had skirted the crater she had kept close to him, and now she lay beside the fire, staring into the flames broodingly. He did not urge her to go out. Lura was more woodswise than any man could hope to be and if she did not choose to hunt there was good reason for her decision. Fors only wished that she could reveal to him the exact nature of the thing she both hated and feared. That hatred and fear came through to him when their minds held fleeting touch, but the creature which aroused such emotions remained a secret.

So they went hungry to bed since Fors determined to use what was left of the corn to bind the mare to him. He kept the fire burning low for he did not want to lie in the dark here where there were things beyond his knowledge.

For a time he listened for the drumming of the night before. He fully expected to hear it again. But the night was still. It had stopped raining at last, and he could hear insects in the grass outside. There was the murmur of a breeze through the foliage on the hill.

It made Fors uneasy, that faint sad soughing. Lura was not asleep either. He sensed her restlessness even before he heard the pad of her paws and saw her move toward the door. He crawled after her, trying to spare his leg. She had halted at the outer portico of the building and was looking down into the blackness of the ruined city. Then he saw what held her—a pin point of red to the north—the telltale flicker of flame!

So there was other life here! Plainsmen for the most part kept clear of the ruins—in memory of the old days when radiation killed. And the Beast Things—did they possess the secret of fire? No man knew how much or how little they had in the way of intelligence or perverted civilization.

The urge to get the mare, to crawl up on her back and cross the rubble to that distant fire, was strong. Fire and companionship in this place of the restless dead—they pulled at Fors now.

But before he so much as filled his lungs again he heard it—a low chorus of yapping, barking, howling which rose higher and higher to a frenzied bedlam. Lura's hair was stiff under his hand. She hissed and snarled, but she did not stir. The cries were coming from some distance—from the direction of the fire. Whatever manner of beast made them had been drawn by that.

Fors shuddered. There was nothing he could do to aid the fire maker. Long before he could find his slow way through the ruins the end would have come. And now—now—there was only blackness down there! The flicker of friendly red was gone!

·*⁺ **5**

The City On The Lake

Fors dragged himself out into the morning sun. Although he had slept poorly, he was content that his wound was healing. And, after he once got to his feet, he managed better, being able without too much effort to take the mare out to graze on the hillside. Lura had been on duty before he roused, as the body of a plump turkey laid on the floor by the remains of the fire testified. He broiled it and ate, knowing all the time that when he was done he must mount and ride across the shattered town searching out the site of that fire which had vanished in the night.

And he did not want to take that ride. Because he did not want to, he finished quickly, gathering up his supplies with nervous haste. Lura came back and sat in the broad beam of sunlight washing her fur. But she was on her feet instantly as Fors got up on the mare and turned into the heart of the ruins.

They clattered out into a burned area where the

black stain of a vast, devouring fire had not faded. There were flowers growing there among the sooty stones, yellow, white, and blue. And a ragged, red-leafed weed overran old cellars. Cat and horse moved slowly through the desolation, testing their footing.

On the far edge of the burned space they found the scene of that night battle. Black birds whirred up from almost under their feet, birds which had been feasting on scraps more powerful scavengers had left them. Fors dismounted and limped up to the trampled grass, reluctant to make investigation.

Two well-picked piles of bones lay on the blood-stained ground. But the skulls were not those of his own race. Those long narrow heads with the cruel yellow teeth he had never seen before. Then the glint of metal caught his eyes and he picked up a broken spear, the haft snapped raggedly off not far from the head. And that spear he *had* seen before! It belonged to the fisherman of the islet.

Fors moved around the circle of the battlefield. He came across one more of the strange skeletons, but, save for the spear, there was no other trace of the hunter. Lura exhibited a violent distaste for the bones—as if the odd scent which clung to them was utterly offensive. And now she stood on her hind legs and sniffed inquiringly up the side of a heap of bricks and stone.

So that was what had happened! The hunter had not been overwhelmed by a rush out of the dark. He had had time to clamber up where the night-running things could not attack in force, had been able from above to fight them off and leave the wounded and dead to the tearing teeth of their own companions. And he must have escaped—since *his* bones were not in evidence.

Fors kicked through the underbrush a last time just

to be sure. Something round and brown rolled away from his toe. He reached for a small, well-polished drum fashioned of dark wood, the stretched head of hide cured to an almost metallic smoothness. The signal drum! Impulsively he tapped the head, and started at the low throbbing note which echoed through the ruins.

When he rode on the drum went with him. Why he did not know, except that he was fascinated by such a message-sending device unknown to his own people.

Within a half hour the ruins lay behind. Fors was glad to be out in the clean freedom of the country again. All morning he rode at a leisurely pace, watching for any signs which the hunter might leave. He was sure that the man was striking north with almost as definite a purpose as the one which drew him in that direction. And, with the drum gone, there would be no more signals.

The next two days were quiet. There was no indication that the Plainsmen had ever ventured into this territory and the land was a hunters' paradise teeming with game. Fors wasted none of his precious arrows but left the chase to Lura who enjoyed every moment of it. He varied his diet with berries and the ripe grain which grew wild in the ancient fields.

They avoided two more small towns, cutting around when they saw the first ruins. The dank, moldy places had little appeal and Fors had once or twice speculated as to what might have happened that night had he been the one caught in the open by the hunting pack, too crippled to climb to the safety the unknown had found. Now his leg was less painful, he walked a part of each day, stretching the muscles and toughening tender flesh. Most of the ache was gone and soon he would be able to move as freely as ever.

On the morning of the fourth day they came out upon a waste of sand- and wind-carved dunes and saw the great lake of legend. There was no end to the gray-blue expanse of water—it must be almost as large as the distant sea. High piles of bleached driftwood lay along the shore. There must have been a recent storm for the bodies of fish lay there too. Fors' nose wrinkled as he plowed through the sand, the mare sinking deeply as she followed him. Lura, investigating the fish, strayed some yards behind.

So—this much was true—this was the lake. And somewhere along its shore must lie the city his father had sought. Right or left, east or west—that was the question. He found shelter from the wind behind a dune and squatted down to consult the scrap of map. When they had avoided that last town they had gone west—so now—east. He would keep to the shore and see—

It was hard to travel in the sand, and after some time he gave up in disgust and edged inland to the more solid earth. Within two yards he was on a road! And, since the roadway hugged the shoreline, he held to it. Shortly the familiar mounds of debris closed in. But this was the remains of no small town. Even in his inexperience he could judge that. In the morning sun far ahead he saw battered towers rising in the sky. This was one of the cities, the great cities of huge sky-reaching towers! And it was not a "blue" one either. He would have seen the sign of that taint on the sky in the night.

His city—all his! Langdon had been right—this was an untouched storehouse waiting to be looted for the benefit of the Eyrie. Fors allowed the mare to amble on at her own pace as he tried to recall all the training rules. Libraries—those were what one was to look for—and shops, especially those which had stores of hardware or paper or kindred supplies. One was not to touch food—no matter if it was found in unbroken containers. Experimentation of that kind had brought death by poisoning too many times in the past. Hospital supplies were best of all, but those had to be selected by the trained expert. Danger lay too in unknown drugs.

For his looting he had best take only samples of what was to be found—books, writing supplies, maps, anything which would prove that he knew how to select intelligently. And with the mare he ought to be able to pack out quite a lot.

Here were signs of fire too. He rode across a bare stretch where the rough footing was all black ash. But the towers stood taller and they did not appear to be too badly damaged. If this city had been bombed, would they be standing at all? Maybe this was one of the places which had perished in the plagues which followed the war. Maybe it had died slowly with the ebbing life of its people—and not suddenly in explosion.

The road they had been following was now a narrow gorge between tall ranks of broken buildings, the upper stories of which had fallen into the street in mounds which almost blocked it completely at places. Here were numerous surface machines in which the Old Ones had ridden in comfort. And here, also, were bones. That single skull he had found in the old bank had had the power to shake him a little, but here lay a nation of dead and soon he ceased to notice them at all, even when the mare trod on brittle ribs or kicked rolling skulls aside. Yes, now it was very apparent that the men of this city had died of plague, or gas, or even of the radiation sickness. But sun and wind and animals had cleared away the foulness of that death, leaving only a framework without power to harm.

As yet Fors did not attempt to explore those caverns which had once been the lower floors of the buildings.

Now he only wanted to get on into the very heart of the place, to the foundations of those towers which had guided him all morning. But before he could reach that goal a barrier was laid across his road.

There was a gash breaking the city in two, a deep valley which nursed a twisted river in its middle. Bridges spanned it. He came to the lip of one such span and he could see two others. But before him was a mass of rusting wreckage piled into a fantastic wall. Machines—not in one and twos or even in tens, but in hundreds—were packed as they must have crashed and telescoped into one another, driven by men who feared some danger behind enough to drive in crazy flight. The bridge was now one gigantic crack-up. Fors might be able to scramble across but the mare could not. It would be best to descend into the valley and cross there—because as far as he could see the other bridges were also choked with rust-eaten metal.

There was a side road down into the valley, and machines filled it too. Men had taken that same trail when the bridge jammed. But the three of them— horse, cat and man—worked their way through to reach the river level. Tracks were rust-red lines and on them were trains—the first he had ever seen. Two had crashed together, the engine of one plowing into the other. Those who had tried to escape by train had been little better off than their brothers in the stalled cars above. It was difficult for Fors to imagine what that last wild day of flight must have been—the trains, the machines. He knew of them only from the old books. But the youngsters of the Eyrie sometimes stirred up nests of black ants and watched them boil up and out. So this city must have boiled—but few had been able to win out.

And those who had—what became of them in the end? What could help a handful of panic-stricken refugees scattered over a countryside, perhaps dropping dead of the plague as they fled? Fors shivered as he picked his way along beside the wrecked trains. But finding a narrow path through the jumble proved lucky. There had been barges on the river and they had drifted and sunk to form a shaky bridge across the water. Horse, man, and cat started over it, testing each step. There was a gap in the middle through which the stream still fought its way. But the mare, under the urging of Fors' heels in her ribs, jumped it and Lura went sailing over with her usual agility.

More dark streets with blank-eyed buildings lining them, and then there was a road leading up at a sharp angle. They took it to find themselves at last close to the towers. Birds wheeled overhead, crying out in thin sharp voices, and Fors caught a glimpse of a brownish animal slithering out of sight through a broken doorway. Then he came up to a wall which was part glass, miraculously unbroken, but so besmeared by the dust and wind-driven grime of the years that he could not see what lay behind it. He dismounted and went over, rubbing his hands across that strange smoothness. The secret of fashioning such perfect glass was gone—with so many other secrets of the Old Ones.

What he saw beyond his peephole nearly made him retreat, until he remembered the Star Men's tales. Those were not the Old Ones standing within the shadowed cavern, but effigies of themselves which they put up in shops to show off clothing. He pasted his nose to the glass and stared his fill at the shapes of three tall women and the draperies of rotting fabric still wreathed about them. None of that would, he knew, survive his touch.

It always turned to dust in the grasp of any explorer who tried to handle it.

There were other deep show windows about him but

all had been denuded of their glass and were empty. Through them one could get into the stores behind. But Fors was not yet ready to go hunting, and probably there would be little there now worth carrying away.

The building to his left was topped with a tall tower which reached higher into the heavens than any other around it. From the top of that a man might see the whole city, to measure its size and environs. But he knew that the Old Ones had movable cars rising in such buildings, the power for which was dead. There might not be any steps—and if there were his lame leg was not yet ready for climbing. Maybe before he left the city—It would be a workmanlike project to make a sketch of the city as seen from that tower—an excellent embellishment to a formal report.

That was the nearest he came to admitting even to himself that he had hopes of a future within the Eyrie, that he dreamed of standing before the elders of the Council and proving that he, the rejected mutant, had accomplished what others had been trained for all their lives long. When he thought of that he was warm deep inside. A new city—the one his father had sought— all mapped and explored, ready for the systematic looting of the Eyrie—what could a man who reported that ask for as a reward? Just about what he wanted—

Fors went on slowly, afoot now, with the mare trailing him and Lura scouting ahead. Neither animal appeared to want to stray too far. The sound of a rolling stone, the cries of the birds, all echoed through the empty buildings eerily. For the first time Fors wished for a companion of his own breed—in a place where only the dead had lain so long it would be good to call upon the living.

The sun overhead reflected from a shelf in the front part of a shop. Fors swung over a strip of iron embedded in concrete to investigate. Rings lay there, rows of them, set with brilliant white stones—diamonds he guessed. He sorted them out of the dust and litter. Most of them were too small to fit any of his fingers, but he chose four of the largest stones to take along— with some vague idea of surprising the young of the Eyrie. Among them was one broader band with a deep red gem and this slipped on to his third finger as if it had been fashioned for it. He turned it around, pleased with the deep crimson shade of the stone. It was a good omen, discovering it, as if the long dead craftsmen had made it for him. He would wear it for luck.

But food would be more useful than sparkling stones now. The mare must eat and they would not find grazing hereabouts. In this section there was only a wild waste of ruins. He must head out toward the edge of the city if he wanted a real camping place. Not through the valley of the trains, though. It would be better to measure the extent of the city by trying to get through it to the opposite side—if he could do that by night-fall.

Fors did not stop to explore any more of the shops, but he made mental notes about those which might be worth a second visit. It was slow work breaking a trail through the blocked streets, and the heat reflected back from the buildings raised sweat on his face and plastered his clothing to him. He had to mount again as his leg began to ache, and the hollow feeling in his middle grew worse. Lura protested—she wanted to get away from this wilderness of stone, into the fields where one could hunt.

Three hours of steady traveling brought them through to the edge of the enchanted wood, for that was what it seemed. It was a band of living green cutting across the pitiless heat and barrenness of the ruins. Once it had been a park, but now it arose a true forest which Lura welcomed with an open meow of delight. The mare whinnied, bursting through bushes until she came into what was undoubtedly a game trail leading down a gentle slope. Fors dismounted and let the mare go on, her pace now a trot. They reached the end of the trail, a lake. The mare stood, nose- and hock-deep, in the green water. Long red-gold fish swam away from the disturbance she caused.

Fors dropped down on a wide stone and pulled off his boots to dabble his burning feet in the coolness. There was a breeze across the water that dried his damp body and lifted the leaves of the wild shrubs around them. He looked across the lake. Opposite him there was a flight of broad white steps, cracked and moss-grown, and he caught a glimpse of a building at their head. But that could be explored later. Just now it was good to sit in the cool. The mare came out of the lake and tore up mouthfuls of the long grass. A duck quacked and fled from under her hoofs, sailing out on the water, swimming energetically toward the steps.

The evening was long, the twilight soft about the hidden lake. While there was still light enough to see Fors ventured into the tall, pillared building at the head of the stairs and discovered that his luck was still holding. It was a museum—one of those treasure houses which rated very high on the Star Men's list of desirable finds. He wandered through the high-ceilinged rooms, his boots making splotchy tracks in the fine dust crisscrossed with the spoor of small animals. He brushed the dust from the tops of cases and tried to spell out the blotched and faded signs. Grotesque stone heads leered or stared blindly through the murk. Warped and split canvas hung dismally from worm-eaten frames in what had once been picture galleries.

But the dark drove him out to shelter in the forecourt. Tomorrow would be time to estimate the worth of what lay within. Tomorrow—why, he had limitless time before him to discover and assess all that this city held! He had not even begun to explore.

It was warm and he allowed his cooking fire to burn down to a handful of coals. The forest was coming to life. He identified the bark of a questing fox, the mournful call of night birds. He could almost imagine the gathering of wistful, hungry ghosts in the city streets seeking what was gone forever. But here, where man had never lived, it was very peaceful and like the glens of his own mountain land. His hand fell on the pouch of the Star Men. Had Langdon actually walked here before him, had it been on a return trip from this place that his father had been killed? Fors hoped that was true—that Langdon had known the joy of proving his theory right—that his map had led him here before his death.

Lura appeared out of the shadows, padding lightly up the mossy steps from the water's edge. And the mare moved in without urging, her hoofs ringing on the broken marble as she came to join them. It was almost—Fors straightened, regarded the gathering night more intently—almost as if they feared an alien world enough to seek company against it. And yet he did not feel the unease he had known in those other ruins—this slice of woodland held no terrors.

Nevertheless he roused and went to gather as much wood as he could find. He worked with mounting haste until it was too dark to see at all, ending with a pile of broken branches and storm drift which might have been gathered to withstand a siege. Lura watched him—and beyond him—sitting sentry-wise at the head of the stairs. Nor did the mare move again into the open.

At last, his hands shaking a little with fatigue, the odd drive still urging him to some sort of effort, Fors strung his bow and set it close to hand, loosened his sword in its sheath. The wind had gone down. It was almost sultry. Above the water the birds had ceased to wheel.

There was a sudden thunder clap and a flash of violet lightning crossed the southern sky. Heat lightning, but there might be another storm on the way. That was probably what made the air seem electric. But Fors did not deceive himself. Something besides a storm was brooding out in that night.

Back in the Eyrie—when they watched the winter-time singplays—just before they drew up the big screen and the play began, he had had a strange feeling like this. A sort of excited waiting—that was it. And something else was waiting now—holding its breath a little. He squirmed. His imagination—he was cursed with too much of that!

A little was good. Langdon had always said that imagination was a tool to be used and no Star Man was any good without it. But when a man had too much—then it fed the dark fears way down inside and became an extra foe to fight in any battle.

But now, thinking of Langdon had not banished his strange feeling. Something was outside, dark and formless, brooding, watching—watching a tiny Fors beside a spark of puny fire—watching for some action—

He poked at the fire viciously. Getting as silly as a moon-mad woodsrunner! There must be a madness which lay in wait in these dead cities to trap a man's thoughts and poison him. A more subtle poison it was than any the Old Ones had distilled to fight their disastrous wars. He must break that grip on his mind—and do it quickly!

Lura watched him from across the fire, her blue eyes fired with topaz by the flames. She purred hoarsely, reassuringly. Fors relaxed a fraction of his guard. Lura's mood was an antidote. From the pouch he brought out the route book and began to enter—with painstaking attention and his best script—observations on the day's journey. If it was ever to be laid before Jarl it must measure up to the standard of such reports. The dark made a black circle beyond the reaches of the firelight.

·*· 6

Mantrap

The next day gave threat of being sultry. Fors awakened beset with a dull headache and vague memories of unpleasant dreams. His leg pained him. But when he examined the healing wound it showed no signs of the infection he dreaded. He longed for a swim in the lake but dared not try it until the throbbing seam had totally closed, being forced to content himself with splashing in the shallows.

Inside the museum the air was dead and there was a faint taint of decay hanging in the long chill corridors. Sightless masks hung on the walls and when he tested some of the displayed swords and knives he found them rusted into uselessness.

In the end he took very little—much of the exhibit was too delicate to transport or too large. He chose some tiny figurines from a case where the dusty card said something about "Egypt" and a clumsy finger ring set with a carving of a beetle from a neighboring shelf.

Last of all was a small sleek black panther, smooth and cool to his fingers, which he fell in love with and could not bear to leave behind. He did not venture into the side wings—not with all the city waiting for him.

But the museum was safe. Here were no falling walls and the alcove where he had spent the night was excellent shelter. He piled up his supplies in one corner before he sallied forth.

The mare was reluctant to leave the woods and the lake, but Fors' steady pull on her lead rope brought her back to the edge of the ruins. They went at a slow pace as he wanted to see what lay behind the spear points of glass which still clung in the shattered frames of the windows. These had all once been shops. How much of the wares they displayed were still worth plundering he could not guess. But he had to turn away in disappointment from fabrics eaten by insects and rotted by time.

In the fourth shop he entered was something better. An unbroken glass case contained a treasure even greater than all the museum had to offer. Shut out from dust and most of the destruction of time were boxes of paper—whole boxes with blocks of separate sheets— and also pencils!

Of course the paper was brittle, yellowed, and easily torn. But in the Eyrie it could be pulped and re-worked into serviceable sections. And the pencils! There were few good substitutes for those. And the third box he opened held colored ones! He sharpened two with his hunting knife and made glorious red and green lines on the dusty floor. All of these must go with him. In the back of the shop he found a metal box which still seemed sturdy enough and into it he crammed all that he could. This—from just one shop! What riches could be expected from the city!

Why, here the men of the Eyrie could explore and

loot perhaps for years before they exhausted all the supplies to be found. The only safe cities they had discovered before had been known to other tribes and were combed almost clean—or else they had been held by the Beast Things and were unsafe.

Fors tramped on, bits of glass crunching under his boots, skirting piles of rubble he could not clamber over. Such piles barricaded some shops entirely or else the roofs were unsafe. He was several blocks beyond the shop of the paper before he came to a second one easy to enter. It had been another dealing in rings and gems. But the interior was in wild disorder as if it had been looted before. Cases lay smashed and the glass mingled with metal and stones on the floor. He stood in the doorway—it would take a long time to sort through that litter and the effort was not necessary. Only—as he turned away—he caught sight of something else on the floor which brought him back.

There was a patch of mud, dried brick-hard. And pressed deep into its surface, holding the pattern as if in a cast, was part of a footprint. He had seen its like before, near the pool of fresh deer blood. Those long narrow toe marks with the talon nail indentations could never be forgotten. That other print had been fresh. This was old. It might have been made months, even years before. The mud which held it crumbled under the prod of his finger tip. Fors backed out of the shop and stood with his back to a tumbling wall. The instinctive reaction which had made him do that also sent his eyes up and down the street.

Birds nested in the broken windows of the building across from him, flitting in and out on their own concerns. And not ten feet away a large gray rat sat on a pile of brick combing its fur and watching him with almost intelligent interest. It was a very large rat and a singularly fearless one. But no rat had made that footprint.

Fors summoned Lura from her ranging. With the cat to scout for him he would feel safer against attack. But he was still conscious of the many places where death could lurk, behind walls, in the pits which broke the street, in the open store fronts.

In the next hour he went about a mile, keeping to the main street and visiting only those buildings which Lura declared safe. The mare carried an odd assortment of bundles and he realized that he could not hope to transport more than a few selected samples of the abundance. He must cache part of his morning's finds in the museum and take only the cream of his gleanings south. Now that the city was discovered the men from the Eyrie would "work" it with greater efficiency, sending experts to choose and dismantle what they needed most and could best use. So the sooner he started back with the news, the more time they would have to work here before the coming of the bad weather in the fall.

The day grew even warmer and big black flies came out of the crevices of the stones to bite viciously, making the mare so crazy he could hardly control her. He had best head back now to the green and the lake and there sort over his loot. But, as they passed the place where he had found the wealth of paper, he stepped in for a last check upon all he must leave behind. The sun made a bright bar across the floor bringing into prominence the pencil marks he had made there. But—he was certain he had not used a yellow or blue pencil, although there had been a few.

Now—yellow and blue lines crisscrossed the red and green ones he had left—almost challengingly. The boxes of pencils he had piled for later transportation had been opened and two were gone!

He could see the tracks in the floor dust—his own boot-heel pattern and across that a more shapeless outline. And in the corner by the door someone had spit out the stone of a cherry!

Fors whistled in Lura. She examined the evidence on the floor and waited for instructions. But she was displaying none of the disgust with which she had greeted that earlier spoor. This might have been left by a roving Plainsman who was exploring the city on his own. If that were so, it behooved Fors to move quickly. He must get back to the Eyrie and return with help before some other tribe staked out a fair claim to the riches here. Once or twice before the mountaineers had been so disappointed.

Now there would be no question about leaving most of the spoil he had gathered. He must cache it in the museum and travel as light as possible to make time. Frowning, he stamped out of the shop and jerked at the mare's lead rope.

They came into the woods, cutting across a glade in the general direction of the museum. The mare snorted as they passed the end of the lake. Fors tugged her along by main force, bringing her up the steps to be relieved of her load. He packed the bundles into the room he now considered his own and freed the mare for grazing. Lura would keep watch until he had time to get everything in order.

But when Fors spread out the morning's loot on the floor he found it very difficult to pick and choose. If he took this—then he could not carry that—and *that* might make a greater impression upon the experts of the Eyrie. He made piles, only to completely change their contents three and four times over. But in the end he made up a pack which he hoped would best display to the mountain clan the quality of this find and be a good example of his own powers of selection. The rest could be easily concealed somewhere in the rambling halls of this building until he returned.

He sighed as he began to sort the discards into order. There was so much to be left behind—why, he should have a pack train of horses, such as the Plains tribes used to carry their gear on the march. The drum rolled and he picked it up, rubbing his fingers across its top to hear again the queer pulsing sound. Then he tapped with his nails and the sound echoed weirdly through the halls.

This must have been the drum which had sounded through the night after his fight with the boar. A signal—! He could not resist other experimental thumps—and then tried out the rhythm of one of his own mountain hunting songs. But this strong music was more eerie than any from the flute or the three- and four-stringed harps his people knew.

As the frightening rumble died away Lura flowed in, her eyes uncannily aglow, haste and urgency expressed in every dark hair on her head. He must come with her and at once. Fors dropped the drum and reached for his bow. Lura stood by the door, her tail tip flicking.

She went down the steps in two bounds and he went after her, not sparing his leg. The mare was standing in the shallows of the lake undisturbed. Lura glided on, between trees and bushes and into the thick depths of the wood. Fors followed at a slower pace, not being able to move so quickly through the green obstruction.

But before he had gone out of sight of the lake he heard it—a faint moaning cry, almost a sigh, which had been wrung out of real suffering. It arose to a hoarse croak, framing muffled words he did not understand.

But human lips had shaped them, he was sure of that. Lura would not have guided him to one of the Beast Things.

The gabble of strange words died away into another moan which seemed to rise out of the ground before him. Fors shied away from an expanse of dried grass and leaves which lay there. Lura had dropped to her belly, reaching out with a forepaw to feel delicately of the ground, not advancing into the small clearing.

One of the pits which he had found throughout the city was Fors' first thought—at any rate a hole of some sort. Now he could see a break through at the opposite end of this cleared space. He started to edge around, treading on the half-exposed roots of trees and bushes and holding on firmly to anything which looked sturdy.

From the torn gap in the mat of dried grass and brush rose a sickening stench. Trying to spare his leg he went to his knees and peered into the dusk below. What he saw there set his stomach to churning.

It was a wicked trap—that pit—a trap artfully constructed and skillfully concealed with the matted covering. And it held its victims. The small deer had been dead for days, but the other body which, as his eyes adjusted to the dim light, he saw writhe weakly, must have lain there for a shorter time. The blood on the impaled shoulder still ran free.

Sharp-pointed stakes had been set in the earth at the bottom, pointing upward to catch and hold the fallen for a tortured death. And the man who half hung, half lay there now had escaped that death by less than six inches.

He had struggled to free himself, as the gaping wound in his own flesh testified, but all his strength had not brought him loose. Fors measured the space between the stakes and then looked around for a good-sized tree. This would not be easy—

It did not take long to fetch what was left of his climbing rope and make a noose in it. The man in the pit looked up with glazed eyes. Whether he could see or understand what his rescuer was planning Fors did not know. He fastened the end of the cord to an arrow and shot the line over the branch which hung the closest to the trap.

To make one end of the rope fast to the tree took only an instant. Then, with the other in his hand, Fors lowered himself cautiously over the edge of the pit, using his elbows to break his speed as he slipped down to the smeared stakes. Black flies rose in a noxious cloud and he had to beat them off as he reached the side of the prisoner. The belt about the fellow's middle was tight enough and he knotted the rope.

The way out of the pit was more difficult, since the makers had fashioned it with every precaution against that very operation. But a landslide at one end gave some footing and Fors fought his way back to the top. It was plain that whoever had set that pitfall had not visited it for some time and Fors left the sentry duty to Lura.

This was going to be a nasty business, but it was the only way he could see of saving the sufferer below. He untied the rope end on the tree and twisted it about his wrists. Lura came without being summoned and seized the dangling tip in her jaws. Together they gave their weight to a quick jerk which was answered by a wild scream of agony. But Fors did not lessen the steady pull and Lura matched him step by step as he crept back.

Out of the black hole rose the lolling head and bloody shoulders of the stranger. When he swung clear Fors made fast the rope and hurried back to pull the limp body away from the edge of the fiendish mantrap. His hands were slippery with blood before he got the unconscious man free. He could not carry the fellow, not with his bad leg. Also he must weigh more than Fors by forty pounds. For, now that he lay in the sunlight, Fors recognized him as the dark-skinned hunter of the island. But his big body was flaccid and his face greenish under its brown pigment. At least the blood was not spurting from that wound—no artery had been touched. He must get the stranger back to the museum where he could see to the ugly tear—

There was a crashing in the brush. Fors hurled himself for the bow which lay where he had dropped it. But it was Lura who came out, urging the mare before her. The scent of blood made the mare roll her eyes and circle away, but Fors wanted no nonsense now and Lura was of a like mind. She walked up to the horse and gave several low snarls. The mare stood still, sweating, her eyes showing white. But she did not rear as Fors somehow got his patient across her back.

Once back in the shelter of the museum he gave a sigh of relief and rolled the stranger onto his blanket. The other's eyes were open again and this time with the light of reason in their dark brown depths. The hunter was very young. Now that he was so helpless this was plain. He could not count many more years than did Fors himself—in spite of his big frame and wide, well-muscled shoulders. He lay in quiet patience watching Fors make a fire and prepare the salve, but he said nothing, even when the mountaineer went to work with his crude surgery.

The stake had passed through the skin of the shoulder, tearing a wicked gouge, but, Fors saw with relief, breaking no bones. If infection did not develop the stranger would recover.

His handling of that torn flesh must have caused the stranger agony but he made no sound, although when

Fors finished at last beads of bright crimson showed along the other's lower lip. He made a gesture with his good hand toward the pouch at his belt and Fors unfastened it. He selected with fumbling fingers a small bag of white material and pushed it into his rescuer's hands, jerking his thumb at the pannikin of water Fors had used during the surgery. There was a coarse brownish meal in the bag. Fors drew fresh water, shook in a little of the stuff and set it back on the fire. His patient nodded and smiled weakly. Then he stabbed himself in the chest with a forefinger and said:

"Arskane"—

"Fors," and then pointing to Lura the mountaineer added, "Lura."

Arskane nodded his head and added a sentence in a deep, almost rolling voice which had a drum note in it. Fors frowned. Some of those words—yes, they were like his own speech. The accent, though, was different—there was a slurring of certain sounds. He tried in his turn.

"I am Fors of the Puma Clan from the Smoking Mountains—" He tried gestures to piece out meaning.

But Arskane sighed. His face was drawn and tired and his eyes closed wearily. Plainly he could not make the effort for coherent speech now. Fors' chin rested on the palm of his hand and he stared into the fire. This was going to alter his own plans drastically. He could not go away and leave Arskane alone, unable to fend for himself. And the big man might not be able to travel for days. He would have to think about this.

The boiling water began to give off a fragrant odor— new to his nostrils but enticing. He sniffed the steam as the water turned brown. When the liquid was quite dark he took a chance and pulled the pan off to cool.

Arskane stirred and turned his head. He smiled at the steam arising from the water and gestured that when it was ready he would drink.

This, then, must be the medicine of his own people. Fors waited, tested it with a cautious finger tip, and then raised the dark head on his arm, holding the pan to those bitten lips. Half the liquid was gone before Arskane signed he had enough. He motioned for Fors to try it too, but a single bitter mouthful was enough to satisfy the mountaineer. It tasted far worse than it smelled.

For the rest of the afternoon Fors was busy. He hunted with Lura, bringing back the best parts of a deer they surprised at the end of the lake, and some of the quail flushed out of the grass. He added an uncounted number of armloads to the stack of firewood. There were berries, too, won from a briar thicket. And, when at last he threw himself down beside the fire and stretched out his aching leg, he was so tired he thought that he could not move again. But now they were provisioned for more than one day ahead. The mare had shown a tendency to wander off, so he shut her into one of the long corridors for the night.

Arskane was awake again after the fitful feverish sleep of the afternoon, and he watched as Fors prepared the birds for broiling. He ate, but not as much as Fors offered. The mountaineer was worried. There might have been poison upon those trap stakes. And he had nothing with which to combat that. He heated up the bitter brown water and made Arskane drink it to the dregs. If there was any virtue in the stuff the big man needed all its help now.

As it grew dark Fors' patient fell asleep again but his attendant hunched close to the fire, even though the evening was warm. The mantrap was occupying his thoughts. True, all the evidence pointed to its not being visited for a long time by those who had set it. The trapped deer in it had been dead for days and there had been another skeleton, picked clean by insects and birds, at the other end of the hold. But someone or something had spent much labor and time in its construction, and it had been devised by a mind both cunning and cruel. No Plainsman he had ever heard of followed that crafty method of hunting, and it was certainly not to the taste of the men of the Eyrie. It was new to Arskane, or he would not have fallen a victim to it. So that meant others—not of the plains or of the mountains or of Arskane's tribe—others roaming this city at their will. And in the cities there lived at ease only—the Beast Things!

Fors' mouth was dry, he rubbed his hands across his knees. Langdon had died under the throwing darts and the knives of the Beast Things. Others of the Star Men had met them—and had not returned from that meeting. Jarl wore a crooked red seam down his forearm which was the result of a brush with one of their scouts. They were horrible, monstrous—not human. Fors was mutant—yes. But he was still human. These were not. And it was because of the Beast Things that mutants were so feared. For the first time he began to understand that. There was a purpose behind the hatred of the mutants. But he was human! And the Beast Things were not!

He had never seen one, and the Star Men who had and survived never talked about them to the commoners of the Eyrie. Legend made them boogies of the dark—ogres—foul things of the night.

What if it had been a Beast Thing trap Arskane had been caught in? Then the Things must live here. There were thousands upon thousands of hiding places in the ruins to shelter them. And only Lura's instinct and hunting skill, and his own ears and eyes to guard them. He looked out into the dusk and shivered. Ears and eyes, bow and sword, claws and teeth—maybe none of those would be enough!

∗⁺∗ 7

Death Plays Hide and Seek

For four days Arskane lay in the cool hall of the museum while Fors hunted for the pot or ranged in scouting trips through the woodland, never venturing too far from the white building. And at night across the fire they grew familiar with each other's speech and exchanged stories of their past.

"Our Old Ones were flying men," Arskane's deep voice rolled across the room. "After the Last Battle they came down from the sky to their homeland and found it blasted into nothing. Then they turned their machines and fled south and when the machines would no longer bear them in the sky they landed in a narrow desert valley. And after a time they took to wife the women of that country. So did my tribe spring forth—

"On the fringes of the desert, life is very hard, but my people learned to use the waste for what it will give man and later they held much good land. Until twice twelve moons ago did they hold it—then the earth trembled and shook so that a man could not stand upright. From the mountains to our southland came fire and many evil smells. Talu of the Long Beard and Mack the Three Fingered died of coughing in the death fog which came down upon the village. And in the morning the world shook again just as the dawn light broke and this time the mountains spewed forth burning rock which flowed down to engulf the best of our hard-won fields and pastures. So we gathered what we might and fled before it, all the tribe together, driving our sheep and taking with us only what might be carried in the pony carts and on our backs.

"We struck to the north and discovered that the earth had broken in other places also so that to the east the sea had eaten into the land. Then we must flee from the rising waters as we had fled from the fire. And it seemed that nowhere might we find a place to call our own again. Until at last we came into this territory where so many of the Old Ones once had lived. Then some of the young warriors, myself among them, were sent on to scout and mark out fields for our sowing and a place to build anew the Village of Birds. This is a fair country—" Arskane's hand gestured south. "I saw much and should have returned with my news, but, having come so far, my heart would not let me rest until I saw more and more of its wonders. I watched in secret the comings and goings of the Plainspeople, but they are not as my folk. It is in their hearts to live in houses of skin which may be set up in any field they choose and taken down again when they grow weary. Your mountain breed I do not know— we have little liking for high places since our mountains brought destruction upon us.

"These cities of the dead have their uses. One can find treasures here—as you know well. One can also find worse things." He touched the bandage pad on his shoulder. "I do not think my people will have a liking for the cities. Now, when I can again walk a straight trail, I must go back to report to the tribe. And maybe it shall follow that we will settle along some river valley where the soil is black and rich. And there shall we open up old fields to the seed grain, and turn out our sheep to graze on the hillsides. Then shall the Village of Birds again take root, in a fair and fruitful land." He sighed.

"You have named yourself a warrior," Fors said slowly. "Against whom do you war? Are there Beast Things also in your deserts?"

Arskane smiled grimly. "In the days of the Great Blow-up the Old Ones loosed certain magic they could not control. Our wise ones know not the secret, having only to guide them the tales of our fathers, the flying men. But this magic acted in strange and horrible ways. There were things in the desert which were born enemy to man, scaled creatures most horrible to look upon. The magic made these both cunning and quick so that it was ever war to the death between them and all human-kind. But as yet they seem few and perhaps the molten rock from the mountains has eaten them up entirely. For we have seen none of their breed since we left."

"Radiation." Fors played with the hilt of his short sword. "Radiation mutations—but sometimes it worked well. Lura's kind was born of such magic!"

The dark-skinned southerner looked at the cat who sprawled at ease beyond. "That was good—not evil—magic. I wish that my people had friends such as that to protect them in their wanderings. For we have had to fight many times against beasts and men. The Plainspeople have not shown themselves friends to us.

There is always danger to watch for. One night when I was in a dead place I was set upon by a pack of nightmare creatures. Had I not been able to climb beyond their reach and use my knife well they would have stripped the flesh from my bones."

"That I know." Fors brought out the drum and put it into the other's hands and Arskane gave a little cry of pure delight.

"Now can I talk with the Master of Scouts!" His fingers started to tap out a complicated beat on the head but Fors' hand shot out and clamped about his wrist.

"No!" The mountaineer forced the fingers away from the drum. "That might signal others—as well as your people. It was a thing unknown to me which dug that trap—"

The scowl which twisted Arskane's black brows smoothed away as the mountaineer continued:

"I believe that that is the work of the Beast Things. And if they still skulk in this city your drum would bring them in—"

"The trap was old—"

"Yes. But never yet have we found Beast Things living together in great numbers. He who set it may now be still dwelling only the length of these ruins from us. This is a large city and all the men of the Eyrie would not be enough to search it well."

"Your tongue is as straight as your wit." Arskane set aside the drum. "We shall get free of this dwelling place of shadows before I try to speak with the tribe. Tomorrow I shall be able to take the trail. Let us be off with the dawn light. There is an evil in these old places which seems to clog the nostrils. I like better the cleanness of the open land."

Fors made up a small bundle of the city loot, caching what remained in an inner room. His leg was fully healed and Arskane could ride the mare for the next day or two. Regretfully the mountaineer looked upon the pile of his gleanings before he covered them up. But at least he had the map he had made and the journal of his explorations both packed away in the Star pouch, along with some of the colored pencils and the small figures from the museum case.

Arskane wandered through the building most of the afternoon, trying his legs he said, but also interested in what lay there. Now he wore on one wrist a wide band of wrought gold and carried a massive club with the head of a spike embedded in a ball which he had found in a room devoted to implements of war. His throwing spears and bow had been recovered from the depths of the trap but the shafts of the spears were broken and he could not draw the bow until his shoulder healed.

The sultry heat of the past days had not yet closed in when they ate their last meal in the museum at dawn the next day and stamped out the fire. Arskane protested against riding but Fors argued him up on the mare and they started out along the one trail the mountaineer had mapped, the one which had brought him into the city. They made no stops, traveling at their best pace down the littered street—with before them the cluster of tall buildings which had been Fors' goal on his first day in the city. If fortune favored them he was sure they could be almost out of the circle of the ruins by nightfall.

Arskane used his hands as sun shields and watched with wonder the towering buildings they moved among.

"Mountains—man made—that is what we see here. But why did the Old Ones love to huddle together in such a fashion? Did they fear their own magic so that they must live cheek to cheek with their kind lest it

eat them up when it was loosed—as it did? Well, they
died of it in the end, poor Old Ones. And now we have
a better life—"

"Do we?" Fors kicked at a loose stone. "They had
such knowledge—we are groping in the dark for only
crumbs of what they knew—"

"But they did not use all their learning for good!"
Arskane indicated the ruins. "This city came out of their
minds and then it was also destroyed by them. They
built only to tear down again. I think it better to build
than to blast."

As the murmur of his words died away Fors' head
snapped around. He had caught a whisper of sound,
a faint pattering. And had he, or had he not, seen the
loathsome outline of a bloated rat body slipping into
a shattered window? There were sounds among the
stones—almost as if some thing—or things—were
following them.

Lura's ears were flat to her skull, her eyes only battle
slits in her brown mask. She stood with her forepaws
planted upon a fallen column staring back along the
track they had come, the tip of her tail quivering.

Arskane caught their unease.

"What is—"

At first Fors thought that the scream which
answered that half question came from the throat of
a bird. And then the mare swung up her head and gave
a second wild cry. Arskane threw himself off just as
she reared to crash back on the stones. Then Fors saw
the dart rising and falling in the gaping wound which
had torn open her throat.

"In—!" Arskane's hand about his wrist jerked him
into a cavern opening in the front of the highest tower.
As they fled Lura's blood-chilling war cry ripped the
air. But a second later she too was with them pushing
back into the dark center of the building.

They paused at the top of a ramp which led down into murky shadows. There were floors below. Fors could see a bit of them. But Arskane pointed to the floor. Beaten in the dust and dried mud was a regular path of footprints—made by feet too narrow—clawed feet!

Lura backed away from that highway spitting and snarling. So—they had escaped but come straight into the stronghold of the enemy! And it did not need the cry of triumph from without, coming in shrill inhuman exultation, to confirm that.

But the trail led down—they might still go up! Lura and Arskane shared Fors' thought, for both ran for the left hand corridor which was parallel to the street level. There were heavy doors along the hall, and no matter how hard they pushed none of these gave. Only one at the very end was open and they crowded up to look down a shaft into utter darkness. But Fors had glimpsed something else.

"Hold my belt!" he ordered Arskane. "There is something to the left—"

With the southerner's fingers hooked in his belt he dared to swing over the edge of the opening. He was right, a ladder of metal strips protruded from the wall. And when he looked up he could see a square of dull light above which must mean another open door maybe a floor or two above. But could Lura and Arskane climb too?

Arskane flexed his arms as Fors explained, testing his shoulder.

"How far above is the opening?" he wanted to know.

"Perhaps two floors—"

While they hesitated Lura edged to the lip of the shaft, measured with her eyes the reach to the ladder, and then was gone before Fors could stop her. They heard the rasp of her claws on the metal—a sound to be drowned out by another—a shuffling noise of many feet. The inhabitants of the lower depths were issuing out to hunt. Arskane tested the lashing which held his war club to his belt. Then he smiled—if a bit crookedly.

"Two floors should not be beyond my strength. And we can only try, my friend."

He judged his distance as the cat had done and then swung away. With a pounding heart Fors waited where he was, not daring to watch that ascent. But the sound he dreaded most to hear—that of a falling body—did not follow. He fitted an arrow to his bow cord and waited.

And that wait was not long. A grayish shadow at the far corner of the corridor was target enough. He shot, pinning the gray patch to the wall with the steel-headed war arrow. Something screeched and tried to jerk free. But before it did Fors had shouldered his bow and had pushed off for the ladder. The strips remained firm under his weight—his minor nightmare had been their breaking loose after taking the strain of the cat and the big southerner—and he scrambled up at a furious pace, his breathing sounding a hurricane in his own ears. He pulled himself through that other gray space to find Lura and Arskane both anxiously waiting for him.

They were in a second corridor fronted by rows of doors, but some of these were already open. Arskane disappeared through the nearest while Fors lay belly down on the floor, his head at the opening of the shaft, listening to the sounds from below. The wailing of the thing he had wounded faded away but the shuffling noise was louder and there were growls which might or might not have been speech. So far the creatures below had not discovered how the quarry had fled.

Fors scrambled to his feet and caught at the door which had once closed the shaft—now it stood a few inches out from where it slid into the wall. Under his tugging it gave a little with a faint grating sound. The mountaineer exerted his full strength and gained a foot more.

But the grating must have betrayed them. There was a shout below and a dart sped up the shaft, to spin harmlessly back again. Arskane came up pushing before him a collection of moldering furniture.

Odd noises arose from the shaft but Fors was not tricked into looking over the edge. He continued his silent struggle with the door. Arskane stood to help him. Together they fought the stubborn metal, salt sweat stung in their eyes and dripped from their chins.

In the shaft the sounds grew louder. Several more darts skimmed into the light and fell. One, aimed with more skill or luck, skidded out across the floor between Fors' feet. Arskane turned to his heap of furniture and gave it one mighty push, toppling the whole pile over. There was a terrified yell in answer and a distant crash. Arskane rubbed a dusty hand across his wet jaw.

"One of them, by the Horned Lizard, climbs no more!"

They had the door halfway across the shaft opening now. And all at once its resistance ended with a snap which almost sent them both flying. Fors cried out triumphantly—but too soon. A foot was all they had gained. There still remained open space enough for a body to squeeze through.

Arskane drew off and considered the door for a long moment. Then he slapped it with the flat of his hand, putting behind that blow all the force he could muster. Again it gave and came forward a few inches. But the sounds in the shaft had begun again. The hunters had not been deterred by the fate of their companion.

Something flipped out of the dark, landing close to Fors' foot. It was a hand, but skeleton thin and covered with wrinkled grayish skin. As it scrabbled with twisted claws for a hold it seemed more a rat's paw than a hand. Fors raised his foot and stamped, grinding the boot, nailed to cross mountain trails, into the very center of the monstrosity. The scream which answered that came from the mouth of the shaft. They threw themselves in a last furious attack upon the door, their nails breaking and tearing on the metal—and it gave—snapping into the groove awaiting in the opposite wall.

For a long moment they leaned panting against the wall of the corridor, holding their bruised and bleeding hands out before them. Fists were beating against that door but it did not move.

"That will stay closed," Arskane gasped at last. "They cannot hang upon the wall ladder and force it. If there is no other way up we are safe—for a time—"

Lura came down the hallway, threading her way in and out of the rooms along it. And there was no menace there. They would have a breathing spell. Or were they now caught in a trap as cruel as the one which had engulfed Arskane in the museum wood?

The southerner turned to the front of the building and Fors followed him to one of the tall windows, long bare of glass, which gave them sight of the street below. They could see the body of the mare but the pack she had carried had been stripped off and there was something odd about the way she lay—

"So—they are meat eaters—"

Fors gagged at Arskane's words. The mare was meat—maybe they, too, were—meat! He raised sick eyes and saw that the same thought lay in the big man's mind. But Arskane's hand was also on the club he had taken from the museum.

"Before this meat goes into any pot, it will have to be taken. And the hunting of it is going to cost them sore. These are the Beast Things of which you have spoken, are they not, comrade?"

"I believe so. And they are reputed to be crafty—"

"Then must we, too, be sly. Now, since we cannot go down—let us see what may lie above us."

Fors watched the pigeons wheeling about the ruins. The floor under their feet was white with bird droppings.

"We have no wings—"

"No—but I am bred of a race which once flew," Arskane answered with a sort of quiet humor coloring his tone. "We shall find a way out of here that that offal below cannot follow. Let us now seek it."

They passed out of one hall into another, looking into the rooms along the way. Here were only decaying sticks of furniture and bones. In the third hall were more of the shaft doors—all closed. Then, in the far end of one back hall, Arskane pushed open a last door and they came upon stairs which led both up and down.

Lura brushed past them and went down, fading away with her customary skill and noiselessness. They squatted down in the shadows to wait her report.

Arskane's face showed a grayish tinge which was not born of the lack of light. The struggle up that ladder and with the door had left its marks on him. He grunted and settled his bad shoulder gingerly against the wall. Fors edged forward. Now that they were quiet his ears could work for him. He heard the pattering which was Lura on her way, the trickle of powdered rubble which her paws had disturbed somewhere.

There was no sign hereabout that the Beast Things had used this stair. But—Lura had stopped! Fors closed his eyes, blanking out his own thoughts, trying as he never had before to catch the emanations of the big cat's mind. She was not in any danger but she was baffled. The path before her was closed in such a manner that she could not win through. And when her brown head appeared again above the top step Fors knew that they could not escape by that route. He said as much to Arskane.

The tall man pulled himself to his feet with a weary sigh.

"So. Then let us climb—but gently, comrade. These stairs of the Old Ones beat a man's breath out of his body!"

Fors pulled Arskane's arm over his shoulder, taking some of the weight of the larger man.

"Slow shall it be—we have the full day before us—"

"And perhaps the night, too, and some other days. Well, climb—comrade."

Five floors higher Arskane sank down, pulling Fors with him. And the mountaineer was glad of the rest. They had gone slowly, to be sure, but now his leg ached and his breath sobbed in a band of pain beneath his ribs.

For a space they simply sat there, taking deep breaths and resting. Then Fors noticed with dismay that the sunlight was fading in the patches on the floor. He crawled to a window and looked out. Through the jagged teeth of broken buildings he could see the waters of the lake and the sun was far into the west. It must be late afternoon.

Arskane shook himself awake at that information.

"Now we come," he observed, "to the matter of food. And perhaps we have too often refreshed ourselves from your canteen—"

Water! Fors had forgotten that. And where inside this maze would they find either food or drink? But Arskane was on his feet now and going through the door which must lead to the rest of that floor. Birds— Fors remembered the evidences of their nesting here— that would be the answer—birds!

But they came into a long room where some soft fabric lay under their feet. There were many tables set in rows down its length, each encircled by chairs. Fors caught the glint of metal laid out in patterns on the nearest. He picked up an unmistakable fork! This then had been an eating place of the Old Ones. But the food—any food would be long since gone.

He said that aloud only to have Arskane shake his head.

"Not so, comrade. Rather do I say that we are favored with such luck as few men have. In my journey north I chanced upon just such a place as this and in the smaller rooms behind I found many containers of food left by the Old Ones, but still good. That night did I eat as might a chieftain when the Autumn Dances begin—"

"To eat food found in the old places is to choose death. That is the law!" repeated Fors stubbornly. But he did trail along behind as Arskane moved purposefully toward the door at the other end of the room.

"They had foods and drinks of many kinds. Now and again some few are safe, but the containers that holds it must be perfect—without blemish. I live, do I not, and I have eaten of the bounty left by the Old Ones. We can do no less than seek for it here."

Arskane, wise from his earlier experience, brought them into a room where shelves stood around the walls. Containers of glass and metal were arranged in rows along the shelves. Fors marveled at the abundance. But the southerner walked slowly around, peering intently at the glass containers, paying no attention to the metal ones red with rust. Selecting four bottles and a glass canister filled with white crystals, he put them down on the table in the center of the room.

"Look well at the label, comrade." Arskane pointed

to the picture of a bubbling spring on each bottle. "Note the sealing. If you see no signs of decay there, then strike it off and drink!"

And drink they did, of water gathered generations before their birth. Then Arskane poured the contents of the third bottle into the opened canister, dissolving its sparkling crystals into a thick, clear syrup.

Fors found it shockingly sweet—stronger than any honey he had ever tasted. But it sated their hunger as the water had appeased their thirst. He noticed sounds from the rooms ahead. Lura feasted also—so birds did nest here.

Arskane tapped the last bottle with his belt knife.

"We need not worry about provisions for the moment. And tomorrow we shall discover a way out of here. For once the Beast Things of the dead places have found their match!"

And Fors met that confidence with his own.

·*·* 8

Where Once Men Flew—

They slept fitfully that night on piles of moldering fabrics they dragged together, and on rousing ate and drank again from the supplies in the storeroom. Then they climbed once more until the steps ended in a platform which had once been walled by large glass windows. Below the city spread out in all its broken glory. Fors identified the route he had pioneered on entering and pointed it out. And Arskane did the same for the one he had followed in the east.

"South should be our road now—straight south—"

Fors laughed shortly at that observation.

"We have yet to win free of this one building," he objected. But Arskane was ready with an answer to that.

"Come!" One of his big hands cupped the mountaineer's shoulder as he drew Fors to the empty window space facing east. Far below lay the broad roof of a neighbor building, its edge tight against the side of the tower.

"You have this." Arskane flipped the end of the mountain rope still wrapping Fors' belt. "We must go down to those windows just above that roof and swing through to it. See, south lies a road of roofs across which we may travel for a space. These Beast Things may be cunning but perhaps they do not watch the sky route against escape—it hangs above the ways they seem to like best. It is in my mind that they hug the ground on their journeyings—"

"It is said that they best love to slink in the burrows," confirmed Fors. "And they are supposed to be none too fond of the open light of day—"

Arskane plucked his full lower lip between forefinger and thumb. "Night fighters—eh? Well then, day is the time for us—the light is in our favor."

They made the long climb down with lighter hearts. A story above the neighboring roof they found a window in the center of the hallway which faced in the right direction, broke out the few splinters of glass still set dagger-like in the frame, and leaned out to reconnoiter.

"The rope will not be needed after all," Arskane commented. "That drop is easy." He took a strong grip on the window frame and flexed his muscles.

Fors crossed to the next window and set an arrow on his bow cord. But, as far as he could see, the roof below, the silent blank windows were empty of menace. Only—he could not cover all of those. And death might fly from any one of the hundreds of black holes, above, below—

But this was their best—maybe their only chance of escape. Arskane grunted with pain from his shoulder. Then he was out, tumbling down to the surface below. As quickly as he had taken the leap he dodged behind the high parapet.

For a long moment they both waited, frozen. Then,

in a flash of brown and cream, Lura went through, making a more graceful landing. She sped across the roof, a streak of light fur.

So far—so good. Fors freed himself from quiver, Star Man's pouch, and bow, tossing them through in the general direction of Arskane. Then he hoisted himself on the sill and swung. He heard Arskane's shout of warning just as he let go. Startled, he could not prepare for a proper landing but fell hard—with a force which jarred him.

He squirmed over on his back. A dart quivered in the frame of the window where his hand had rested. He rolled into the safety of the parapet with a force which brought him up with a crack against Arskane's knees.

"Where did that come from?"

"There!" The southerner pointed at the row of windows in the building across the street. "From one of those—"

"Let us go—"

Belly flat, Fors started a snake's progress toward the opposite end of the roof. They could not go back now—to try to climb up to that window would be to present a target which even a fumbling marksman could not miss. But now the hunt was on and they would have to make a running fight of it through a maze which the enemy knew intimately and they did not know at all—a maze that might be studded with traps more subtle and more cruel than the one which had imprisoned Arskane—

A thin fluting—like the piping of a child's reed whistle—cut the air somewhere behind. Fors guessed it to be what he had dreaded most to hear—the signal that the quarry had been flushed out of hiding and was now to be pursued in the open.

Arskane had forged ahead. And because the big man

seemed to know just what he was going to do next Fors accepted his lead. They came into a corner of the parapet between the east and south sides of the roof. Lura had already gone over it; she called softly from below.

"Now we must trust to luck, comrade—and to the favor of Fortune. Slip over quickly on the same instant that I move. It may be that if we give them two targets they will not be able to choose either. Are you ready?"

"Yes!"

"Then—go!"

Fors reached up and caught the top of the parapet at the same moment Arskane moved. Together their bodies went over and they let themselves roll across the second roof, painfully shedding some skin in the process. Here the surface was not clear. Blocks, fallen from a taller building beyond, made a barrier which Arskane greeted with an exclamation of satisfaction. Both gained the protection of the rubble and squatted down to listen. The pipe of the whistle sounded again, imperatively. Arskane rubbed dust off his hands.

"Beyond here lies another street, and below is the river valley which you crossed—"

Fors nodded. He, too, could remember what they had seen from the tower. The river valley made a curve, cutting due east at this point. He shut his eyes for an instant the better to visualize the old train yards, the clustered buildings—

"Well," Arskane shook himself, "if we give them more time they will be better able to greet us in a manner we shall not relish. Therefore, we must keep on the move. Now that they expect to find us on roof tops it might be wise to seek the street level—"

"See here." Fors had been examining the rubbish

about them. "This did not fall from above." He dug into the pile of rubble. Set in the roof was a slanted door. Arskane pounced upon it joyfully.

They dug as furiously as ground squirrels in autumn until they cleared it. Then they tugged it open and looked down into a musty darkness from which old evil odors arose. There were stairs, almost ladder steep. They used them.

Long hallways and more stairs. Although all three walked with the silence of forest hunters their passing sent small thuds and old sighings through the deserted building. Now and again they stopped to listen. But Lura manifested no signs of uneasiness and Fors could hear nothing beyond the fall of plaster, the shifting of old boards their tread had disturbed.

"Wait!" He caught Arskane as the latter started down the last flight of stairs. Fors' swinging hand had struck lightly against a door in the wall and something in the hollow sound which had followed that blow seemed promising. He opened the door. They stepped out on a kind of ledge above a wide cavern of a place.

"By the Great Horned Lizard!" Arskane was shaken and Fors gripped the rail which framed the platform.

They looked down into what once must have been a storage place for the heavy trucks which the Old Ones had used for transportation of goods. Ten—fifteen of the monsters stood in line waiting for the masters who were long gone. And several were of the advanced engine type which had been the last invention of the Old Ones. These appeared unblighted by time, still perfect and ready for use.

One of them had its nose almost against a wide closed door. A door, decided Fors instantly, which must give upon the street. A wild idea began to flower in his mind. He turned to Arskane.

"There was a road leading down into the valley of the trains—a road which was mostly steep slope—"

"True—"

"See that machine—the one by the gate? If we could start it out it would roll down that street and nothing could stop it!"

Arskane licked his lips. "The machine is probably dead. Its motor would not run and we could not push it—"

"We might not need to push. And do not be sure that the motor would not serve us. Jarl of the Star Men once piloted a sealed motor car a full quarter of a mile before it died again. If this would only bring us to the top of the slope it would be enough. At least we can try. It would be a safe and easy way to gain the valley—"

"As you say—we can try!" Arskane bounded down the steps and headed for the truck.

The door to the driver's seat hung open as if to welcome them. Fors slid across the disintegrating pad to sit behind the controls—just as if he were one of the Old Ones who had used this marvel as a matter of course.

Arskane crowded in beside him and was leaning forward to examine the rows of dials and buttons confronting them. He touched one.

"This locks the wheels—"

"How do you know?"

"We have a man of learning in the tribe. He has taken apart many of the old machines to learn the secret of their fashioning. Only we have no longer the fuel to run them and so they are of no use to us. But from Unger I have learned something concerning their powers."

Fors yielded his place, not without some reluctance, and watched Arskane delicately test the

controls. At last the southerner stamped with his foot
upon a floor-set button and what they had believed
in their hearts would never happen, did. The ancient
engine came to life. The sealed engine was not dead!

"The door!" Arskane's face was white beneath its
brown stain, he clung to the wheel with real fear of
the terrifying power that was throbbing under him.

Fors leaped out of the cab and dashed for the big
door. He pulled down on the counter bar and it gave
so that he could push back the ponderous barrier. He
looked out upon a street clear of wrecks. A glance up
slope told him why. At the head—only a few feet back
from the door—one of the great trucks had slewed
sidewise, its nose smashed into the wall of a building
on the opposite side—an effective barricade. He did
not linger after that fleeting examination. Behind, the
sound of the dying engine was horrible—grating and
grinding out its last few seconds of life.

Fors gained the cabin, bringing Lura in with him.
They crouched together with pounding hearts as
Arskane fumbled with the wheel. But the last spurt of
power set the big truck moving, rubber shredding away
from the remains of the tires as they turned. The
engine faltered and died as they rolled out of the
garage and reached the rise, but the momentum carried
on and they sped faster and faster down the steep hill
to the valley below.

Only pure luck had given them that clear street
ahead. Had it not been for the smashed truck corking
the street at its head they might have crashed into
wreckage which would have killed them all. Arskane
fought the wheel, steering only by instinct, and brought
them along the pavement at a pace which grew ever
wilder as the truck gained speed.

Twice Fors closed his eyes, only to force them open
again. His hands were buried deep in the fur of the

squalling Lura who wanted none of this form of travel. But the truck went on and on and they were at last on level land, bumping over the rusted tracks of the railroad. The truck slowed, and at last it stopped as it buried its front bumper in a heap of coal.

For a moment the three simply remained where they were, shaken and weak. Then they roused enough to tumble out. Arskane laughed, but his voice was going up scale as he said:

"If anyone followed us they must be well behind now. And we must labor so that such a distance grows even wider."

They took advantage of any cover afforded by the wreckage in the train yards, and struck south at a trotting pace until, at last, the valley of the river looped away again from the southern path they had set themselves. Then they climbed the slope and went on across the tree-grown ruins of the city outskirts.

The sun was overhead, hot on head and shoulders. There was a fishy scent in the breeze which blew inland from the lake. Arskane sniffed it loudly.

"Rain," was his verdict, "and we could not hope for better fortune. It will cover our trail—"

But the Beast Things would not follow any prey out of a city—or would they? They must be ranging farther afield now—there was that track left by the deer hunter. And Fors' father had been brought down by a pack, not within a city but in the fringes of the true forest land. It was not well to count themselves safe merely because they were drawing out of the ruined area.

"At least we travel without weight of baggage," Arskane observed some time later as they paused to rest and drink the sweetened water with which Fors had filled the canteen that morning.

Fors thought regretfully of the mare and the plunder

which she had carried only yesterday. Not much remained now to prove his story—just the two rings on his fingers, and the few small things in the Star pouch. But he had the map and his travel journal to turn out before the Council when he had that accounting with the Eyrie which he thirsted for.

Arskane had even less than the mountaineer. The museum club in his hand was the only weapon he still had left except his belt knife. In his pouch he carried flint and steel, two fishhooks and a line wound about them.

"If we but had the drum," he regretted. "Were that in my hand we should even now be talking with my people. Without signals it will be a chancy matter to find them—unless we cross the trail of another scout."

"Come with me—to the Eyrie!" Fors said impulsively.

"When you told me your story, comrade, did you not say that you fled your tribe? Will they be quicker to welcome you back with a stranger at your heels? This is a world in which hate lives yet. Let me tell you of my own people—this is a story of the old, old days. Among the flying men who founded my tribe were those born with dark skins—and so they had in their day endured much from those born of fairer races. We are a people of peace but there is an ancient hurt behind us and sometimes it stirs in our memories to poison with bitterness.

"As we moved north we strove to make friends with the Plainspeople—three times that I have knowledge of did we send heralds unto them. And each time were we greeted by a flight of war arrows. So now we have hardened our hearts and we stand for ourselves if the need be. Can you promise that those of the mountains will hold out friendly hands if we seek them out?"

Hot blood stung Fors' cheeks. He was afraid that

he knew the answer to that question. Strangers were enemies—that was the old, old ruling. Yet why should it be so? This land was wide and rich and men were few. Surely there was enough of it for all—it went on and on to the sea. And in the old days men had fashioned ships and sailed across seas to other wide lands.

He said as much aloud and Arskane gave hearty and swift agreement.

"You reason with straight thoughts, comrade. Why should there be distrust between the twain of us because our skin differs in color and our tongues sound different to the ear? My people live by tilling the land, they plant seed and food grows from it, they herd sheep from which comes the wool to weave our wind cloaks and night coverings. We make jars and pots from clay and fire them into stone hardness, working with our hands and delighting in it. The Plainspeople are hunters, they have tamed horses and run the herds of cattle—they love to keep ever moving—to know far trails. And your people—?"

Fors screwed his eyes against the sun. "My people? We are but a small tribe of few clans and often in the winter we needs must go lean and hungry for the mountains are a hard country. But above all do we love knowledge, we live to loot the ruins, to try to understand and relearn the things which made the Old Ones great in their time. Our medicine men fight against the ills of the bodies, our teachers and Star Men against the ignorance of the mind—"

"And yet these same people who fight ignorance have made of you a wandering one because you differ from them—"

For the second time Fors' skin burned red. "I am

mutant. And mutant stock is not to be trusted. The—
the Beast Things are also mutant—" He could not
choke out more than that.

"Lura is mutant also—"

Fors blinked. The four quiet words of that answer
meant more than just a statement of fact. The tenseness
went out of him. He was warm, and not with shame,
nor with the sun which was beating down on him. It
was a good warmness he had not remembered feeling
before—ever.

Arskane propped his chin on his hand and stared
out over the tangle of bush and vine. "It seems to me,"
he said slowly, "that we are like the parts of one body.
My people are the busy hands, fashioning things by
which life may be made easier and more beautiful. The
Plainspeople are the restless, hurrying feet, ever itching
for new trails and the strange things which might lie
beyond the sunrise and the sunset. And your clan is
the head, thinking, remembering, planning for feet and
hands. Together—"

"Together," Fors breathed, "we would make such a
nation as this land has not seen since the days of the
Old Ones!"

"No, not a nation such as the Old Ones knew!"
Arskane's answer was sharp. "They were not one
body—for they knew war. And out of that warfare came
what is today. If the body grows together again it must
be because each part, knowing its own worth and taking
pride in it, recognizes also the worth of the other two.
And color of skin, or eyes, or the customs of a man's
tribe must mean no more to strangers when meeting
than the dust they wash from their hands before they
take meat. We must come to one another free of such
dust—or it will rise to blind our eyes and what the Old
Ones started will continue to live for ever and ever to
poison the earth."

"If that could only be—"

"Brother," for the first time Arskane used the more intimate word to Fors, "my people believe that all the actions in this life have behind them some guiding power. And it seems to me that we two were brought to this place so that we might meet thus. And from our meeting perhaps there will be born something stronger and mightier than what we have known before. But now we linger here too long, death may still sniff at our heels. And it is not to my mind that we shall be turned from the path marked out for us."

Something in the solemn tones of the big man's voice reached into Fors. He had never had a real friend, his alien blood had set him too far apart from the other boys of the Eyrie. And his relationship with his father had been that of pupil with teacher. But he knew now that he would never willingly let this dark-skinned warrior go out of his life again, and that where Arskane chose to go, there he would follow.

When the sun was almost overhead they were in a wilderness of trees where it was necessary to go slowly to avoid gaping cellar holes and lengths of moldering beams. But in this maze Lura picked up the trail of a wild heifer and within the hour they had brought it down and were broiling fresh meat. With enough for perhaps two more meals packed in the raw hide they went on, Fors' small compass their guide.

Abruptly they came out on the edge of the old place of flying men. So abruptly they were almost shocked into dodging back into the screen of trees when they first saw what lay there.

Both were familiar with the pictures of such machines. But here they were real, standing in ordered rows—some of them. And the rest were piled in battered confusion, torn and rent or half engulfed in shell holes.

"Planes!" Arskane's eyes gleamed. "The sky-riding planes of my fathers' fathers! Before we fled the shaking of the mountains we went to look our last upon the ones which brought the first men of our clan to that land—and they were like unto some of these. But here is a whole field of planes!"

"These were struck dead before they reached the sky," Fors pointed out. A strange feeling of excitement burned inside him. The ground machines, even the truck which had helped them out of the city, never moved him so. These winged monsters—how great—how very great in knowledge must the Old Ones have been! That they could ride among the clouds in these—where now their sons must crawl upon the ground! Hardly knowing what he did Fors ventured out and drew his hand sadly along the body of the nearest plane. He was so small beside it—a whole family clan might have once ridden in its belly—

"It was with such as these that the Old Ones sowed death over the world—"

"But to ride in the clouds," Fors refused Arskane's somber mood, "above the earth—They must have been godlike—the Old Ones!"

"Say rather devil-like! See—" Arskane took him by the arm and led him between the two orderly rows on the edge of the field to look at the series of ragged, ugly craters which made a churned mess of the center of the airport. "Death came thus from the air, and men dropped that death willingly upon their fellows. Let us remember that, brother."

They passed around the wreckage, following the lines of unwrecked planes until their way led to a building. There were many bones here. Many men had died trying to get the machines into the air—too late.

When they reached the building, both turned and looked back at the path of destruction and the two lines of curiously untouched bombers still waiting. The sky they would never again travel was clear and blue with small, clean-cut white clouds drifting across it in patterns. In the west other and darker clouds were gathering. A storm was in the making.

"This," Arskane pointed down the devastated field, "must never happen again. No matter what heights our sons rise to—we must not tear the earth against each other—Do you agree, brother?"

Fors met those dark burning eyes squarely. "It is agreed. And what I can do, that I shall. But—where men once flew they must fly again! That also we must swear to!"

·*· 9

Into the Blow-Up Land

Fors hunched over the table, leaning on his elbows, hardly daring to breathe lest the precious cloth-backed square he was studying crumble into powdery dust. Maps—such a wealth of maps he had never dreamed of. He could put finger tip to the point of blue which was the edge of the great lake—and from that he could travel across—straight to the A-T-L-A-N-T-I-C Ocean. Why, that was the fabulous sea! He looked up impatiently as Arskane came into this treasure room.

"We are here—right here!"

"And here we are like to stay forever if we do not bestir ourselves—"

Fors straightened up. "What—?"

"I have but come from the tower at the end of this building. Something alive moves at the far end of the field of machines. It is a shadow but it slides with too much purpose to be overlooked by a cautious—"

"A deer," began Fors, knowing that it was not.

Arskane gave a short bark of humor-lacking laughter. "Does a deer creep upon its belly and spy around corners, brother? No, I think that our friends from the city have found us out at last. And I do not like being caught in this place—no, I do not like that at all!"

Fors left the maps regretfully. How Jarl would have delighted in them. But to attempt to move them would be to destroy them and they would have to remain— as they had through the countless years. He picked up his quiver and checked the remaining arrows. Only ten left. And when they were gone he would have only short sword and hunting knife—

Arskane must have picked that thought right out of his companion's mind for now he was nodding. "Come." He went back to the flight of stairs which led them in a spiral up and up until they stood in a place that had once been completely walled with glass. "See there—and what do you make of that?"

The southerner stabbed a finger southeast. Fors picked out an odd scar in the vegetation there, a wide wedge of land where nothing grew. Under the sun the soil had a strange metallic gleam. He had seen the raw rocks of mountain gorges and the cleared land where the Old Ones had once had concrete surfaces, but this was different. In a land where trees and grass had reclaimed their own nothing green encroached upon the wedge.

"Desert—" was all he could suggest doubtfully. But there should be no deserts in this section of the country.

"That it is not! Remember, I am desert born and that is no natural wasteland such as I have ever known. It is something the like of which I have not stumbled upon in all my journeying!"

"Hush!" Fors' head snapped around. He was sure

of that sound, the distant scrape of metal against metal. His eyes ran along the lines of the silent machines. And there was a flicker of movement halfway down the second line!

He screened his eyes against the sun, crowding up to the frame of the vanished glass. Under the shadow of the spreading wing of a plane squatted a gray-black blot. And it was sniffing the ground!

His whisper hardly rose above the rasp of Arskane's quick breathing. "Only one—"

"No. Look within the curve of that bush—to the right—"

Yes, the southerner was right. Against the green, one could see the bestial head. The Beast Things almost always hunted as a pack. It was too much to hope that this time they did not. Fors' hand dropped to his sword hilt.

"We must go!"

Arskane's sandals already thudded on the stairs. But before he left the tower, Fors saw that gray thing dart forward from under the plane. And two more such lumps detached themselves from the covering of trees along the ruined runway, taking cover among the machines. The pack was closing in.

"We must keep to the open," Arskane warned. "If we can stay ahead and not allow them to corner us we shall have a fair chance."

There was another door out of the building, one which gave upon the other half of the field. Here was a maze of tangled wreckage. Shell holes pocked the runways; machines and defense guns had been blasted too. They swung around the sky-pointing muzzle of a mounted gun. And in the same instant the air was rent with a horrible screech, answered by Lura's snarl of rage. A thrashing tangle of fighting cat and her prey rolled out almost under their feet.

Arskane swung his club with a sort of detached science. He struck down, hard. Thin, bone-gray arms went wide and limp and Lura was clawing a dead body. A missile from the wreckage grazed Fors' head sending him spinning against the gun. He stumbled over the body from which came a filthy stench. Then Arskane jerked him to his feet and pulled him under the up-ended nose of a plane.

Still shaking his ringing head Fors allowed his companion to guide him as they turned and dodged. Once he heard the ring of metal as a Beast Thing dart struck. Arskane pushed him to the left, the momentum of the southerner's shove carrying both of them into cover.

"Driving us—" Arskane panted. "They herd us like deer—"

Fors tried to struggle free of the other's prisoning hand.

"Lura—ahead—" In spite of the blow which had rocked him he caught the cat's message. "There the way lies clear—"

Arskane did not seem disposed to leave cover but Fors tore free and wriggled through an opening in the churned earth and broken machines. It seemed to last hours, that crawling, twisting race with death. But in the end they came out on the edge of that odd scar in the earth which they had sighted from the tower. And there Lura crouched, her lips lifted in a snarl, her tail sweeping steadily to signify her rage.

"Down that gully—quick—" Arskane was into the notch before he had finished speaking.

The strange earth crunched under Fors' boots. He took the only way left to freedom. And Lura, still giving low voice to her dismay, swept by him.

Here there was not even moss and the rocky outcrops had a glassy glaze. Fors shrank from touching anything with his bare flesh. The sounds of pursuit were gone though. It was too quiet here. He realized suddenly that what his ears missed was the ever-present sound of insects which had been with them in the vegetation of the healthy world.

This country they had entered blindly was alien, with no familiar green and brown to meet the eye, no homely sounds for the reassurance of the ear. Arskane had paused and as Fors caught up he asked the question which was on his tongue tip.

"What is this place?"

But the southerner countered with a question of his own. "What have you been told of the Blow-Up Lands?"

"Blow-Up Lands?" Fors tried to remember the few scanty references to such in the records of the Eyrie. Blow-Up Lands—where nuclear bombs had struck to bite into the earth's crust, where death had entered so deeply that generations must pass before man could go that way again—

His mouth opened and then shut quickly. He did not have to ask his question again. He knew—and the chill horror of that knowing was worse than a Beast Thing dart striking into his flesh. No wonder there had been no pursuit. Even the mutant Beast Things knew better than to venture here!

"We must go back—" he half whispered, already knowing that they could not.

"Go back to certain death? No, brother, and already it is too late. If the old tales be true we are even now walking dead men with the seeds of the burning sickness in us. Instead—if we go on—there is a chance of getting through—"

"Perhaps more than a chance." Fors' first horror faded as he recalled an old argument long ago worn to rags by the men of the Eyrie. "Tell me, Arskane, in the early years after the Blow-Up did the people of your tribe suffer from the radiation sickness?"

The big man's straight brows drew together. "Yes. There was a death year. All but ten of the clan died within three months. And the rest sickened and were ever weakly. It was not until a generation later that we grew strong again."

"So was it also with those of the Eyrie. Men of my clan who have studied the ancient books say that because of this sickness we are now different from the Old Ones who gave us birth. And perhaps because of that difference we may venture unharmed where death would have struck them down."

"But this reasoning has not yet been put to the proof?"

Fors shrugged. "Now it is. And we shall see if it is correct. I know that I am mutant."

"While I am like the others of my tribe. But that is not saying that they are the same as the Old Ones. Well, whether it be what we hope or not, we are set on this path. And there is truly death, and an unpleasant one, behind us. In the meantime—that is a storm coming. We had best find shelter, this is no land to blunder across in the dark!"

It was hard to keep one's footing on the greasy surface and Fors guessed that if it were wet it would be worse than sand to plow through. They held to the sides of the narrow valleys which laced the country, looking for a cave or overhang that would afford the slightest hint of shelter.

The dark clouds made a sullen gray mass and a premature twilight. A bad night to go without a fire—in the open of the contaminated land under a dripping sky.

A jagged flash of purple lightning cracked across the heavens and both of them shielded their eyes as it

struck not far from where they stood. The rumble of
the thunder which followed almost split their ear
drums. Then the rain came in a heavy smothering
curtain to close them in. They huddled together,
miserable, the three of them against the side of a
narrow valley, cowering as the lightning struck again
and again and the water rose in a stream down the
center of the gully, washing the soil from the glassy
rocks. Only once did Fors move. He unhooked his
canteen and pulled at Arskane's belt flask until the big
man gave it to him. These he set out in the steady
downpour. The water which ran by his feet was
contaminated but the rain which had not yet touched
soil or rock might be drinkable later.

Lura, Fors decided, must be the most unhappy of
the three. The rain ran from their smooth skin and was
not much held by their rags of clothing. But her fur
was matted by it and it would take hours of licking with
her tongue before it was in order again. However, she
did not voice her disapproval of life as she usually did.
Since they had crossed into the atom-blasted land she
had not given tongue at all. On impulse Fors tried now
to catch her thoughts. He had been able to do that
in the past—just enough times to be sure that she
could communicate when she wished. But now he met
only a blank. Lura's wet fur pressed against him now,
but Lura herself had gone.

And then he realized with a start that she was
listening, listening so intently that her body was now
only one big organ for the trapping of sound. Why?

He rested his forehead on his arms where he had
crossed them on his hunched knees. Deliberately he
set about shutting out the sounds around him—the
drum of the rain, Arskane's breathing, the gurgle of
the water threading by just beyond their toes. Luckily
the thunder had stopped. He was conscious of the

pounding of his own blood in his ears, of the hiss of his own breath. He shut them out, slowly, as thoroughly as he could. This was a trick he had tried before but never with such compulsion on him. It was very necessary now that he *hear*—and that warning might have come either from Lura or some depth within him. He concentrated to shut out even the drive of that urgency—for it too was a danger.

There was a faint plopping sound. His mind considered it briefly and rejected it for what it was—the toppling of earth undercut by the storm-born stream. He pushed the boundaries of his hearing farther away. Then, even as a strange dizziness began to close in, he heard it—a sound which was not born of the wind and the rain. Lura moved, rising to her feet. Now she turned and looked at him as he raised his head to meet her eyes.

"What—?" Arskane stirred uneasily, staring from one to the other.

Fors almost laughed at the blank bewilderment in the big man's eyes.

The dizziness which had come from his concentration was receding fast. His eyes adjusted to the night and the shadows. He got to his feet and put aside bow and quiver, keeping only the belt with his sword and knife. Arskane put out a protesting hand which he eluded.

"There is something back there. It is important that I see it. Wait here—"

But Arskane was struggling up too. Fors saw his mouth twist with pain as he inadvertently put weight upon his left arm. The rain must have got to the healing wound. And seeing that, the mountaineer shook his head.

"Listen—I am mutant—you have never asked in what manner I differ. But it is this, I can see in the dark—even this night is little different from the twilight for me. And my ears are close to Lura's in keenness. Now is the hour when my difference will serve us. Lura!" He swung around and looked for a second time deep into those startlingly blue eyes. "Here will you stay—with our brother. Him will you guard—as you would me!"

She shifted her weight from one front paw to another, standing up against his will in the recesses of her devious mind, refusing him. But he persisted. He knew her stubborn freedom and the will for it which was born into her kind. They called no man master and they went their own way always. But Lura had chosen him, and because he had no friends among his own breed they had been very close, perhaps closer than any of the Eyrie had been with the furred hunters before. Fors did not know how much she would yield to his will but this was a time when he must set himself against her. To leave Arskane here alone, handicapped by his wound and his lack of night sight, would be worse than folly. And the big man could not go with him. And the sound— that must be investigated!

Lura's head came up. Fors reached down his hand and felt the wetness of her fur as she rubbed her jaw along his fist in her most intimate caress. He had a moment of pure happiness at her acceptance of his wish. His fingers scratched behind her ears lovingly.

"Stay here," he told them both. "I shall return as quickly as I may. But we must know what lies there—"

Before he finished that sentence he was off, not giving either of them time to protest again, knowing that the rain and the darkness would hide him from Arskane within a few feet and that Lura would be on guard until his return.

Fors slipped and stumbled, splashing through small

pools, following the route he had memorized as they came. The rain was slacking, it stopped entirely as he reached the top of a pinnacle of rock and looked out again over the old airport. He could distinguish the bombed section and the building where they had found the maps. But he was more interested in what was directly below.

There was no fire—although his mind kept insisting that there should be one, for it was plain that he was spying upon a council. The circle of hunched figures born an uncanny and, to him, unwholesome resemblance to the meetings of the elders in the Eyrie. The Things were squatting so that their bodies were only blotches—for that he was glad. Somehow he had no desire to see them more clearly. But one pranced and droned in the center of that circle, and the sounds it uttered were what had drawn Fors there.

He could distinguish guttural sounds which must be words, but they had no meaning for him. Arskane's tongue and his own had once had a common base and it had not been difficult to learn each other's speech. But this growling did not sound as if it were shaped by either lips or brain which were human.

What the leader urged he could not know, but what they might do as a result of that urging was important. The Beast Things were growing bolder with the years. At first they had never ventured beyond the edges of the cities. But now they could follow a trail beyond the ruins and perhaps they were sending scouts into the open country. They were a menace to the remaining humans—

The leader ended his, her, or its speech abruptly. Now its too thin body turned and it pointed to the wasteland where Fors crouched, almost as if it had sighted the hidden watcher. The gesture was answered by a growl from its companions. One or two got to their feet and padded to the edge of the Blow-Up ground where their heads sank as they sniffed warily at the polluted soil. But it did not take them long to make up their minds. For they were gathering up their bundles of darts and forming into a sort of crude marching line.

Fors stayed just long enough to be sure that they were indeed coming, that whatever taboo had held them back no longer operated. Then he fled, skimming lightly at his sure woods' pace, back to where he had left Lura and Arskane. The Beast Things did not seem too cheerful about their venture and their starting pace was slow. They walked as if they expected to find traps under their feet. There was hope that the pursued could keep ahead of them.

The mountaineer found Arskane impatient, Lura crouched on an outcrop, her eyes glowing in the dark. Fors grabbed up the equipment he had discarded as he gasped out his news.

"I have been thinking," Arskane's slower but deeper voice cut through his report. "We do not understand the weapons of the Old Ones, those which could make a desert such as this. Was there only one bomb which fell here, or were there more? But the heart of such a place would be more dangerous than its lip. If we head straight across we may be going to that death tradition promises for those who invade the 'blue' places. But if we circle we may—"

"There is the matter of time. I tell you trackers run on our heels now."

"Yes, and they track by scent. There is at hand an answer to that."

Arskane's moccasins plowed through a pool, sending up spray. Fors understood. The thread of stream might be their salvation after all. But, since the rain had ceased, the water was shrinking rapidly in volume,

almost as if the rocky soil over which it ran was a
sponge to suck it up.

Fors started ahead, his night sight picking out the
pitfalls and bad footing for both of them. Sometimes
it was only his hand which kept Arskane on his feet.
The big man stumbled stubbornly on, his breath torn
out of him in harsh gasps. Fors knew from the
cramping in his own leg muscles what tormented the
other. But they must gain ground—gain it while the
pursuers, still suspicious of the Blow-Up Land, traveled
slowly.

Then, long after, Arskane fell and, although Fors
allowed them both a rest, he could not get to his feet
again. His head slumped forward on his chest and Fors
saw that he was either unconscious or asleep, his mouth
twisted with pain. But what was worse were the seeping
stains on the bandage which still bound the wounded
shoulder.

Fors pressed the palms of his hands against his
burning eyes. He tried to think back—was it only last
night they had slept in the city tower? It seemed a
week behind them. They could not keep on at this
rate, that was certain. Now that he relaxed against
a sandy bank he was afraid he could not make the
effort to get up again. He must sleep. And there was
the matter of food also. How large was this Blow-
Up desert? What if they must go on and on across
it—maybe for days?

But they would be dead before days passed. Would
it be better to choose a likely place now and make a
last stand against the Beast Things? He dug his eyes
again. He dared not sleep now. Then he remembered
Lura.

She lay flat on a ridge a little above them, licking
one paw, pausing now and then to prick her ears and
listen. Lura would nap too, but in her own fashion,

and nothing could come to attack while she watched. His head fell back against Arskane's limp arm and he slept.

·⁺ 10

Captured!

The glare of sun reflected from the grease-slick surface of the bare rocks made Fors' eyes ache. It was hard to keep plodding steadily along when raw hunger gnawed at one's middle. But they had seen no game in this weird waste. And at the very worst he was not suffering as Arskane was. The southerner mumbled unintelligibly, his eyes were glazed, and it was necessary to lead him by the hand as if he were a tired child. The red stain on his bandaged shoulder was crusted and dried—at least he no longer lost blood he could ill afford to spare.

Where was the end of the Blow-Up country? If they had not traveled in circles they must have covered miles of its knife-edged valleys and rocky plateaus. And yet, still facing them at the top of each rise, was only more and more of the sick earth.

"Water—" Arskane's swollen tongue pushed across cracked lips.

All the abundance of yesterday's flood had vanished, absorbed in the soil as if it had never existed. Fors steadied the big man against a rock and reached for his canteen. He did it slowly, trying to keep his hand from shaking. Not one precious drop must be spilled!

It was Arskane who did that. His eyes suddenly focused on the canteen and he grabbed for it. Water splashed over his hand and gathered in a depression of the stone. Fors looked at it longingly, but he still dared not swallow the fluid which had touched the tainted land here.

He allowed Arskane two swallows and then took the canteen away by force. Luckily the big man's strength had ebbed so that he could control him. As Fors fastened the canteen onto his belt he glanced at the ground. What he saw there kept him still and staring.

From out of the shadow cast by a rock something was moving toward the spilled water. It was dark green, mottled with reddish-yellow patches, and man's age-long distrust of a reptile almost made him send his boot crashing down on it. But in time he saw that it was not a snake that writhed across the ground, it was the long fleshy stem of a plant. Its flattened end wavered through the air and fell upon the water drops, arching over the moisture. Now the rest of the thing moved out to drink and Fors saw the three stiff leaves encircling a tall middle spike which bore a red bulb. The plant drank and the suckered stem lifted to curl back against the leaves as the whole fantastic growth withdrew into the shade, leaving the watcher to wonder if thirst and hunger had played tricks with his eyes. Only on the stone was a damp mark covering the hollow where the water had been.

So there was life here—even if it were an alien life. Somehow Fors was heartened by that glimpse of the plant. It was true that he was used to vegetation which

remained rooted. But in a slice of land as strange as
this men might well stay in place while the plants
walked abroad. He laughed at that—it seemed a very
witty and enlightening thought and he repeated it
proudly to Arskane as they moved on. But the
southerner answered only with a mumble.

The journey went on with the quality of a nightmare.
Fors managed to keep going, pulling Arskane to his
feet again and again, heading on to landmarks he
established ahead. It was easier to keep moving if one
picked out a rock or one of the slippery earth dunes
and held to it as a guide. Then, when that point was
achieved, there was always another ahead to fix on in
the same manner.

He was sometimes aware of movement in the
shadows which lay blue-black under rocks and ledges.
Whether colonies of the water plants lurked there or
other inhabitants of this hell who spied upon travelers,
he neither knew nor cared. All that mattered was to
keep going and hope that sometime when they topped
one of the ridges they would sight the healthy green
of their own world.

Now and then Lura came into sight, her once
smooth fur rough and matted, her flanks shrunken and
thin. Sometimes she would pad beside them for a few
feet and then melt away on her own road, watchful
and ready. If anything had found their back trail and
was following it and them, it had not yet come within
striking distance.

It was becoming almost impossible to keep Arskane
going. Twice he would have fallen heavily full length
if Fors had not steadied him, and the second time the
collapse bore the mountaineer to his knees. It was then
that he was reckless with the water, hoping to spur his
companion on. And he did get the southerner to his
feet. But now the canteen was empty.

They were struggling through a maze of knife-narrow ravines. But these led in the general direction they had chosen and they followed them. Fors was bending almost double under Arskane's weight when he caught a glimpse of something which brought hope and life back into him in one great surge. Only it was almost twilight and his eyes might have played him a trick—

No, he had been right! Those were tree tops ahead and never had the sight of branches against an evening sky seemed so beautiful! Fors pulled Arskane's arm about his shoulders, dropped his bow, quiver and the Star pouch, and made that last dash.

After what seemed like days, weeks, later he lay face down in soft and natural earth, the good smell of leaf mold dank in his nostrils. And he heard the swish of rising wind through leaves which were true and green and clean. At last he raised his head. Arskane sprawled beyond. He had turned over on his back and his eyes were closed, but he was asleep. Fors sighed.

He must go back and recover the bow and the pouch before night closed in. But the struggle of getting to his feet made him grit his teeth. Odd—for the first time he noticed Lura was nowhere about. Hunting—maybe—But he must get that pouch! It was all the proof remaining that he had succeeded.

His feet dragged and his head was dizzy and queer. But he could keep to the line of footprints they had made and it was an easy guide back. He wavered on.

The walls of the first gully closed about him. When he glanced back he could see the trees but not where Arskane lay. It was growing darker—he must hurry.

A splitting pain broke in his head. He knew that he was falling and tried to throw out his hands to break that fall. But he only dimly felt the shock when he hit the ground. Instead he whirled out into a blackness which was complete.

First he was conscious of his body being jerked roughly, roughly enough to send pain shooting through it to the bursting agony in his head. Then he came out of the blackness, trying weakly to hold his thoughts together. The end to that fight came when he fell again, struck painfully against solid rock and rolled. A kick in the ribs brought him to a racking stop. He must have been carried and thrown down. And the sickening stench in his nostrils told him by whom. He lay limply, not daring to open his eyes. As long as they deemed him senseless he might be safe for a while.

He was bound, his wrists behind the small of his back, his ankles together. Already his hands were numb and the bonds had cut his flesh. He could only listen and try to guess at what his captors were doing. They appeared to be settling down. He heard the grunt one gave, the scratching of nails across tough hide. Then, through rank body smell, he caught the scent of smoke and dared to peek beneath half-open lids.

Yes, they had kindled a fire, a fire which they were feeding with handfuls of a coarse grass they pulled up from where it grew along the sides of the valley. One came into the full light of the flames and flung down an armload of the water plants, still alive enough to attempt to writhe away from the heat.

But these were speedily seized upon and the red bulbs at their centers squeezed between yellowed fangs with snorts of satisfaction. Sucked dry, the plants were tossed on the fire. Fors swallowed with a bruised throat—his turn next?

But one of the Beast Things turned with inhuman swiftness and sprang to the wall behind it, clutching up something which wriggled and squeaked shrilly. It came back holding a squirming captive in each paw and batted the small bodies against a convenient rock until they were limp and still. The hunter's success aroused the envy of its fellows and they all pawed among the rocks of the valley, a few successfully.

Fors heard swift movement in the loose rocks somewhere behind him, as if small, agile things were speeding away to safety. The slowest of the hunters had returned to the fire grumbling and empty-handed. When the catch was laid out on the stone Fors saw it clearly for the first time—lizards! They resembled those he had seen all his life hiding among rocky places—and yet there was something odd about the shape of the heads—But before he could guess what it was the bodies had been slung over the flames to broil.

There were four Beast Things busy there. Either the whole clan had not after all ventured into the Blow-Up or else the party had split. But these four were bad enough. For the first time he was able to see them clearly.

They were probably no taller than he but their emaciated bodies perched on stick legs made them seem to top him. The grayish skin which was stretched tight over their sharp bones was deep grained, almost scaly, and their bodies were bare save for strips of filthy tattered stuff worn about their loins. But their faces—!

Fors forced himself to study, to study and file in memory what he saw. He tried to view those masks of horror with detachment. In general outline they were remotely human. But the eyes deep set in bone-rimmed pits, the elongated jaws above which the nose was only two slits—jaws equipped with a hunting beast's fangs—sharp fangs never fully covered by thin vestiges of lips—those were not human. They were—he recoiled from the picture formed in his mind—they were rats! Or had once been rats.

Fors shivered and could not control the trembling of his aching body. Then he tensed. Something was climbing down the slope behind him, not with the light patter of the lizards but with the assured tread of one who knows he has nothing to fear and is coming to meet friends. A moment later Fors felt a jar, then soft fur rolled against him. The steps went on.

Lura lay beside him now, her eyes wild with helpless rage, thongs about her paws, a loop holding her jaws tight together. Her tail beat across him. But when her eyes met Fors' she relaxed slightly. He could not move yet—

A fifth and sixth Beast Thing joined the others by the fire and were now demanding their share of the food. They were greeted with jeers until one growled some order and the meat was grudgingly shared. They ate in silence and when the leader was done it wiped its clawed fingers perfunctorily across its thighs before turning to examine some objects beside it.

Fors recognized his bow. The leader twanged the string curiously, hitting its thumb. With a savage growl it snapped the shaft between its fists and threw the broken weapon into the fire. The quiver followed, but the Beast Things appreciated the worth of the steel arrowheads enough to break them off and put them aside.

When the creature took up the last piece of plunder—the Star pouch—Fors bit deep into his underlip. The precious contents were dumped out and went piece by piece into the flames. Map, journal, everything, except the small figures from the museum which seemed to fascinate the Beast Thing leader.

Having so examined the spoil the creature came over to the captives. Fors lay limp, willing each muscle to relax. Again a set of clawed toes, planted with breath-taking force in his short ribs, rolled him away from Lura and out into the full light of the fire. He struggled to keep under control his outrage and nausea as foul paws stripped from him every rag and fumbled over his body. What would come next, a knife, a blow strong enough to cave in his aching head? But strangely he was left while Lura underwent the same sort of inspection.

Then the claws twisted a hold in the thong which bound his wrists and he was pulled back to his former position, his back raked raw by the gravel. Lura was writhing violently. She had not relished her taste of the same treatment. Now she was tight against him, her thonged jaws pushed into his shoulder.

After a while Fors slept. When he roused again it was dim and gray with the false dawn. One of his captors hunched by the fire nodding, now and then feeding the flames. The rest lay curled in sodden sleep.

But Fors' mind was alert now. And he heard again very clearly the faint sounds made by the lizards passing among the rocks. Why should they venture back into a danger zone, he wondered. And then he saw what ringed the walls of the valley.

Terraces, hundreds of them, some only a few inches, some of them several feet, wide, made a continuous stairway up the walls of the gulch. Each had been laboriously built up artificially, each was walled with pebbles and small stones. And on these tiny fields grew the grass stuff with which his captors fed their fire. They had stripped half the valley already. Even as he noticed the terraces for the first time the fire tender pulled an armload from its roots, denuding two more of the small fields.

Lizards and terraces—did the lizards make them? And those black holes showing at intervals along the topmost rim of the valley—what were they? He was answered by the sight of a scaled head—a sort of crest rising from its brow—which appeared in one as jewel bright eyes inspected the valley and the invaders.

Fors, now knowing what to look for, glanced around the rim of the valley. Heads! Heads popping in and out of the cave holes, appearing and disappearing around stones and over the edges of the higher terraces. Always they moved almost silently, so close to the rock in coloring and outline that only one who suspected them might even guess where and what they were.

If last night the lizards, surprised by a superior force, had fled, now they were back—with reinforcements. But at the best they stood only twenty inches high against the iron strength and greater bulk of the Beast Things who could crack their spines between thumb and forefinger. Why, an army would go down under the stamping feet of the enemy. But the lizards did not seem to be overawed by the odds against them.

Scouts advanced down the sides of the valley. From time to time Fors sighted slender shapes shooting from one piece of cover to another, always down toward the foe. Then he saw something else and could hardly believe his eyes. A party of lizards was issuing boldly out of one of the cave holes on the opposite side of the cut. They made no noise but neither did they make any effort to conceal their march. Instead they pattered down to the fields which the Beast Things had not yet torn up.

They walked on their hind legs in a curiously humanlike stance and they each carried something in their shorter front paws. Down into their tiny meadows they paraded and set to work. Fors stared—they were reaping the grass, shearing off the blades and bundling them into shocks. And they worked without a single glance at what lay below, as if going about their business in the usual way.

Fors wanted to get up and shout a warning to those busy workers—for them to get away before the brutes by the fire sighted them. On the other hand, he was aware that an army, grim and intent upon some purpose, had gathered silently at the slope. Then he caught some glimmering of their plan and his head jerked up to see the better.

Bait! The lizards reaping up there were to be bait! Why, that was hard to believe. These—these little scaled creatures knew perfectly well what they were about—they were the heroes of the clan who had probably volunteered to man those terraces as bait. But even yet he did not realize to what extent the lizard folk would go to save their land.

The fire watcher yawned, belched, and stretched. Then it caught sight of the activity above. It grinned, its stained fangs widely displayed, and, reached over, prodded one of the sleepers awake. At first the newly aroused one was inclined to resent it, but when the farmers above were pointed out to it, it rubbed the sleep from its eyes and proceeded to business.

From the gravel at its feet it picked out a handful of walnut-sized stones. And both the Beast Things let these fly with deadly accuracy. Two of the lizards kicked out their lives in the fields. The resulting shout of triumph from the hunters brought the whole camp awake.

But surely the lizards could take to cover quicker than they did! Fors watched with a queer sick feeling as one after another of the farmers failed to reach the safety of the cave holes. Then he understood—they had never intended to escape. They were giving their lives for the purpose of some plan they had made.

He would not watch the pitiful carnage any longer and he looked at the opposite side of the valley—just in time to see a small round object shoot out of the side of the hill and fall close to the camp fire. Another and another rattled down, as if brown hailstones were falling. Once they landed among the stones and loose gravel it was almost impossible to detect them. And if one had not rolled across a flat stone within touching distance he would never had known what they were.

A small ball, fashioned maybe of clay, was all he saw. But why were the small thorn points sticking out of its surface all the way around? If it was meant to wound, why shoot it while the Beast Things were all well away from the spot? Fors still puzzled over that as the victors came back swinging limp bodies and proud of their killing.

In spite of his revulsion Fors could not subdue the hunger pangs when the smell of the roasting meat was heavy on the air. He could only faintly remember his last meal—his stomach was one vast empty hollow. But neither did he want to attract the attention of those who were now wolfing down the half-cooked flesh.

One of the Beast Things, while reaching for another broiled lizard, gave a sudden exclamation and plucked something from its arm, hurling it away with the force of annoyance. It had been pricked by one of the lizard balls. But Fors could not see how that caused the victim any more than momentary discomfort. He watched closely and witnessed two of the creatures treading upon the thorn-studded globes. One of them did so when it went for a fresh supply of the water plants. And when it returned it walked slowly, stopping now and again to shake its narrow head and once to brush vigorously before its eyes as if to clear some obstruction hanging there.

They drank from the dying plants, sucked the last slender lizard bones clean, and got to their feet. Then they turned their attention to the captives. This was it! Fors grimaced. He had seen them impale and roast a screaming broken-legged lizard—

The Beast Things circled around the captives. There was a period of rough humor during which Fors was both kicked and slapped. But they were apparently not going to kill him now. Instead the leader stooped to slit the bonds about his ankles, the mountaineer's own knife in its paw.

That steel never bit into the hide. One of the brutes in the circle voiced a deep roar and bit at its own arm. Flecks of white foam showed in the corners of its jaws. It tore savagely at its own flesh and then started on an unsteady run down the valley. With grunts of astonishment the others remained where they were, watching their companion double up with a scream of anguish and fall into the fire.

Poison! Fors knew now the cleverness of the lizards, the reason for the sacrifice of the gleaners. The thorn balls were poisoned! And there had to be time for the poison to work. But—were they all infected?

In the end it was the leader who lived long enough to almost reach the other end of the valley, its paws scrabbling on the rock as it tried to drag its tortured body out of that place of death. But it crashed back, moaned twice, and then was as still as the rest.

Fors could hear the patter of lizard feet before he noticed that the hillsides were alive with them, moving in a red-brown cloud down toward the slain. He licked raw lips. Could he communicate with them, get them to use that knife lying there to saw through his bonds? His hands were too numb and so were his feet.

For a long time he hesitated as the lizards crowded about the dead, their thin whistling echoing up and down among the rocks. Then he ventured to make a croaking sound which was all his dry throat and dryer mouth could shape.

His answer was a flash of movement as those heads snapped around and cold hard eyes regarded him with detachment. He tried again as Lura kicked for freedom to no purpose. Some of the lizards drew together, their

crested heads bent as they conferred. Then a party
started forward. Fors tried to lift himself. Then sheer
horror caught at his nerves.

In each four-fingered paw they were carrying
something—a branch thick with thorns!

·*· 11

Drums Speak Loudly

"No! Friend—I am friend—" Fors gabbled the words wildly. But they were words the lizards did not recognize and the silent and menacing advance did not falter.

What stopped them was something else—a hissing from some point on the slope behind the helpless mountaineer. It was as if the giant grandfather of all snakes coiled there, resentful of the disturbance. To the lizards the hissing had meaning. They halted almost in midstep, their threadlike tongues flickering in and out, their ragged top crests stiff and upright, pulsing dark red.

Stones rattled down the hill. Fors tried desperately to turn his head to see what or who was coming. Lura's struggles increased in violence and he wondered if he could roll to that knife which lay just out of reach. Though his hands were dead and numb he might be able to saw through the cat's bonds.

133

One of the lizards drew ahead of the rest of the pack, but its thorn spear was still at "ready." The scaled throat swelled and an answering hiss sounded. That was replied to promptly and afterward came three words which set the captive's heart to pounding.

"Can you move?"

"No. And watch out! Poison thorns set in balls—on the ground—"

"I know." The answer was calm. "Keep still—"

Arskane hissed for the third time. The lizards drew back, leaving their leader alone, alert and on guard. Then Arskane was there, stooping to slash the bonds of both captives. Fors tried to lever himself up with dead arms which refused to obey him.

"Can—not—make—it—"

But Arskane was rubbing at the puffed and swollen ankles and the torture of reviving circulation was almost more than the mountaineer could bear without screaming. It seemed only a second before Arskane hauled him to his feet and pushed him toward the back slope.

"Get up there—"

That order had an urgency which made Fors climb in spite of himself, Lura dragging up ahead. He dared not waste the time to look back, he could only put all his strength to the task of getting up to the top.

If the way had been steeper he might never have made it. And as it was Arskane caught up to him and pulled him along the last few steps. From the southerner's arm hung Fors' knife belt with knife and sword both in their sheaths—he had waited to retrieve that.

Neither of them lost time in talk, Fors glad to reel along with the larger man's support. After a while he knew that there was real grass under his feet and then he slumped down where water sprayed his parched skin.

He did not know how much time passed before he roused enough to know that Arskane was trying to pour some broth down his throat. He swallowed eagerly until his eyes closed against his will and he drifted off again.

"How did you get us out?" Fors lay at ease, hours later. Under him a mat of ferns and leaves seemed almost unbelievably soft and Arskane hunched on the other side of the fire fashioning a shaft for a short hunting spear.

"It was easy enough—with the Beast Things gone. I will tell you this with a straight and truthful tongue, brother." The southerner's teeth flashed white and amused in his dark face. "Had those yet breathed, then this venture might well have ended otherwise.

"When I awoke in this wood and found you gone I at first thought that you were hunting—for food or water or both. But I was not happy in my mind— not happy at all. I ate—here are rabbits, fat and foolish and without fear. And yonder there is the brook. So did my unease grow, for with food and drink so near I knew that you would not have gone from me and remained so long a time. So I went back along our trail—"

Fors studied the hands lumped on his chest, the hands which were still purplish and blue and which hurt with a nagging pain. What would have happened if Arskane had not gone back?

"That trail was very easy to follow. And along it I found the place where the Beast Things had lain in hiding to strike you down. They did nothing to cover their tracks. It is in my mind that they fear very little and see small need for caution. So came I at last to the valley of the lizards—"

"But how did you stop *their* attack?"

Arskane was examining a pile of stones he had culled out of the brook, weighing them in his hands and separating them into two piles. The smoothed spear shaft he had set aside.

"The lizard folk I have seen before. In my own land—or the land we held before the shaking of the mountains drove us forth—there was such a colony. They marched across the desert from the west one year and made a settlement in a gulch a half day's journey from the village of my people. We were curious about them and often watched them from a distance. At last we even traded—giving them bits of metal in return for blue stones they grubbed out of the earth—our women having a liking for necklaces. I do not know what I said back there—I think it was only that my imitation of their speech surprised them so that they let us go.

"But it was well we got out of that place with all speed. The poison ball is their greatest weapon. I have seen them use it against coyote and snake. They wish only to be left alone."

"But—but they were almost—almost human—" Fors told of the gleaners and the sacrifice they had made for their clan.

Arskane laid out three stones of equal size and girth. "Can we then deny that they have a right to their valley? Could we show equal courage, I wonder?" He became busy with some thin strips of rabbit skin, weaving them into a net around each rock. Fors watched him, puzzled.

Just overhead there was a break in the mass of tree tops and as he lay back flat he could see blue sky and part of a drifting white cloud. But this morning there was a chill tooth to the wind—summer was going. He must get back to the Eyrie soon—

Then he remembered what had happened to the Star pouch and his puffy fingers dug into the stuff he lay upon. There was no use in returning to the mountain hold now. When the Beast Things had destroyed his proof they had finished his chance of buying his way back into the clan. He had nothing left except what Arskane had brought out of the lizard valley for him—his knife and sword.

"Good!"

Fors was too sunk to turn his head and see what had brought that note of satisfaction into his companion's voice. Arskane did not have anything to worry about. He would go south and find his tribe, take his place among them again—

"Now we shall have food for the pot, brother—"

Fors frowned but he did not look around. The southerner stood there tall and straight and around his head he whirled a strange contraption that, to the mountaineer, seemed of no use at all. The three stones in their rabbit skin nets had been fastened to thongs of hide and the three thongs tied together with one central knot. This knot Arskane gripped between his fingers as he sent the stones skimming in a circle. Having tested it he laughed at Fors' bewilderment.

"We shall be moving south, brother, and in the level fields this will do very well, as I shall show you. Ha, and here now is dinner—"

Lura walked up to the fire carrying a young pig. She dropped her burden and with an almost human sigh plumped down beside the kill to watch Arskane butcher it skillfully.

Fors ate roasted pork and began to wonder if his lot was as hopeless as he had thought it to be. The Beast Things were dead. He might lie up until his full strength returned and then make a second visit to the city. Or if he did not dally there would still be time to reach the Eyrie and lead an expedition before winter closed in. He licked rich grease from his fingers and planned. Arskane sang the tune of mournful notes Fors had heard him hum at the fishing lake. Lura purred and washed her paws. It was all very peaceful.

"There faces us now," Arskane said suddenly, "the problem of clothes for you—"

"It faces me," Fors corrected him sleepily. "Unfortunately my wardrobe was left to amaze the lizards. And, strangely enough, I do not find in me any desire to reclaim it from them—"

Arskane tightened the knots on the ball and cord weapon. "There you may be wrong, my friend. A visit to the lizard valley—keeping a safe distance, of course, might serve us very well."

Fors sat up. "How?"

"Five of the Beast Things died there. But how many followed us into the Blow-Up land?"

Fors tried to remember the size of the party he had spied upon. How large had it been? He could not truthfully say now, but he did have a disconcerting suspicion that there had been more than five in it. If that were so—why were they lingering here so close to the edge of the Blow-Up? His feet were good enough to enable him to put some miles between himself and the desolate waste which now lay only a half mile beyond them.

"Do you think that the lizards may have added to their bag?"

Arskane shrugged. "Now that they have been warned, perhaps they have. But we need the spoil they took. Your bow is gone, but those arrowheads would be useful—"

"Useful to the extent of daring the thorns?"

"Maybe." And Arskane fell to cross questioning him as to how much of his equipment the Beast Things had destroyed.

"Everything that is of value to me!" Fors' old feeling of helpless inadequacy closed in upon him. "They ripped the Star pouch to shreds and burned my notes and map—"

"There are the arrowheads," persisted Arskane. "Those were not burned."

Since he seemed to mean it when he urged such an expedition Fors began to believe that the southerner had some purpose of his own in mind. He himself saw no reason to return to the lizard valley. And he was still protesting within him when they came to the top of the rise down which Arskane had gone to the rescue. Lura had refused to accompany them any further than the edge of the Blow-Up and they had left her there pacing back and forth, her flattened ears and moving tail emphatic arguments against such foolishness.

They stood looking down at a wild scene which almost turned Fors' stomach. He gulped and balled his puffed fingers into fists, so that the pain took his attention. The lizards might live upon the grass of the terraces but it appeared that they were also meat eaters and they were now making sure of the supply chance had brought them.

Two of the Beast Things were already but skeletons and the valley's inhabitants were fast at work on the others, a line of laden porters tramping up to the cave entrances while their fellows below swung tiny knives with the same skill with which the martyrs had earlier wielded their sickles.

"Look there—to the left of that rock—" Although Arskane's touch made pain shoot along the length of his arm Fors obediently looked.

There was a pile of stuff there. Fors identified the

remnants of his leggings and a belt such as was worn by the Beast Things. But a glint of color just beyond the haphazard pile of loot was more interesting. It stood in a tiny hollow of the wall—three blue rods— just about a finger high—familiar—

Fors' puzzlement vanished. Those rods—they were the little figures he had brought from the museum in the Star pouch. Now they were set up—and before the feet of each was a pile of offerings!

They were gods. And with a sudden shock of illumination he knew why the lizard folk did them honor.

"Arskane! Those figures—there in that hollow—they are the ones I brought from the museum—and they are making offerings to them—worshiping them!"

The southerner rubbed his hand down his jaw in the familiar gesture which signified puzzlement. Then he fumbled in the traveling pouch at his own belt and brought out a fourth figure.

"They do it, don't you see—because of this!" Fors indicated the small head of the carving. Although the figure was human the head was that of a hook-billed bird of prey.

"One of those figures down there has the head of a lizard—or at least it looks like a lizard!"

"So. And thus—yes—I can see it!"

Arskane started down the slope and from his lips came the hissing cry he had used before. There was a flicker of movement. Fors blinked. The workers were gone, had melted into the cover of the rocks leaving the floor of the valley deserted.

The southerner waited, with a hunter's patience, one minute, two, before he hissed again. He was holding out between two fingers the bird-headed statue and its blue glaze was sharp and clear. Perhaps it was that which drew the lizard leaders from their cover.

They came warily, gliding around stones so that only the most intent watcher could sight them. And, Fors also saw with apprehension, they had their thorn spears with them. But Arskane was well above the line where those balls of clay had fallen. And now he put the blue figure down on the ground and retreated with long-legged strides uphill.

It was the statue which drew them. Three came together, flitting along with their peculiar scuttle. When they were within touching distance of the figure they stopped, their heads darting out at strange angles, as if to assure themselves that this was no bait for a trap.

As one of them laid a paw upon the offering, Arskane moved, not toward them but in the direction of the pile of loot. He went cautiously, examining the ground by inches, paying no outward attention to the lizards. They stood frozen where they were, only their eyes following him.

Deliberately and methodically the southerner turned over what lay there. When he came back he carried Fors' boots and what was left of the mountaineer's clothing, passing the lizards as if they were not there. After he had passed by the leader grabbed the blue figure and darted away around a rock, his two fellows almost treading on his tail. Arskane came up slope with the same unhurried pace but there were beads of moisture across his forehead and cheeks.

Fors sat down and worked the boots over his sore feet. When he got up he looked once more into the valley. The workers were still skulking in their holes but there were now four instead of three blue figures standing in the rock shrine.

The next day they started south, leaving the strange Blow-Up land well behind them. And the second day they were deep in open fields where patches of self-sown grain rippled ripely under the sun.

Fors paused, half over a stone wall, to listen. The sound he had caught was too faint and low pitched for thunder, and it kept within the boundaries of a well-defined rhythm. "Wait!"

As Arskane stopped Fors realized where he had heard that before—it was the voice of a signal drum. And when he said so Arskane dropped down beside the stones, putting his ear to the ground. But the message ended too soon. The southerner got to his feet again, frowning.

"What—?" ventured Fors.

"That was the recall. Yes, you were right and it was a talking drum of my people and what it said is all bad. Evil comes now upon them and they must call back all spears to stand in defense of the clan—"

Arskane hesitated and Fors plunged.

"I am not a spearman, or now even a bowman. But still I wear a sword at my belt and I possess some skill in handling it. Shall we go?"

"How far?" he added another question some breathless minutes later. Arskane had taken him at his word and the steady lope which the southerner had set as their pace was easier matched by Lura's four feet than Fors' two.

"I can only guess. That drum was fashioned to summon across the desert country. Here it may be farther from us than it sounds."

Twice more that day they heard the summons rumble across the distant hills. It would continue to sound at intervals, Arskane said, until all the roving scouts returned. That night the two sheltered in a grove of trees, but they did not light a fire. And before daylight they were on the trail once more.

Fors had not lost his sense of direction but this was new country, unknown to him from any account of the Star Men. The trip across the Blow-Up land had taken

them so far off the territory on any map he had ever
seen that he was entirely lost. He began to wonder
privately if he could have returned to the Eyrie as he
had so blithely planned, or made that trip without
retracing his way through the city. This land was wide
and the known trails very, very few.

On the third day they came to the river, the same
one, Fors believed, he had crossed before. It was
swollen with rain and they spent the better part of the
day making a raft on which to cross. The current tore
them off their course for several miles before they
could make the leap ashore on the opposite side.

At sunset they heard the drum again and this time
the throbbing was close to thunder. Arskane seemed
to relax, he had had his proof that they were heading
in the right direction. But as he listened to the
continued roll, his hand went to the hilt of his knife.

"Danger!" He was reading the words out of the beat.
"Danger—death—walks—danger—death—in—the—
night—"

"It says that?"

He nodded. "The drum talk. But never before have
I heard it speak those words. I tell you, brother, this
is no common danger which sets our drums to such
warnings. Listen!"

Arskane's upheld hand was not needed for Fors had
caught the other sound before his companion had
spoken. That light tap-tap was an answer, it was less
carrying than the clan signal, but it was clear enough.

And again Arskane ready the message: "Uran here—
coming—That is Uran of the Swift Arm, the leader of
our scouts. He ventured west as I came north at the
faring forth. And—"

Once more the lighter sound of a scout's drum
interrupted him.

"Balakan comes, Balakan comes. Now," Arskane

moistened his lips, "there remains only Noraton who has not replied. Noraton—and I who cannot!"

But, though they waited tensely for long minutes, there was no other reply. Instead, after the period of silence, the clan signal broke again, to roll across the open fields, continuing so at intervals through the night.

They paused only to eat at dawn, keeping to the steady trot. But now the drum was silent and Fors thought that quiet ominous. He did not ask questions. Arskane's scowl was now permanent and he pressed on almost as if he had forgotten those who ran with him.

For smoother footing they took to one of the Old Ones' roads which went in the right direction and when it turned again moved into a game trail, splashing through a brook Lura took with a single bound. Deer flashed white tails and were gone. And now Fors saw something else. Black shapes wheeled across the sky. As he watched one broke away and drifted to earth. He caught at Arskane's swinging arm.

"The death birds!" He dragged the southerner to a stop. Where the death birds fed there was always trouble.

12

Where Sweep the Tides of War

What they found was a hollow pocket in the field and what lay there on stained and trampled ground was not a pretty sight. Arskane went down on one knee by the limp body while Lura snarled and sprang at the foul birds that protested such interruption with loud screeching cries.

"Dead—a spear through him!"

"How long?" asked Fors.

"Maybe only this morning. Do you know this marking?" Arskane did some grisly work to hold up a broken shaft ending in a smeared leaf-shaped point.

"Plainsman made. And it is part of one of their lances, not a spear. But who—"

Arskane swabbed off the disfigured face of the dead with a handful of grass.

"Noraton!" The name was bitten off as his teeth snapped together. The other scout, the one who had not answered the summons.

145

Arskane wiped his hands, rubbing savagely as if he did not want to think of what they had touched. His face was stone hard.

"When the tribe sends forth scouts, those scouts are sworn to certain things. To none were we to show an unsheathed sword unless they first attacked us. We would come in peace if we may. Noraton was a wise man and of cool, even temper. This was none of his provoking—"

"Your people are moving north to settle," mused Fors slowly. "The Plainspeople are proud-hearted and high of temper. They may see in your coming a threat to their way of life—they are much bound by custom and old ways—"

"So they would take to the sword to settle differences? Well, if that is as they wish—so be it!" Arskane straightened out the body.

Fors drew his sword, sawing through the turf. Together they worked in silence until they had ready a grave. And afterward, above that lonely resting place they piled up a mound to protect the sleeper. On its summit Arskane thrust deep the long knife Noraton had worn and the shadow of its cross hilt lay straight along the turned earth.

Now they pushed on through a haunted world. Death had struck Noraton down and that same death might now stand between them and the tribe. They held to cover, sacrificing speed once more to caution. Arskane took out his weapon of balls and thong and carried it ready for action.

The end of their journey came as they skirted a small ruin and saw before them a wide stretch of open field. To use the cover afforded only at its far edge would mean a wide detour. Arskane chose to strike boldly across. Since the haste was his Fors accepted that decision, but he was glad that Lura scouted ahead.

Here the grass and wild grain was waist-high and a man could not run. It would entangle his feet and bring him down. Fors thought of snakes just as Arskane sprawled on his face, one foot in a hidden rabbit burrow. He sat up quickly, his mouth working a little as he rubbed his ankle.

Fors' throat went tight. A clot of horsemen were pounding at them out of the shadow of the ruins, riding at a wild gallop, lance points forging a flashing wall before them.

The mountaineer flung himself on Arskane and they rolled just in time to escape being spitted by those iron tips, avoiding hoofs by so thin a hair of safety that Fors could hardly believe his skin intact. Arskane struggled out of his grasp as Fors got up, sword in hand. Just the proper weapon, he thought bleakly, with which to face armed horsemen.

Arskane whirled the ball weapon around his head and turned to meet the enemy. The force of their charge had taken them on too far to rein back quickly. But they had played this game before. They scattered out, fanning in a circle which would ring in their victims.

As they rode they laughed and made derisive gestures. That decided Fors. Short sword or no, he would take at least one of them down with him when the end came. The circling riders speeded their pace around and around, making their captives turn to face them at a dizzy rate.

But Lura spoiled that well-practiced maneuver. She reared out of the grass and wiped a paw full of raking claws down the smooth flank of a horse. With a terrible scream of fright and pain the animal reared and fought against the control of its rider. The horse won and raced out and away taking its rider with it.

Only—the rest were warned now and when Lura

sprang again she not only missed but suffered the bite of an expertly aimed lance. However, her attacks gave Arskane the chance he had been waiting for. His ball weapon sang through the air and with uncanny precision wrapped itself about the throat of one of the lancers. He thudded limply into the tall grass.

Two—out of eight! And they could not run—even with the circle broken. Such a move would lead only to Noraton's death with cold steel breaking from back to breast. The unharmed six had stopped laughing. Fors could guess what was being planned now. They would ride down the enemy, making very certain they should not escape.

Arskane balanced his long knife on the palm of his hand. The riders made a line, knee to knee. Fors jerked a hand to the left and the southerner's teeth showed in a mirthless smile. He pointed a finger right. They stood and waited. The charge came and they dared to watch a whole second before they moved.

Fors flung himself to the left and went down on one knee. He slashed up at the legs of the mount which came at him, slashing viciously with all his strength. Then he was up again with one hand twisted in the legging of the rider who stabbed down at him. He caught the blow on his sword and managed to hold on to the blade although his fingers went numb with the shock.

The rider catapulted into his arms and fingers dug into his cheeks just below his eye sockets. There were tricks for close fighting, tricks which Langdon had passed to his son. Fors got on top and stayed there— or at least he did for a few victorious moments until he glimpsed a shadow sweeping in from the left. He dodged, but not quickly enough, and the blow sent him rolling free from the body of his opponent. He blinked painfully at the sky and was levering himself up on his elbows when a circle of hide rope dropped about his shoulders snapping his arms tight to his body.

So he sat dumbly in the grass. When he moved his ringing head too suddenly the world danced around in a sickening way.

"—this time no mistake, Vocar. We have taken two of the swine—the High Chief will be pleased—"

Fors picked the words out of the air. The slurring drawl of the Plainsmen's speech was strange but he had no difficulty in understanding it. He raised his head cautiously and looked around.

"—ham-strung White Bird! May night devils claw him into bits and hold high feast with him!"

A man came tramping away from a floundering horse. He walked straight to Fors and slapped him across the face with a methodical force and a very evident desire to hurt. Fors stared up at him and spat blood from torn lips. The fellow had a face easy to remember—that crooked scar across the chin was a brand not to be forgotten. And if fortune was at all good they would have a future reckoning for those blows.

"Loose my hands," Fors said, glad that his voice came out so steady and even. "Loose my hands, tall hero, and worse than night devils shall have your bones to pick!"

Another slap answered that, but before a second could be struck his assailant's wrist was caught and held.

"Tend your hose, Sati. This man was defending himself as best he knew. We are not Beast Things from the ruins to amuse ourselves with the tormenting of prisoners."

Fors forced his aching head up another inch so that he could see the speaker. The Plainsman was tall—he must almost top Arskane's height—but he was slighter and the hair tied back for riding was a warm chestnut brown. He was no green youth on his first war trail but a seasoned warrior. Lines of good humor bracketed his well-cut mouth.

"The other one is now awake, Vocar."

At that call the war chief turned his attention from Fors. "Bring him hither. We have a long trail to follow before sundown."

The floundering horse was stilled with an expert knife. But Sati arose from that task with the blackest of scowls for both captives.

Lura! Fors tried to glance across the grass without betraying interest or concern. The big cat had disappeared and since his captors did not mention her, surely she had not been killed. They would have been quick enough to claim her hide as a trophy. With Lura free and prepared to act there was a chance they might escape even yet. He held to that hope as they lashed his right hand fast to his own belt and fastened the left by a punishing loop to the saddle of one of the riders. Not to Sati's he was glad to note. That warrior had swung onto the horse of the man Arskane had killed with the ball loops.

And the southerner had taken other toll too. For there were two bodies lashed to nervous led horses. After some consultation two of the band went ahead on foot leading the burdened mounts. Fors' guard was the third in line of march and Vocar with Arskane at his side came near the end.

Fors looked back before the jerk at his wrist started him off. There was blood on the southerner's face and he walked stiffly, but he did not appear to be badly hurt. Where was Lura? He tried to send out a summoning thought and then closed his mind abruptly.

There had long been contact between the Eyrie and the Plainspeople. These men might well know of the big cats and their relationship with man. Best to leave well enough alone. He had no desire at all to watch Lura thrash out her life pinned to the hard earth by one of those murderous lances.

The line of march was westward, Fors noted mechanically, forced to keep a loping run as the horse he was bound to cantered. The sun was hard and bright in their faces. He studied the paint marks of ownership dabbed on the smooth hide of the animal beside him. It was not a sign used by any tribe his people knew. And the speech of these men was larded with unfamiliar words. Another tribe on the move, maybe roving far distances. Perhaps, like Arskane's people, they had been driven out of their own grounds by some disaster of nature and were now seeking a new territory—or maybe they were only driven by the inborn restlessness of their kind.

If they were strange to this country their attitude of enmity against all comers was not so to be wondered at. Usually it was only the Beast Things who attacked without declaring formal war—without parley. If only he wore the Star—then he would have a talking point when he faced their high chief. The Star Men were known—known in far lands where they had never walked—and none had ever raised sword against them. Fors knew the bite of his old discontent. He was not a Star Man—he was nothing, a runaway and a wanderer who did not even dare claim tribe protection.

The dust pounded up by the hoofs powdered his face and body. He coughed, unable to shield his eyes or mouth. The horses went down a bank and splashed through a wide stream. On the other side they turned into a well-marked trail. A second party of riders issued out of the brush and shouted questions made the air ring.

Fors was a center of attention and the newcomers stared at him curiously. As they discussed him with a frankness he tried to ignore, he held firmly to the rags of his temper.

He was not like the other one at all, was the gist of most of their comments. Apparently they already knew of Arskane's people and had little liking for them. But Fors, with his strange silver hair and lighter skin, was an unknown quantity which intrigued them.

The combined troops at last rode on, Fors thankful for the breathing spell he had been granted by the meeting. Within a half mile they came into their camp. Fors was amazed at the wide sweep of tent rows. This was no small family clan on the march, but a whole tribe or nation. He counted clan flags hung before the sub-chieftains' tent homes as he was led down the wide road which divided the sprawling settlement into two parts. He had marked down ten and there were countless others to be seen fluttering back from this main path.

At the sight of the dead the women of the Plains city set up the shrill ritual wailing, but they made no move toward the prisoners who had been released from the saddle ties to have their hands lashed behind them and to be thrust into a small tent within the shadow of the High Chieftain's own circle.

Fors wriggled over on his side to face Arskane. Even in that dim light he could see that the southerner's right eye was almost swollen shut and that a shallow cut on his neck was closed with a paste of dust and dried blood.

"Do you know this tribe?" Arskane asked after two croaking attempts to shape the words with a dust-clogged tongue.

"No. Both the clan flags and their horse markings

are new to me. And some of the words they use I have never heard before. I think that they have come a long way. The tribes the Star Men know do not attack without warning—except when they go against the Beast Things—for always are all men's swords bare to *them!* This is a nation on the march—I counted the banners of ten clans and I must have seen only a small portion of them."

"I would like to know what use they have for us," Arskane now said dryly. "If they did not see profit in our capture we would now be awaiting the attention of the death birds. But why do they want us?"

Fors set himself to recall all that he had ever heard concerning the ways of the Plainspeople. They held freedom very high, refusing to be tied to any stretch of land lest it come to hold them. They did not lie—ever—that was part of their code. But they also deemed themselves greater than other men, for they had a haughty and abiding pride. They were inclined to be suspicious of new things and were much bound by custom—in spite of their talk of freedom. Among them a man's given word was held unbreakable, he must always hold to a promise no matter what might come. And anyone who offended against the tribe was solemnly pronounced dead in council. Thereafter no one could notice him and he could claim neither food nor lodging—for the tribe he had ceased to exist.

Star Men had lived in their tents. His own father had taken a chief's daughter to wife. But that was only because the Star Men possessed something which the tribe reckoned to be worth having—a knowledge of wide lands.

A wild burst of sound broke his thoughts, a sound which grew louder, the full-throated chanting of fighting men on the march.

"With sword and flame before us,
  And the lances of clans at our backs,
  We ride through plains and forests
  Where sweep the tides of war!
  Eat, Death Birds, eat!
  From a feast we have spread for your
    tearing—"

A flute carried the refrain while a small drum beat out the savage "eat, eat." It was a wild rhythm which made the blood race through the listener's veins. Fors felt the power of it and it was a heady wine. His own people were a silent lot. The mountains must have drawn out of them the desire for music, singing was left to the women who sometimes hummed as they worked. He knew only the council hymn which had a certain darksome power. The men of the Eyrie never went singing into battle.

"These fighting men sing!" Arskane's whisper echoed his own thoughts. "Do they welcome in such a manner their high chief?"

But if it were the chief who was being so welcomed he had no present interest in captives. Fors and Arskane remained imprisoned as the dreary hours passed. When it was fully dark fires were lighted at regular intervals down the main way and shortly after two men came in, to release them from the ropes and stand alert while they rubbed stiff hands. There were bowls of stew plunked down before them. The stuff was well cooked and they were famished—they gave the food their full attention. But when he had licked the last drop from his lips Fors bent his tongue in the Plains language he had learned from his father.

"Ho—good riding to you, Plainsborn. Now, windrider, by the custom of the shelter fire and the water bowl, we would have speech with the high chief of this tribe—"

The guard's eyes widened. It was plain that the last thing he expected was to have the formal greeting of ceremony from this dirty and ragged prisoner. Recovering, he laughed and his companion joined jeeringly.

"Soon enough will you be brought before the High One, forest filth. And when you are that meeting will give you no pleasure!"

Again their hands were tied and they were left alone. Fors waited until he judged that their sentry was fully engaged in conversation with the two visitors. He wriggled close to Arskane.

"When they fed us they made a mistake. All Plainspeople have laws of hospitality. Should a stranger eat meat which has been cooked at their fires and drink water from their store, then they must hold him inviolate for a day, a night, and another day. They gave us stew to eat and in it was cooked meat and water. Keep silent when they lead us out and I shall claim protection under their own laws—"

Arskane's answering whisper was as faint. "They must believe us to be ignorant of their customs then—"

"Either that, or someone within this camp has given us a chance and waits now to see if we have wit enough to seize it. If that guard repeats my greeting then perhaps such an unknown will know that we are ready. Plainspeople visit much from tribe to tribe. There may be one or more here now who knows the Eyrie and would so give me a fighting chance to save us."

Maybe it was that Fors' greeting had been passed on. At any rate, not many minutes elapsed before the men came back into the tent and the captives were pulled to their feet, to be herded between lines of armed men into the tall hide-walled pavilion which was the center of the city. Hundreds of deer and wild cattle had died to furnish the skins for that council room. And within it, packed so tightly that a sword could not lie comfortably between thigh and thigh, were the sub-chieftains, chiefs, warriors and wise men of the whole tribe.

Fors and Arskane were pushed down the open aisle which ran from the doorway to the center. There the ceremonial fire burned, sending out aromatic smoke as it was fed with bundles of dried herbs and lengths of cedar wood.

By the fire three men stood. The one, a long white cloak draped over his fighting garb, was the man of medicine, he who tended the bodies of the tribe. His companion who wore black was the Keeper of Records—the rememberer of past customs and law. Between them was the High Chief.

As the captives came forward Vocar arose out of the mass of his fellows and saluted the Chief with both hands to his forehead.

"Captain of Hosts, Leader of the Tribe of the Wind, Feeder of the Death Birds, these two be those we took in fair fight when by your orders we scouted to the east. Now we of the clan of the Raging Bull do give them into your hands that you may do with them as you wish. I, Vocar, have spoken."

The High Chief acknowledged that with a brief nod. He was measuring the captives with a keen eye which missed nothing. Fors stared as boldly back.

He saw a man of early middle age, slender and wiry, marked with a strand of white hair which ran back across his head like a plumed crest. Old scars of many battle wounds showed under the heavy collar of ceremony which extended halfway down his chest. He was unmistakably a famous warrior.

But to be High Chief of a tribe he must be more

than just a fighting man. He must also have the wit and ability to rule. Only a strong and equally wise hand could control a turbulent Plains community.

"You"—the Chief spoke first to Arskane—"are of those dark ones who now make war in the south—"

Arskane's one open eye met the Chief's without blinking.

"My people only go out upon the battlefield when war is forced upon them. Yesterday I found my tribesman food for the death birds and through his body there was a Plains lance—"

But the chief did not answer that. He had already turned to Fors.

"And you—what tribe has spawned such as you?"

Ring of Fire

"I am Fors of the Puma Clan, of the tribe of the Eyrie in the mountains which smoke." Because his hands were bound he did not give the salute of a free man to the commander of many tents. But neither did he hang his head nor show that he thought himself not the full equal of any in that company.

"Of this Eyrie I have never heard. And only far-riding scouts have ever seen the mountains which smoke. If you are not of the blood of the dark ones, why do you run with one of them?"

"We are battle comrades, he and I. Together we have fought the Beast Things and together we crossed the Blow-Up land—"

But at those words all three of the leaders before him looked incredulous and he of the white robe laughed, his mockery echoed a moment later by the High Chief, to be taken up by the whole company until the jeering roar was a thunder in the night.

"Now do we know that the tongue which lies within your jaws is a crooked one. For in the memory of men—our fathers, and our fathers' fathers, and their fathers before them, no men have crossed a Blow-Up land and lived to boast of it. Such territory is accursed and death comes horribly to those who venture into it. Speak true now, woodsrunner, or we shall deem you as twisted as a Beast One, fit only to cough out your life upon the point of a lance— and that speedily!"

Fors had clapped his rebel tongue between his teeth and so held it until the heat of his first anger died. When he had control of himself he answered steadily.

"Call me what you will, Chief. But, by whatever gods you own, will I swear that I speak the full truth. Perhaps in the years since our fathers' fathers' fathers went into the Blow-Up and perished, there has been a lessening of the evil blight—"

"You call yourself of the mountains," interrupted the White Robe. "I have heard of men from the mountains who venture forth into the empty lands to regain lost knowledge. These are sworn to the truth and speak no warped tales. If you be of their breed show us now the star which such wear upon them as the sign of their calling. Then shall we make you welcome under custom and law—"

"I am of the mountains," repeated Fors grimly. "But I am not a Star Man."

"Only outlaws and evil livers wander far from their clan brothers." It was the Black Robe who made that suggestion.

"And those are without protection of the law, meat for any man's ax. These men are not worth the trifling over—"

Now—now he must try his one and only argument. Fors looked straight at the Chief and interrupted him

with the old, old formula his father had taught him
years before.

"By the flame, by the water, by the flesh, by the tent
right, do we now claim refuge under the banner of this
clan—we have eaten your meat and broken our
thirsting here this hour!"

There was a sudden silence in the large tent. All
the buzz of whispering from neighbor to neighbor was
stilled and when one of the guards shifted his stance
so that his sword hilt struck against another's the sound
was like the call to battle.

The High Chief had thrust his thumbs between his
wide belt and his middle and now he drummed on the
leather with his finger tips, a tattoo of impatience. But
the Black Robe moved forward a step reluctantly and
gestured to the guard. So a knife flashed and the hide
thongs fell from their cramped arms. Fors rubbed his
wrists. He had won the first engagement but—

"From the hour of the lighting of the fires on this
night until the proper hour you are guests." The Chief
repeated those words as if they were bitter enough to
twist his mouth. "Against custom we have no appeal.
But be assured, when the time of grace is done, we
shall have a reckoning with you—"

Fors dared now to smile. "We ask only for what is
ours by the rights of your own customs, Chieftain and
Captain of many tents." His two hands made the proper
salute.

The High Chief's eyes were narrowed as he waved
forward his two companions.

"And under custom these two be your guardians,
strangers. You are in their care this night."

So they went forth from the council tent free in their
persons, passing through the crowd to another hide-
walled enclosure of smaller size. On the dark skins of
which it was made various symbols were painted. Fors

could make them out with the aid of the firelight. Some he knew well. The twin snakes coiled about a staff—that was the universal sign of the healer. And those balancing scales—those meant the equalizing of justice. The men of the Eyrie used both of those emblems too. The round ball with a flower of flames crowding out of its top was new but Arskane gave an exclamation of surprise as he stopped to point at a pair of outstretched wings supporting a pointed object between them.

"That—that is the sign of the Old Ones who were flying men. It is the chief sign of my own clan!"

And at those words of his the black-robed Plainsman turned quickly to demand with some fierceness:

"What know you of flying men, you creeper in the dirt?"

But Arskane was smiling proudly, his battered face alight, his head high.

"We of my tribe are sprung from flying men who came to rest in the deserts of the south after a great battle had struck most of their machines from the air and blasted from the earth the field from which they had flown. That is our sign." He touched almost lovingly the tip of the outstretched wing. "Around his neck now does Nath-al-sal, our High Chief, still wear such as that made of the Old One's shining metal, as it came from the hand of his father, and his father's father, and so back to the first and greatest of the flying men who came forth from the belly of the dead machine on the day they found refuge in our valley of the little river!"

As he talked the outrage faded from the Black Robe's face. He was a sadly puzzled man now.

"So does all knowledge come—in bits and patches," he said slowly. "Come within."

But it seemed to Fors that the law man of the

Plainspeople had lost much of his hostility. And he even held aside the door flap with his own hands as if they were in truth honored guests instead of prisoners, reprieved but for a space.

Once inside they stared about them with frank curiosity. A long table made of polished boards set on stakes pounded into the earth ran down the center and on it in orderly piles were things Fors recognized from his few visits to the Star House. A stone hollowed for the grinding and bruising of herbs used in medicines, its pestle lying across it, together with rows of boxes and jars—that was the healer's property. And the dried bundles of twigs and leaves, hanging in ordered lines from the cord along the ridge pole, were his also.

But the books of parchment with protecting covers of thin wood, the ink horn and the pens laid ready, those were the tools of the law man. The records of the tribe were in his keeping, all the customs and history. Each book bore the sign of a clan carved on its cover, each was the storehouse of information about that family.

Arskane stabbed a finger at a piece of smoothed hide held taut in a wooden stretcher.

"The wide river?"

"Yes. You know of it, too?" The law man pushed aside a pile of books and brought the hide under the hanging lantern where oil-soaked tow burned to give light.

"This part—that is as I have seen it with my own two eyes." The southerner traced a curved line of blue paint which meandered across the sheet. "My tribe crossed right here. It took us four weeks to build the rafts. And two were swept away by the current so that we never saw those on them again. We lost twenty sheep in the flood as well. But here—my brother scouted north and he found another curve so—" Arskane corrected the line with his finger. "Also—when the mountains of our land poured out fire and shook the world around them the bitter sea waters came in here and here, and no more is it now land—only water—"

The law man frowned over his map. "So. Well, we have lived for ten tens of years along the great river and know this of its waters—many times it changes its bed and wanders to suit its will. There are the marks of the Old Ones' work at many places along it, they must have tried to hold it to its course. But that mystery we have lost—along with so much else—"

"If you have ridden from the banks of the great river you have come far," Fors observed. "What brought your tribe into these eastern lands?"

"Whatever takes the Plainspeople east or west? We have the wish to see new places born in us. North and south have we gone—from the edges of the great forests where the snows make a net to catch the feet of our horses and only the wild creatures may live fat in winter—to the swamp lands where scaled things hide in the rivers to pull down the unwary drinker—we have seen the land. Two seasons ago our High Chief died and his lance fell into the hand of Cantrul who has always been a seeker of far lands. So now do we walk new trails and open the world for the wonder of our children. Behold—"

He unhooked the lamp from its supporting cord and pulled Fors with him to the other end of the tent. There were maps, maps and pictures, pictures vivid enough to make the mountaineer gasp with wonder. They had in them the very magic with which the Old Ones had made their world live for one another.

"Here—this was made in the north—in winter when a man must walk with hide webs beneath his feet so that he sinks not into the snow to be swallowed as in quicksands. And here—look you—this is one of the forest people—they lay paint upon their faces and wear the hides of beasts upon their bodies but they walk in pride and say that they are a very ancient people who once owned all this land. And here and here—" He flipped over the framed parchment squares, the records of their travels set down in bright color.

"This—" Fors drew a deep breath—"this is greater treasure than the Star House holds. Could Jarl and the rest but look upon these!"

The law man ran his fingers along the smooth frame of the map he held.

"In all the tribe perhaps ten of our youth look upon these with any stir in their hearts or minds. The rest—they care nothing for the records, for making a map of the way our feet have gone that day. To eat and to war, to ride and hunt, to raise a son after them to do likewise—that it the desire of the tribe. But always—always there are a few who still strive to go back along the old roads, to try to find again what was lost in the days of disaster. Bits and pieces we discover, a thread here and a tattered scrap there, and we try to weave it whole."

"If Marphy spoke now the full truth," the harsher voice of the healer broke in, "he would say that it was because he was born a seeker of knowledge that all this"—he waved at the array—"came to be. He it was who started making these and he trains those of like mind to see and set down what they have seen. All this has been done since he became keeper of the records."

The law man looked confused and then he smiled almost shyly. "Have I not said that it is in our blood to be ever hunting what lies beyond? In me it has taken this turn. In you, Fanyer, it also works so that you make your messes out of leaves and grass, and if you dared you would cut us open just to see what lies beneath our skins."

"Perhaps, perhaps. Dearly would I like to know what lies beneath the skins of these two that they have crossed the Blow-Up land and yet show no signs of the burning sickness—"

"I thought," retorted Arskane quickly, "that was the story you did not believe."

Fanyer considered him through narrowed eyes, almost, Fors thought, as if he did have the southerner opened for examination.

"So—maybe I do not believe it. But if it is true, then this is the greatest wonder I have yet heard of. Tell me, how did this thing happen?"

Arskane laughed. "Very well, we shall tell our tale. And we swear that it is a true one. But half of the tale belongs to each of us and so we tell it together."

And as the oil lamp sputtered overhead, guards and prisoners sat on the round cushions and talked and listened. When Fors spoke the last word Marphy stretched and shook himself as if he had been swimming in deep water.

"That is the truth, I think," he commented quietly. "And it is a brave story, fit to make a song for the singing about night fires."

"Tell me," Fanyer rounded abruptly upon Fors, "you who were lessoned for knowledge seeking, what was the thing which amazed you most in this journey of yours?"

Fors did not even have to consider his answer. "That the Beast Things are venturing forth from their dens into the open country. For, by all our observations, they have not done so before in the memory of men. And this may mean danger to come—"

Marphy looked to Fanyer and their eyes locked. Then the man of medical knowledge got to his feet and went purposefully out into the night. It was Arskane who broke the short silence with a question of his own.

"Recorder of the past, why did your young men hunt us down? Why do you march to war against my people? What has passed between our tribes that this is so?"

Marphy cleared his throat, almost as if he wished for time.

"Why? Why? Even the Old Ones never answered that. As you can see in the tumbled stones of their cities. Your people march north seeking a home, mine march east and south for the same reason. We are different in custom, in speech, in bearing. And man seems to fear this difference. Young blood is hot, there is a quarrel, a killing, from the spilled blood springs war. But chiefly the reason is this, I think. My people are rovers and they do not understand those who would build and root in one place within the borders of a land they call their own. Now we hear that a town is rising in the river bend one day's journey to the south. And that town is being settled by men of your blood. So now the tribe is uneasy and a little afraid of what they do not know. There are many among them who say that we must stamp out what may be a threat to us in time to come—"

Arskane wiped the palms of his hands across the tattered remnant of his garment, as if he had found those palms suddenly and betrayingly damp.

"In no way is my tribe any threat against the future of yours. We ask only for land in which to plant our seed and to provide grazing for our sheep. Perhaps we may be lucky to find a bank of clay to give us the material we need for our potters' craft. We are indifferent hunters—coming from a land where there is but little game. We have arts in our hands which might well serve others beside ourselves."

"True, true." Marphy nodded. "This desire for war with the stranger is our curse—perhaps the same one which was laid upon the Old Ones for their sins. But it will take greater than either of us to make a peace now—the war drums have sounded, the lances are ready—"

"And there, for once, you speak the full truth, oh, weaver of legends!"

It was the High Chief who came to the table. Laid aside were his feather helmet and cloak of office. In the guise of a simple warrior he could walk the camp unnoted.

"You forget this—a tribe which breeds not warriors to hold its lances will be swallowed up. The lion preys upon the bull—if it can escape the horns. The wolves run in packs to the kill. Kill or be killed, eat or be eaten—that is the law upheld better than all other laws."

Something hot rose in Fors' throat and he snapped out an answer to that which was born of this new emotion.

"The paws of the Beast Things are against all of us— in just that manner, oh Captain of the Tents. And they are no lightly considered enemy. Lead your lances against them—if war you must!"

Surprise came first into Cantrul's eyes and then the flush of anger stained his brown cheekbones. His hand moved instinctively to the hilt of his short sword. Fors' hands remained on his knees. The scabbard at his belt was empty and he could not accept any challenge the Plainsman might offer.

"Our lances move when they will and where they will, stranger. If they wish to clean out a nest of mud-hut-dwelling vermin—"

Arskane made no move, but his one unswollen eye calmly measured the High Chief with a control Fors admired. Cantrul wanted an answer—preferably a hot one. When it did not come he turned to Fors with a harsh question.

"You say that the Beast Things march?"

"No," Fors corrected him. "I say that for the first time in our knowledge they are coming fearlessly out of their burrows in the cities to roam the open lands. And they are cunning fighters with powers we have not yet fully gauged. They are not men as we are—whether or not their sires' sires' sires were of our breed. So they may be greater than we—or lesser. How can we yet know? But this is true—as we of the Eyrie, who have warred against them during generations of city looting, can say—they are enemies to mankind. My father died under their fangs. I, myself, have lain in their bonds. They are no common enemy to be dismissed without fear, Plainsman."

"There is this, remember." Marphy broke the short silence. "When these two fled across the Blow-Up land a pack of the creatures sniffed their trail. If we march south without taking care we may find ourselves with an enemy behind as well as before—to be caught between two fires—"

Cantrul's fingers drummed out a battle rhythm on his belt, a sharp furrow cut between his thin brows. "We have scouts out."

"True. You are a leader old in war knowledge. What is needful has been ordered. Forgive me—I grow old, and conning records sometimes gives one a weary view of life. Man makes so many mistakes—sometimes it appears that never shall he learn—"

"In war he learns or dies! It is plain that the Old Ones did not or could not learn—well, they are gone, are they not? And we live—the tribe is strong. I think that you worry too much, both of you—Fanyer, too. We ride prepared and there is nothing that—"

But his words were drowned in such a thunder of sound that it seemed a storm had broken directly above the tent in which they stood. And through the general uproar came the shouts of men and the higher screaming of frightened women and children.

Those in the tent were across it in an instant, elbowing each other to be first at the door flap. The Plainsmen pushed out as Arskane pulled Fors back. As they hesitated they saw the wild stampede of horses pound down the center lane of the camp, threading around the fires with so little room that tents were going down under their hoofs. Behind, across the horizon, was a wavering wall of golden light.

Arskane's hand closed about Fors' wrist with almost bone-crushing pressure as he dragged the slighter mountaineer back into the tent.

"There is fire! Fire running through the prairie grass!" He had to shout the words in order to be heard over the tumult outside. "Our chance—"

But Fors had already grasped that. He broke out of the other's grip and ran down the length of the table looking for a weapon. A small spear was all he could see to snatch up. Arskane took the pestle of the herb grinder as Fors used the point of the spear to rip through the far wall of the tent.

Outside they headed away from the chieftain's enclosure, running and dodging among the tents, joining other running men in the shadows. In the stirred-up ant hill of the camp it was ridiculously easy to get away without notice. But the sky behind was growing steadily brighter and they knew they must get out of the camp quickly.

"It's sweeping around." Fors pointed out the swing of that ghastly parody of daylight. East and west the fire made a giant mouth open and ready to engulf the camp. There were fewer men running now and order was developing out of the first confusion.

They rounded the last of the tents and were out in the open, looking out for clumps of bushes or trees among which they could take cover. Then Fors caught a glimpse of something which brought him up short. A glare of yellow showed before them where it should not be—reflection—but how? A moment later Arskane verified his suspicion.

"It's a ring of fire!"

Fors' hunter's instincts began to work as those tongues of flame lapped skyward.

"Downhill!" He threw the order over his shoulder.

He could see a trampled trail marked by many hoofs, hoofs of horses led to water. Downhill was water!

Downhill they ran.

·✦· 14

Arrow's Flight

The wind had changed and blinded by the smoke which bit at eyes and throat they discovered the stream by falling into it. In its depths they were not alone. A wave of rabbits and other small furry things which squeaked and scurried flooded out of the high grass to run along the edge of the water, making small piteous sounds of fear and terror until they plunged in to clog the water with their bodies.

Out in midstream the smoke did not hang so thick. Fors' night eyes adjusted and he took the lead, heading down current, out toward where the flames bannered high. The confused noise of the Plains camp died out as the river turned a bend and a screen of willows closed in.

A deer crashed through the bushes, running, and behind it came a second and a third—then four more all together. The stream bed deepened. Fors' foot slipped off a stone and his head went under. For a moment he knew panic and then the art learned in mountain pools came back to him and he swam steadily, Arskane splashing along at his shoulder.

So they came out into the middle of a lake, a lake which ended in the straight line of a dam. Fors blinked water out of his eyes and saw round mounds rising above the stream line—beaver houses! He flinched as a big body floundered by to pull out its bulk on top of one of those lodges. A very wet and very angry wild cat crouched there, spitting at the liquid which had saved its life.

Fors trod water and looked back. Arskane's head was bobbing along as if the big man were in difficulties and the mountaineer turned back. Minutes later both clung to the rough side of the nearest lodge and Fors considered their future with cool calculation.

The beaver lake was of a good size and recent rains had added to its contents. Also the builders of the lodges and the dam had cleaned out the majority of the trees which had grown along its banks, leaving only brush. Seeing this the mountaineer relaxed. Luck had brought them to the one place which would save them. And he was not the only living thing to believe that.

An antlered buck swam in circles near them, its pronged head high. And smaller creatures were arriving by the dozens to clamber over each other up the sides of the lodges to safety. Arskane gave a violent cry of disgust and jerked back his hand as a snake wriggled across it.

As the fire crept along the shore, making the water as ruddy as blood, the creatures in the water and on the lodges seemed to cower, sniffing in the cindery hot breath of the flames reluctantly. A bird dropped out of the air, struck Fors' shoulder, and plumped into the water leaving a puff of burned feather stench behind it. The mountaineer dropped his head down on his hands, holding his mouth and nose only an inch or so above the water, feeling the blistering heat whip across his shoulders.

How long they remained there, their bodies floating in the water, their fingers dug into the stuff of the lodges, they never knew. But when the crackle of the fire diminished Fors raised his head again. The first of the blaze was gone. Here and there the stump of a tree still showed stubborn coals. It would be some time before they would dare walk over that still smoking ground. The water must continue to give them passage.

Fors fended off the body of a deer which had taken too late to refuge and worked his way to the next lodge and so on to the dam. Here the fire had eaten a hole, taken a good bite out, so that water was spilling freely into the old channel of the stream.

By the light of smoldering roots he could make out the course for some distance ahead.

"Holla!"

A moment later, Arskane joined him.

"So we follow the water, eh?" The southerner applauded. "Well, with the fire behind us we shall not worry about pursuit. Perhaps good fortune journeys on our right hand tonight, my brother."

Fors grunted, climbing over the rough surface of the dam. Again they could keep their feet. The water was only waist-deep here. But the stones in the course made slippery footing and they crept along fearing a disastrous fall.

When they were at last well away from the fire glow in the sky Fors stopped and studied the stars, looking for the familiar clusters which were the unchanging guides he had been taught. They were heading south—but from a westerly direction and this was unknown territory.

"Will we hear the drums now?" he asked.

"Do not count on it. The tribe probably believes me as dead as Noraton and sounds the call no longer."

Fors shivered, perhaps just from the long immersion in the chill water. "This is a wide land, without a guide we may miss them—"

"More likely to since this is war and my people will conceal what they may of the camp. But, brother, it is in my mind that we could not have won free so easily from this night's captivity had there not been a mission set upon us. Head south and let us hope that the same power will bring us to what we seek. At least your mountains will not move themselves from their root and we can turn to them if nothing better offers—"

But Fors refused to answer that, giving his attention again to the stars.

For the present they kept to the stream, stumbling between water-worn boulders and over gravel. At length they came into a ravine where walls of gray rock closed in as if they were entering the narrow throat of a trap. Here they pulled out on a flat ledge to rest.

Fors dozed uneasily. The mosquitoes settled and feasted in spite of his slaps. But at last his heavy head went flat and he could no longer fight off the deep sleep of a worn-out body and fatigue-dulled mind.

The murmur of water awoke him at last and he lay listening to it before he forced open puffy eyelids. He rubbed an itching, bite-swollen face as he focused dazedly upon moss-green rock and brown water. Then he sat up with a snap. It must be mid-morning at least!

Arskane still lay belly down beside him, his head pillowed on an arm. There was an angry red brand left by a burn on his shoulder—a drifting piece of wood must have struck there. And beyond Fors could see floating on the current other evidence of the fire—half-consumed sticks, the battered body of a squirrel with the fur charred from its back.

Fors retrieved that before the water bore it on. Half-burned squirrel was a rare banquet when a man's stomach was making a too intimate acquaintance with his backbone. He laid it out on the rock and worried off the skin with the point of the spear he had clung to through the night.

When he had completed that gory task he shook Arskane awake. The big man rolled over on his back with a sleepy protest, lay staring a moment into the sky, and then sat up. In the light of the day his battered face was almost a monster's mask mottled with purple brown. But he managed a lopsided grin as he reached for the bits of half-raw meat Fors held out to him.

"Food—and a clear day for traveling ahead of us—"

"Half a day only," Fors corrected him, measuring the length of sun and shadow around them.

"Well, then, half a day—but a man can cover a good number of miles even in a half day. And it seems that we cannot be stopped, we two—"

Fors thought back over the wild activity of the past days. He had lost accurate count of time long since. There was no way of knowing how many days it had been since he had left the Eyrie. But there was a certain point of truth in what Arskane had just said—they had not yet been stopped—in spite of Beast Things, and Lizard folk, and the Plainsmen. Even fire or the Blow-Up land had not proved barriers—

"Do you remember what once I said to you, brother—back there when we stood on the field of the flying machines? Never again must man come to warfare with his own kind—for if he does, then shall man vanish utterly from the earth. The Old Ones began it with their wicked rain of death from the sky—if we continue—then we are lost and damned!"

"I remember."

"Now it lies in my mind," the big man continued slowly, "that we have been shown certain things, you and I, shown these things that we may in turn show others. These Plainsmen ride to war with my people— yet in them, too, is the thirst for the knowledge that the Old Ones in their stupid waste threw away. They breed seekers such as the man Marphy—with whom I find it in my heart to wish friendship. There is also you, who are mountain bred—yet you feel no hatred for me or for Marphy of the Plains. In all tribes we find men of good will—"

Fors licked his lips. "And if such men of good will could sit down together in common council—"

Arskane's battered face lit up. "My own thoughts spoken from your lips, brother! We must rid this land of war or we shall in the end eat each other up and what was begun long and long ago with the eggs of death laid by our fathers from the sky shall end in swords and spears running sticky red—leaving the land to the Beast Things. And that foulness I shall not believe!"

"Cantrul said that his people must fight or die—"

"So? Well, there are different kinds of warfare. In the desert my people fought each day, but their enemies were sand and heat, the barren land itself. And if we had not lost the ancient learning perhaps we might even have tamed the burning mountains! Yes, man must fight or he becomes a soft nothing—but let him fight to build instead of to destroy. I would see my people trading wares and learning with those born in tents, sitting at council fires with the men of the mountain clans. Now is the time we must act to save that dream. For if the people of the tents march south in war they shall light such a fire as we or no living man may put out again. And in that fire we shall be as the trees and grass of the fields—utterly consumed."

Fors' answer was a grim stretch of ash-powdered skin which in no way resembled a smile. "We be but two, Arskane, and doubtless I am proclaimed outlaw, if the men of the Eyrie have noted my flight at all. My chance of gaining a hearing at their councils was destroyed by the Beast Things when they burned my city records. And you—?"

"There is thus much, brother. I am a son of a Wearer of the Wings—though I am youngest and least of the family clan. So perhaps some will listen to me, if only for a space. But we must reach the tribe before the Plainsmen do."

Fors tossed a cleaned bone into the water below. "Heigh-ho! Then it is foot slogging again. I wish that we might have brought one of those high-stepping pacers out of the herds. Four legs are better than two when there is speed to consider."

"Afoot we go." But Arskane could not suppress an exclamation of pain as he got to his feet and Fors could see that he favored the side where the shoulder wound still showed red. However, neither made any complaint as they jumped down from the ledge and plodded on through the ravine.

Arskane was dreaming a dream and it was a great dream, Fors thought, almost with a prick of real envy. He himself drew bow cord against the Beast Things without any squeamishness, and he could fight with everything in him when his life was at stake as it had been when they were cornered by the Plainsmen. But he took no joy in slaying—he never had. As a hunter he had killed only to fill his belly or for the pots of the Eyrie. He did not like the idea of notching an arrow against Marphy or of standing against Vocar with bare swords—for no good reason save a lust to battle—

Why had the men of the Eyrie drawn apart from their kind all these years? Oh, he knew the old legends—that they were sprung from chosen men and women who had been hidden in the mountains to escape just such an end as tore their civilization into bloody shreds. They had been sent there to treasure their learning—so they did, and tried to win more.

But had they not also come to believe themselves a superior race? If his father had not broken the unwritten law and married with a stranger, if he himself had been born of pure clan blood within the walls of the Eyrie—would he think now as he did? Jarl—his father had liked Jarl, had held him in high respect, had been the first to give him the salute when he had been raised to the Captaincy of the Star Men. Jarl!—Jarl could speak with Marphy and they would be two quick minds talking—hungrily. But Jarl and Cantrul—no. Cantrul was of a different breed. Yet he was a man whom others would follow always—their eyes on that head, held high, with its startling plume of white hair— a battle standard.

He himself was a mutant, a thing of mixed strains. Could he dare to speak for anyone save himself? At any rate he knew what he wanted now—to follow Arskane's dream. He might not believe that that dream would ever come true. But the fight for it would be his battle. He had wanted a star for his own—the silver star which he could hold in his two hands and wear as a badge of honor to compel respect from the people who had rejected him. But Arskane was showing him now something which might be greater than any star. Wait—wait and see.

His feet fell easily into the rhythm of those two words. The stream curved suddenly when it issued out of the ravine. Arskane pulled himself up the steep bank by the help of bushes. Fors gained the top in the same moment and together they saw what lay to the south. A dense column of smoke mushroomed into the sky of late afternoon.

For one startled minute Fors thought of the prairie fire. But surely that had not spread here, they had passed the line of burning hours back. Another fire, and a localized one by the line of smoke. One could take a route leading along the row of trees to the right, snake through the field of tangled bushes beyond where red fruit hung heavy and ripe, and reach the source without being exposed to attack.

Fors felt the rake of berry thorns on his flesh, but at the same time he crammed the tartly sweet fruit into his mouth as he crawled, staining his hands and face with dark juice.

Halfway across the berry patch they came upon evidence of a struggle. Under a bush lay a tightly woven basket, spilling berries out into a mush of trampled earth and crushed fruit. From this a trail of beaten-down grass and broken bushes led to the other side of the field.

From the tight grasp of briers Arskane detached a strip of cloth dyed a dull orange. He pulled it slowly through his fingers.

"This is of my tribal making," he said. "They were berrying here when—"

Fors felt the point of the spear he trailed. It was not much of a weapon. He longed fiercely for his bow—or even to hold the sword the Plainsmen had taken from him. There were sword tricks which could serve a man well at the right occasion.

With the scrap of cotton caught between his teeth Arskane crawled on, giving no heed to the thorns which ripped his arms and shoulders. Fors was conscious now of a thin wailing sound, which did not rise or fall but kept querulously to one ear-torturing note. It seemed to come with the smoke which the wind bore to them.

The berry field ended in a stand of trees and through these they looked out upon a lost battlefield. Small, two-wheeled carts had been pulled up in a circle, or into a segment of a circle, for there was a large gap in it now. And on these carts perched death birds, too stuffed to do more than hold on to the wood and stare down at a feast still spread to entice them. A mound of gray-white bodies lay at one side, their clothing clotted and stiffened with blood.

Arskane got to his feet—where the birds roosted unafraid the enemy was long gone. That monotonous crying still filled the ears and Fors began to search for the source. Arskane stooped suddenly and struck with a stone grabbed from the ground. The cry was stilled and Fors saw his companion straighten up from the still quivering body of a lamb.

There was another quest before them, a more ghastly one. They began it with tight mouths and sick eyes—dreading to find what must lie among the burning wagons and the mounds of dead animals. But it was Fors who found there the first trace of the enemy.

He half stumbled over a broken wagon wheel and beneath it was a lean body which lay with arms outstretched and sightless eyes staring up. From the hairless chest protruded the butt of an arrow which had gone true to its mark. And that arrow—! Fors touched the delicately set feathers at the end of the shaft. He knew the workmanship—he himself set feathers in much the same fashion. Though here was no personal mark of ownership—nothing but the tiny silver star set so deeply into that shaft that it could never be effaced.

"Beast Thing!" Arskane exclaimed at the sight of the corpse.

But Fors pointed to the arrow. "That came from the quiver of a Star Man."

Arskane did not display much interest—there were his own discoveries.

"This is the encampment of a family clan only. Four wagons are burning, at least five escaped. They could not run with the sheep—so they killed the flock. I have found the bodies of four more of these vermin—" He touched the Beast Thing with the toe of his moccasin.

Fors stepped across the hind legs of a dead pony which still lay with the harness of a cart on it. A Beast Thing dart stood out between its ribs. From the presence of the Beast Thing corpses, Fors was inclined to believe that the attack had been beaten off and the besieged had been successful in the break for freedom.

A second search of the litter equipped them with darts, and Fors snapped off the shaft of the arrow which bore the star marking. Some wanderer from the Eyrie had made common cause with the southerners in this attack. Did that mean that he could expect to meet a friend—or an enemy—when he joined Arskane's people?

The wheels of the escaping carts had cut deep ruts in the soft turf and there were footprints clear to read beside them. The death birds settled back to the feast as the two moved on. Arskane was breathing hard and the grimness which had cut his mouth into a cruel line over the grave of Noraton was back.

"Four of the Beast Things," puzzled Fors, lengthening his stride to a lope to keep up. "And the Lizard folk killed five. How many are out roving— There has never been such an onslaught of the things before. Why—?"

"I found a burned-out torch in the paw of one of

them back there. Maybe the fire of the Plains camp came from their setting. Just as they tried here to fire the carts and drive out the clan to slaughter."

"But never before have they come out of the ruins. Why now?"

Arskane's lips moved as if he would spit. "Perhaps they too seek land—or war—or merely the death of all those not of their breed. How can we look into the minds of such? Ha!"

The cart track they followed joined another—a deeper, wider track, such a road as must have been beaten down by the feet and wheels of a nation on the march. The tribe was ahead now.

In the next second, Fors checked so suddenly that he came near to tripping over his own feet. Out of nowhere had come an arrow, to dig deep into the earth and stand, quivering a little, an arrogant warning and a threat. He did not have to examine it closely. He knew before he put out his hand that he would find a star printed in its shaft.

·✦· 15

Bait

Arskane did not break stride but threw himself to the left and crouched in the shadow of a bush, the darts he had picked up at the scene of the ambush in his hands, ready. Fors on the contrary stood where he was and held up empty palms.

"We travel in peace—"

The rolling words of his own mountain land seemed odd to mouth after all these weeks. But he was not surprised at the identity of the man who came out of the clump of trees to the right of the trail.

Jarl would be imposing even in the simple garb of one of the least of the Eyrie. In the insignia of the Star Captain he had more majesty, thought Fors proudly, than Cantrul, for all the Plainschief's feather helmet and collar of ceremony. As he walked toward them the sun glinted meteor bright on the Star at his throat and on the well-polished metal of belt, sword hilt and knife guard.

Arskane pulled his feet under him. He was like Lura ready to spring for the kill. Fors made a furious gesture at him. Jarl, in turn, showed no astonishment at the sight of the two who waited for him.

"So, kinsman." He fingered his bow as if it were a councilor's staff of office. "This is the trail you have found to follow?"

Fors saluted him. And when Jarl did not acknowledge that courtesy he bit down hard on the soft inner part of his lip. True, Jarl had never shown him any favor in the past, but neither had the Star Captain ever by word or deed betrayed belief that Fors was any different from the rest of the young of the Eyrie. And for that he had long ago won a place apart in the boy's feelings.

"I travel with Arskane of the Dark Ones, my brother." He snapped his fingers to bring the southerner out of the bush. "His people are in danger now, so we join them—"

"You realize that you are now outlawed?"

Fors tasted the salty sweetness of the blood from his lip. He could, in all fairness, have hoped for little less than that sentence after his manner of leaving the Eyrie. Nevertheless the calm mention of it now made him cringe a little. He hoped that he did not show his discomfiture to Jarl. The Eyrie had not been a happy home for him—he had never been welcome there since Langdon's death. In truth they had outlawed him long since. But it had been the only shelter he knew.

"By the fire of Arskane is his brother always welcome!"

Jarl's eyes, those eyes which held one on the balance scale, went from Fors to his companion.

"Soon the Dark Ones will not have fire or shelter to offer. You are late in your returning, clansman. The drums of recall have been still these many hours."

"We were detained against our will," returned Arskane almost absently. He was studying Jarl in his turn and, seemingly, the result was not altogether to his liking.

"And not detained in gentleness it would appear." Jarl must have marked every cut and bruise the two before him boasted. "Well, fighting men are always welcome before a battle."

"Have the Plainsmen—?" began Fors, truly startled. That Cantrul could have moved so quickly out of the wild confusion they had left him in was almost beyond belief.

"Plainsmen?" He had shaken Jarl. "There are no Plainsmen in this. The Beast Things have forsaken their ways and are boiling out of their dens. Now they move in numbers to make war against all humankind!"

Arskane put his hand to his head. He was tired to exhaustion, his lips showing white under the swelling which made a lopsided lump of half his mouth. Without another word he started on doggedly but when Fors would have followed him the Star Captain put out a hand which brought him up short.

"What is this babble of Plainsmen attacking—?"

Fors found himself answering with the story of their capture and stay in the Plains camp and their escape from Cantrul's tent city. By the time he had finished Arskane was already out of sight. But still Jarl made no move to let him go. Instead he was studying the patterns he traced in the dust with the tip of his long bow. Fors impatiently shifted weight from one foot to the other. But when the Star Captain spoke it was as if he followed his own thoughts.

"Now do I better understand the events of these past two days."

He whistled high and shrill between his teeth, a sound Fors knew would carry far.

And he was answered when out of the grass came two lithe furry bodies. Fors did not notice the black one that rubbed against Jarl—for he was rolling across the ground where the force of the other's welcome had sent him, rolling and laughing a little hysterically as Lura's rough tongue explored his face and her paws knocked him about with heavy tenderness.

"Yesterday Nag came back from hunting and brought her with him." Jarl's hand rubbed with steady strokes behind the ears of the huge cat whose black fur, long and silky and almost blue in the sun, twisted in his fingers. "There is a lump on her skull. During your fight she must have been knocked unconscious. And ever since Nag brought her in she has been trying to urge me into some task—doubtless the single-handed rescue of your person—"

Fors got to his feet while Lura wove about him, butting at him with her head and rubbing against his none too steady legs with the full force of her steel-tendoned body.

"Touching sight—"

Fors winced. He knew that tone from Jarl. It had the ability to deflate the most confident man and that speedily. With an unspoken suggestion to Lura he started down the trail after the vanished Arskane. Although he did not look back he knew that the Star Captain was following him at the easy, mile-eating pace his own feet had automatically dropped into.

Jarl did not speak again, remaining as silent as Nag, that black shadow which slipped across the land as if he were only in truth the projection of a bush in the sun. And Lura, purring loudly, kept close to Fors' side as if she were afraid that should she return to her old outflanking ways he would disappear again.

They found Arskane's people encamped in a meadow

which was encircled on three sides by a river. The two-wheeled carts were a wooden wall around the outer edges and in the center showed the gray backs of sheep, the dun coats of ponies in rope corrals with the lines of family cooking fires running between low tents. There were only a few men there and those were fully armed. Fors suspected that he must have come through some picket lines unchallenged because of the Star Captain's companionship.

It was easy to find Arskane. A group of men and a large circle of women ringed him. It was a crowd so intent upon the scout's report that not one of them noted the arrival of Fors and Jarl.

Arskane was talking to a woman. She was almost as tall as the young warrior before her and her features were strongly marked. Two long braids of black hair swung down upon her shoulders and now and again she raised a hand to push at them impatiently with a gesture which had become habitual. Her long robe was dyed the same odd shade of dusky orange as the scrap of cotton they had found in the berry field and on her arms and about her neck was the gleam of stone-set silver.

As Arskane finished, she considered for a moment and then a stream of commands, spoken too rapidly in the slurred tongue of the south for Fors to follow, sent the circle about her apart, men and women both hurrying off on errands. When the last of these left she caught sight of Fors and her eyes widened. Arskane turned to see what had surprised her. Then his hand fell on the mountaineer's shoulder and he pulled him forward.

"This is he of whom I have told you—he has saved my life in the City of the Beast Things, and I have named him brother—"

There was almost a touch of pleading in his voice.

"We be the Dark People." The woman's tone was low but there was a lilt in it, almost as if she chanted. "We be the Dark People, my son. He is not of our breed—"

Arskane's hands went out in a nervous gesture. "He is my brother," he repeated stubbornly. "Were it not for him I would have long since died the death and my clan would never have known how or where that chanced."

"In turn," Fors spoke to this woman chief as equal to equal, "Arskane has stood between me and a worse passing—has he neglected to tell you that? But, Lady, you should know this—I am outlawed and so free meat to any man's spear—"

"So? Well, the matter of outlawry is between you and your name clan—and not for the fingering of strangers. You have a white skin—but in the hour of danger what matters the color of a fighting man's bone covering? The hour is coming when we shall need every bender of bow and wielder of sword we can lay orders upon." She stooped and caught up a pinch of the sandy loam which ridged between her sandaled feet. And now she stretched out her hand palm up with that bit of earth lying on it.

Fors touched the tip of his forefinger to his lips and then to the soil. But he did not fall to his knees in the finish of that ritual. He gave allegiance but he did not beg entrance to a clan. The woman nodded approvingly.

"You think straight thoughts, young man. In the name of the Silver Wings and of Those Who Once Flew, I accept your fighting faith until the hour when we mutually agree to go our ways. Now are you satisfied, Arskane?"

Her clansman hesitated before he answered. There was an odd soberness on his face as he regarded Fors.

Plainly he was disappointed at the mountaineer's refusal to ask for clan standing. But at last he said:

"I claim him as a member of my family clan, to fight under our banner and eat at our fire—"

"So be it." She dismissed them both with a wave of her hand. Already she looked beyond them to Jarl and was summoning the Star Captain imperiously.

Arskane threaded through the camp, giving only hasty greetings to those who would have stopped him, until he came to a tent which had two carts for walls and a wide sweep of woolen stuff for a roof. Round shields of rough-scaled skin hung in a row on mounts by the entrance—four of them—and above these warrior shields the wind played with a small banner. For the second time Fors saw the pattern of the widespread wings, and below those a scarlet shooting star.

A small, grave-eyed girl glanced up as they came. With a little cry she dropped the pottery jar she had been holding and came running, to cling tightly to Arskane, her face hidden against his scarred body. He gave a choked laugh and swept her up high.

"This is the small-small one of our hearthside, my brother. She is named Rosann of the Bright Eyes. Ha, small one, bid welcome my brother—"

Shy dark eyes peered at Fors and then little hands swept back braids which would in a few years rival those of the woman chief and an imperious voice ordered Arskane to "put me down!" Once on her two feet again she came up to the mountaineer, her hands outstretched. Half guessing the right response Fors held out his in turn and she laid small palms to press his large ones.

"To the fire on the hearth, to the roof against the night and storm, to the food and drink within this house, are you truly welcome, brother of my brother."

She said the last word in triumph at her perfect memory and smiled back at Arskane with no little pride.

"Well done, little sister. You are the proper lady of this clan house—"

"I accept of your welcome, Lady Rosann." Fors showed more courtliness than had been in his manner when he had greeted the chieftainess.

"Now," Arskane was frowning again, "I must go to my father, Fors. He is making the rounds of the outposts. If you will await us here—"

Rosann had kept hold of his hand and now she gave him the same wide smile with which she had favored her brother. "There are berries, brother of my brother, and the new cheese and corn cake fresh baked—"

"A feast—!" He met her smile.

"A true feast! Because Arskane has come back. Becie said that he would not and she cried—"

"Did she?" There was an unusual amount of interest in that comment from her tall brother. Then he was gone, striding away between the tent lines. Rosann nodded.

"Yes, Becie cried. But I did not. Because I knew that he would be back—"

"And why were you so sure?"

The hand tugged him closer to the shield stands. "Arskane is a great warrior. That—" a pink-brown finger touched the rim of the last shield in the row, "that is made from the skin of a thunder lizard and Arskane killed it all alone, just himself. Even my father allowed the legend singer to put together words for that at the next singing time—though he has many times said that the son of a chief must not be honored above other warriors. Arskane—he is very strong—"

And Fors, remembering the days just past, agreed.

"He is strong and a mighty warrior and he has done other things your legend singer must weave words about."

"You are not of our people. Your skin"—she compared his hand with hers—"it is light. And your hair—it is like Becie's necklace when the sun shines upon it. You are not of us Dark People—"

Fors shook his head. In that company of warm brown skins and black hair his own lighter hide and silver head-capping must be doubly conspicuous.

"I come from the mountains—far to the east—" He waved a hand.

"Then you must be of the cat people!"

Fors' gaze followed her pointing finger. Nag and Lura sat together at a good distance from the sheep and the tough little ponies as they had apparently been ordered to do. But, at Fors' welcoming thought, Lura came up, leaving Nag behind. Rosann laughed with pure delight and threw her arms around the cat's neck, hugging her tight. The rumble of Lura's purr was her answer and a rough pink tongue caressed her wrist.

"Do all you people of the mountains have the big cats for your own friends?"

"Not all. The cat ones are not so many and it is for them to choose with whom they will hunt. This is Lura who is my good friend and roving companion. And that yonder is Nag who runs with the Star Captain."

"I know—the Star Captain Jarl, he who has the kind eyes. He talks in the night with my father."

"Kind eyes." Fors was a little startled at a description so at variance with what he thought he knew. Though Rosann probably did not see Jarl as he appeared to a mutant and tribal outlaw.

Smoke was rising from the line of fires and borne with it was the fragrance of cooking. Fors could not repress a single sniff.

"You are hungry, brother of my brother?"

"Maybe—just a little—"

Rosann flushed. "I am sorry. Again have I let my tongue run and not remembered the Three Duties. Truly am I shamed—"

Her fingers tightened on his and she pulled him under the entrance flap of the tent.

"Down!"

Fors' heels struck against a pile of thick mats and he obediently folded up his long legs and sat. Lura collapsed beside him as Rosann bustled about. Before Fors could even make out the patterns of the hangings on the walls Rosann returned, carrying before her a wide metal basin of water from which rose steam and the spicy scent of herbs. A towel of coarse stuff lay over her arm and she held it ready as Fors washed.

Then came a tray with a spoon and bowl and a small cup of the same bitter drink he had brewed under Arskane's direction in the museum. The corn mush had been cooked with bits of rich meat and the stimulating drink was comforting in his middle.

He must have dozed off afterward because when he roused it was night outside and the crimson flames of the fire and the lesser beams of a lamp fought against the shadows. A hand placed on his forehead had brought him awake. Arskane knelt beside him and there were two others beyond. Fors levered himself up.

"What—" He was still half asleep.

"My father wishes to speak with you—"

Fors gathered his wits. One of the men facing him now was a slightly older edition of his friend. But the other wore about his throat a pair of silver wings fastened to a chain of the same stuff.

The chieftain was smaller than his sons and his dark skin was seamed and cracked by torrid winds and

blistering suns. Across his chin was the ragged scar of
an old and badly healed wound. Now and again he
rubbed at this with a forefinger as if it still troubled
him.

"You are Fors of the mountain clan?"

Fors hesitated. "I was of those clans. But now I am
outlaw—"

"The Lady Nephata gave him earth—"

Arskane was both interrupted and effectively silenced
by a single sharp look from his father.

"My son has told us something of your wanderings.
But I would hear more of this Plainsmen encampment
and what chanced with you there—"

For the second time Fors repeated his outline of
recent events. When he had finished the Chief favored
him with the same sort of intimidating glare which had
worked on his son a few minutes before. But Fors met
it forthrightly.

"You, Rance," the Chief turned to the young man
with him, "will alert the scouts against this trouble
and make the rounds of the western outposts every
hour. If an attack offers, the two beacons on the
round hills must be fired. That you must keep ever
in the minds of the men—"

"You see, rover"—the Chief spoke over his shoulder,
addressing a shadow near the door, and for the first
time Fors noted a fourth man there—"we do not go
to war as to a banquet—as these Plainsmen seem to
do. But if it be necessary then we can fight! We who
have faced the wrath of the thunder lizards and taken
their hides to make our shields of ceremony—"

"Do not greatly fear the lances of mere men." The
Star Captain appeared faintly amused. "Perhaps you
are right, Lanard. But do not forget that the Beast
Things are also abroad and they are less than men—
or more!"

"Since I have ordered the war drums for more than the lifetime of this my youngest son, I do not forget one danger when faced by another, stranger!"

"Your pardon, Lanard. Only a fool tries to teach the otter to swim. Let war be left to the warriors—"

"Warriors who have sat too long at their ease!" snapped the chieftain. "To your posts, all of you!"

Arskane and his brother went, the chieftain stamping out impatiently after them. Fors started to follow.

"Wait!"

There was the crack of a whip in that one word. Fors stiffened. Jarl had no power of command over him—not even the faintest shadow of power if he was an outlaw. But he dropped his hand on Lura's head and waited.

"These people," Jarl continued with the same harsh abruptness, "may be broken between two enemies. It is not in their nature to back trail and in their own country there has been nothing they could not vanquish. Now they have come into this new land and fight on strange territory against those who are familiar with it. They face worse than they can imagine—but if that truth is told them they will not believe it."

Fors made no comment and after a moment the Star Captain went on:

"Langdon was my good friend always, but there was a streak of rashness in him and he did not always see the road ahead with clear eyes—"

At this criticism of his father Fors stirred but he did not speak.

"You have already, youth that you are, broken the clan laws—going your own way in pride and stubbornness—"

"I ask for nothing of the Eyrie's giving!"

"That is as it may be. I have twice heard your tale— you have a liking for this Arskane, I think. And you have eyes and a talent for getting under the skin of a man. This Marphy is one whom we might well remember. But Cantrul is a fighting man and of a different breed. Give him something to fight and he may be more open to other thoughts when the victory lies behind him. Very well, it is up to us to give him something to fight—something other than this tribe!"

"What—?" Fors brought only the one word out of his vast amazement.

"Beast Things. A well-baited trail could lead them north to the Plains camp."

Fors began to guess what was coming. He swallowed, his mouth and throat suddenly dry. To be bait for the Beast Things, to run north a pace or two before the most hideous death he knew—

"Such a task could be only ours alone—"

"You mean—not tell Lanard?"

"It would be best not. The plan would have no merit in their eyes now. You—you are an outlaw—a stranger who might well have little stomach for a fight not his. If you were to desert this camp, run away—"

Fors' nails bit into the palms of his balled fists. To appear a skin-saving coward in Arskane's eyes—just because Jarl had dreamed up so wild a plan—And yet part of him acknowledged the point of the Star Captain's reasoning.

"If the Plainsmen and this tribe fight—then it may well follow that the Beast Things shall finish off both of them."

"You do not have to point it out to me as one and one are two," Fors spat out.

Somewhere a childish voice was humming. And the brother of that child had brought him whole out of the valley of the lizards.

"When do I march?" he asked the Star Captain, hating him and every word he himself spoke.

·* 16

The Hunted and the Hunters

Again Fors was grateful for the mutation which had given him the keenness of his night sight. For almost an hour he had been wriggling down an ancient roadside ditch as a hanger-on of the small party of dark-skinned warriors whom Arskane now led. The broken surface of the nearby road was steel bright in the beams of the full moon, but he was sure that only he could see clearly what passed in the shadows beyond.

He was glad for the weight of bow and quiver across his shoulders—although the bow was the short, double-stringed weapon of the southerners and not the long one he was accustomed to. However, one sword was much like another and the new one at his belt already fitted his hand as if it had been forged to rest therein.

If it had not been for Jarl's plan he could have been really happy in that hour. To follow Arskane as one of his own tribe—to be accepted without question by those around him——But he was now pledged to put an end to that by his own actions—as soon as the time was right. Jarl was scouting to the west, the same compulsion driving him. They might be able to rendezvous after their break away from the tribe or they might never see each other again. Fors sent a silent call to Lura. If they did strike out into the wilderness tonight he would have to depend upon her wits and instinct—even more than upon his own.

The old road curved around the base of a rise. Fors stopped—had he really seen a flicker of movement in a bush halfway up that hill? His hand fell on the ankle of the man before him and he pressed hard, knowing that that signal would be as swiftly passed down the line.

That flash of cream white, that must be Lura crossing the road and heading up. But what he had caught only the faintest glimpse of had been far above that. Lura should rout it out—

There was a sudden scurry on the slope and Fors saw the outline of a crouching body. The sharp line of the thing's shoulders was only too familiar.

"Beast Thing!"

Lura's scream tore through the air drowning out the warning he shouted. The bushes threshed wildly at her attack. But she had had her instructions, not to kill now—only to harry and drive. The black thing snapped up out of hiding, arms flailing as the men around Fors went to their knees, arrows ready on strings. A cloud of feathered shafts flew. Most, Fors guessed, had fallen woefully short. Shooting up slope was always a tricky business.

The Beast Thing scuttled away over the crown of the hill at a desperate speed. And it was gone before other arrows could follow the first volley. Arskane edged along the line of disappointed archers to join Fors.

"Was that a scout?" he asked.

"Could be. They have always hunted in packs before. If it was a scout, it will now report."

Arskane chewed the tip of his thumb thoughtfully. Fors knew the worries which plagued him now. Ambush—that was the worst fear. They knew so little of the tactics of the Beast Things—but lying in wait in the dark seemed to fit the nature of the foul creatures best. In the ruined cities they had always fought from cover when they could.

In the end Arskane did as Fors thought he would, gave the signal to push on until they reached the boundaries of their beat, one of the hills where the beacon had been heaped some days before. So they crawled on, Lura flanking the line of march. And they reached the beacon hill without interference. Once there, Arskane formally relieved the guard on duty.

The hour was close to dawn. A thin gray light gave ordinary trees and bushes a queer new life as if they were now cut off from the real world by some flimsy barrier. The beacon keepers had torn out or hacked away most of the brush and saplings, so that the crown of the hill was bare and one could see for a good range on all sides.

Fors located the camp by the river first and then set about noting other landmarks which might help him keep the proper course if he decided to make the break north soon. The men whom they had relieved were marching in fairly good order down the hill, ready to drop into the protection of the road ditch, when the last one in that line threw up his arms with a startled jerk and fell without a sound. The man nearest him spun around just in time to see him fall and started back to his aid, only to choke and go to his knees tearing at the dart quivering in his own throat.

They broke and ran back. But before they could

reach the miserable shelter offered by the beacon, two more died, Beast Thing steel in their contorted bodies. Only one lived to break through to the men above.

And they, arrows ready, stood cursing, unable to shoot at a foe which would not show itself.

Lura bounded out of cover below. She crowded up to Fors, her blue eyes wide. Once getting his attention her head swung meaningly from side to side. So, they were surrounded! Maybe it was already too late to play the game Jarl had set him. But even as that hope leaped he knew that he would have no escape—that this was just the right sort of background for his break through—that this would truly bring the Beast Things out on any trail he laid for them. He must openly desert Arskane—perhaps even to the southerner's death!

"We are surrounded." Tonelessly he passed on Lura's report.

Arskane nodded. "That I thought when she came to us. Well, now we may be forced to the waiting game." He turned to the men around him. "Down on your bellies! Crawl to the brush. We are clear targets to them now."

But before those orders were out of his mouth, the man beside him gave a gasping cry and held out his arm, a dart embedded in its flesh. As one man they moved into what cover they could find, Arskane pulling the wounded tribesman with him. But the cover of the beacon was a sorry shield.

The worst was not being able to sight the enemy. If they had been able to fight back it would not have been such a strain on the nerves. Picked and seasoned warriors knew better than to waste arrows on empty tree glades where nothing moved. It would be a battle in which patience would mean the most.

Fors sent Lura on another scouting trip. He must

learn if there was any gap in the line the Beast Things
held. If there was he should cross, break out to start
north. If he won through they would probably wait to
see if he headed for the river camp before they
followed. So he must give the impression from the first
that he was confused—then the sport of driving him
might draw a portion of them after him.

During the morning there were two more
casualties. Arskane, on making the rounds from one
hidden man to another, found one dead with a dart
pinning him down, and another with a torn leg,
bandaging his own wound. When he came back to
Fors he was very sober.

"At noon the camp will send us relief. If we light
the beacon in warning they will prepare to move camp
and that may lead them straight into an ambush. But
Karson thinks he remembers something of the old
smoke talk and he has volunteered to try it. Only those
who signal will be exposed to fire." The southerner
scowled at the silent woods. "We are but five now and
two of those wounded. If we die and the tribe is
saved—what does it matter?"

Fors fought his impulse to volunteer. He was
sensitive to the slight hesitation with which Arskane
regarded him when he did not answer. Then the
southerner turned and crawled to the center of the
beacon. Fors stirred. He might have gone after his
companion had he not caught sight of something else
which brought him into a crouch, tense and ready.
Lura's head showed for the slightest instant below. She
had found the gap he had sent her to search for. Now
he, too, began to work his way around the hill to a
point just above that section.

His dash would lead him across an open space and
he must not be brought down. If he could time it right
his move might draw fire which would otherwise be

concentrated on the men at the beacon. He licked dry lips. Bow and quiver must be left behind, leaving him only sword and hunting knife.

Yes, he had not been mistaken. Lura's brown ears showed again in outline against a moss-grown rock. She was waiting for him. He gathered his feet under him, and, as an arrow from a bow, he dashed out of cover and zigzagged down the slope. There was a single shout of surprise from behind and then he was into the woods, Lura with him.

Now he was absorbed in the task at hand. He burst through a screen of small trees, making only the most elementary effort to hide his trail. Lura's warning that they were now followed set his heart to pounding. Now—now it was just his own two feet, his hunting lore, and his sense of direction against all the cunning of the enemy. He must be a tempting morsel always just about to fall into the pursuers' hands, and yet he must keep from capture and lead the run into Plains territory so that Cantrul might be provoked into action. As Jarl had outlined it the plan was as simple as it was deadly—but was it going to work?

There were short periods during the rest of the day when he could snatch some rest, always after Lura assured him that something still ran the trail behind. Once he dared verify that for himself, having climbed a cliff after crossing a stream. He lingered in a shallow crevice at the top long enough to see three gray shapes come out of the woods a half mile back, the first on all fours sniffing the ground as it came.

Three—out of how many? But the beacon must have warned the camp. He must think of nothing else now but his own task. If ever his eyes and ears served him well they must do better than that now. As a fugitive gaining his second wind perhaps he would dare display a little more cunning. The Beast Things might accept the idea that sheer panic had brought him away from the beacon, but that would not prevent a greater show of caution now. He tried several of the simpler trail-hiding tricks and waited for Lura's verdict. It was favorable, the chase was still on.

Some hours before evening he struck west, trying to intercept a line which must run to the beaver lake and so to Cantrul's camp—unless the fire had driven the Plainsmen from that base. He ate as he went, berries and handfuls of ripe grain pulled from the ragged self-sown patches in the old fields. There were hard, half-ripe peaches in an old orchard he pounded through and he had enough to keep him going when washed down with water from brook and spring.

The night was the worst. He had to lay up for rest, swinging into the branches of a tree, close enough to an outcrop of rock to be able to leap away if the need came. Lura catnapped on that rock, her brown and cream melting into the weathered stone. He dozed and woke, to stretch cramped muscles and doze again. Before morning he moved twice, putting a mile between each resting place and choosing each for the ability to make a quick retreat.

When the gray of dawn caught him again he was lying flat on a bluff overhanging a stream he was sure was the outlet of the beaver lake. Pieces of charred wood caught among the boulders below proved that. The size of the stream had dwindled, perhaps the beavers had started repairs in the broken dam. Fors lay there, every aching joint, every exhausted muscle protesting the move he was willing his body into making. It was as if he had been running for days— since they had left the ruined city they had been on the move with little or no rest. And none to look for in the immediate future either—

Luckily he was facing downstream, with his eyes on the moving surface, for now he saw what might have been the strangest sight to ever appear on that forgotten shore. An animal was swimming up river, nosing along the bank in a peculiar fashion, almost as if it were intelligently questing. When it reached the spot between two stones where Fors had knelt to drink before he climbed, it scrambled out of the water and sat up on its haunches, its forepaws held close to its lighter underbelly, its head high with sniffing nose testing the flowing air currents.

It was a rat—one of the huge, gray-coated ones of the old breed with which man had fought eternal warfare since the first days of time. A rat—Fors remembered back to the sunny morning in the ruins of the old city shops when just such a beast had sat to watch him without alarm. The rats flourished in the cities—everyone knew that. But for the most part men did not see them—even there. Their ways were underground, in the noisome burrows they had hollowed and claimed from cellar to cellar, through the old sewers and waterways.

The rat shook itself. Then the growing light brought a flash from its throat as it raised higher its head. A metal collar—surely that was a metal collar. But a collar on a rat—why—who—

Who lived in the cities? Who might tame and use rats? He knew the answer to that. But why? The rat alone was not a formidable fighter—not an ally as good as Lura—they were only to be feared in hordes. Hordes!

The rat jumped to the top of a boulder and began to lick itself dry, as if it had successfully completed a set task and could now take time for its own concerns. Fors had not been mistaken by some trick of the light—as the beast's head twisted and turned the collar was easy to see. It was made of flat links and seemed flexible.

Suddenly the creature stopped its grooming and crouched very still, its beady eyes aimed downstream. Fors could not move. He had to see what was going to happen. And the same idea flashed to his mind from Lura who was flattened out against the rock some feet away, her lips frozen in a snarl.

They heard the splashing first, a sound too regular to be natural. If he were wise he would leave now, but he could not.

An ungainly figure came skittering through the shallows around the waterworn rocks. Its shape was odd but Fors peered until he made out that the hunched back of the creature was in reality a basket cage. At its coming the collared rat showed its teeth wickedly but it did not attempt to escape.

The Beast Thing came on, leisurely reached out a long arm and picked up the rat by its collar while it snapped its teeth and clawed wildly. With the ease of long practice the rat master threw his captive through a trap door into the cage and snapped it shut again. From the wild chattering which ensured Fors deduced that more than one rat rode therein. But Lura was gliding away from her vantage point and he knew that she was right. It was time for them to go.

But as he fled he continued to wonder. Why the rats? Unless the Beast Things had rested and sent the rats to trail him during the night. If that was true his taking to the trees must have baffled them for a good while. Or did rats climb? He wished that he knew more about their habits. And why had none of the Star Men discovered during their brushes with the Beast Things this use of rats? Was it new— another manifestation of the urge which was bringing the sub-human forces out of their century old burrows to challenge the descendants of the Old Ones?

All the old tales about the Beast Things went through his head as he mechanically set a trail which would delay but not altogether throw off the pursuers. They were supposed to be the offspring of city dwellers and perhaps invading soldiers as well caught in the full strength of the radiation waves. Their children were so much mutant in form and mind that they were no longer human at all. That was one explanation.

But there was another story about them too. Before the Blow-up, men had been altering the very stuff of life to suit their fancy, combining human and animal traits in curious and bizarre ways. Could the ancestry of the Beast Things have included both men *and* rats before radiation had done its deadly work?

Whichever theory was the true one, the Beast Things, though they aroused revulsion and instinctive hatred among the humans, were also victims of the Old Ones' tragic mistake, as shattered in their lives as the cities had been.

Fors jogged into the first section of the fire-swept land. Ahead lay a black and desolate waste. And there was little or no cover left. He would have to dare discovery from the rat-carrying Beast Thing and take to the riverside again.

The smell of burnt stuff was thick in the air, the stench making him cough as much as the powdery ashes which drifted up between his feet. Perhaps it was best to take to water. Here and there a fallen tree still showed a heart of glowing coals.

Coughing, rubbing his eyes to clear them, Fors scrambled over rocks and once even swam to breast the current. Here water marks were high above the present level of the stream. It was evident that the dam must have been at least partly repaired.

Then he clambered up over that structure itself. Before him lay the lake, ringed completely around with the black scar of fire. The beavers faced a famine season unless they moved. It would be a full year before the saplings would begin to sprout again and not for several generations would trees stand tall there once more.

Fors dove into the water. Even here the smell of smoke and the tang of burning clung. There were bodies floating too, a deer, a wild cow, and close to the far shore, a horse bearing on its puffed flank the painted sign of the Plains camp. He swam by it and headed up the feeder stream down which he and Arskane had won to freedom. But before he left the lake he glanced back.

And over the beaver dam was clambering the hunchbacked figure of the rat carrier. Behind it three others came up. As they hesitated on the dam, teetering as if they feared either the water or the still smoldering footing offered ashore, five more of their kind appeared.

Fors drew back into a half circle of rocks. Jarl's plan had succeeded. He had no way of guessing how many of the Beast Things had ambushed the party at the beacon hill, but the pack now running at his heels had numbers enough to interest Cantrul. The Beast Things were dour and terrible fighters, and they were fighters who never wanted to head an open attack. Their present openness showed how much they held him in contempt. Fors watched, to see the rat cage unstrapped while its bearer went over into the lake.

A comrade tore away part of the dam's substance to make a raft to carry the cage. Then they were all swimming, clumsily but surely, taking turns pushing the cage before them.

Fors took to his heels, skidding over slime-coated stones, the stream rising from thigh to waist as he panted through it and tried to dodge the smoking timber which had fallen across the banks here and there.

The patch of green grass he sighted where he had come to expect only the black of the burning was almost a shock. But there were reeds standing tall and unscorched in a thick mass. He plunged through them to shore. The mud bank beyond was thickly scored with hoofprints, some still fresh, good evidence that the Plainsmen were still there. Lura's tracks overlay the others and the marks of her claws on the clay overhang were deep. Fors grabbed for the tough roots of a bush and pulled himself up.

He pulled himself up and took two steps. Then he tripped and rolled, his feet jerked out from under him. And as he went down he heard the shrilling of a vicious laughter. His hand was tight on his sword hilt and he had the blade out almost before he had again sucked the air into his lungs. He came up, the bare blade in swing, ready and waiting.

17

The Last War

Fors saw what he knew would be there—a ring of wiry gray bodies around him. The Beast Things must have been concealed in the grass. A little beyond him, Lura—also a captive—threshed, the noose tight about her neck as she clawed up great patches of turf in her struggle for freedom.

Another jerk on the trapping cord brought him sprawling forward to the accompaniment of inhuman laughter. There was only one thing he could do now. Without trying to regain his feet or even to get to his knees, Fors struggled across the ground on his belly to Lura, a move which seemed to take his captors entirely by surprise. None of them could prevent his sword biting through the cord which strangled her. And his order had flashed from mind to mind in that same instant.

"Find Nag—and he who hunts with Nag—find!"

She would be more likely to join the other cat than

go directly to Jarl. But where the black cat ran the Star Captain would not be far away.

Lura's powerful legs gathered under her. Then she sprang in a great arching leap, passing over the head of one of the Beast Things. Free of their circle she went as a streak of light fur into the grass and was lost. Fors took advantage of the excitement to slash at the tangle of cord about his ankles and he had one foot free before the rage of the Beast Things flamed and they concentrated again on the remaining captive.

There was no hope now. He wondered how many seconds of life he had before he would go down for the last time, pin-cushioned by the darts they all held. But—when in doubt—attack! The advice Langdon had once given him stiffened his sword arm now. Speed— Do as much harm as he could. There was no chance of keeping alive until Lura found Jarl but he could take some of these beasts with him.

With the same lithe speed Lura had displayed he sprang at one of the circle, blade up and ready to twist in the vicious thrust which was the most dangerous he knew. And almost he made it, had his one foot not remained in bond. As it was he laid open gray hide, not in the deep death-dealing gash he had planned, but in a shallow cut which ran red half across the thing's bulbous pouch.

He ducked the blow aimed at his head, ducked and struck up again. Then his sword arm went limp, the blade falling out of his numbed fingers as a dart went home. A cuff delivered across the side of his face before he could raise his left hand sent him sailing back surrounded by a burst of red which turned into black nothingness.

Pain dragged him back, a red agony of pain which ran through his veins like fire, a fire which ran from his torn arm. He tried to move feebly and found that his ankles and wrists were fast—he had been tied down, spread-eagled to stakes in the ground.

It was hard to get his eyes open, the left eyelid was glued to his cheek. But now he was looking up into the sky. So he was not dead yet, he thought dully. And since the tree he could see was green he must still be close to the point where he had been captured. He tried to raise his head, had one moment of blurred sight, and then was so sick that he dropped it flat again and shut his eyes to hide reeling sky and heaving ground.

Later there was noise—much of it which rang in his head until he forced his eyes open again. Beast Things were driving up another prisoner. By his hair and dress he was a Plainsman. And he was sent flat with a blow and pegged out beside Fors. The Beast Things favored him with a couple of rib-cracking kicks before they left, making suggestions in gestures—suggestions which did not promise well for the future.

Fors' head felt thick and tight, he could not force his thoughts together in the fog which seemed to gather in his brain. It was better just to lie still and endure the pain in his arm as best he could.

A shrill squeaking pulled him out of the fog of pain and sickness. He turned his head to see the wicker basket of rats a few feet away. The Beast Thing who had worn it on its back gave a sigh of relief as it dropped its burden and joined the three or four of its fellows who were lounging under a nearby tree. Their guttural greeting meant nothing to Fors.

But through the open slits of the basket cage he fancied he could see sparks of reddish light—small wicked eyes watching him with a horrid kind of intelligence. All at once the rats were quiet, save when at intervals one or another squeaked briefly as if making some comment to its companions.

How long did they watch each other? Time in true measure no longer existed for Fors. After a space the Beast Things made a fire and broiled ragged pieces of meat, some still backed with horsehide. When the scent of that reached the rats they went wild, running about their cage until it rocked, squeaking at the tops of their thin voices. But none of the masters made any move to share the feast with them.

When one was done it came over to the cage and shook it, yelling. The rats were quiet, again their eyes showed at the open spaces, looking now only at the prisoners—red eyes, angry, hungry eyes.

Fors tried to tell himself that what he suspicioned was not true, that in his torment he had no control over imagination. Surely that Beast Thing had not made a promise then—a promise which Fors dared not believe lest he lose all control over wits and will.

But those red rat eyes watched and watched. He could see the sharp claws pointing between the wicker ribs, and the gleam of teeth—And always the watching eyes—

By the lengthening shadow he guessed that it was far along in the afternoon when the third and last party of Beast Things came into camp. And with them was the leader.

He was no taller than other members of his tribe, but a certain arrogant confidence in his bearing and stride made him seem to overtop the others. His hairless head was narrow with the same slit nose and protruding fanged jaws, but the brain case was domed, larger by half again over any of the rest. His eyes held a cunning intelligence and there was a subtle difference in the way he looked over his world. A true man—no, but neither was he as brutish as the pack he led. One could almost believe that here lay the power which had brought the foul band out to range the open lands.

Now he came to stand between the two captives. Fors turned away from the rat cages to meet those curious eyes firmly.

But the mountaineer could read nothing understandable in their depths and the protruding jaws expressed no emotion which might be deduced by a human. The leader of the Beast Things might have been wildly elated, annoyed, or merely curious, as he stared at first one and then the other of the staked-out prisoners. But curiosity must have directed his next move for he dropped down crosslegged between them and mouthed the first real words Fors had ever heard issue from one of the city-bred monsters.

"You—where?" He demanded that of the Plainsman who could not or would not answer.

When he did not reply the Beast Leader leaned over and, with a deliberation which was as cruel as the blow, slapped the captive with lip-bursting force across the mouth. It then swung to Fors and repeated the question.

"From the south—" Fors croaked.

"South," the leader repeated, distorting the word oddly. "What in south?"

"Men—many, many men. Ten tens of tens—"

But that sum was either beyond the calculations of the creature beside him, or the Beast Thing did not believe in its truth, for it cackled with a ghastly travesty of laughter and, reaching out, brought a fist down across his wounded arm. Fors fainted, dropping into blackness with a sick swoop.

A scream brought him back to consciousness. He had the echoes of that cry still ringing through his head when he forced open his eyes and tried to stabilize crazily flowing blocks of light and shade. A second cry of pain and horror settled the world into place.

The leader of the Beast Things still squatted

between the captives and in outstretched hand it held the struggling body of one of the hungry rats. There was red on the vermin's fangs and more scarlet drops spattered its breast and forepaws as it fought like a mad thing against the hold which kept it from its prey.

Down the arm and side of the Plainsman a line of dripping gashes told the story. His distorted face was a mask of tortured despair as he cursed, his words a frenzied mumble which soared into a scream every time the Beast Leader held the rat closer.

But a cry of pure rage cut through the captive's breathless sobbing, a cry uttered by the leader. The rat had turned to slash one of the fingers which held it. With a snarl the Beast Leader twisted the writhing body. There was a cracking and the thing he threw from him was limp and broken. He got to his feet, the torn finger at his mouth.

A respite—for how long? The Beast Things seemed to feel themselves safe in this camping site they had chosen. They were not moving on for the night—but just as Fors decided that, the picture changed suddenly. Two more of the enemy came out of the bush and between them they pulled along a mangled, trodden body—the body of one of their own kind. Over this there was a hasty consultation and then the leader barked an order. The bearer of the rat cage took up its burden and four of the largest of its fellows came over to the captives.

Knives slashed free their bonds and they were pulled and slapped to their feet. When it was apparent that neither could walk, there was a second conference. From gestures Fors gathered that one party was in favor of killing them at once, but that the leader opposed this. And in the end the leader carried the debate. Two of the clan trotted off and returned shortly with stout saplings which were trimmed of branches.

And in a moment or two Fors found himself lashed to one of these, dangling face to the ground, carried between two of the Beasts who moved on with their deceptively easy pace.

He never remembered much of that night. The bearers of his pole changed from time to time, but he swung in a daze, rousing only when he was dropped painfully to the ground during these operations. And they must have been halted for some time when he became aware of the sound.

He was on the ground, his ear tight to the earth. And at first he thought that the pounding beat he heard must be the heated blood running in his own feverish body—or else that it was but another shadowy bit of a delirious nightmare. But it continued—steadily—alive—alive, and somehow reassuring. Once, long before, he had heard a sound like that—it had had a meaning. But the meaning was lost. Now he was only aware of his body, the mass of pain which had become a thing apart from Fors. Fors was gone away—far away from that pain—what remained could not think—could only feel and endure.

Why, now that distant throbbing was broken by another, a deeper, heavier beat—two sounds. And he had once known them both. But neither mattered now. He must watch red eyes which stared at him from space in wickerwork, red, hungry eyes which watched and waited, growing still more starved and demanding. And in the end those eyes would come closer and closer and teeth would be with them. But that did not matter very much either.

Somewhere there was shouting, it tore a hole through his head, made his ears ring. But it did not frighten the eyes, they still watched and waited.

The throbbing, now it filled the air, beating into him.

Why, he was up now, being held on his feet by rough hands. He was being tied fast again—or so he thought, he was too numb to feel bonds. But he was standing right enough, looking down from the crest of a hill.

And he watched the dream roll on—the dream which had nothing to do with him. There were horsemen down there, riding in a charging wave. Around and around they were circling. He closed his eyes to the glare of light. Around and around—almost they were passing in answer to the beat—almost but not quite. The beat was not coming from the horsemen—it had another source.

Fors hung unresisting. But a tiny spark of the real Fors was moving in the broken, hurting body. Now he forced open his eyes and there was intelligence and purpose looking out of them.

The horsemen were keeping in their moving circle and as they rode they hurled spears up the grade. But among the horsemen others tramped now, men who ran lightly with ready bows. And the arrows made a cloud against the sun. The noose of men and horses drew smaller and tighter about the hill.

Then Fors realized suddenly that his body was part of the defense wall of those besieged here, that he had been fastened up for a screen behind which the dart throwers could crouch in safety. And those darts, expertly aimed, were taking toll below. Man and horse went down to cry and kick or lie still. But that did not halt the circle, nor deaden the flying arrows.

Once there was a loud screech of anguish and a body fell out from behind the barrier of which he was a part. On hands and knees it blundered downhill, heading for one of the nimble archers. They met in a headlong crash of fighting rage. Then a horseman swung low from the saddle and used his lance expertly. Both bodies lay still as he rode on.

A heavy blow landed on Fors' side. He forgot about the fighting as he looked down. His own arm hung there, free, a dead weight with the cut thong still ringing the purple swollen wrist. Arrow or spear had cut that tie. He ceased to have any interest in the battle—his world narrowed in that instant to the one free hand. In the puffed flesh there was no feeling, he could not even move it yet. So he concentrated on the fingers, he must move his thumb, his forefinger— even a fraction of an inch—he must!

There! He could have shouted at his success. The arm still was limp and heavy against his side but he had clawed the fingers against his thigh. One hand and arm free—and it was his right—the unhurt one! He turned his head. His other wrist was fast to another sapling post driven into the ground. But the very way the Beast Things were using him, as part of their defense works, was now in his favor. The left arm was not stretched full length from his shoulder. If he could bring the right fingers up, bring them up and make them work, he was sure he could unfasten that one too.

The barrier of which he was now a part must have screened his actions from his captors—or else they were too occupied to take any interest in him. He was able to bring the hand across, bring it across and force the fingers to the bonds on his left wrist. But it was another thing to untie the cords there. His numb fingers could not even feel and they kept slipping off.

He fought against his own stubborn and mistreated flesh, fought a battle as hard as the one raging about him. Arrows thudded home inches away, one of the spears brought a gasp of pain from him as the shaft struck full across his shin, but he willed his hand to the work. The torture of returning circulation hit full, but he made himself think only of those painful fingers and what he must have the courage and patience to make them do.

Then, all at once, something gave. He held an end of loose hide and his left arm fell inert as he gritted his teeth against the pain brought by that sudden release. But there was no time to nurse it now, he went down to the ground. In their haste the Beast Things had set but one loop of the hide around his ankles. He sawed at it with the edge of an arrowhead until it parted.

It would be safer to stay where he was for the moment. The Beast Things could not get at him without climbing the barrier and thus exposing themselves. And, flat to the ground as he was, he might escape the worst of the hail from below. So, too shaky to move or even to think clearly, he continued to cower where he had fallen.

After a space of time Fors was aware of another sound, coming through the din. He turned his head a fraction of an inch and was face to face with the rat cage. It, too, had been added to the breastworks. And the prisoners within it were racing about, their frenzied squeaking born of fear and hate loud enough to reach his ears. The sight of those obscene, too plump bodies aroused him as nothing else could have done and he hitched away from the swaying cage.

Where was the other prisoner—the Plainsman? Fors levered up cautiously on his elbows to see some distance away a fallen head and limp body. He allowed his head to sink back on his arms. He could move now—after a fashion—both legs and one arm would obey him. He could roll down the hill—

But that Plainsman—still exposed to certain death—

Fors began to creep, past the cage of rats, past a bundle of brush, a lopsided, hastily planted stockade of saplings, past the stuff the Beast Things had grabbed

up and thrown together in an attempt to keep out
arrows and spears. He traveled only a few inches at
a time and there were long pauses between those
inches. But he gained ground.

A dart struck the earth just beyond his straining
hand. The Beast Things were aware of him at last and
were trying to bring him down. But the one who
exposed itself in such a try fell back choking, an arrow
through its throat. It was not wise to give the archers
below even a partial target. Fors crawled on.

He was confident now that he could reach the
Plainsman. And he paid no attention to what chanced
below or inside the stockade. He must save all strength
and will for his journey.

Then he was squatting at a pair of bound ankles—
reaching up for knots which held torn wrists. But his
hands fell back. Two arrows held the captive pinned
more securely than any hide rope. The Plainsman
would never need help now.

Fors sank onto the rough trampled soil. The will and
purpose which had driven him went out as strength
of body flows out of an open wound. He could feel
them ebbing and he did not care.

Mountain rocks rose up about him and across crags
the gray flags of a storm flew their tatters. He could
hear the howl of wind down one of the narrow valleys,
see the gathering of the black clouds. It must be winter
for those were snow clouds. It would be well to head
back to the protection of the Eyrie—back to the fires
and stout stone walls—before those winds bit and the
snow fell.

Back to the Eyrie. He did not know that he was on
his feet now—no more than he knew that behind him
there came cries of consternation and red rage as the
Beast Thing leader went down to death under a chance
arrow. Fors did not know that he was tottering down

the slope, his empty hands out, while over the barrier behind him boiled a rabble of maddened, long-armed things intent on taking vengeance with fangs and claws, blind now to the precaution which had kept them safe.

Fors was walking a mountain trail and Lura was beside him. She had caught his hand in her mouth to lead him—which was right for the snow or the wind was blinding him and it was hard to keep on the trail. But the Eyrie lay just ahead and Langdon was waiting for him. Tonight they would study together that tiny scrap of map—a map of a city which lay on the shores of a lake. Langdon was going to put that map to the test soon. And after he, Fors, had been accepted by the Star Men he would also follow old maps—follow and find—

His hand went uncertainly to his head. Lura was hurrying him so. She wanted the fire and the meat. It was not right to keep Langdon waiting. Because somewhere there was a city waiting, too, a city of tall towers and filled storehouses, cracked roads and forgotten wonders. He must tell Langdon all about it. But that was not right—the city belonged to Langdon— not to him. He had never seen a ruined city. The storm must be making him lightheaded.

He staggered, one of the Beast Things aimed a blow at him as it passed to join the fighting mob below.

So many rocks—he had trouble keeping to his feet among these rocks. He'd best be careful. But he was going home. There were the fires—showing brightly through the dark. And Lura still held his hand. If the wind would only die down a little—the sound of it was wild and strange—almost like the battle cries of an army. But there stood the Eyrie—right there—

18

A New Star Shines

It was late afternoon. Smoke curled up from a ceremonial fire. Fors looked downslope to where green grass had been ground into a pulp by the pressure of many feet. And that pulp was stained with stale splotches of red. But the men below were squatting unconcernedly on it—their eyes only for each other. Two lines—facing across the fire warily—weapons unsheathed and to hand. Between those lines were the chieftains of the tribes. But both sides bore the scars of a hard fight and there were holes in the ranks which would never be filled again.

Fors forgot his own bruises as he watched Arskane step into place at the right of his father. The woman chief who had given the mountaineer the rights of the tribe was there, too, her robe a spark of bright color among the drabness of the hide jerkins and the tanned skins of the men.

And opposed was Marphy and his fellow long robe.

Only Cantrul was missing. The heads of family clans had usurped the place the High Chief should have held.

"Cantrul—?"

From beside Fors, Jarl made answer to that half question.

"Cantrul was a warrior—and as a warrior he entered on the long trail in a fitting fashion—taking a goodly number of the enemy with him. They have not yet raised up a new High Chief in his place."

What else the Star Captain might have added was blotted out in a roll from the talking drums, a roll which wrung harsh echoes from the surrounding hills. And when those faded, Lanard edged forward, though he needs must lean upon the arm of his son to spare weight from a leg which was bandaged from knee to ankle.

"Ho—warriors!" His voice followed the drums' beat in its force. "Here have we carried spears to a great killing and given the death birds a feast beyond the memory of our father's fathers! From the south have we marched to this war and victory is ours. Our arrows have struck full upon their marks and our swords have been blooded to their hilts. It this not so, my brothers?"

And out from the ranks of his tribe behind him came a low growl of agreement. Here and there some of the younger men cried the shrill war slogan of a family clan.

But from the ranks of the under chieftains in the mass of the Plainspeople arose another man and he answered with prideful words of his own:

"Lances bite as deep as swords, and the Plainsmen have never known fear of a fight. Death birds eat today from our providing also. We stand shame-filled in the sight of no man!"

Someone began the war song Fors had heard on his

night of captivity among the tents. Hands were reaching for bows and lances. Fors got to his feet, forcing his body to obey his will. He pushed aside the hand the Star Captain put out to stay him.

"There is a fire breaking out here," he said slowly. "If it comes to full flame it may eat us all up. Let me go—!"

But as he half staggered down the slope to the council fire, he sensed that the Star Captain was still at his back.

"You have fought!"

From somewhere within him that clear cold voice had come at his willing—It was a chill wind to cut through the evil vapors of a swampland. In his head the thoughts Arskane had planted long ago were coming to life so clearly that he was confident at last of their truth and rightness.

"You have fought!"

"Ahhh—" That answering sound was close to the purr which Lura might voice when remembering her hunt.

"You have fought," he repeated for the third time and knew that he had them now. "The Beast Things are dead. *These* Beast Things—"

That accented word have riveted their full attention.

"You have looked upon the enemy slain—is that not so? Well, I have lain in their hands—and the horror that you know is tenfold in my memory. But I say that you might also look in fear as well as in pride of your victory, for there lies among them a dire promise. My fathers' fathers fought with these creatures—when still they held to their home burrows. My father died under their claws and fangs. Long have we known them. But now there has been born amongst them something stronger—something which threatens us as the burrow creepers of old never did. Ask it of your wise men, warriors. Ask them what they found in the circle of the dead within that barrier up there—what may come again to plague us in future years. Tell these your people, oh, healer of bodies." He addressed himself to the Plains white robe. "And you, oh, Lady." He spoke to the woman chief. "What have you seen?"

It was the woman who replied first.

"I saw and heard many things. In the seeing there was nothing to doubt. I hope with all my heart that your notions are mistaken. There lay among the Beast dead one who was different. And if the fates are against us, then this one will be born again among them—again and again. And, its knowledge being greater, so will it prove a worse menace to us and all human beings. Thus, because this may be true, I say that those who are humankind must stand together and put a united sword wall against these things bred out of the ancient evil of the cities which was sown by the Old Ones—"

"It is true that mutants may come of mutant stock." The white robe spoke after her almost against his will. "And these Beast Things were led and ordered as never has their race been before. When their strange chief fell they were broken, as if their knowledge was all blotted out in that single death. If they breed more such as he, then they shall prove a force we must reckon with. We know but little of these creatures and what their powers may be. How can we guess now what we shall be called to go up against a year, ten years, a generation from now? This land is wide and there may be much hiding within its vastness which is a menace to our breed—"

"The land is wide," Fors repeated. "What do you and your tribe seek for here, Lanard?"

"A homeland. We search out a place to build our houses and sow our fields anew, to pasture our sheep and dwell in peace. After the burning mountains and quaking land drove us forth from the valley of our fathers—the sacred place where their machines landed from the sky at the end of the Old Ones' war—we have wandered many circles of the seasons. Now in these wide fields, along the river, we have found what we have sought for so long. And no man or beast shall drive us from it!" As he ended, his hand was on his sword hilt and he stared straight along the ranks of the Plainsmen.

Fors turned now to Marphy: "And what do your people seek, Marphy of the plains?"

The Recorder raised his eyes from the ground where a pattern of crushed grass blades had apparently held his attention.

"Since the days of the Old Ones we of the Plains have been a roving people. First we were so because of the evil death which abode in the air of many quarters of the land, so that a man must be on the move to shun those places where plagues and the blue fires waited to slay him. We are now hunters and rovers and herdsmen, warriors who care not to be tied to any camp. It is in us to travel far, to seek new places and new hills standing high against the sky—"

"So." Fors let that one word fall into the silence of those war-torn ranks.

It was a long minute before he spoke again. "You," he pointed to Lanard, "wish to settle and build. That is your nature and way of life. You"—it was Marphy he turned to now—"would move, grazing your herds and hunting. These," he bent a stiff arm painfully to gesture up the hill to that uneven pile of earth and stone under which lay the bodies of the Beast Things, "live to destroy both of you if they can. And the land is wide . . . "

Lanard cleared his throat—the sound was sharp

and loud. "We would live in peace with all who raise not the sword against us. In peace there is trade, and in trade there is good for all. When the winter closes in and the harvest has been poor, then may trade save the life of a tribe."

"You are warriors and men," the woman chief of the Dark People broke in, her head high, her eyes straight as she measured the line of strangers facing her. "War is meat and drink at the table of men—yes—but it was that which brought the Old Ones down! War again, men, and you will destroy us utterly and we shall be eaten up and forgotten so that it shall be as if man had never lived to walk these fields—leaving our world to the holding of those!" She pointed to the Beast Things' mound. "If now we draw sword against one another then in our folly we shall have chosen the evil part for the last time, and it is better that we die quickly and this earth be clean of us!"

The Plainspeople were quiet until along the ranks of the men a murmur arose and it spread to where their women were gathered. And the voices of the women grew louder and stronger. From their midst arose one who must have ruled a chieftain's tent since there was gold binding her hair:

"Let there be no war between us! Let there be no more wailing of the death song among our tents! Say it loudly, oh, my sisters!" And her appeal was taken up by all the women, to be echoed until it became a chant as stirring as the war song.

"No more war! No more war between us!"

So did the cup of blood and brotherhood pass from chief to chief on the field and the ranks of the Dark Ones and the Plainsmen were made one by the ritual so that never again might man of one raise lance against man of the other.

Fors sank down upon a flat-topped rock. The strength which had upheld him drained away. He was very tired and the excitement beyond no longer had anything to do with him. He had no eyes for the melting of the stiff tribal lines and the mingling of clan and people.

"This is but a beginning!" He identified the quick eager voice of Marphy and looked around slowly, almost sullenly.

The Plainsman was talking to Jarl, gesturing, his eyes bright. But the Star Captain was his usual calm contained self.

"A beginning, yes, Marphy. But we still have much to master. If I may see those northern records of yours. We of the Star House have not penetrated that far—"

"Of course. And—" Marphy seemed hesitant before he plunged into his counter request—"that cage of rats. I have had it brought into my tent. There are three still alive and from them we may learn—"

Fors shivered. *He* had no desire to see those captives.

"You claim them as your spoil of war?"

Marphy laughed. "That I shall do. And other spoil beside the vermin shall we ask for—a greater gift from you. This fellow rover of yours—"

He touched gentle fingers to Fors' stooped shoulder. It seemed to the mountaineer that Jarl displayed a flash of surprise.

"This one has the gift of tongues and the mind which sees. He shall be a guide for us." Marphy's words spilled out as if now that he had a kindred spirit in which to confide he could no longer bottle his thoughts. "And in return we shall show him strange lands and far places. For it is in him to be a rover—even as we are—"

Jarl's fingers plucked at his lower lip: "Yes, rover was he born, and in him flows Plains blood. If he——"

"You forget." Fors did not force a smile this time. "I am mutant."

Before either man could answer someone else came up—Arskane. His face still bore the marks of the fight and he favored his shoulder as he moved. But when he spoke it was with an assumption of authority which he plainly did not expect to have disregarded.

"We break camp to march—I have come for my brother!"

Marphy bristled. "He rides with us!"

Fors' laugh had no humor in it. "Since I cannot travel on my feet I shall be a drag in any company——"

"We shall rig a pony litter," was Arskane's quick reply.

"There are also horse litters," began Marphy jealously.

Jarl moved. "It seems that you now have a choice to make," he observed dispassionately to Fors. For a moment it seemed to the younger mountain man that only the two of them were there. And neither Arskane nor Marphy pressed his claim farther.

Fors held his free hand to his swimming head. He had Plains blood from his mother—that was true. And the wild free life of the roving horsemen appealed to him. If he went with Marphy no secrets of the ruined country would be hidden from him now—he could learn much. He could make such maps as even the Star Men had never dreamed of possessing, see forgotten cities and loot them for his pleasure, always going on to new country beyond.

If he took the hand Arskane had half offered in support a few minutes ago he would be accepting brotherhood and the close-knit ties of a family clan such as he had never had. He would know all warmth of affection, and go to build a town, maybe in time a city, which would mark the first step back along the road the sins of the Old Ones had lost for their sons. It would be a hard life but, in its way, a rewarding one, as adventurous—though he would never rove far—as Marphy's.

But—there was the third road. And it ran from a choice he knew only too well. When he thought he was dying—back there during the battle—his feet had taken it without his will. It led to the rare coldness of the mountain heights, into the austere chill of punishment and hurt and eternal discouragement.

So when he raised his head he dared not look at Arskane or Marphy, but he found and held Jarl's uncompromising eyes as he asked:

"It is true that I am outlawed?"

"You have been called three times at the council fire."

He recognized flat truth and accepted it. But he had another question:

"Since I was not there to answer in my own voice I have the right of appeal for the period of six moons?"

"You have."

Fors picked at the sling which bound his left arm across his chest. There was an even chance that it would heal straight and strong again. The healer had promised him that after probing the wound.

"I have then," he found that he had to stop and work out his words, to regain discipline over his voice, "I shall go and claim that right. Six moons are not yet gone—"

The Star Captain nodded. "If you can travel in three days' time you will make it."

"Fors!" At that protest from Arskane, the mountaineer winced. But when he turned his head his voice still held firm.

"It was you yourself, brother, who spoke of duty once—"

Arskane's hand dropped. "Remember—we be brothers, you and I. Where lies my hearth—there is your place waiting." He went and he did not look back, he was swallowed up in the throng of his tribesmen.

Marphy came to life. He shrugged. Already he was intent on other plans, other enthusiasms. But he lingered long enough to say:

"From this hour on for you there runs a mount in my herd and the promise of meat, and shelter in my tent. Look for the Standard of the Red Fox when you have need of aid, my young friend." His hand sketched a half salute as he strode away.

Fors spoke to the Star Captain: "I shall go—"

"With me. I have also a report to make to the tribe—we journey together."

Was that news good or otherwise? Under other circumstances Fors could have longed for no greater pleasure than to travel in the company of the Star Captain. But now he went in a manner as Jarl's prisoner. He sat glumly looking over the battlefield— only a small scrimmage—one which the Old Ones, with their fleets in the air and their armed columns on land, would not even have mentioned. Yet here a full-sized war had been fought and out of it had come an idea—perhaps one which would prove the starting point for men. It would be a long weary trail for them to travel—the road back to such a world as the Old Ones had known. And maybe not even the sons' sons' sons of those who had fought here would live to see more than the glimmerings of its beginning growth. Or maybe the world which would come would be a better world.

The Plainsmen and the Dark Ones were still suspicious, still wary of one another. Soon the tribes would separate for a space. But, perhaps in six months' time, a party of Plainsmen would venture again to the south, to visit the bend in the river and see with wondering eyes the cabins which stood there. And one rider would trade a well-tanned hide for a clay dish or a string of colored beads to take home to astonish his women. Afterward would come others, many others, and there would in time be marriages between tent and cabin. And in fifty years—one nation.

"There will be one nation." Fors hunched on the riding pad of the steady old horse Marphy had forced upon him. Two days had sped but the tramped earth would show scars for a long time.

Jarl shot a measuring glance over the field they crossed.

"And how many years pass before such a miracle?" he inquired with his old irony.

"Fifty—fifty years—perhaps—"

"If nothing intervenes to stop them—yes—you may be right."

"You are thinking of the Beast Thing mutant?"

Jarl shrugged. "I think that he is a warning—there may be other factors to set barriers in the way."

"I am mutant." For the second time Fors made that bitter statement and he spoke it again before the one person he wished had never known of his difference.

Jarl did not rise to the bait. "I have been thinking that we may all be mutants. Who is to say now that we are of the same breed as the Old Ones? And I am of the belief that it is time we all face that fact squarely. But this other—this Beast Thing—" And he proceeded to drown Fors in a barrage of questions which drew out of him all that he had observed while a prisoner of the enemy.

Two days later the mountains stood sharply outlined against the sky. Fors knew that by nightfall, it they kept the pace they had held through the journey, they would be past the outposts of the Eyrie. He fumbled awkwardly with his one hand at his belt and pulled his sword from the sheath. As Jarl caught up to him he held it out, hilt first.

"Now I am your prisoner." He did not have to steady his voice, it was naturally so. It was as if he no longer cared what happened to him during the next few days. This was a piece of unfinished living which must be completed before he left it behind him. But he was impatient now to have it over, to be read out of the tribe as an outlaw, to go into the wilderness again—he was ready and unafraid.

Jarl took his sword without a word and Fors glanced beyond the Star Captain to the waiting Lura. She was tugging in his mind, suddenly weary of the leash of loyalty which had held her to him through all these days of danger. She wanted the mountains, too, in a different way—the mountains and her freedom. He gave it to her with a single shaft of thought and she was gone that same instant. And because he had released her so willingly he knew that she would return as willingly when she had followed her own desire to its end.

After that Fors rode in a kind of dream. He paid little or no attention to the men of the Eyrie who came out of their scout posts to greet the Star Captain. They did not speak to him and he had no wish for them to do so. His impatience to come to the judging only burned the stronger in him.

He was alone at last in the inner chamber of the Star House, that same chamber which he had violated. The empty hook where Langdon's star pouch had once hung was a mute reminder of that offense. Too bad his venture had failed so completely. He would never be able now to prove the truth of his father's dream.

But even that thought did not prick him overmuch. He could go out again—and not by any favor of the council men.

There was the reflection of the council fire on the naked rock of the mountain wall out there. The elders were gathering to judge him. But it would be the Star Men who would have the final voice against him. It was the Star House he had looted, the Star tradition and mysteries he had flouted.

At an almost soundless footfall in the outer room Fors turned his head. One of the Star Novices had come for him—Stephen of the Hawk Clan. Fors followed him out into the circle of firelight, walled in by rows of white blurs which were faces without expression.

The elders were together, all of them, Healer, Recorder, Master of the Fields, Commanders of the Hunters and Defenders. And behind them were the tillers, the hunters, the scouts and guards. On the other side was the solid block of Star Men, Jarl at their head.

Fors came out on the smooth shelf of rock alone, his silver head high, his back and shoulders straight.

"Fors of the Puma Clan—" That was Horsford, the Eyrie Guardian.

Fors made courteous salute.

"You stand here because you have defied the traditions of the Eyrie. But against the wearers of the Star was your greater offense. So now it is the decision of the Council that the Star Men shall be given the right to pronounce against you and they shall deal with you as they see fit."

Short and to the point. And fair enough, he had expected little else. So now what did the Star Men wish for him? It was up to Jarl. Fors turned to the tall Captain.

But Jarl was staring beyond him at the leaping

flames. And so did they wait in silence for a long, long moment. When the Star Captain spoke it was not to pass sentence but to catch the attention of all who gathered there.

"We come, men of the Eyrie, to a place where two roads separate before us. And upon our choice of them depends the future of not only the clans gathered here, but also that of all true men in this land, perhaps on this earth. Therefore tonight I am breaking a solemn vow, the oaths taken in my green youth—that secret which has made of my kind men apart. Listen, all of you, to the inner story of our Stars.

"Now we who wear them are hunters of dim trails, seekers of lost knowledge. But once this," his hand went to the star, bright and hot in the firelight, at his throat, "had another meaning. Our forefathers were brought to this mountain hiding place because they were designed to be truly men of the Stars. Here were they being trained to a life which would be theirs on other worlds. Our records tell us that man was on the eve of conquering the planets, and even the stars, when his madness fell upon him and he reached again for slaying weapons.

"We who were meant to roam the stars go now on foot upon a ravaged earth. But above us those other worlds still hang, and still they beckon. And so is the promise still given. If we make not the mistakes of the Old Ones then shall we know in time more than the winds of this earth and the trails of this earth. This is the secret we now publish abroad so that all men may know what was lost to us with the dread folly of the Old Ones and to what we may aspire if we make not the same error in our turn."

Fors' fingers clenched until nails bit into his palms. So this was what man had thrown away! The same longing which had torn him on the field of the dead, bombed plains came to him again. They had been so great in their dreams—the Old Ones! Well, men must dream again.

"We stand before two roads, my people," Jarl repeated slowly. "And this time we must take a better choice. It is the will of the Star Men that Fors of the Puma Clan, being of mixed blood and clan, shall no longer be held as lesser than we, in spite of the laws of our fathers. For now has come the time to break such laws.

"From this hour forth he shall be set apart in a different fashion. For he shall be one who will carry the knowledge of one people to another, binding together in peace swords which might be raised in war.

"A mutant may have skills which will serve his tribe well. And so do we urge a new law—that a mutant be deemed a full man. And if he is born in a clan, then is he to be counted a man of that clan. Which of us can prove—" Jarl swung around to face the throng from which was now arising a growing murmur, whether of assent or dissent who could tell—"which of us can prove that we are of the same breed as the Old Ones? Do we wish to be as the Old Ones? Our fathers threw away the stars—remember that!"

It was the Healer who answered him. "By nature's laws, if not man's, you speak the truth. It is guessed that men are different today from what they once were. A mutant—" He coughed behind his hand. "Truly any here might be termed mutant to some degree."

Horsford held up his hand to still the babble of sound. His powerful voice boomed around the circle.

"There has been a weighty thing done here tonight, brothers. The Star Men have broken faith with the past. Can we do less? They speak of two roads—I shall speak of growing. We have put our roots in narrow and stony ground. We have held stubbornly to it. But now comes a time when we must move or die. For the only end to growth is death. And in the name of the Council I am choosing growth. If the stars were once promised us—then shall we reach for them again!"

Someone raised a cheer—it came from the outer edges where the youths stood. And that cheer gathered voices and grew. Men were on their feet now, their voices eager, their eyes alight. Never had this reserved and serious people seemed so like their cousins of the Plains. The tribe was coming to a new life.

"So be it," Jarl's voice broke through the din. At his gesture of command some of it died away. "From this hour we shall walk new ways. And in remembrance of that choice do we now set upon Fors a star which is like unto no other worn here. And in his turn, when the time comes, he shall raise up those who will wear it after him. Thus there will be always those among us who shall speak with other peoples as a friend, think with neutral minds, and hold the peace of nations in their hands!"

Jarl came to Fors holding out a chain from which hung a star, not of five points but of many, so that it was a compass sign pointing in all directions at once. And this fell cool and smooth below the mutant's throat.

Then the tribe shouted the cry which was the welcome to a Star Man newly raised up. But in this too there was a difference. For now was born a new star and from it would follow what no man standing there that night might rightly foresee—not even he who wore it as a trust.

NO NIGHT WITHOUT STARS

The thick plume of the greasy-looking black smoke rising from beyond the ridge was warning enough. Sander slipped off Rhin, crept up-slope, his mount padding behind him with the same caution. They had seen no campsite for days, and the provision bag, still knotted to the pad strapped about Rhin, was empty. Hunger was a discomfort within Sander. This land had been singularly empty of game for the past twenty-four hours. And a handful or two of barely ripe grain, pulled out of a straggle of stalks, was far from filling.

Five days ago Sander had passed the boundaries of the territory known to Jak's Mob. When he had ridden out of the ring of tents, blackly bitter at his treatment, he had swung due east, heading for the legendary sea. Then it had seemed possible that he could achieve his purpose—to find the ancient secrets whereby he could better forge the metal brought by Traders, so that, upon his return, he could confront Ibbets and the others and force from them an acknowledgment that he was not an apprentice of little worth, but a smith of the Old Learning. This long trek through a wilderness he did not know had taught him caution, though it had not yet dampened the inner core of his rebellion against Ibbets's belittling decision.

Now he wedged his shoulders between two rocks, pulling his hood well down over his face so that its gray color would blend well with the stones around him. Though he was no hunter by training, each member of the Mob was lessoned from childhood in the elements of hiding-out when confronted by the unusual. He would not move until he could make very sure there was no danger ahead.

Below lay a wide valley down which a river angled. And where that opened into a much larger bowl of water (of which he could see only one shoreline, the one into which the river cut), there stood a collection of buildings, a small village. Those log-walled shelters appeared to be permanent, unlike the hide tents of the Mob that were easily moved from one place to another. However, small sullen tongues of fire now showed here and there, threatening to destroy the buildings.

Even from this distance Sander sighted what could only be a huddle of bodies lying along the river bank. There had been a raid, he deduced. Maybe the dreaded Sea Sharks of the south had struck. He doubted there was any life left in that collection of huts.

The fire burned slowly, mainly along the river bank and the shoreline of the large body of water beyond. There were a few buildings seemingly still untouched. They would have been looted, of course. Still, there was a chance that not all of the provisions collected by those settled here had been carried away. And this was harvest season. His own people (or those whom he had believed to be his close kin—he grimaced at that thought) had been engaged in late season hunts and the drying of meat when he had ridden out.

Though the nomadic Mob roamed the wide inner lands, Sander had heard enough tales from the Traders to know that elsewhere men lived differently. In some places clans had settled permanently upon the land, planting and tending food which they grew. Here, in this near-destroyed settlement, they must also have fished. His stomach growled and he shifted a little, surveying the scene of the raid carefully to make sure that if he did go down he was not running into trouble.

Rhin whined deep in his throat, nudged Sander with his muzzle. His yellow-brown coat was already thickening with new winter growth. Now his jaws opened a little, his pointed tongue showed. His ears pricked as he watched the burning buildings with the same intense stare as Sander. But he betrayed no more than the common caution with which he approached all new situations.

His green eyes did not blink, nor did his brush of tail move. Instead he sat on his haunches as if it did not matter that his head rose well above the skyline, visible from the town. Sander accepted Rhin's verdict of no imminent danger—for the sly intelligence of his kind supplied information that no man, with his blunter senses, could hope to gain.

Though he got to his feet, Sander did not remount. Instead he slipped down the ridge, using every bit of cover. Rhin followed like a red-yellow ghost a step or two behind. Sander carried his dart thrower, a missile notched ready against its taut string and loosened his long knife in its leather scabbard.

As they drew closer to the looted town, Sander's nose wrinkled at the stench of burning and of other smells far worse. Rhin growled, sniffing. He liked that scent no better than Sander. But at least he seemed to have picked up no hint of enemies.

Sander circled away from the river bank where lay those blood-stained bundles, heading toward the seemingly unharmed buildings farther inland from the shore. He could hear the pounding of waves and smell a new odor, swept toward him by a rising wind—a strange, fresh scent. Was this indeed the sea, not just some larger lake?

As he approached the nearest building, he hesitated, something in him resisted making this intrusion. Only the need for food forced him into an alleyway so narrow that Rhin crowded him with a furry shoulder as they padded on together.

The walls of logs Sander saw were thick. The only openings were set very high, nearly masked by the over-hanging eaves of the sharply-pitched roofs. He reached the end of the alley and turned right before he found the entrance door.

It had been fashioned of heavy planking. Now it hung crazily from a single hinge, scarred by forced entry. Rhin snarled, his tongue sweeping out over his lips. There was a body just within that broken door; between the shoulders was a splotch of clotted blood. The villager lay face downward and Sander had no desire to turn him over.

The stranger was not wearing the leather and furs of a Mobsman, rather a coarsely woven overtunic dyed a nut brown. His legs were encased in baggy trousers of the same material, with laced hide boots on his feet. For a long moment Sander hesitated before he stepped gingerly around the dead man into an interior that showed both search and wanton destruction.

There was another huddle of twisted body and stained clothing in the corner. After a single glance, Sander kept his eyes resolutely from it. Smashed and nearly destroyed as the contents of this room were, he could still see that the town dwellers had possessed more worldly goods than any Mobsman. That was only sensible in their way of life. One could not cart chairs, tables, and chests about the land when one was ever traveling to follow the herds. He stopped to pick up a broken bowl, intrigued by the design across its side. Its few dark lines against the clear brown of the pottery made him envision birds in flight.

He made his way quickly to the food bins, wanting no more of this chamber of the dead. Rhin whined from without. Sander caught the uneasiness of his companion, the need to be gone. But he forced himself to examine what was left.

There was a measure of grain flour mixed with chopped and powdered nut meats. Using the broken bowl for a scoop he packed it into his provision bag. He found two dried fish wedged in another over-turned bin. But the rest had been deliberately wasted or wantonly befouled. Sickened by the signs of relentless hatred, he hurried out to join Rhin.

Yet Sander made himself approach the next building. No corpse blocked the forced door this time. However, one glance at what lay inside made him gag and turn hastily away. He could not go any nearer to *that*. It seemed that the raiders, whoever they might have been, had not been content to kill, but had also taken time to amuse themselves in a beastly fashion. Sander kept swallowing to control his nausea as he backed out into the way that fronted the unfired buildings.

There was one other place he must search for—in spite of his growing terror. There *must* have been a smith's forge somewhere in this ravaged village. He slapped his hands against the bag of tools that was lashed to the back of Rhin's riding pad. What he carried there was all he had from his father. Ibbets would have liked to have claimed those, as he claimed the office of smith with the Mob, but custom had supported Sander to that extent.

Two major hammers and chisels had been buried with his father, Dullan, of course. A man's main tools of trade were filled with his own powers and must so be laid away in the earth when he no longer could use them. But there were some smaller things that a son could rightfully claim, and no one could deny him those. However, Sander needed more, much more, if he were to realize his dream. He longed to find the place wherein those masses of congealed metal, which the traders brought to the Mobs, were concealed and to learn the secret of the alloys which now baffled smiths.

Resolutely he started on, dodging a charred wall that had fallen outward, closing his mind to everything but his search, holding his nose against the stink. Rhin continued to whine and growl. Sander was well aware that his companion wanted none of this place of death and followed him under protest. Yet because of the brotherhood between them, Rhin would continue.

Rhin's people and those of the Mob were entwined in mutual service. That companionship began during the Dark Time. Legends Sander had heard recited by the Rememberers said that Rhin's people had once been much smaller, yet always clever and quick to adapt to change. "Koyots" they were called in the old tongue.

There had been many animals, and more men than one could count, who had perished when the Earth danced and the Dark Time had begun. Mountains of fire had burst through the skin of the world, belching flame, smoke, and molten rock. The sea had rolled inward with waves near as high as those same mountains, hammering the land into nothingness in some places, in others deserting the beds over which it had lain for untold ages. Cold followed and great choking clouds of evil air that killed.

Here and there a handful of men or animals survived. But when the skies cleared once again, there were changes. Some animals grew larger generation by generation, just as distant species of men were rumored to be now twice the size of Sander's own people. That information came from Traders' tales, however, and it was well known that Traders like to spread such stories to keep other men away from any rich finds. They would invent all manner of monsters to be faced were a man to try to track them back to their own places.

Sander stopped, picked up a spear, gruesomely stained, and prodded with that into the ashes of a small building. He swiftly uncovered what could only be an anvil—a good one fashioned from iron, but far too heavy to be transported. Finding that, a sure sign he had found the smithy, he scratched with more vigor.

His delving uncovered a fine stone hammerhead, with the haft near burned away, but the best part remaining. That and another of a lesser weight were all that remained. There were also some traces of metal—copper he was sure—puddled from the heat.

He raised his hand and recited the secret smith words. If the owner, who might lie farther back under the debris at the rear, was still spirit-tied, as men who died quickly and violently sometimes were, he would know by those words that one of his own craft was present. He would not, Sander was sure, begrudge that his possessions be used again, carefully, and to a purpose that might in the end benefit all men.

Sander fitted the two hammerheads in among the tools he carried. He would hunt no farther. Let the dead smith keep all else as grave-hold. But such hammers he did not have and he needed them.

He wanted no more of this nameless village wherein death stank and spirits might be tied to their destroyed homes. Rhin sensed that decision, greeting it with a yelp of approval. However, Sander was not minded to leave the shore of the sea—if sea this was. Rather he passed as quickly as he could among the smoldering buildings, refusing to look at the bodies he passed, to reach the slippery sand of the shore.

To prove that he might have reached one of his

objectives, he advanced to where the small waves ended in foam upon the sand. There he dipped a finger into the water and licked it. Salt! Yes, he had found the sea.

However it was not the sea alone that he sought, but rather the heart of the old legends around it. Along the shore of the sea had once stood many great cities of old. Sander's father had often speculated about the secrets that lay in those cities.

It was certain that men before the Dark Time had possessed such knowledge that they lived as the spirits of the upper air did, with unseen servants and all manner of labor-saving tools. Yet that learning had been lost. Sander did not know the number of years that lay between him and that time. But his father had said that the sum was more than the lifetimes of many, many men, each a generation behind the other.

At the death of his father from the coughing sickness, Ibbets, his father's younger brother, had denied Sander the smith-right, saying he was only an untried boy and unfit to serve the Mob. Then Sander knew he must prove himself, not only to the people whom he had believed kin-blood, but to himself. He must become such a worker of metal that his own number of years—or lack of them—would mean nothing, only what could be wrought by his design and his skill. Thus, when Ibbets would have bound him to a new apprenticeship, he had instead claimed go-forth rights, and the Mob had been forced to grant him that choice of exile.

Now he was kinless by his own hard decision. And he burned with the need to know that he was a better smith, or would be, than Ibbets claimed. To do that he must learn. And he was sure that such knowledge lay near the original source of the lumps of congealed metal that the traders brought.

Some of the metal could be worked by strength of arm and hammer alone. Other kinds must be heated, run into molds, or struck when hot to form the needed tool or weapon. But there were some metals that defied all attempts to work them. And it was the secret of those that had fascinated Sander from childhood.

He had found the sea; now he could go north or south along its shore. There had been great changes in the land, he knew. Perhaps such cities as he sought were long since buried under the wash of the waves, or else so overturned by earth-shaking that little remained. Yet somewhere the Traders found their metal, so somewhere such sources existed—and those he could seek.

It was close to nightfall, and he did not wish to camp close to the half-destroyed town. He pushed on northward. Above, sea birds wheeled and screamed hoarsely, and the steady roll of the waves made a low accompaniment to their cries.

Rhin's head swung around twice toward their back trail. He growled, and his uneasiness gripped Sander in turn. Though it seemed the town was wholly given over to the dead, it was true that Sander had not delved too deeply in the ruins. What if some survivor, perhaps shaken out of his wits by the terror of the raid, lurked there, had seen Sander and Rhin come and go? They might now be hunted by such.

Climbing on the top of a dune, along the sides of which grew tough sea grass, Sander studied the still-smoking buildings. Nothing moved save the birds. He did not, however, discount Rhin's uneasiness, knowing he could depend upon the koyot's acute senses to give him fair warning if they were followed.

He would have liked to have ridden, but the slippery sand gave such uncertain footing that he kept on as they were. He angled away from the wave line now, for there lay drifts of wood which might entrap the unwary. Now and then a shell lay exposed in the damp sand. Sander eyed their fantastic forms with amazement. They delighted him like bright bird's feathers or tumble-smoothed stones, so he dropped some into his left pouch. Momentarily he dreamed of setting shells in bands of copper, a metal that easily responded to the skill he had learned, and make such articles of adornment as the Mob had never seen.

The sand became covered with coarse grass, which in turn changed to meadowland. But Sander disliked this too-open country. He could see a dark line across the horizon that marked the beginning of wooded land. While his people were of the open plains to the west, they also knew northern woods, and he recognized the value of finding cover.

However, he was enough a judge of travelers' distances to be sure he could not reach that forest before nightfall. What he wanted now was a defensible camp site, if Rhin's instinct was proven correct and they were to face some danger out of the dark.

He would not dare a fire tonight, wanting no beacon that might draw anyone—or anything—that prowled this country. So at last he settled on a stand of rocks, huddled together as if the stones themselves had drawn close for comfort in an hour of need.

Jerking up handfuls of grass, he arranged it into a nest. Then he brought out the dried fish and shared with Rhin. Ordinarily, the koyot would have gone off hunting on his own. But it would seem that this night he was not about to leave Sander.

As the young man watched the twilight draw in, felt the chill of the night winds which bore strange scents from the sea, his weariness grew. He could hear nothing save the wash of the waves and the sounds of birds. And although Rhin pricked up his ears to listen with all his might, he did not yet show any signs of real alarm.

Tired though Sander was from the day's journeying, he could not sleep. Over him arched the sky sparkling with the eyes of the night. The Rememberers said those were other suns, very far away, and around them perhaps moved worlds like their own. But to Sander they had always seemed like the eyes of strange, aloof creatures, who watched the short lives of men with more indifference than interest. He tried to think about the star eyes, but his mind kept returning to the horrors of the raided village. What would it be like, he wondered with a shiver, to be suddenly set upon by men out of the sea who wanted to slay, to destroy, to dip their hands in blood?

The Mob had fought for their lives, but only once, in Sander's memory, against their kind. That had been when a terrifying people with light skin and wild pale eyes had come down to raid their herd. Mainly their struggle was against cold and famine and sickness, warring against a hard land rather than mankind. Their smiths forged the weapons and the tools for that struggle, not many of the kinds meant to drink man-blood.

Sander had heard tales of the sea slavers. Sometimes he had thought that those, too, were inventions of the Traders, who created fearsome horrors to fill the land they did not want others to explore. For the Traders were notoriously tight-fisted when it came to their own profits. But after this day he could believe that man was more ruthless than a full winter storm. Now he shivered a little, not from the touch of the sea breeze, but because of what his imagination suggested might exist in this wilderness so unknown to him.

Sander put out a hand for the reassuring touch of Rhin's furry hide. At the same moment the koyot leaped to his feet and growled in warning. Rhin faced not the sea, but inland. Plainly the animal had decided that there was some menace slinking through the night.

With so little visibility, the dart thrower was no good. Sander drew his long belt knife, which was really a short sword. He crouched upon one knee with the rocks a firm wall at his back, and listened. There seemed to be a slight shuffling ahead. Rhin growled again. Now Sander caught a trace of musky odor. He thought he had seen a shadow, moving so swiftly its shape blurred.

A hissing out of the dark became a loud snarl. Rhin advanced a step, stiff-legged, plainly alert against attack. Sander desperately regretted the fire he had not lit. To face such an unknown menace kindled one of mankind's age-old fears.

Yet the thing did not attack as Sander expected it to do. He heard that challenging hiss, and he judged from Rhin's reaction that the koyot thought this unknown to be a formidable opponent. Still, whatever it was stayed beyond the boundaries where Sander might sight it against the lighter rocks. A shrill whistle came out of the night, followed by a flash of light. It shone straight into Sander's eyes, dazzling him, though he flung up his arm in an involuntary gesture to ward off the blinding glare.

Under the shadow of his hand he watched an animal glide forward, a sinuous body seeming more like a snake than a furred species. It arose upon its haunches, still hissing, until its head was nearly level with his own. Behind it a smaller edition of itself, much darker in color, hugged the ground. Neither of that pair carried the light.

"Stand—" The command from behind the source of

the light was an emphatic order. Another followed: "Drop your knife!"

Sander was sure only the will of the speaker held the threatening animals in check, but he shook his head in refusal.

"I do not obey the orders of unknown who skulk in the dark," he returned. "I am not a hunter or harmer of men."

"Blood cries for blood, stranger," snapped the voice. "Behind you streams blood—kin-blood. If there is an accounting, then it is mine, seeing that no one else lives in Padford now—"

"I came to a town of the dead," Sander returned. "If you seek blood for blood, look elsewhere, stranger. When I rode from the south, there were only the dead within half-burned walls."

The light held steady on him and no answer came forth. But that the stranger had been willing to speak without immediate attack was, Sander believed, in his favor.

"It is true that you are no Sea Shark," the voice observed slowly.

Sander could understand the words. But the accent with which they were spoken differed both from that of the Mob and that of the Traders.

"Who are you?" Now the voice sharpened in a new demand.

"I am Sander, once of Jak's Mob, and I am a smith."

"Soooo?" The voice drawled that as if not quite believing. "And where tents your Mob this night, smith?"

"Westward."

"Yet you travel east. Smiths are not wanderers, stranger. Or is there blood guilt and kin-death lying in your back trail?"

"No. My father, who was smith, died, and they would

have it that I was not skilled enough to take his place. Thus I took out-rights—" He was growing irritated. That he must patiently answer this quizzing out of the dark stirred his anger. Now he boldly asked in return:

"Who are you?"

"One not to meddle with, stranger!" snapped that other. "But it seems you speak the truth and so are not meat for us this night."

The light snapped out instantly. He could hear a stirring in the dark. Rhin whined in relief. Though the koyot could be a formidable fighter when he wished, it was plain he preferred the absence of those animals and whoever controlled them to their presence.

Sander himself felt tension seep away. The voice was gone, taking with it the strange hounds of its hunting. He settled back, and after a while he slept.

Sander's slumber was full of dreams in which dead men arose to face him with broken weapons in their slack hands. He roused now and again, sweating, hardly sure of what was dream and what reality. He could then hear sometimes a soft growl deep in Rhin's throat, as if the koyot scented something dangerous. Yet the voice and the light were surely gone.

By the first hint of dawn Sander was ready to move on. This seemed to him a haunted land. Perhaps the unburied dead of the town oppressed his spirit. The sooner he was well away from such an ill-omened place, the better. However, he made a quick survey of the ground where the night before that half-seen beast had reared up in the light.

That truly had been no dream, for there were paw marks deep-set in the soil, pads and claws in clear impression. Beyond, he discovered a single other print, small and distinct, unmistakably human. Rhin sniffed at the tracks and again growled. It was plain from the swing of the koyot's head that he little liked what his own special senses reported. Another reason to be on their way.

Sander did not even wait to eat. He swung up on the riding pad, and Rhin trotted off at a pace that soon carried them well into the tough grass of the lowlands, parallel with the sea. The passing of the koyot stirred into life some birds, and Sander uncoiled his sling, made ready a pebble, brought down two of those fugitives. Once away, where he could light a fire, there would be food.

He headed directly for the distant line of forest, misliking the feeling of nakedness that he had in the open, a sensation the plains bred youth had never experienced before. As he rode, he tried to see traces of the path the voice had taken. But, save for the tracks near his improvised camp, Sander found nothing that would suggest he and Rhin were not alone.

Resolutely, he kept from glancing back at the now-distant village. Perhaps his visitor had returned there, since it was plain from the words they had exchanged that the unknown had been in search of those who had despoiled the town. What had the stranger named it? Padford. Sander repeated the word aloud. It was as strange as the accent of the other's speech.

Sander knew so little of the land beyond the Mob's own range. That such villages existed he had picked up from the Traders' guarded accounts. But the herdspeople of the wide lands in the west had no personal knowledge of them. He wished now that he had made a closer examination of the dead. It seemed to him, trying to recall those glimpses of the bodies, that they had been unusually dark of skin, even darker than he was himself, and that their hair had been of a uniform black. Among his own people, who were an even brown in skin color, hair color varied from light reddish gold to dark brown.

The Rememberers told strange tales, saying that before the Dark Time, men did not always share the same skin color or features. Their tales carried other unbelievable statements also—that men could fly like birds and traveled in boats that went *under* the surface of the water and not over it. So one could not believe every remnant of the supposed old knowledge they cherished.

Rhin abruptly halted, startling Sander out of his thoughts. The koyot gave a sudden shake of body, which was his warning that he must be free of his rider to confront something. Sander slid off as Rhin whirled about to face their back trail, his lips wrinkled to show his formidable fangs, the growl in his throat rising to a snarl.

Sander thrust his sling into his belt, whipped free his thrower, making sure there was a dart set within the firing groove. There were no stones to back them here. They had been caught in the open.

Plain to see were two shapes humping along with a curious up and down movement, at a speed Rhin could only equal by short bursts of determined flight. A third figure on two legs ran behind, like a hunter urging on hounds, though the two forerunners bore no likeness to any of the small dogs the Mob knew. Sander dropped to one knee, steadying the dart thrower. His heart beat faster. Those animals, whatever they might be, were remarkably agile, continually twisting and turning, yet always advancing. To sight a dart on one was almost impossible.

"Aeeeeheee!"

The cry came as sharp as the scream of a seabird, while the running figure behind the first two flung up both arms as if urging on its furred companions. It was that runner who must be his target, Sander decided.

"Aeeeeheee!"

The foremost of the animals halted and rose on its haunches to stare at the smith. A moment later its mate froze likewise. But Sander did not relax his grip of the dart thrower. The distance, he judged, was still a fraction too far for a telling shot. Rhin snarled continually. The koyot was already on the defensive, prepared for attack. It would seem that Rhin regarded these as formidable opponents.

The human companion of the pair drew level with them, so the three moved together toward Sander and the koyot. But they no longer ran. Sander rose to his feet, his weapon at the ready.

He stared at one of the strangest sights he had ever seen. The newcomer was plainly a woman, as her scant body covering revealed. Like the villagers, she had very dark skin, and her only clothing was a piece of scarlet cloth wound from armpit to knee. Around her neck rested a massive chain of soft, hand-worked gold, which held pendant a disc set with gemstones in an intricate pattern. Her dark hair had been combed and somehow stiffened, to stand out about her face like a halo of black. On her forehead was a tattooed design, much like the one Sander himself wore. But while his was the proud badge of a smith's hammer, hers was a whirl he could not read.

She wore boots that reached nearly to her knees, not as well-fashioned as the leatherwork of his own people, and a belt twisted of gold and silver wire from which hung, on hooks, a number of small cloth bags in different colors. Now she walked proudly, as if she were one to whom others paid deference, like a clan-mother, each hand resting on the head of one of the animals.

These were of the same breed, Sander believed, but they differed greatly in coloring and size. The larger one was creamy fawn in color. The smaller was dark brown with black feet and tail. Their long tails lashed back and forth as they came. It was plain to Sander that they did not have the same confidence in his harmlessness as their mistress did, for they were ready to do battle. Only her will kept them in check.

Some distance away she stopped, her dark eyes surveying him coolly. The animals once more reared on their haunches to flank her, the lighter-colored one's head now topping hers.

"Where do you go, smith?" she asked imperiously.

By the sound of her voice, he knew that this was his questioner of the night before.

"What matters that to you?" He was stung by her tone. What right had she to demand any answer from him in this fashion?

"The seeing tells me that our paths now run together." Her eyes were very bright. They caught his gaze. He did not like her calm assumption that he was some tribesman under her command.

"I do not know what a seeing may be." With determined effort he broke that linkage of eyes. "What I seek is my own affair."

She frowned as if she had not believed he could withstand her control any more readily than the hissing beasts by her side. That she *had* tried to control him in some unknown manner he was now certain.

"What you seek," she returned, a sharper note in her voice, "is the knowledge of the Before Men. That is what I must also find, that my people may be avenged. I am Fanyi, one who talks with spirits. And these be Kai and Kayi who are one with me where there is need. My protection lay over Padford, but it was necessary for me to go to meet the Great Moon. And while I was gone"—she made a slight gesture with her hand—"my people were slain, my faith to them broken. This should not be!" Her lips drew back in a snarl as marked as Rhin's. "The blood debt is mine, but for its paying I must draw upon the Before Ones. I ask you, smith, have you knowledge of the place you seek?"

He longed to say yes, but there was something in her gaze, which, though he would not allow it to bind him, compelled the truth.

"I am Sander. I seek one of the Before cities. Such may lie to the north along the sea—"

"A Traders' tale perhaps?" She laughed and there

was a note of scorn in that sound, angering him. "Traders' tales are not to be depended upon, smith. These seek always to deceive, not revealing what they deem their own hunting grounds. However, for once, this is partly right. To the north—and the east—there lies a great place of the Before Men. I am a Shaman— to us remains some of the ancient knowledge. There *is* a place—"

"To the northeast," Sander continued, "lies the sea. Perhaps your city is now buried under waves."

She shook her head. "I think not. The sea has eaten deep into the land in some places; in others it has drained from ancient beds, leaving land long hidden once more revealed. But," she shrugged, "of that we cannot be sure until we see. You seek, I seek—but in the end our quest is not too divided. I want knowledge of one kind, you of another, is this not the truth?"

"Yes."

"Well enough. I have powers, smith. Perhaps more potent than you carry in your hands." She glanced at the weapon he held. "But to fare forth into the wilderness alone, that is folly when we are traveling in the same direction. Therefore, I say to you—let us journey together. I will share my certain knowledge of where the Before Place lies."

He hesitated. But he believed that for some reason she was in earnest. Why she made such an offer he could not quite understand. She might have been reading his thoughts, for now she added:

"Did I not say that I had had a seeing? I know little of your people, smith, but have you none among you who can foretell, who can sometimes see that which has not yet happened but which will certainly come to pass?"

"We have the Rememberers. But they dream of the

past, not the future. The Traders—they have said that they have heard of those who foresee not backsee."

"Backsee?" Fanyi seemed startled. "What do they backsee, these Shamans of yours?"

"Some of the Before things, but only small pieces," Sander had to admit. "We came into this land after the Dark Time, and what they tell of is another part, now sea covered. Mostly they remember our own Mob and a past that is ours alone."

"That is a loss. Think what might be done if your backseers could uncover the lost things. But it is much the same with us who foresee—we can do such for only a short way. Thus, I know that we shall journey together, but little more than that."

She spoke with such authority that Sander found himself unable to utter any objection, though he was suspicious of her self-confidence. Obviously this Fanyi believed she was conferring some honor upon him by so deciding. Yet there was sense in what she said— he had been traveling blindly. If she indeed had some clue to a definite lost city, he would be far better served to agree to her guidance than to simply wander on blindly.

"Very well." He now looked at her beasts. "But do those agree also? They seem to me to be less certain of the wisdom of our joining forces than you are."

For the first time he saw her lips curve into a smile. "My friends become theirs. And what of your furred one, Sander-smith?" She nodded to Rhin.

Sander turned to the koyot. He exercised no such control on Rhin as the girl apparently did over her companions, nor could he. There was a form of communication between man and koyot, but it was tenuous. He was not sure himself just how deep it ran, nor how well it would work in all circumstances. Rhin was willing to share his travels and was an efficient warner against enemies. But whether the koyot would accept close companionship for days with the strange beasts, Sander had no way of telling.

Fanyi shifted her gaze slightly to meet the eyes of the taller of her furred ones. After their stare had locked and held for a long moment the creature dropped to forefeet and was gone at its backhumping gait, disappearing into the tall grass. Its companion remained quietly where it was, but Fanyi came forward now to turn the same intent gaze up into Rhin's bright eyes. Sander fidgeted, again more than a little irritated at the girl. What right had she to impose her will on his koyot, for that was what she was doing he was sure.

Again she might have read his rebellious thought, for she spoke:

"I do not rule these other ones, smith. It is enough that they learn that we can live together after a fashion, neither imposing wills upon another. My fishers know that if I halt their actions by a will-thought, it is only with good reason. And there are times when I accept their desire as quickly as they do mine. We are not master-slave. No—we are comrade with comrade. That is the way it should be with all life forms. So does the Power teach us who are born to serve Its purposes. Yes, your koyot will accept us, for he knows we mean no harm to one another."

The fisher who had disappeared was returning. Clamped in its jaws was the end of a bundle that it bumped and tugged along the ground until it could be dropped at Fanyi's feet. She loosened lashings to draw forth a square of drab cloth, which had a hole in the center. Through this she thrust her head and then belted the loose folds about her with a woven strip, hiding her scarlet garment and her adornments under the dim gray overtunic.

The rest of her equipment for the trip was in two

separate bags, their strings knotted together. Sander took them from her when she would have slung them across her shoulder and arranged them with his own bags on Rhin. He could not ride while she walked, and the two of them would be too great a weight for the koyot.

Fanyi whistled, sending the fishers bounding away, ranging ahead. For the first time Sander relaxed a little. Those creatures must form an effective scouting force, if Fanyi depended upon them.

"How far do we go?" he asked, finding that she matched strides with apparently little effort.

"That I do not know. My people do—did—" she corrected herself, "not travel far. They were fisherfolk, and they worked the fields along the river. We had Traders come from the north—and more lately from the south. From the south," she repeated and her tone was bleak. "Yes, now I think that those came before the raid to sniff out how helpless we were. If I had not been afar—"

"But what could you have done?" Sander was honestly puzzled. She seemed to believe that her presence, or the lack of it, had sealed the fate of the village. He could not believe that.

She glanced toward him, clearly astounded at his question.

"I am one with Power. It is my thought-holding that walled my people in safety. There was no danger that came to them that I, or Kai or Kayi, could not sniff out and give warning of. Just as I knew, even though I sought with open heart and mind the will of the Great Moon, when death came to those who believed in me! Their blood lies on my hands, that I must avenge—for upon me rests the burden of this deed."

"And how can you avenge them? Do you know those who came raiding?"

"At the proper time I shall cast the stones." Her hand went to the breast of her drab overgarment. "Then their names shall be made clear. But first I must find in the Before Place such a weapon as shall make those who delighted in slaughter wish that they had never been born!" A cruel cast twisted her generous lips and the grimness of her face chilled Sander.

He himself had never felt such great anger—even against Ibbets—as to death-wish another. When the White Ones had struck he had been only a child, too young to be affected by the battle, even though his mother had been one of its victims. His whole being had been focused on learning what he could do with his hands. To him, weapons were only matters of fine workmanship. He rarely thought beyond their fashioning to the uses they would eventually serve.

Although what he had seen in the destroyed village had sickened and revolted him, it had not touched his inner being. For those dead were strangers, none close to him. Had he discovered one of the enemy left behind through some chance he would have fought, yes, but mainly to save his own life. The flame that he saw burning in Fanyi, the implacable drive for vengeance, he could not quite understand. Perhaps if it had been his people who had been so handled, he would have felt differently.

"What weapons do you believe might be stored in a Before Place?"

"Who knows? The old tales are many. They say that once men slew with fire and thunder, not with steel or dart. It may be that such stories are only tales. But knowledge is a weapon in itself and such a weapon I have been born to use."

That Sander could accept. He discovered that he had unconsciously quickened pace a little, as if the very thought that such a storehouse of the Before Days might exist had urged him to speed. But they dared not, he was certain, count on too much. The churning of the earth during the Dark Time had changed the whole of the land. Could they be sure that anything from Before endured?

When he mentioned this, Fanyi nodded. "That is true. But still the Traders have their sources. And so there must be something remaining. I have this—" Both hands were now clasping her breast where the pendant lay hidden. "I am of a clan-line of Shamans. From mother to daughter, time and again past reckoning, has descended our learning. There are secrets that can be understood only when one is in the presence of that which hides them. What I wear is in itself a secret. Only I can read its message when I hold it in my hand. For no other will this charm work. I seek with it a certain wall—"

"And this wall lies northeast—"

"Just so. Long have I wanted to search for it. But my duty was to my people. Their ills, both of mind and body, were mine to ease. Now it is that same duty which drives me at last—so that I may repay blood for blood."

Her face became such a secretive mask that Sander ventured no more questions. So they journeyed in silence, the fishers playing scout, Rhin trotting at his shoulder.

At noon they halted, and Sander made a small fire while Fanyi stirred together some of the meal he had taken from the village, and moistened it with water from his leather bottle. She spread the resulting paste on a small metal griddle that she took from one of her own bags and set to bake before the fire. In a few minutes she deftly swept off a sheet of near-bread. Sander roasted the birds he had brought down while Rhin, stripped of riding pad and burdens, went hunting on his own. Fanyi said her fishers would do the same.

The fare was better than the dried fish he had eaten the night before. Fanyi held the water bottle to her ear and shook it vigorously.

"Water," she said. "That we shall need by nightfall."

Sander laughed. "Rhin shall find it. His breed does that very well. I have seen them dig into a bare streambed and uncover what no man would believe existed below. They come from a parched land—"

"Yours?"

Sander shook his head. "Not now, though it used to be. The Rememberers say we were all from the south and west. When the sea came in, all fled before it, even though mountains spewed fire from their bellies. Some men lived, and later Rhin's people came. They were small once, it is said. But who knows now— so much is told of the Before Time."

"Perhaps there are records." Fanyi licked grease from her fingertips, imparting to that gesture a certain fastidiousness.

"Marks like this—" She plucked a long grass steam and with its tip drew lines in the dust.

Sander studied her pattern. He thought he could see a certain resemblance to similar lines that Traders made on bleached skins when his father had described kinds of metal he wanted them to bring up on their next trip.

"See—this means my name." She pointed out the marks she had made. "F-A-N-Y-I— That I can write. And certain other words. Though," she added with truthfulness, "the meaning of all I do not know. But it was part of my learning because it is of my Power."

He nodded. The smith words were part of his learning, along with the work of his hands. The metal did not run nor harden nor work unless one chanted the right words—all men knew that. Which was why a smith allowed only his apprentice to be with him during certain parts of his labor—lest those without the right learn the work-words of his art.

"Even if you find such marks," Sander asked, "what if they cannot be read?"

She frowned. "That would be a mystery one must master, even as one learns the healing art and how the moon works upon men and women, how to call the fish, or speak with animals and birds. It is one of the Shaman learning."

Sander stood up to summon Rhin with a whistle. Shaman learning did not greatly interest him. And whether smith mysteries had ever been reduced to such markings—that he would not believe unless he saw them before his eyes. They were still a goodly distance from the forest, and he had little liking to camp out in the open another night.

He stamped out the last coals of their small cooking fire, kicking earth over the ashes carefully as any plainsman would. The fear of grass fires in the open was one danger that was more real in his mind than such raids as had been made on the village. He had seen the results of such devastation and known the horror of finding two clansmen who had been caught in such and died in the red fury no man could escape.

They plodded on. The fishers were not in sight, though Rhin had returned promptly at Sander's call to assume pad and bags. But Fanyi seemed unconcerned at the absence of her animals. Perhaps they always traveled so.

It was close unto evening when the trees loomed ahead behind a screen of brush. Sander came to a stop, for the first time doubting the wisdom of his choice. It looked very dark and forbidding under that spread of green that was already beginning to be touched by the flames of fall. Perhaps it would be best to stay in the open for tonight and enter in the morning, rather than blunder into such a gloomy unknown in the dusk.

"Where are Kai and Kayi?" he asked the girl.

She had been squatting on her heels and now she glanced up. "They go about their own concerns. I do not rule them, as I have said. This woodland," she pointed ahead with an uplift of her chin, "would be to their liking. They are not usually creatures of the open—but have a taste for trees."

Well, if that was the way of it, what did it matter to him? Still, the more Sander looked into that darkness ahead the less he wanted to enter it with only failing daylight to guide him.

"We will stay here for the night," he said, then worried if she would refuse his guidance.

"If you wish," was all she answered, as she got to her feet to lift her bags from Rhin's back.

Sander stripped the pad and his own bags from the koyot, and Rhin padded into the night for the food he would hunt on his own. Neither of the fishers had returned, and Sander began to wonder if Fanyi's control over the beasts was as complete as he had believed. But the girl showed no signs of concern as she slipped out of her drab overdress. The first flickers of the fire turned both her girdle and massive necklace into bands of glitter.

Once more she made the cakes of meal and set them to bake on the thin griddle. Sander checked his supply of darts carefully, for he wanted to enter the forest with a weapon ready. Then he gathered a pile of wood, a supply he hoped would last the night.

As she watched her baking, Fanyi began to croon to herself. The words were strange to Sander. Now and again he caught one that had a meaning, but the rest— it was as if she sang in some tongue that was hers alone.

"Have your people always been by the river?" he asked abruptly, breaking the somnolent spell of her crooning.

"Not always—what people has lived always in any land?" she asked in return. "Were we not all shaken, dispersed, sent wandering by the Dark Time? Our story is that we were on a ship upon the sea—driven very far, carried inland by the waters that swept the world. Many of those aboard died or were dragged away by the lick of the waves. But some survived. When the sea withdrew, their ship was left rooted upon land.

"That was in the days of Margee, who was mother to Nana, and Nana was mother to Flory, and she bore Sanna." Slowly she recited names, more than he could count as she spoke them, until at last she ended, "and I am true daughter to the fourth Margee. The ship's people met with others who wandered, and so was Padford born in the days of my grandmother's mother. Before that we had lived by the sea to the south. But we came north because of evil in that place, for suddenly there was a new mountain born, even as it was in the Dark Time. It spewed out fire and running rock so that all life must flee or be utterly eaten up. What of your people, Sander-smith?"

"We came from the south and west, as I have said. Our Rememberers know—but they are the only ones with such knowledge. I am a smith." He held his two hands into the firelight flexing their strong fingers. "My mysteries are not theirs."

"To each man his own mystery." She nodded as she swept the cakes deftly from the griddle and held one out to him. "It is said that the first Margee had the power of healing, and thus she taught those of her blood-line. But also we have other powers." She bit into the round of hot bread, her ornaments flashing with every movement.

"Tell me," she said after she had chewed and swallowed. "Why did you take out-rights, cutting yourself away from those of your blood-kin, to hunt what you may never find? Is it because you lost face when your people would not name you smith?"

Somehow she was able to compel the truth from him.

"I was tested and ready—my father would have spoken up if matters were otherwise. But Ibbets was his brother and long had wanted to be smith. He is good enough." Though Sander grudged saying that, he must admit it. "Yet he never seeks beyond what has already been done. I would learn more—why there are some metals that we cannot handle though the Before Men did, what were the secrets that they held that we have lost. My father knew that this lay in my mind, but he always said that a smith has a duty to his Mob. He must not go off a-roving, hunting that which may not even exist."

"When my father died, Ibbets made the council listen—saying that I was one with a head full of dreams, that I was too young and heedless to be a full smith. He"—Sander's lips tightened—"he generously offered to take me as apprentice. Apprentice! I who had been taught by a far greater worker of metal than he dreamed to be! He was jealous of my father, but in me he saw a way to make sure that the smith magic passed to him. Thus I took out-rights. Let me but learn every one of the Before secrets, and I can make Ibbets seem the apprentice!"

"And this is what you wish the most—to humble before your Mob the man who humbled you?" she asked, brushing her fingers together to rid herself of the crumbs of the bread.

"Not wholly that—I want also the smith secrets." The old longing came to life in him. "I want to know how they worked that they could do so much more than we. Were they truly so much greater in mind than we that such learning came easily to them? What we must seek so hard and long, did they know instantly? Some of the ignorant—my father claimed them so—speak now of men who learned so much that the Great Power thought to wipe them from the earth. Because they were evil they had to be melted down as one melts a collection of metal fragments to cast anew. Perhaps this may be so. But I seek to know what I can learn—"

"And your Rememberers were of no aid?"

Sander shook his head. "We were not a people who lived in the great cities. Rather we were scattered in a country that was left much to itself. We have always been herdsmen, traveling with our animals. Our Rememberers recall the churning of the country and that a handful of our people fled and survived with a few of our animals. But beyond that I have only my own clan-line teaching, for we are from a family of smiths and were not one with the Mob from its beginning. My first Man came out of the wilderness to join with those wanderers when they had already been roving for nearly a man's lifetime, fleeing ever from the loss of all they knew. What we have kept is not knowledge of the Before Time, but the skill to use our hands."

She sat with her legs curled under her, her fingers playing with the small bags that hung from her girdle. Now she nodded.

"Knowledge that was needful to keep life within the body, men held to that. But what lay beyond was often forgotten. I wish, however, that I might talk with your Rememberers. Much could be learned, even from unknown words that now lack meaning. Such words are many—we do not know for what they stand—things? actions?" She shook her head slightly. "So much lost. Even more will go with those ravening Sea Sharks." Now her rounded jawline set, and she looked bleakly into the fire.

"Life was good in Padford." She spoke as if assuring herself of the past, as if she were no longer aware he existed. "Our planted land grew wider each year. We did not have to depend alone on the bounty of the sea—which can fail at times—as first we did when we settled here. The Traders came in the mid-summer. Twice my mother bargained for books—real books—

those records which the Before Men kept. She read them—a little—and what she knew she taught me. We might have learned so much more, given the time." Her hand cupped the pendant on her breast.

"This was given her by him who fathered me. He came with the Traders, yet was not of their breed. Rather, he was a seeker of lost knowledge, journeying from a far place. He was making a book himself, recording all that he learned, for his clan was a clan of men wiser than any I have heard of. And he left this necklace so that, if my mother bore a child, that child might seek out the greater source of learning. He taught her its secret—" When she fell silent, Sander could not help asking:

"What became of him?"

"He died," she returned flatly. "A sickness and dire pain came upon him. He knew the secret of it—there was a part within his body that was diseased, that should be cut out. But my mother had no skill to cut to save. So he died. Then she swore by the Great Moon that when she bore a child, that child must learn and learn so that the old knowledge would be once more ready to serve her people. But she and I, we were bound to the kin, we could not go a-seeking such learning at our own will. We must be there to talk to the waters at the setting forth of the fishing boats and there to bless the sowing of the fields so that more grain would grow. Our blood line set these duties upon us. Now—I go to seek what this key will open." She still fingered the pendant. "But by the Great Moon, I would that my seeking had not come through such a means!"

The night had gathered in. Only their fire made a barrier against the crowding shadows. Sander stood up and whistled sharply, suddenly conscious that Rhin had not yet returned. When the koyot did not bark in answer, he was once more uneasy. Perhaps Rhin had to range far in the hunt. It was not unknown for him to sometimes spend half the night on his own. But in this unknown land Sander wished him closer.

"He is not near." The girl spoke calmly. "They have their own lives, do the furred ones. We cannot demand more of them than they willingly give."

"I do not like it," muttered Sander, though he must agree with her. His association with the koyot was a voluntary one on both their parts. To compel Rhin was to lose him. But he was unhappy now as he settled himself to a doze beside the fire, nodding awake now and then to feed a handful of wood to the flames.

The girl did not bed down as quickly in her day cloak. Instead, she took from one of those belt bags four small white cubes, each of their sides bearing dots. Smoothing out a hand-sized portion of her cloak, she tossed the cubes with a flick of her wrist, so that they tumbled onto the site she had prepared, and lay with one surface up. She bent over them eagerly, scanning the dots that were uppermost, and then frowned. Sweeping them up she tossed again. The result seemed to satisfy her no better, nor did a third try. Her frown was much deeper as she tumbled them back into her bag. She sat for a time staring into the fire, and Sander caught the faintest of mumbles, as if she now spoke words of her own Power, intended for her ears alone.

At last she gave a sigh and curled up in her cloak as if she had performed some necessary action but was not reassured by that. He thought that she slept. If she was as alarmed about the non-return of the fishers as he was about the missing Rhin, she gave no outward sign.

The koyot was not back when Sander stretched the stiffness from his limbs with the coming of light. He was thirsty, and a heft on the leather water bag told

him that it was too near empty. Rhin's instinct was
what Sander depended upon to locate some stream
or spring, and Rhin was not here. Of course, the
koyot could easily follow their trail as they traveled
on, but Sander wanted him now. Once more he
whistled. His call was answered, not by the short yelp
he hoped to hear, but rather with the screech of some
bird within the wood.

Fanyi sat up. She pulled from one of her own bags
a handful of dried, dark red fruit, which she divided
meticulously into two shares.

"Your furred one is not near," she said.

"And yours?" he demanded with unusual harshness.

"No nearer. I think they hunt in there." She pointed
with her chin at the wood. "As I said, they have a liking
for trees."

"Can they find water?" He shook the bag a little to
emphasize their need.

"If they wish." Fanyi's reply was calm enough to be
irritating. "But there are other ways. I know some of
them. It would seem we must now carry our gear
ourselves." She regarded the bags Rhin had borne.
"Well, that I have also done before." She spread out
her cloak and began wrapping in it the bags she had
brought, lashing them into a neat bundle.

Sander finished the dried fruit in two swift gulps.
The taste was tart, and the small portion came
nowhere near satisfying his hunger. He hoped that
somewhere in the forest facing them he could get a
shot at meat on the hoof. He needed the strength
of such a meal.

Now he made a back pack, using Rhin's pad for
its outer casing. The smith tools were the heaviest
items, and silently he fretted over the non-appearance
of the koyot. Rhin was a formidable fighter, he was
also fleet of foot. Foreboding pricked at Sander. They

had no knowledge of what might exist in this new country. He had no idea either of how he could trail the koyot and find him, if the animal had fallen into some peril.

The pack weighed heavily on his shoulders. However, he was determined to make no complaint, for the way Fanyi marched confidently ahead into the shadow of the trees was, in a measure, a challenge. Sander went forward with his bolt thrower ready in his hands.

The trees were enormous, with a huge spread of limb. Some leaves were already turning yellow or scarlet, a few wafted down now and then to join the centuries'-thick deposit of their kind under foot, a soft carpet that deadened the sound of their own passing.

For the first time Sander was conscious of something he had not foreseen. On the open plains one could fix upon some point ahead and have it as a guide. Here, with one tree much like another, how could one be sure one was heading in a straight path, not wandering in circles?

Sander stopped. Perhaps it would have been better to have stayed on the seashore, using that body of water for a guide. Fanyi paused and glanced over her shoulder.

"What is it?"

He was ashamed of his own stupidity, yet there was nothing he could do but admit it now.

"We have nothing to follow—this is all alike."

"But there is something. I have been a way in before, and there is a road—a north road—"

A road? Her confidence was such that he could not help but believe that she knew what she was doing. But a road—!

Fanyi beckoned, and, hesitantly, he followed. Already he could look back and see nothing but trees. Nor could he be sure where they had entered this maze

of trunks and low-hanging branches. But she showed
no bafflement.

And it was only a short time later that they came
out onto a more open space. Here the drift of leaves
and earth did not quite cover a surface badly holed,
fast being destroyed by creeping roots that attacked it
from both sides, yet unmistakably still an artificial
surface.

It ran straight, and the trees that framed or attacked
it were yet young, so there was enough light and
freedom to see quite a space ahead. Fanyi waved him
on.

"See? It is as I said. This was once a Before Road.
Much has been destroyed over the years, but still there
is enough to see. Here it bends"—she gestured left to
the west—"that way it comes, but from here it goes
north—at least what I know of it does."

Sander could trace the old curve; the road must
never have been in the open. He wondered why. It
seemed to him much easier to build such a highway
across the plains than within the grip of the woods.
And it was narrower than the two great roads the Mob
knew in their ranging. They had been so wide that even
the Rememberers were not able to tell how great the
armies of people must have been when they used such
ways.

The surface here was so rough they had to go slowly
and warily that they not be tripped up or catch an ankle
disastrously in some hidden hole. But the road did lead
them to water.

Sander had caught the sound of a stream before
they reached the jagged edge of the span that had
once bridged it. Small flies danced over the sun
dappled surface, those in turn hunted by much
larger insects. There was a swift current, but the
stream was so clear that he could see the fuzzy

brown stones forming its bed. Taking the water bottle and leaving his back pack with Fanyi, he scrambled down to rinse out the container, then fill it brimming.

Since the bridge was gone, they made use of some of its blocks, now green-slimed and water-washed, as stepping stones to reach the far side. Heartened by the discovery of water, their most pressing need, Sander began now to look around seriously for a method of relieving their other want, food.

There were birds enough, but they were small and flitted about, hidden, except for sudden flashes of wings, by the trees. He had seen no animals since they had entered this place. And though he watched the stream very carefully now, its glassy surface revealed no movement below. There appeared to be no fish sizeable enough to show.

Fanyi caught at his arm, nearly knocking him forward into the water. He turned his head to speak impatiently when the sight of her face startled him. She was so plainly listening!

Rhin! A burden heavier than he had been aware he had carried lifted from him. Sander pursed his lips to give the summoning whistle. But Fanyi's hand shot out, pressed fiercely across his mouth to silence him.

Now he strained his ears to catch what she must have heard, something, he guessed from her actions, that was a dire warning.

It was not quite sound, rather a pulsation of the air—as if sound had given it birth very far away. He pushed her fingers aside and asked in a voice hardly above a whisper:

"What is it?"

She was frowning, much as she had the night before when she threw her cubes to read some message from them.

"I do not know," she answered, in a voice even lower than his. "But it is of some Power. I cannot mistake that."

Of her vaunted Powers he knew practically nothing. Among his people they had a healer. But that one claimed nothing beyond a knowledge of how to set bones, treat wounds, and use some herbs to ease disease. They had also a vague idea that an Influence greater than themselves existed. But that It concerned itself with man was hardly probable. If so, why then had the Dark Time been sent to nearly kill off their species, unless Before Man had in some manner provoked a blood-feud with that Influence. If that was so, the Mob had reasoned during the few times they applied themselves to such speculation, it was now better for man not to appeal to or worship such an Influence.

Sander thought that it might be different with Fanyi. Some of her claims—such as farseeing—were matters strange to him. Also there could be other peoples on earth now, not so wary of the Influence, who might have made some pact with It. From such might come these Powers of which she so confidently spoke. Since this land was known to her, he was willing to be guided by her—up to a point.

"What kind of power?" he whispered once more.

She had gathered up her pendant, held it now cupped in her hand, and was staring into it as if she could read an answer from the points of light glittering on its surface.

As he waited for her to reply, Sander began to wonder if they were even closer to her legendary cache of knowledge, and if this emanation, whatever it might be, was the signal of its being. But whatever Fanyi thought, she was not pleased with what she learned by looking at the pendant. She shook her head slowly.

"It is not what we seek." Her words were decisive. "There is some darkness ahead of us. Yet this is the way—"

"We can go back," Sander pointed out. "It would be easier to go along the seashore. We should have tried that in the first place."

The wood, which earlier had been a promise of cover, now began to take on the semblance of a trap. He wanted none of it—rather to be out in the open where one could see an enemy approaching, even if one was equally naked to that other's sight. "Come on!" As she had earlier grasped his shoulder to rivet his attention, so now his hand closed about her arm.

She gave one more long look at the pendant and then let it fall back against her breast.

"All right," she agreed.

He had half expected an argument and was relieved that she surrendered to his will so easily. Perhaps Rhin's higher sensitivity had already warned the koyot against this place of trees, and that was why the animal had not joined them.

They recrossed the stepping stones and made the best time they dared, scrambling back the way they had come. Always now, Sander was aware of that distant beating. It seemed to him that his own heart thudded heavily in time to it, that he could feel its vibration throughout his body. Nor did it lessen as they fled. Rather it remained the same, as if whatever caused it kept always at the same distance behind them, slipping steadily along their trail.

It was when they reached the curve in the ancient road that the trap was at last sprung and from a direction Sander had not expected. As they passed beneath the wide-spreading branches of one of the giant trees, there fell over them the tangles of a net. Before Sander could struggle, it was jerked tight, entrapping him past any hope of freedom. The strings of the net were not the braided hide ropes he had always known. Rather they were coated with some sticky substance, which, once touched, clung tightly to what it covered. Movement on the part of the captives only wound them more completely in its fold.

He could not reach his knife, he could not even drop the useless dart thrower, which was glued now to his hands. A second sharp and vigorous jerk took him from his feet, landing him face down on the carpet of decayed leaves. He fought to turn his head enough so that his nose and mouth were not closed by that stifling muck and so caught a distorted side view of those who had so easily taken them captive.

The small creatures dropped from the tree branches, chattering, to aid those already on the ground. They were furred in patches and all they wore in the way of clothing were short aprons of woven vines. Fur grew along the outer parts of their arms and legs, in mats across their chest and shoulders, thicker yet on those bellies that bulged a little above the vine cords supporting their aprons. In contrast, their faces were smooth, but unlike the olive-toned skin showing on their hairy bodies, their faces were red and wrinkled.

Sander could understand nothing of their clicking speech, could detect no weapons save wooden clubs. He saw one of those just as it descended toward him. Pain exploded in his head felt as if the blow struck, but he did not altogether lose consciousness.

Still bundled in the net, he was being lifted. The sour body odor of the forest dwellers was sickening. They were grunting, perhaps in protest to his weight, as they carried him along. One must have noticed that his eyes were open and that he had some awareness of what was happening, for a forest man—if men they truly were—thrust his crimson face closer to Sander's and snarled. The stranger shook his club ominously directly above the captive. Sander needed no further hint. It would serve no purpose to allow himself to be beaten to a pulp here and now. Obediently, he lay quiet.

Trussed as tightly as the pack still on his back, Sander found himself pulled aloft. It appeared that their captors were creatures who considered trees their natural roadways. The smith was tense with foreboding as they swung him across wide expanses, sure that sooner or later he must crash helplessly to the ground beneath, while the pain in his head made him dizzy. At last he closed his eyes tightly, determined to hoard his strength for any effort he could make at the end of a nightmare journey.

That Fanyi suffered the same fate he had no doubt, yet he had heard no sound from her. Had they beaten the girl into unconsciousness before they whirled her thus aloft? It was plain that even if she knew something of the woodland, she had not foreseen the coming of these savages.

To Sander's half-dazed mind these were less than men. Nor were they to be numbered among those animals with whom men had established some rapport during the years. The snarling red face, which had been bent over him, had held a mindless ferocity mirrored in its small eyes, while the fetid smell that arose from those pulling him along made him gag.

They were, Sander knew, going deeper into the forest. And that vibration swelled within his body, so that his heart pounded as fast as if he had been running to the point of exhaustion. Not even the Traders had ever mentioned such as these.

Beat—beat—

It still was not a sound, save that it came with the

pound of his blood in his ears. Sander felt as if his
whole body shook with the force of each great blow—
if blows those were. The chittering of the forest
things—he did not want to dignify them with the term
"men"—grew stronger, much louder.

There came a final downward swing that ended in
a vicious jerk, sending pain red and hot through his
head. Then Sander lay flat on the ground in an open
place. The sun beaming harshly into his eyes made him
squint them shut again.

When he turned his head as far as he could and
cautiously opened his eyes again, it was just in time
to see the last of the hairy creatures swing upward into
the trees again on the other side of the clearing.

Had they left a guard? If not, was there any
way—? Sander squirmed within his casing of net. He
could wriggle a little on the ground, but none of the
lashings loosened. In fact, he was sure that they
were slowly tightening instead. However, his efforts
had moved him enough to catch a glimpse, through
the lashing that held her, of Fanyi.

There was no sign of any tree creatures. The
opening in which the prisoners lay was nearly covered
with a jumble of blocks. Paramount in the clearing was
a thing squatting upright on a heap of rocks.

It appeared to have been hacked out of wood,
crudely, but with enough skill to represent hazily one
of the tree people, enlarged three times. And it was
blatantly female. The ugly face was stained scarlet, and
necklaces of polished nuts and seed pods decked the
hunched shoulders. Squatting on its hams, its two hands
knuckle down on either side, its head pointed forward
as if it were looking down upon the prisoners with avid
interest.

Then—

One of those small, shiny eyes, which Sander had

thought an inset bit of colored rock, blinked. The thing was—alive!

Sander's mouth went dry. He could accept an image. But that this huge brute thing lived was true nightmare. The nightmare compounded when the vast mouth opened a little to show fangs, one cracked and broken. The tip of a pallid tongue issued forth like a loathsome worm.

The thing raised its head a little and hooted—a queer cry like that of some night-hunting creature. From the trees around, though they remained unseen, the forest things answered with a loud chorus of chittering cries.

Here was no resemblance to any speech Sander had ever heard, but it thrust fear into his heart. He could not fight the constricting net that crushed his back pack against him, constraining his limbs as if he were held in some giant vise.

"Aeeeeheee!" Fanyi burst forth with a rising scream. Sander had a dim memory of having heard it before. Yet he read into it no call for help, rather defiance.

The thing on the rock stopped hooting. It shuffled its paunchy body closer to the edge of its perch, swinging its head so that its small eyes regarded the girl. Then, almost negligently, it picked up a round rock lying close to hand and threw.

Only by a finger's breadth did the stone miss Fanyi's head. Sander believed that, had the creature wished, it could have smashed the girl's skull. The warning was clear. But if so, Fanyi was not heeding it.

"Aeeeeeheeee!" Once more she sent that call, which echoed faintly from the blocks.

Sander remembered now. So had she on the plain called to Kai and Kayi. Did she somehow sense that her companions were nearby?

The huge female grunted, sweeping out a hand

in search of another stone. Then she got lumberingly to her feet. Sander gasped. Even allowing for the fact that her perch was above the level of the clearing floor, she was tall enough to top him by far more than a head. Her ponderous body was that of a giant not only among her own kind, but his as well.

She descended the blocks slowly, as if she were not quite sure how stable they might be under her weight. When she reached the ground, she stooped to grab at Fanyi. Sander twisted frantically to free himself. He was sure he was going to witness some horrible act of mutilation or death.

But through the air, as if the fisher had borrowed wings, came Kai, a hissing scream issuing from his fanged jaws. The beast landed true, on the slightly bent shoulders of the giant female, his head darting forward toward her massive neck.

The forest female straightened with a hooting cry, tried to swing back her arms, tear loose the animal sinking its fangs in her flesh. Now the smaller Kayi appeared in turn, not leaping through the air, but streaking across the ground to clamp her teeth into one of those pendulous breasts.

Loud cries from the trees echoed the hoots of the giant. Sander expected to see the forest things drop from the branches to the rescue of their beleaguered female. Yet they did nothing but keep up their clamor as she stamped about, striving to pluck away her attackers. She loosened Kayi by tearing loose her own flesh still clamped in the fisher's jaws, flinging the animal from her. But when she sought to reach Kai again, the smaller fisher flashed in once more apparently unharmed by that rough handling.

Suddenly, a fountain of blood burst from the side of the giant's throat. Kai, worrying away, had severed an artery. The forest woman gave a last hoot and sank forward to her knees, while Kayi returned, to snap and tear at her body. She pawed feebly, trying to reach the creature on her back, and then slumped. Her terrible head came to rest upon a block like a mask of hideous death while a river of blood ran across the stones. The chittering of her people, still hidden in the trees, sank into silence even as she died.

The fishers backed away from the body, as if, since the death of the giant, they found the scent and taste of her torn flesh noisome. Sander waited, expecting that unseen audience in the trees to burst down upon them, clubbing both animals and the helpless prisoners. He and Fanyi might have escaped whatever particularly grisly fate the giant female planned, but they had certainly not won their freedom.

That beat had stopped. Sander was no longer aware of it. But he could hear rustlings and movements in the trees and braced himself for a final attack. When that did not come, he grew even more apprehensive, fearful that they might not be killed at once by the forest creatures, but rather be the victims of some crueler and more prolonged fate.

The fishers crouched by Fanyi, their heads up and turning from side to side as they kept their attention fixed on the trees. Fierce as the animals had shown themselves to be in that surprise attack, Sander thought they would be helpless as Fanyi should the tree men use their nets.

Moments passed. He could no longer even hear movement overhead. The sun beat down hotly in the clearing and the smell of death was strong.

"They are gone." Fanyi broke the waiting silence.

"What?" Sander tried to raise his head higher to catch a glimpse of what might lie beyond the curtain of the leaves.

"They have gone," she repeated.

Perhaps they might have for now. But that did not free their captives. The constriction of the ropes binding him was now a torment, as his awareness turned toward his own condition and away from the menace of the giant.

"Lie still," Fanyi said now. "I have heard of these vines. There is an answer to them also. But be still—let me try to make Kayi understand what must be done."

He could not move at all now, and his fear took another form—that the continued constriction of the rope would slowly cut his body to pieces, crush his back with the weight of his own pack and its smith tools. There was nothing he could do but *be* still, whether at her orders or not.

The heat of the sun on his face brought back the pain in his head, and he longed for water, for the easement of his bonds. Kayi had crouched by the girl, muzzle nearly touching Fanyi's face. They were utterly quiet as they matched stares with one another.

Meanwhile Kai prowled about the clearing, stopping under each tree to gaze upward, as if in search of more prey. Now and then his body, large as it was, was hidden behind some of the blocks. Twice the fisher reared his length against a tree trunk, peering up, his head swinging a little right and then left, as if he sought by scent what he could not see.

Sander looked back to Fanyi and Kayi. The fisher shuffled away from the girl and deliberately dabbed one forepaw and then the other into the pool of blood that had dropped from their dead enemy. With the same care she then scraped her claws into the earth so that loose dust adhered to them.

Thus prepared, she came back to Fanyi and set her filthy claws within the bonds of the net, plainly using her full strength as she strove to tear the mesh.

It was necessary for her to make many trips to recoat her claws against the sticky surface of the ropes. But each time she returned to her task. Sander had some lapses from consciousness. The pain in his head, the steady pressure on his back caused blackouts, and he did not know how long they lasted. He expected the forest creatures to return at any moment, and now he no longer cared. Finally he passed entirely into that dark world which had been lapping at him.

He awoke, choking a little, liquid spewing from his mouth. Then, still not quite aware, he swallowed painfully once and again, as more water was dribbled between his dry lips. But he could breathe, the pain in his back was no longer constant. He shifted and knew that he was free from the net. Fanyi leaned above him, pouring the water a few sips at a time into his mouth.

"We—" His voice sounded fuzzy and far away.

"Can you move?" she demanded. "Try! Can you sit—stand—?"

Her urgency reached him only dimly through the haze that wrapped about him. But obediently the smith dragged himself up to his knees, then, with her tugging at him, lurched to his feet.

The sun no longer baked them so fiercely, but they were still in the clearing and the giant's body—Sander averted his eyes hastily.

"Come!" Fanyi pulled at him until he staggered a pace or so ahead. Then he stopped, swaying.

"My tools!" The first truly coherent thought struck him. He would not abandon all that belonged to his past.

"Kai brings them!" the girl snapped impatiently. "Come!"

The male fisher was lumbering along, dragging Sander's pack, jerking at it when it caught against the edge of a block or the branches of a bush. And since Sander doubted if he could stoop to reclaim it and then keep going, he had to be content.

He wavered on, glad to feel strength return as he went, even though the torment of renewed circulation accompanied the motion. His mind began to clear also.

"The tree things—" He strove to find words for his ever-present foreboding.

"They have not returned—I do not know why," Fanyi admitted. "Unless when the fishers slew their great woman they were so in fear that they will not face Kai or Kayi again. Still they may come hunting. But the furred ones will not let them reach us without warning this time."

"Where do we go?"

"There is a path," she replied. "It leads right—eastward. I think we are safer heading for the sea than trying to return through the forest."

To that he agreed. Fanyi had been carrying his dart thrower, now she pressed it back into his hold.

"This is your weapon; have it ready. We know not what manner of revenge these beast-things may plan."

He took it eagerly. If she was right and the fishers could warn them of any future attack by the net, then they would have a chance. He had seen no weapons other than the clumsy clubs.

Since he could now walk alone, Fanyi moved a little ahead, her own pack firmly against her shoulders, Kayi bounding with her, while the larger male formed their rear guard. Sander found himself listening.

The beat, which was more vibration than sound, had been silenced. The whole woods was quiet now, too—no more twittering of birds or other hints that any life beside their own had even ventured under this green roof. It was only then that Sander caught, faint and seemingly from very far away, a yelp he knew. Rhin!

But if the koyot trailed them into this deadly tree trap, he might well be netted as they had been! And Sander had no way of warning the animal not to venture here. Or had he?

The smith paused, drew breath deep into his lungs, and then uttered a cry that bore no relation to the whistle that usually summoned Rhin. Instead this was a deep-lunged yowl—the war call of the great mountain cat. Whether Rhin could catch his meaning he did not know—he could only hope.

Both fishers whirled to face him, snarling. Fanyi's surprise was open. Twice more he sounded that cry, thinking that the desperation which had set him to mimic it had indeed this time produced almost the proper timbre.

"Rhin," he explained. "He must not come and be caught. That is the cry of an old hill enemy. But perhaps unlike it enough in his ears to be a warning."

The girl nodded, already again pushing on. Sander could see that what she called a path must once have been a road. Perhaps not as wide a one as they had followed earlier, but still having remains of paving. Those tumbled blocks back in the clearing—now that he thought about them he believed that they were too regular in outline to be a natural outcrop. Perhaps they had also been set in place by man for some reason.

To his relief Sander now saw that the forest growth was getting thinner. And he caught a murmur that he fiercely hoped was the sound of distant surf. Let them get out into the open on the beach and they would be safe enough—there could be no overhead attack launched there.

They quickened pace. Now the smith felt strong enough to catch up his pack and sling it back across his shoulders as they thudded along. There were blocks of stone poking through the lighter brush. More buildings once? He did not know or care—to get into the open was the important thing.

The growth of trees became much lighter. Bushes, tall grass, and heaped stones formed barriers around and over which they had to make their way. The fishers flowed along easily while the humans had a more difficult time of it.

Open sun again—but now well down the sky. And the sea! Sander stood on the top of one block he had had to climb, making sure of that. And running along the sand, which spurted out from under his pads as he came, was Rhin! The koyot startled the shore birds, which arose with shrill cries; then his yelp sounded loud and clear.

They pushed through a stand of stubborn briars, and sand crunched under their boots. The fresh air of the beach blew away the last vile memory of the haunted woods. Rhin reached them, nosing at Sander delightedly, then growling a little, as he must have scented either the forest savages or their nets. His ears pricked toward woods as he growled again more deeply.

"Not now!" Sander told him joyfully. "We're free!"

They had no wish to linger too close to that dark stand. Instead, they turned north again, this time keeping to the beach where one could see for miles anyone or anything that might come.

"Who—or what—were they?" Sander asked that night when they made camp among the dunes, with a cheerful fire of driftwood cooking the crabs Rhin had pawed from sand holes. "Have you seen or heard of them before?"

"The tree men?" Fanyi was repacking her bag, having searched carefully through it as if she feared that some of its contents had suffered from rough handling. "I do not know. I think they must be new-come here, for my people have gone nutting in that wood each autumn and never before have we found such. You ask 'what'—do you then believe that they are not in truth men?"

"I do not know. To me, they seemed closer to animals, lesser than Rhin or your furred ones. And why did they serve a giant?"

"There were many strange changes in both man and animal during the Dark Time. My father," her hand cupped the pendant again, "he had knowledge of such changes. He told my mother some animals now moved toward the estate of men. Perhaps it is also true then that some men were dropping backward into animals. These forest people are less even than the Sea Sharks—though perhaps they are fully akin in spirit." That fierce light was again in her eyes when she spoke of the enemy who had wiped out Padford. "I think that we were intended as an offering to placate their female."

Sander did not shiver, but he would have liked to. What might have happened had not the fishers come to their rescue? He did not care to dwell upon that. He noticed that this night neither Kai, Kayi, nor Rhin roamed away from the fire, but were settling down close to its light. Perhaps, they, too, were affected by the strangeness of this region, sensing a menace that lay just below the surface.

He suggested that they watch in turn, being sure to keep the fire lit, and Fanyi agreed at once. But she pressured him into taking the first rest, pointing out that his heavy pack had been such a hazard to him in the shrinking net that he had suffered more than she. And, although he would have liked to argue the question, her good sense made his pride seem childish.

When she aroused him, the night had closed in. Rhin lay with his head pillowed on his forepaws, his eyes yellow slits of awareness as Sander went to feed the fire. The fishers were curled into two furry balls, and Fanyi settled herself in a sandy hollow by them.

Above, the stars were very bright and clear, and the ceaseless wash of the waves lulling. Sander got to his feet, motioning Rhin to lie still when the koyot at once raised his head. He walked a little down the beach, gathering more driftwood, feeling too restless to remain still. As he started back, he faced toward that black shadow marking the edge of the woods. Had the forest men come slinking after them? Would those leave the trees to hunt down the slayers of their—what had she been: a chief, mother of the tribe, even a supernatural figure with supposed powers of a Shaman? They would never know. Only that she had had no common heritage with either Fanyi or him, that she had been farther removed from their blood-kin than even the furred ones.

This might be a world of many surprises. It would be best that from now on their party should move with great care, accepting nothing as harmless until it was proven so.

He tramped back to the fire and fed in some wood. Rhin's eyes closed when he saw Sander settle down. Fanyi lay, breathing evenly. In sleep her face looked very young, untried. But she was not. He owed his life to her or at least to her furred ones. Somehow that idea was one he did not altogether like. *He* had blundered around like an untried boy on his first herd ride. There was little for him to be proud of in this day's work.

Frowning, he pulled his tool bag to him, drawing forth the tools, examining them one by one. The two hammers he had found in Padford—those ought to be fitted with proper handles. But there was nothing here except driftwood, and the strength of that he did not trust. When he had time, he would search out some proper wood and see them shafted again. He thought they would have excellent balance, once they were ready for use.

Now he wondered about the man who had used them. What manner of smith had served Padford? He would like to ask Fanyi. But he thought it better not to call to her mind any thought of her people and their doom.

That made him think in turn of what she sought— some weapon out of the Before Time, one potent enough to wipe out those raiders from the south. Did such exist still? He doubted it. But that Fanyi did have knowledge of some hidden place, that he did not doubt.

Metal—

He thought of copper and gold and silver and iron— those he knew, could fashion to obey his will. But the others—the strange alloys that no man now held the secret of—if he could master those also! His hand curled about the broken handle of the large hammer he had found, and a kind of restless eagerness filled him so that he longed to get up at this very moment and run—run to find the secrets Fanyi promised existed somewhere.

He must discipline his too vivid imagination. Fanyi's idea of what she sought was very vague. He must not count on good fortune until he met it face-to-face. Slowly Sander repacked the tools and knotted their bag. It was good fortune enough this night that they were still alive.

For two days they plodded among the dunes. Save for the birds, shellfish and crabs they foraged for, this land might have been bare of any life. Far to the west showed the dark line of the forest. Between them and it was a waste in which little grew but tough grass in scattered clumps and some brush twisted by the salt winds into strange shapes.

On the third morning they reached an even stranger desert land. The sea, too, now curled away to the east, so what they faced was a slope leading downward into territory that had once been covered by ocean but was now dry land. Here rocks had necklaces of long-dead shellfish, while brittle carcasses of other sea life lay half-buried around outcrops of wave-worn stone.

Sander wanted to alter their path westward—hoping to skirt this desert. But Fanyi hesitated, her eyes again on her pendant, in which she seemed to trust so deeply.

"What we seek lies there!" She pointed straight ahead, out into the sea-desert.

"How far?" countered Sander. He had little liking for the path she suggested.

"I cannot say."

"We must be more sure. To go out there—" He shook his head. "We have finished the last of the meal. Even crabs and shellfish will not be found there. Though we filled our waterskin at the pool among the dunes this morning, how long think you that supply will last?"

"And if we turn west, how many days may we be adding to our journey?" she countered.

He surveyed what lay to the west. The beach land they had been following narrowed to a cliff barrier, on which he could see trees. To return to any wood after their experience—no, not if there were a way to avoid it. But he had to have some assurance that they were not heading into nowhere without a better guide than Fanyi's vague directions.

True, he could sight some grass and a few bushes that had rooted out on the old sea bottom. It was not quite so desolate as he had first believed. And there were rocks in that uncovered landscape that would provide them with landmarks, so that they need not wander in circles once they were out of sight of this land that had once been the shore.

"A day's journey," he conceded. "Then, if we find nothing—return."

The girl seemed hardly to hear him, though she nodded. Now she allowed the pendant to drop again and surveyed what lay ahead with an eagerness obviously not lessened by any forebodings.

Rhin trotted confidently along. But the fishers prowled back and forth, venting their displeasure by hissing, following the others only when Fanyi coaxed. It was very apparent that they, at least, had no liking for this open country.

For a space, the bottom was sandy and fair walking. Then there began a gravelly stretch studded with many water-worn stones. This footing shifted and turned under any weight. The land they left must have formed, Sander deduced, one arm of a great bay in the Before Days.

Sun shone through a huge upstanding fence of wide-spaced rib bones belonging to some sea creature, or perhaps they were the timbers of a ship so overlaid with the bodies of shelled things that all that remained was as if turned to stone. Sander was not sure which.

The sea-desert was not evenly floored, for there were hillocks and dips. In the hollow of one small valley they came upon a little pool ribbed with white salt, perhaps a last remnant of the lost sea.

On and on; now that Sander glanced back he could hardly see the true land from which they had come. And his doubt concerning the wisdom of traveling in this direction grew in him. There was a kind of rejection here—as if the life he represented was resented, even hated by the ancient desolation.

At length, they reached a deep cut and looked down its rugged sides. Below flowed a river. How to cross? The fishers were clambering down the side, heading for the water below. He and Fanyi might also do that, but Rhin could not. They would have to go off course—west again, even farther out into the desert, hoping to discover a place where there was an easier crossing.

The river solved one of their problems, however, for Sander saw the fishers dipping their muzzles into the stream, obviously drinking sweet water.

They trudged along the edge of that gorge. Sander's hope was proven right, the rock walls began to sink down while the river widened. They detoured around masses of encrusted objects that he thought were ships, to come at last upon something else, the remains of a wall of massive blocks, which were far too regular in pattern to be the work of nature. Beyond that were other stones that might have once marked the beginning of a road, as well as two great fallen columns, all so overlaid with sea growth that it was plain they were very old, perhaps even old when the Before Time had begun. He marveled at the work, and Fanyi traced along the edge of a block with her finger tips.

"Old—old—" She marveled. "Perhaps there was

even another Dark Time when the world changed to bring in the same sea that our Dark Time drove out. If we only knew—" There was a wistfulness in her voice that he could well have echoed.

They dared not linger to explore what the ancient sea had concealed, pushing on resolutely to where the river now flowed out to the sea, well away from the Before shore they had followed.

Dusk found them on the new seashore, so once more they camped by the sound of beating waves. Here, too, was driftwood enough for a fire. And the fishers, who had followed the river, came into camp each dragging a large fish. Fanyi hailed their catch, a delicacy her people knew but were seldom able to eat.

As the fish broiled on sticks before the fire, Sander leaned his back against a water-worn stone and stared out over the river. There was a current to be sure. But with the bed so much wider and shallower here, he thought they could gain the other side in the daylight without too much exertion. Then following it westward once more they could also depend upon water as long as they paralleled its flow. Though the river had taken them far off the course Fanyi had set, perhaps it was not to be counted a major difficulty after all.

Fanyi laid out a pattern of small shells. "It is a wonder of the sea, Sander-smith, that no two of these is ever quite the same. The shape may be alike, yet the markings—there is always some slight differing. There are some the Traders prize, and those will buy a length of copper wire, even a lump of rusted iron, which still has a good core. I—"

But what she would have said Sander never knew. He had been watching Rhin. Now he made a swift gesture with one hand and reached for his dart thrower. The koyot bristled, his lips drawn back to show his teeth, his eyes near-slits.

Sander listened intently. Fanyi crouched by the fire her hands resting on the backs of Kai and Kayi, who were also hissing softly.

Now came a splashing—from the sea or the river? Sander could not be sure just which direction. Rhin growled again.

"A fire torch!" Sander half-whispered to Fanyi.

Instantly she caught up a thick branch of the driftwood, thrust one end into the flame. When that branch caught, she whirled it around, to make the flame-blaze glow. With that in hand, before Sander could stop her, she clawed her way to the top of one of the large stones, swinging her improvised torch outward.

He scrambled up to join her, a dart laid ready to shoot. A croaking sound came from out of the dusk. Then the light of the torch caught a dark figure standing on the edge of the river, its body glistening as if it had just crawled out of the flood.

The thing stood like a man, erect upon its hind limbs. But for the rest—this was not even as human as the forest men had seemed. Pallid skin hung in folds about its torso, while its upper and lower limbs looked flat. It had a great gaping mouth from which issued the croaking, and above the mouth were bulbous eyes. But—

Around its middle was a strip of something that appeared to be scaled hide. Into that were thrust two long, curved, deadly-pointed lengths that might have been fashioned, Sander thought, of bone, not metal.

"Do not shoot!" Fanyi cried out. "It is afraid. I think it will go——"

Even as she spoke, the thing took a great leap backward, sinking into the river. The flame of the torch did not reach very far, so it was almost instantly out of sight as it swam.

"Fire—it does not like the fire." The girl spoke with conviction, as if she had, in those few seconds of confrontation, been able to read the water thing's mind.

Rhin passed below them, racing to the edge of the river, howling madly at the swift-flowing surface. It was plain the koyot had made up his mind that the river dweller was dangerous.

If they were to cross the river to continue their journey, Sander thought, they must plunge into the water in which the thing was clearly at home. He did not like the prospect that faced them with the coming of daylight.

"What was it?" Since this land was more Fanyi's than his, he turned to her for enlightenment. She shook her head.

"Again—such a creature I have not seen before. But there are tales that once something from the sea came and broke the nets at Padford, taking also fishermen who were unwary. It was after a great storm and the water turned red. It stank and so many fish died men had to burn them in great heaps upon the shore. Later there was no more trouble. But that was in my mother's mother's time, and none saw clearly the sea things. It was thought that they had some intelligence—for the nets were slashed where the cutting would do the most harm."

"It"—Sander slid down to sit on her perch—"the thing did not look much like a man."

"The creature is a water thing," she agreed. "Listen!"

Above the wash of the sea waves, the gurgle of the river, they caught a sound, though distant—a croaking. Was the visitor they had sighted only the scout of a larger party? Perhaps for them to remain near the river was folly. Still Sander hesitated to move out into the dark.

In the end they decided that, with the fire and the

sentry service of Rhin and the fishers, they might stay
where they were. As Sander improvised a second torch
to aid in hunting more wood, Fanyi brought from one
of the belt pouches a thick rod about the length of her
own palm. She turned the bottom of it firmly to the
right and then touched a place on its side. Straightway
there flashed the light that had transfixed him on their
first meeting.

"This is a Before thing," she told him with pride of
ownership. "It was also my father's. But he said that
it has limited life and after a while it will die. However,
now we can use it to advantage."

Sander shook his head. "If it will die, then it should
be saved for a time of greater need. Since you say these
water things fear fire, fire we shall use."

With Fanyi holding a torch he made a harvest of
driftwood from some distance on either side of their
camping place, piling pieces high, hoping this would
last the night. The fire itself—unless there was warning
of the water dweller's return—they would keep low.

Once more they divided the watch. This time neither
the fishers nor Rhin relaxed into deep slumber. Rather
they dozed, rising at intervals to pad out into the
darkness where Sander believed they were making
rounds of the camp.

He himself listened for croaking. However, it had
died away. Even when it was his time to rest, he kept
nodding awake to listen and watch the fire.

With the morning he went down to the river, carefully judging the chance of crossing at this point. Fanyi
insisted that what she sought lay beyond, north and
now a little west. If they returned to land, retracing
all the way they had covered yesterday, they would still
have the river to cross in order to reach their goal, and
it could well be patrolled, even back to the edge of
the inner country, by the water creatures.

Therefore, dare they attempt to cross here and now?

The river current cut sharply into the new sea. Sander did not like the way pieces of wood he threw to test the strength of that current were whirled so swiftly past.

Secondly, he gauged the river depth with a long piece of wood. Close to the shore he thought it about thigh-high. Beyond that, he believed they might have to swim. And they would have to fight the current also in order not to be swept out to sea.

This meant going back upstream for a distance to allow some leeway. He knew the rivers of the plains. But, except in the spring when they were in spate, none of them had ever presented such a problem as this.

"Can you swim?" he asked Fanyi, when she joined him. His own prowess, he knew, was nothing to boast of. But at least, he thought, he could keep himself afloat by his efforts long enough to reach the other bank. Always providing their visitor of the night before, or his fellows, did not arrive to make things difficult.

"Yes, and you?"

"Well enough to cross this."

"It will be better"—the girl echoed his own thought—"to cross here, I think. If we return we shall lose much time, and it may be more difficult farther back than easier."

They prepared for the attempt as well as they knew how. Their bags were lashed high and tight on Rhin's back; they stripped off their clothing to add to the burdens on the koyot. Staff in hand, Sander gingerly stepped into the water. The flood was chill and his flesh shrank from it. The tug on his body grew stronger as it crept upward from his thighs to his middle. Cautiously he probed the bottom ahead for a possible quick drop in footing that might be disastrous. Rhin plunged in beside him, a little downstream, and Sander

could hear a loud splashing behind that told him Fanyi
and her companions were following.

He had taken the precaution of bringing a hide rope
from his stores. This was anchored to Rhin's back pack,
then looped around Sander's waist, the other end in
turn knotted to Fanyi's belt.

Now the water was shoulder high, and he had to
fight to keep upright in it. A sudden slip of his pole
left him threshing without footing. Choking and
sputtering, he began to swim clumsily. Within moments
his body brought up against Rhin's. The koyot fought
to keep his own way, as both of them were borne
downstream.

Fear grew in Sander. What if they could not break
the hold of the current? Before starting, he had given
Fanyi strict orders that, if he and Rhin were overborne,
she was to slash the rope that looped them together
so she would have a better chance for herself. However, the pull was still taut because she had not done
so.

Rhin swam lustily, and Sander made some way
beside the koyot, not daring to try to see how much
closer to the sea the current had already dragged them.
He floundered on, feeling as if he were as much
entrapped now by the water as he had been by the
forest net.

Finally the koyot found footing and plunged up and
on. Sander swiftly linked a hand in the rope making
fast the load the animal carried. A moment later one
of his feet grazed an underwater rock painfully, and
he scrambled on until he could rise once more.

Keeping that hold on Rhin, he splashed and fought
his way up the opposite bank. The rope about his
middle was so taut as to nearly jerk him backward. He
slewed around and caught at it with both hands,
fighting to pull it in.

Down in the river, Fanyi's arms flashed into the air and disappeared again. Already she had been carried a little past the point where Sander and Rhin had found footing. Sander nudged the koyot with his shoulder, so that the animal added his strength to the pull.

By their combined efforts, Fanyi's body curved around in the stream. She was at last being drawn up current toward them. Before Sander had time to think what might have happened if they had failed, she waded ashore, her mass of hair water-slicked against her head.

Down the bank toward them flashed the fishers. Of the whole party, they had made the smoothest crossing. Now they paused to shake their bodies furiously, sending drops flying in all directions. But Rhin had swung around to face the river, and he snarled.

Sander caught sight of V-shaped ripples cutting the surface of the water. He jerked the rope that still linked him with Fanyi.

"Come on!"

He began to run, pulling the girl along with him, very conscious of his present defenseless state. Rhin trotted abreast of them, but the fishers played rearguard, snarling at what traveled in the depths of the flood.

Sander did not pause until they rounded some blocks of stone that gave him a momentary sense of safety. Then he wriggled free the dart thrower from the burden Rhin bore, loosening the ropes in the process to leave the koyot also stripped for action.

Scrambling on Rhin's back, he climbed from it to the top of the tallest rock. There he lay flat, to survey the back trail. By the morning light he had a clear view. Out of the water trooped a number of the same creatures as the one they had sighted before. There were perhaps a dozen of them, though they presented a slightly different appearance from the first one, as each wore over his body—or its body—a rounded carapace that might have been fashioned from some outsize shell. Their round heads were covered in the same fashion, and there were even plates strapped about the arms and legs. They had certainly come armored and ready to do battle.

Their weapons were long spears bearing wicked-looking barbed heads, designed, according to Sander's craft-wise eyes, so that the barbs would break off in a wound. Their croaking sound was more hollow, perhaps because of their helmets, but they kept up a continual chorus as they hopped forward.

Although if they were river dwellers, they were able to handle themselves on the sea-desert, for they did not hesitate to advance. The fishers did not close on them instantly as they had with the forest people. Instead, Fanyi's beasts wove back and forth, just out of spear range, threatening and hissing, yet retreating warily.

Sander took careful aim and fired. His dart struck home, but was partly deflected by a sudden shift of his target, so that it lodged in the shell near the "shoulder" of the creature, but missed the vulnerable patch between chest shield and helmet.

Still his attack appeared to shake the enemy strangely. They ceased advancing and bunched. The one who had been his target worried at the dart shaft until he worked it out of his shell covering. Then he held the weapon up as if considering it unique. Their hollow croaking grew stronger, sounding agitated. Or was that only wishful thinking on his part, Sander wondered?

He had already set another dart in the groove. But the river creatures offered such small unprotected areas that he dared not fire again until he was sure of better success. Fanyi, once more clothed, stretched out now beside him. Her hand covered his on the stock of the thrower.

"Let me hold them while you dress," she urged. "Under this sun your skin will burn badly if you do not."

Sander could already feel the heat of the sun. But to leave his post to her—

"Go!" She nudged him hard with her shoulder. "I have used such weapons as this before." There was an angry note in her voice, as if she resented his hesitation.

The competent way she handled the weapon was evidence that she spoke the truth. He laid three more darts on the stone, then half tumbled down to dress.

Back again on the rock's crest, he discovered that the fishers had withdrawn to the edge of the "wall" on which he and the girl lay, while the river creatures had apparently recovered from their surprise over the dart and were determinedly crossing the sand and gravel toward them. The creatures hopped rather than walked in men's fashion, yet they were not slow.

Just as Sander joined her, Fanyi fired. The leader of the water pack dropped his spear. With a loud croak of dismay, he dangled his "hand," a webbed member with four equal-length digits. The dart had pierced that to form another finger set at an angle.

Once more the enemy bunched to examine their fellow's hurt. Sander wondered at tactics that seemed stupid to him. These amphibians were well within range of the weapon, yet they gathered around their wounded fellow, interested only in what had happened to him rather than the party on the rocks. The creatures' seeming disregard of any counterattack by the besieged was puzzling. Perhaps, having spears for weapons, they could not understand a dart that came out of the air. They might even be so stupid or of such an alien way of thought that they did not connect those darts with the party they attacked.

As Fanyi surrendered the thrower to him, she also offered some advice.

"Do not kill unless you are forced to. Death might excite them to vengeance."

"How do you know that?" Sander demanded.

"I do not know—no, rather, it is that I cannot find words to explain." She seemed as puzzled now as the river creatures were over the dart. "It is just as I know what my furred ones think and feel. They are disturbed—they fear. But I believe that they can be roused by hate so that their fear will be smothered. Then they will not care how many of them die if only they can reach us. Now—they are of two minds, they half-believe we are such as they cannot profitably hunt."

Sander could not quite accept that the girl knew this for certain. She must be just guessing. Yet he did not loose any darts even at targets that were tempting. He would wait out this present round of the enemy's croaking to see what they would try next.

N ow that Sander had time to examine more closely their own temporary refuge, he noticed for the first time the continuity of the blocks of stone on which they rested. This, too, must be some very ancient work of intelligent beings. The sun beat down so fiercely that he squirmed back and forth across the surface on which he lay. To linger here was to invite another kind of disaster.

The party of water creatures moved at last. Two hunched down, holding their spears straight up in the air. The others, including the one with the dart-transfixed "hand," hopped toward the river.

Sander slipped down. The time to move was now. He guessed that the enemy had gone for reinforcements. And he was sure they themselves could handle the two remaining, if they were trailed on into the desert.

Fanyi agreed to his suggestion. She had been standing, her pendant once more in hand, turned north-west, gazing back along the course of the river down which they had traveled the day before.

"We shall have to stay away from the river," Sander cautioned. "Water is their element, and they will make the most of it." Luckily he had filled his bottle this morning before they had crossed the stream. Only, as he surveyed the shimmering heat of the sea-desert, he regretted that there was not a second or third vessel to sling with their gear.

On the other hand, the bare expanse of sand and stone, open to the full rays of the sun, ought to daunt the water people. If they were indeed the amphibian race he judged them to be, they would not choose willingly a long excursion over this scorched land.

In fact, Sander decided, as he examined the territory ahead with narrowed eyes, it might be well if they themselves chose to travel more cautiously. He was well trained in his people's way of herding under the night stars, using those distant points of light for a guide. At night also they would have fire for a weapon so could travel nearly as well as by day. However, first they must find a place in which to shelter until sundown.

Once more he stated aloud his estimate of their situation. That preoccupied expression smoothed from Fanyi's face and she dropped the pendant.

"Our seamen also steer by the stars," she replied slowly. "And I think that the heat of the day here is such as would make any journey an ordeal. Yes, you have judged rightly."

Again Sander felt a prick of irritation. Of course, he had judged the situation correctly! He did not relish that tone from her, hinting that she must weigh what he said and then agree or disagree. Her statements that her will and power alone had kept her people safe and that it was only because she was elsewhere they had been raided had sounded, and still did, preposterous to him. Shaman she might claim to be, with her tricks of foreseeing and the like, but his people held no faith in anything save their own decisions and actions, and neither did he.

They started off at a jog trot, the fishers bringing up the rear, Rhin once more carrying all their gear except for the bolt thrower Sander held at the ready. The smith had also thrust a half-dozen more bolts into his belt, close to hand. But he wished that he

had more. The loss of the two bolts he had already
shot was grievous when his armament was so limited.

Rhin, in spite of his pack, forged ahead, ranging back
and forth as he was wont to do on the plains when
hunting. Sander paused frequently at the beginning of
their trek to look back.

If two armored amphibians were indeed pursuing,
they managed to make such excellent use of the
unevenness of the ancient sea floor as to remain
invisible. The farther the fugitives ventured into what
was increasingly a salt-encrusted and sere desert, the
surer Sander became that beings used to living in water
could not trail them hither.

That did not make him relax his vigilance as they
headed northwest by his reckoning. Fanyi now and then
gazed at her pendant as if it were a sure guide. He
himself chose the old method of fixing upon a
permanent point, a feature that could not be lost to
sight, and aiming at that. Then, having reached that
goal, he selected another.

Thirst followed as their boots stirred up a fine dust
impregnated with salt. To know that the river with its
endless bounty was closed to them, unless sheer
desperation forced them to its dangerous flow, irked
Sander.

He had experienced heat on the plains, and had
ridden far during seasons when water was scarce. But
then he had also known the country well enough to
assess the chances of finding a spring or one of those
seasonally dried streambeds into which Rhin dug with
the instinct of his kind to uncover seeping moisture.
Where in this forsaken land could they find such?

Every time they paused to rest, the smith climbed
the nearest elevation to look, not only back but ahead.
If they could just hole up, out of this punishing sun
and wait until nightfall.

During the fifth such survey, he caught sight of a thing that lay a little to the east of their present course. They were used by now to the relics of ancient ships, their encrusted shapes even furnishing several of the landmarks by which Sander traveled. But this was something out of the ordinary.

In the first place, Sander was sure that he had caught a glint of metal. Secondly, the shape he now studied was totally unlike anything they had sighted before. It was long and narrow, in comparison with the other skeletons of lost vessels, and it lay a little canted to one side, its broken superstructure pointed toward the rock on which Sander balanced.

Also it did not seem so aged. One end was crumpled up against a rise of reef, but otherwise, Sander believed, it appeared nearly intact. He thought that it might have been left thus by the falling of the sea that had uncovered this new land. It offered the best shelter he had seen so far.

If they could find a way inside that hulk, it would be what he had sought for them. And Fanyi eagerly agreed.

As they approached the strange ship, Sander saw that his first valuation of it had been deceptive. It was larger than he had thought. The outline seemed to puzzle Fanyi, for she commented wonderingly that it was not like any ship she knew.

Once at its side they were dwarfed by it. Though the plates that formed it bore streaks of rust, yet the metal beneath had withstood the passage of time surprisingly well. Sander thumped the surface, judging that under a thin crusting of rust it was firmly intact.

Any entrance must be made through the deck that slanted well above them. He unwound the hide rope that had lashed the pack to Rhin and hunted out one of his largest hammers. This he tied with well-tested knots. Then he bade Fanyi stay where she was, while he rounded the narrow end of the ancient ship to the other side.

There he whirled the end of rope weighted with the hammer about his head and threw. Twice it clattered back, bringing flakes of rust with it. But the third time it caught so securely on some portion of the superstructure that his most energetic jerks could not dislodge it. He began to climb and moments later balanced on the slope of the deck. Facing him was a stump of a tower broken off as if some giant hand had twisted a portion free. There was no other opening he could see.

He crossed the slanting deck to look down at Fanyi. Rhin, released from his back pack, was trotting away. And, though Sander straightway whistled, the koyot did not even look back.

Frustrated, Sander knew this was one of the times Rhin was minded to go his own way. He guessed that might be in search of water. Yet the koyot was heading west on into the desert, rather than east as Sander would expect him to go. The fishers, however, continued to prowl nearby among the rocks, plainly uneasy. Or perhaps they were unhappy at being so far from the green-grown country that was their own.

Sander dropped the rope end, having made very sure the hammer was well wedged into the broken spear of the tower, and Fanyi climbed to join him. She stood there, her legs braced against the tilt of the deck, her hands on her hips, her head turning slowly from side to side.

"What manner of ship was this?" she asked musingly, more as if she meant that question for herself and not for him. "It is surely very strange looking."

Sander edged along to the broken superstructure.

Rust streaked its sides, but there was a space to enter
within, though dark. Here they needed Fanyi's Before
Light, and he asked her to use it. She probed with its
beam through the break. He glimpsed the remains of
a ladder against one wall leading downward through
an opening in the floor. With Fanyi on the deck at the
top, shining her light past him, Sander descended,
testing each ladder rung as well as he could before he
trusted his full weight to it.

He found himself in a confined area, crowded with
smashed objects, all sea-stained, that he could not
identify. However, the ladder continued. So he went
on, reaching a larger room where there were banks of
strange-looking cases along the walls. All had been
water-washed and were broken. He called and Fanyi
lowered the light, then clambered down herself as he
held the gleam upward to illuminate those steps. When
she stood beside him, she gazed in wonder at the
enigmatic fittings along the walls.

"What did they use, these Before Men, to power
their ship?" she asked of the stagnant, sea-scented air
about them. "There was no sign of a proper mast
aloft—nor oars."

Sander was intent on the wealth of metal about him.
It was plain that this ship had been the helpless
plaything of the great flood in the Dark Time, and
waters washing through the hole above had damaged
much. Yet most of the metal was still stout. He could
scrape away the coating of sea deposits and rust to see
it bright and strong underneath.

To his right, behind the jumble of battered wall
fittings that made no sense, there was an oval of a door,
tight shut. He moved cautiously through the debris that
covered the floor to feel about for some latch. There
was a wheel there—perhaps one must turn that.

But, though he exerted his full strength of arm, the

fitting remained immovable. He drew his hammer from his belt and began a rhythmic attack on the wheel, though the quarters were so cramped that he could not get a proper swing.

At first he merely chipped free an age-long deposit of rust and sea life from its surface. Then the stubborn latch yielded a fraction, feeding his excitement. His blows grew stronger, until, with a sudden give, the wheel moved gratingly. Now Sander delivered a fast tattoo, striking with a smith's eye at the most vulnerable angle.

He had, he believed, brought the wheel to face the notch that would release the door catch. Around the edge of the door were encrustations that sealed it. He turned his attention to chipping them away.

At last he rebelted his hammer and set both hands to the wheel, urging the door open. A puff of odd-smelling air blew out from the dark cave of the interior. Air—under the sea?

Sander snatched the light from Fanyi without any by-your-leave, sending its beam into the room beyond. There was a table there that must have been securely fastened to the floor since all the battering this strange ship had taken in its death days had not loosened it. And it was still flanked by benches. Under them, rolled near to the lower side—

He heard Fanyi catch her breath. They had both looked on death, for that was common enough in their world. But this was no death they had seen before. Those shrunken withered things did not now bear any likeness to man.

"They sealed themselves in," Fanyi said softly, "and then the sea took their ship and there was no escape. Before Men—we look now upon Before Men!"

But these things, still clad in rags of clothing— Sander could not believe that such as these had once been men who walked proudly, masters of their world. The Rememberers had chanted of the Before Men, that they were greater, stronger, far more in every way than those who now lived in distorted lands left after the Dark Time. These—these were not the heroes of those chants! He shook his head slowly at his own thoughts.

"They are—were—only men," he said, never aware until this moment that he had, indeed, always held a secret belief that those ancestors must have been far different from his own kind.

"But," Fanyi added softly, "what men they must have been! For this ship sprang from their dreams! I believe that this is one of those meant to sail under water, not on its surface, such as the legends say men possessed in the Before Time."

Sander had a sudden dislike for this place. What manner of men had these poor remnants been who had sealed themselves in a metal shell to travel *under* water? He felt choked, confined, even as he had in the net of the forest people. Yes, perhaps after all, the Before Men were of a different breed, possessing a brand of courage that he frankly admitted he did not have.

He stepped backward, having no wish to explore this ship farther. They could clear some of the litter out of that upper chamber and shelter there until night. But these remains should be left undisturbed in their chosen tomb.

"It is theirs, this place." He spoke softly, as he might if he wished not to disturb some sleeper. "Let us leave it wholly theirs."

"Yes," Fanyi assented.

Together they pushed shut that door upon the past and climbed the ladder to the upper level. As they brushed all they could of the debris in the small compartment down the ladder hole to free floor space, Sander came across lengths of wire, pieces of metal that were hardly corroded at all. He recognized them as something the Traders named "stainless steel," another secret from Before, for such did not corrode easily—neither could it be copied. From these pieces, knowing to his disappointment that he could not hope to carry much, he made a judicious selection. Some of the bits could be worked into dart heads, always supposing they could find a place where he might be able once more to labor at his trade.

Fanyi, for her part, combed through the litter for scraps of material on which appeared lines and patterns that she declared were part of the old art of writing. The most portable of these she tucked into a small sack.

In the end they cleared a goodly space in which, cramped though it might be, they could shelter. The fishers refused to come on deck, though Fanyi coaxed them. The pair settled down instead under the shade of the tilted ship. Of Rhin there was no sign. Nor was there any hint that Sander could see, after a searching survey of that part of the surrounding desert he could examine, of any pursuit by the amphibians.

They shared out a handful each of Fanyi's dried fruit, allowing themselves and the fishers each a limited drink. Then they curled up to await the coming of dark.

The day was hot, but lacked the baking, drying heat of the outer world, so they managed to doze. Sander awoke at last in answer to a sharp familiar yelp. There was no mistaking the cry of a koyot. He crawled over Fanyi, who murmured in her sleep, ascending the ladder to the deck.

Rhin reared on his hind feet, his front paws planted against the curve of the ship's side. He yelped again, sharply, with a note that demanded attention. Yet it was not a cry of warning.

Sander swung down by the rope. Rhin nosed at him eagerly. The koyot's muzzle and the hair on his front legs were wet—or at least damp, with an overcoating of the sea-bottom sand plastered there by moisture. Rhin had found water!

"What is it?" Fanyi appeared above.

"Rhin has found water!"

"Another river?"

Sander wondered about that with foreboding. Since their experience with the amphibians, from now on he would look upon all streams warily. But water they must have, or else back trail west completely.

Now for the first time he wished there was some more direct method of communication between man and koyot, that he could ask Rhin a question and learn what lay out toward the east where the other had disappeared earlier. But he was assured in this much: Rhin already knew the menace of the amphibians; therefore the koyot would not lead them into any ambush. He said as much, and Fanyi agreed.

The sinking of the sun removed the desert's direct heat. But they still suffered from the rise of salt dust about their feet. Rhin, once more bearing his pack, trotted confidently forward in a direction that, to Sander, only took them farther from the land. However, his confidence in the koyot was such he was sure the animal knew where he was bound.

Before the moon rose, the fishers suddenly pushed to the fore of the small party, loping forward with their usual sinuous gait until they disappeared into a section of towering rocks that must have once been reefs showing above water. They formed knife-edged, sharp ridges, rather than hillocks that could be climbed.

On the other side of one of these, they came to a second deep drop in the sea-desert floor. But edging this was another tumble of those ancient worked blocks. Among them Fanyi's light (which she had been forced to put to use in this uneven footing) picked out a curving curb. Lying within it was the sheen of water, like a dull mirror that had nothing to reflect.

The pool (Fanyi's light moved in a circular pattern to pick out its circumference) was an oval, far too symmetrically formed to be of nature's fashioning. At one side, some of the curbing had given way, allowing the water to lap over and run away in a small riverlet to the edge of the drop, spinning over it in a miniature falls. The drop there was beyond the power of the light to plumb.

Sander tasted the water. Sweet and fresh. He drank from his cupped hands, dashed it over his dusty face. Small rivulets dribbled down his neck and chest, carrying away the grime of the desert. The fishers plunged their muzzles in deep, sucking with audible gulps. Fanyi followed Sander's example, drank and then washed, uttering at last a small sigh of contentment.

"I wonder who built this," she said, as she sat back on her heels.

Sander brought out their water bottle, dumped its contents into the sterile sand before he rinsed it, preparatory to refilling. A sweet water spring in the midst of the ocean—or what had been the ocean! But long before that, it had been on land. The sense of eons of vanished ages hung heavy about this curbed pool. Men reckoned seasons now from the Dark Time. And the Rememberers had counted some three hundred years from the end of one world and the beginning of this one.

But how long before *that* had this sea land been uncovered for the first time so that men—or at least intelligent beings—raised these stone piles that even long ages had not completely worn away, titanic building that raging seas had not entirely erased? He felt dazed when he tried to think of years that must certainly be counted, not by generations of men, but rather by the slow passage of thousands and thousands of seasons.

There was nothing here of that aura of despair and loss that he had felt in the undersea ship. Not even a tenuous kinship linked him with these ancient-upon-ancient builders. Perhaps they had not even been human as he and his kind now reckoned humanity. He wished that Kabor, the senior Rememberer of the Mob, could witness this, though there would be no hint of memory that the sight could awaken within his well-trained mind.

They drank deeply again, leaving the forgotten pool. Twice they had had the good fortune to find water in the desert. Sander could not be sure such luck would hold for a third time. It seemed to him that they had best now angle back west. There was no game to be hunted here. Hunger could strike them as swiftly and in as deadly a fashion as lack of water. The sooner they reached true land, the better, whether they were able to locate Fanyi's goal or not.

The smith half expected her to protest when he suggested an abrupt swing west. But she did not, though she held her pendant for a long moment or two, focusing the light on its surface, as if by that she could check the path they must go.

Here they could not make good time. The ground was very rough, for the ridges left by old reefs sent them on long or short detours. Their clothing and their bodies, their faces, even their hair, were thick with sandy dust, and the coats of the three animals seemed matted with it. As the night wore on, Sander kept looking ahead for some shelter in which to wait out the day.

After the moon rose, they gained a measure of light. Fanyi snapped off her Before Torch. It was perhaps an hour or so before dawn when Sander felt a sudden drop in temperature. He had been sweating so that the chill of this new breeze made him shiver. They halted for Fanyi to rearrange her belongings and put on her overcloak. Now they could see their breath issuing forth in white puffs.

The change had come so quickly Sander wondered if some kind of a storm was on its way. Although no clouds yet masked the stars above, nevertheless he was anxious for them to find some secure shelter.

Ahead a dark mass projected well above the surface they toiled across. He strained to see that rise better, wondering if they were approaching a one-time island that now stood like a mountain above the denuded plain.

Fanyi flashed her light, holding her pendant directly in its beam.

"That way!" Her voice rang out as she shifted the light to point ahead, toward the dark plateau. She seemed so sure that Sander, for the moment, was willing to follow her lead without question.

By dawn they arrived at the foot of a cliff. Falls of dressed stone, stained by rusty streaks, made Sander sure that above them now lay the remains of a Before city. The scattered and shattered debris about them gave warning that devastation had hit hard here. There could be little left of any value above—even if they could make the climb.

If this city had once held the storehouse Fanyi sought, then her quest must certainly be doomed to failure. Sander, too, felt a pinch of disappointment, even though, he told himself, he had never truly believed in her rumored treasure house of knowledge.

When he glanced at the girl, he saw no sign of any chagrin in her expression. Rather she eyed the tumble of stone as if she saw in it possibilities for ascent to what lay above. And her manner was brisk as if she were sure she was on the right trail and what she sought was near.

"This is the place?" he asked.

Fanyi had her pendant in her hand again. Slowly she pivoted, until she no longer faced the cliff, but rather once more the western lands.

"Not here," she said with quiet confidence, "but there." She waved to the more distant shadow of the land.

Sander believed that the city above had been built on a cape projecting out into the vanished sea, or even an island. To reach the true shore of the Before Days one would have to travel still farther west.

They needed food and water. That either could be

found in the tangle of shattered ruins above, the smith doubted. He thought that perhaps their best plan was to keep to the sea bottom, heading directly for the land.

However, he had not foreseen the coming of the storm, which that earlier cold wind had heralded. Clouds arose out of nowhere in only a few breaths of time, while the wind became a lash of freezing cold, under which they cringed.

The animals made their decision for them. Like two streaks of looping fur the fishers were already swarming up the fall that formed a vast and uneven stairway to the ruins above. Rhin was not far behind. There was that in the quick flight of all three that Sander found alarming enough to goad him to follow. Rhin's senses were far more acute than his own. In the past he had been saved by the koyot's superior gifts of scent and hearing. If Rhin chose that path, there was an adequate reason.

Both the fishers and the koyot were surefooted on that broken trail. Sander and Fanyi, shivering under each blast of wind, had to go more slowly. Too many of the blocks rocked under their weight, some crashing down under the pull of the wind. They flattened themselves to each stable surface they reached, forcing themselves to grope farther up when they caught their breaths again.

At last they crawled over a dangerous overhang of perilously piled materials to reach a wilderness of mounds from which protruded rusty shells of metal, likely to crumble at a touch.

But there was also a show of vegetation, vines withering now with the touch of frost, saw-edged grass in ragged patches, even a wind-sculpted tree or two.

Sander's first thought was that they must keep well away from any pile of rubble that seemed likely to crash. He kept glancing overhead as he felt his way along, cautious lest he step on something that would shift disastrously under his weight. Fanyi moved behind him, choosing in turn each step he had pioneered.

At least the force of the wind was blunted here by these mounds. And, although the cold was intense, they were less tormented by freezing blasts.

It began to rain. And the rain was as cold as the wind, the force of it penetrating their garments, plastering their hair to their skulls, seeming to encase their shivering flesh with a coating of glass-thin ice. Sander had known storms on the plains, but nothing such as this.

The wind roared and howled over their heads in a queer wailing, perhaps because it whirled through openings in the mounds. Now and then they could hear crashes as if the gale brought down new rock falls. Then, when there came a lull, Sander heard the bark of Rhin.

"This way—" He turned to the girl. But the words he mouthed were lost in the rise of the wind's fury. He reached out to catch her hand.

They rounded a mound, to see before them a line of sizeable trees. The storm whipped their branches, ruthlessly tearing off leaves in whirling clouds that were quickly borne to earth by the weight of the rain.

Sander staggered forward, away from the treacherous mounds into the fringe of the trees. The branches absorbed some of the force of the rain but not all of it. Rhin paced impatiently back and forth, his head swinging as he looked from Sander to the way ahead, patiently urging the human to hurry. Of the fishers there was no sign.

They felt underfoot the relative smoothness of one of the paved ways, though the trees and bushes had encroached thickly upon it. Here there were no looming piles of blocks to threaten them as they hurried after the koyot. In a few moments they came out into a clearing where there was a shelter made of wood at one side. Its staked walls met a thatch of thickly interwoven branches. A single door stood open, and there was no sign of any inhabitant, even though this building was plainly of their own time.

Sander plucked thrower and bolt from his belt and waved Fanyi behind him, as he cautiously slipped toward the open door.

When Kai poked a nose from the doorway that he knew his fears were needless. In a last dash, the koyot, Sander, and Fanyi reached the opening and scrambled within, Sander jerking the door to in their wake.

It must have been open for some time because there was a drift of soil he had to loosen before he could close it firmly against the fury of the storm. And since there were only slits, high-set under the roof, to give any light, he found it difficult at first to view their surroundings.

This was not the rude or temporary hut he had guessed it to be at first sight, but a large and sturdy building. The floor had been cleared down to a reasonably smooth surface of stone, which might once have been a part of a road. Against the far wall was a wide fireplace constructed of firm blocks, its gaping maw smoke- and fire-stained but now empty. There was a box to one side in which he could distinguish some lengths of wood standing end up.

Fanyi had pulled out her light and shone its circle of brilliance along the log walls. Shelves hung there. For the most part they were bare, save for a small box or two. Under the shelves were the frames of what could only be sleeping bunks. These were still filled with masses of leaves and bits of brush, all much broken and matted together.

Sander caught the faint scent of old fires and, he thought, even of food. But there was also an emptiness here which, he believed, meant that it had been a long time since the place was inhabited.

"This is a clan house," Fanyi said. "See—" She held her light beam high on one wall showing a big metal hook set into the log. "There they hung divider curtains. But this was a small clan."

"Your people?" He had assumed that Padford had been the only settlement of those folk.

Fanyi shook her head. "No. But Traders perhaps. They live in clans also. They do not take their women or children with them on the trail, but sometimes they have talked of their homes. And this city would be a fine place for their metal searches. They may have cleared this portion of it and moved on—or else heard of richer hunting grounds elsewhere. I think this has been empty for more than one season."

The building was stout enough, Sander conceded. Now that a bar had been dropped into the waiting hooks, sealing the door, he was far less aware of the storm's force. He headed to the hearth, choosing wood from the box. The lengths were well seasoned, and he had no difficulty in striking a spark from his firekit, so that the warmth of flames soothed them as well as gave light to their new quarters. The fishers lay by the fire, licking moisture from their fur. Even Rhin seemed not too large for the long room.

Shelter, warmth—but they still needed food. Fanyi delved into the few containers on the wall shelves. She returned with two with tight sliding covers. These contained a small measure of what looked like the same kind of meal Sander had found in Padford and some flakes of a dried substance.

"They cannot have gone too long ago after all," Fanyi

observed, "for this meal is not musty or moldy. And the other is dried meat."

Straightway, she shed her square cloak, leaving it to steam dry before the fire. That done, she mixed cakes of the meal and meat flakes, having passed to the fishers and Rhin the major portion of the latter.

Sander prowled about the long room, taking note of its construction. Much work had gone into its building. He could not believe that this was only a temporary structure. Rather it must have been meant to stand. Perhaps it was intended for seasonal occupation.

In the far corner he came upon a circular piece of metal, pitted and worn, but still solid, set in the stone of the floor. There was a bar crossing its top, and he thought that with pressure applied through that the lid could be raised. Perhaps there was a store room below, with more supplies than the meager amount Fanyi had found.

He went back to the woodbox, chose a length and returned to lever up that strange door. It took some effort, but at last he could slide the round metal to one side. Crouching low he stared down into thick darkness. There was, he saw as the fireplace flames flickered a little in this direction, the beginning of a ladder of metal. So there was indeed a way into the depths.

Lying belly down, he ran his hands down the ladder as far as he could reach. The steps that formed it had been patched with a crude stripping of other bits of metal. But the smell that arose to him did not, he believed, come from any storage place. It was damp and unpleasant, so much so that he jerked back his head and coughed. The larger fisher had come to the opposite side of the hole, thrusting its head forward to sniff. Now Kai hissed, expressing his own dislike of the unknown. Sander wriggled the cover back into place. He had no desire to go exploring down there in the dark.

Sander took the further precaution of wedging a length of wood through the lifting handle so that it protruded against the hard floor on either side, hoping that this might provide a lock. He had no idea what might threaten from below, but his adventures in the forest and with the amphibians had been warning enough to take care in any strange circumstances.

Now and again the house shook from a gust of the wind. They had drawn as close as they could to the fire, shedding their soaked clothing by degrees to dry it piece by piece.

The wood box had been well filled, but Sander, fearful that the supply might not last through the storm, had been eyeing the shelves along the wall. He believed they could be battered free and used to feed the flames. For now it was enough to feel the heat and be sure they had found a shelter, not haunted and dangerous as the ruins might have been, one made by those of their own species.

The roar of thunder was often followed by a distant crash. Sander believed that the gale took new tribute from the rubble mounds. And the small windows high in the eaves gave frame to brilliant flashes of lightning. The fishers and Rhin seemed uneasy, no longer settling in the fire warmth as they had at first.

Sander watched them narrowly. He could not be sure that it was only the wildness of the display outside that affected the animals. Instead, his imagination suggested menaces creeping toward their shelter. Twice he got up, first to inspect the bar across the door, then that other he hoped would seal off the hole in the floor. Both seemed tight enough.

Once they had eaten, Fanyi seated herself near the hearth, her cloak belted about her while she spread to dry her scanter undergarment. Her mat of hair straggled in wild tufts, which she made no attempt to put into order. Instead she sat with her eyes closed, her hands once more clasped over her pendant. There was about her an aura of withdrawal. She might have been asleep, even though she sat straight-backed and rigid. If she was not sleeping, she must be using another method to block out the present, retiring fully into her own thoughts. That this might be part of her Shaman's training Sander accepted.

In time the fishers quietly came to crouch, one on either side of her, their heads resting on their paws. But they were not asleep, for whenever Sander made the slightest move, he could see their bright eyes regarding him.

He was restless, feeling shut out and cut adrift by Fanyi's absorption. Rhin at last lay down between the fire and the door. But Sander could see that the koyot's ears were ever aprick, as if he still listened.

The thunder rolls were dying and the lightning no longer flashed in the high windows. However, the drum of rain on the roof over their heads did not grow lighter. After their trek by night, Sander longed to sleep and he found now that he nodded, started awake, only to nod again. He had no desire to climb into one of the bunks, his wariness keeping him from relaxing entirely. And his vigilance was proven necessary when Fanyi gave a start, her eyes snapping open, her head up as if she listened.

Yet none of the three animals displayed similar unease.

"What is it?" Sander demanded.

He saw the tip of her tongue sweep across her lips. "There is thought—seeking thought—" she answered, but she spoke almost absently, and as if she did not want to lessen her concentration.

Her words meant nothing to him. Thought? What was *seeking* thought?

"There is some one—some one who is Shaman trained," she continued. "But this—" Her hands moved away from her pendant. She held them up and out, lightly cupped, as if to catch in her palms some elusive stream of invisible water, "This is so strong! And it is not wholly pure thought—there is something else—"

"I do not understand what you are saying," Sander replied brusquely, trying to break through the air of otherness that clung to her. "I do not know the ways of Shamans. Do you mean that someone is coming?"

Again he glanced at the animals. But they were quiet, even though they watched. He could not believe that Rhin would allow any stranger to approach without giving full warning.

Fanyi's expression was one of excitement, not fear. It was as if she were a smith and before her lay some problem of smelting for which she now clearly saw the answer. He, himself, well knew the feeling of exultation such rare moments could bring.

"It—there is no enemy." She appeared to be choosing words. "There is no awareness of us—that I could read at once. I feel the power of a sending, but it is not entirely like my power, and I cannot tell the nature of the matter with which it is concerned. Only there is one who sends. Ah—now it is gone!" She sounded disappointed. "There is no more reach—"

That she believed passionately in what she spoke of, Sander knew. But he could not accept those facts that seemed so much a part of her beliefs. A Rememberer, now, spent long years of "remembering"—of listening over and over again to chants of past events, which it was necessary the Mob be able to draw upon for help in untangling some new problem. The lineage of all the kin was so remembered that there not be too close uniting of birth relationships, weakening the people as a whole. The care of the herd, the very contours of the lands over which they had roamed in the seasons upon seasons since the Dark Time, all that lay in the mind of a Rememberer, to be summoned at will. But this seeking thought—? How could one seek save physically by eye, voice, body?

"The Traders have these seekers?" he asked now. That breed of organized wanderers, who had sought out the Mob, seemed little different from his own people. They were jealous of their secrets, yes. But those were secrets of trails and of the places where they found their basic stocks, the metal that was so necessary for making tools and weapons. They told wild tales of the lands they crossed to bring that metal, yet most of the Mob had been agreed that there was method in those stories—meant to warn off any curiosity on the part of outsiders. Traders had been known to kill lest some favorite supply place be tapped by those not of their own particular clan. But they said nothing of this mind-seek.

"I have never heard that such was so," Fanyi replied promptly. "The Traders who came to Padford"—she shook her head again—"they were no more nor less than any of the villagers. Yet we have already seen strange peoples who are not of our blood. Think you of the forest savages or of those who swarm in the river. This world is very full of wonders, and he who travels learns."

"The Traders tell wild enough tales, but those are meant to afright men and keep their own secrets safe."

"Or so we have always thought," she returned. "But perhaps there is a small seed of truth at the center core of such."

Sander would have laughed, but then he reconsidered. It was true that he had been shaken out of his complacency about the superiority of his own species by their two brushes with forest and river dwellers. Though the Mob had never met any except herdsmen like themselves or the far-ranging Traders, could they say that those were the *only* people left in the world? The fishermen of Padford differed in coloring and life ways from his own kin. And he had heard of the Sea Sharks who made up the slaving bands from the south, though no man had ever understood why they collected the helpless to take into captivity. Those, too, were men—of a kind.

Now he began to recall some of the Trader stories. Suppose she was right? Suppose there *were* armored beasts of giant size roving elsewhere, slaying any man they met; flying things that were neither man nor bird but mingled something of each in an uncanny and horrifying way, their talons raised against normal men? It was easier to believe that the earth still bubbled and boiled in places, that if any ventured too far into such tormented country they died from the poisons filling the air or sank by inches into a steaming mud from which they could not fight free.

"You see"—she smiled now—"I have led you to rethink what you have heard. Therefore, perhaps it is also reasonable to believe that elsewhere there are Shamans to whom I am as but a small child, still unlearned in even the simplest of the healing ways. What"—she flung her hands wide as if to garner in against her breast some thing that seemed precious to her—"what marvels may exist in this world, open to our finding if we only have the courage to seek for them! If someone has learned to mind-seek—then I shall also do this! Am I not of the kin-blood to whom such knowledge is as meat and drink? Young and untried I may seem to such ones, yet I can say in truth—we share some gifts of mind, therefore let me learn of you."

Sander watched her excitement, troubled. Yes, he could understand her thirst for learning, was it not also his? But what he wanted was a learning that brought concrete results, that did not deal with such unreasonable matters as thoughts that were loosed, as it were, to roam. Rather he wanted to know more about what he could make with his two hands when their skill was well harnessed by his mind. It gave him an uneasy feeling to think of using thought in some other way, not to accompany physical action, but in place of that—if he had guessed aright what she hoped to gain.

"I believed"—he strove now to return her to the obvious—"that what you sought was a weapon of vengeance for your people."

"And do you not know," Fanyi flashed, "that thought itself can be as able a weapon, if it is skillfully used, as those forged darts of yours? Yes, I have a debt to the dead; do not believe that I have ever forgotten that." There was a flush rising beneath her dark brown skin. "Now—" She rose to her feet. "I say we should sleep. My fur people, your Rhin, they shall serve as our watch."

"The fire—"

Away from the hearth it was cold.

Fanyi laughed. "Do not worry. Kai knows much." She laid her hand on the head of the larger fisher. "He shall watch the fire, and well. This he has done for me before."

She chose a bunk along the nearer wall, taking her now dried and warmed under-robe to wrap around her. Sander watched her settle in before he followed her example. The last thing he remembered seeing was the larger fisher lifting a piece of kindling from the box, catching the length between his powerful jaws and pushing it into the fire with the dexterity of one who indeed had performed that same act many times in the past.

So Sander settled himself to sleep. And he was deep in a dream wherein he trudged through a long dark tunnel, drawn ever by the sharp tap-tap of a hammer on metal, seeking a smith who had all secrets and from whom he must learn.

A cold touch on his cheek brought him out of that corridor before he ever caught sight of the industrious smith. Rhin loomed over him, and it was the koyot's nose that had touched his face. The animal lowered his muzzle for a second such prod as Sander came fully awake and sat up.

The sound of the wind, the heavy pelt of the rain, was gone. It was so still that he could hear the sound of his own breath, a faint crackling of the fire. But the fishers no longer lay by it. They were ranged on either side of the barred door, facing it. And when Rhin saw that Sander was fully awake, he looked in the same direction.

Sander sat up and reached for his boots. They had dried after a fashion, but he found it hard to force his feet into them. While he struggled to do that, he listened.

He could pick up nothing, but he relied fully on the warning of the animals and he did not doubt that there was someone or something near enough to arouse their instincts of alarm. The Traders returning to their house?

That need not be a real matter for fear. The laws of hospitality, which were scrupulously kept save among the Sea Sharks, would excuse their intrusion here in such a storm, jealous though the Traders were. Sander hoped furiously that this was the case.

Still, he caught up his dart thrower and loosened his long knife in its sheath, as he padded, as softly as he could, across the room to lay his ear tight to the barred door.

T hat Sander heard nothing did not mean that the alarm was false. Now he reslung his weapons in his belt and turned to the wall on which hung the shelves. They might be used as a ladder, allowing him to peer out one of the high windows.

Sander swiftly cleared the remaining containers from the shelves he selected and tested the anchorage of the boards by swinging his full weight upon them. Though the wood creaked protestingly, they held firm. He scrambled up, to crouch perilously on the narrow top plank. Struggling to retain his balance, he reached farther overhead and caught at either side of the narrow window opening.

These had been covered, sealed against the air, by pieces of glass, a refinement that surprised him. Had glass, the most fragile of inheritances from the Before Time, actually existed in this rubble in pieces large enough to be salvaged?

Sander brought his face as close as he could to that surface. As he tried to peer outside he discovered that the glass was not perfectly clear, for it carried bubbles and distortions within it. Yet those imperfections did not prevent a good sight of the clearing immediately before the house.

The darkness of the storm was past. By the angle of the pale sunlight that struck full against the door, he judged it was late afternoon. But it was not time that interested him—rather what might be prowling out there.

A wide expanse lay clear immediately before the door.

The brush, which formed the first rank of the wood's growth, stood some distance away. On the ground was a light scuff of snow and that was not unmarked!

The snow must have fallen near the end of the storm. Already it began to melt under the direct rays of the sun, especially around the edges of numerous tracks. Through the bubbled glass Sander could not make out any clearly defined print, but they were larger than those made by any animal he knew.

Shapeless as they seemed, there was something about their general proportions—Sander would not allow himself to speculate. Nor could he even be certain that more than one creature had left its signature there. A single unknown thing might have scented them, plodded back and forth for a space.

Sander shifted on his narrow perch. He could see where those tracks had emerged from the wood, but no sign they had returned thither. Was the creature prowling around the back of the house now?

At that moment the silence inside and out was broken by a high, wailing cry, startling Sander so he almost tumbled from his spy post. He heard from below the answering growl of Rhin, the hissing of both fishers, then a soft call from Fanyi:

"What was that?"

"I do not know." Sander twisted his body around, striving to see further both right and left. "There is something prowling outside. But I have not yet sighted it."

His last word had hardly left his lips before a bulk shuffled into the sun, coming from the left as it had just completed another circuit of the house.

The thing halted before the door, its out-thrust head nearly on a level with the window from which he viewed it. What was it? Animal—? Yet it walked upright. And now that Sander studied it more closely, he thought that its covering of matted and filthy-looking skin was not part of its own hide, but rather clothing of a sort.

Clothing? This was a *man*?

Sander swallowed. The thing was as huge as the forest female had been. Its head, hunched almost against its shoulders suggesting that its neck must be very short indeed, had an upstanding crest of stiffened hair, the ends of which flopped over to half conceal small eyes. Now it impatiently raised a vast clawed hand, or paw, to push the hair away.

They had felt no kinship with the forest people, and this was an even greater travesty of the human shape. The legs were short and thick, supporting a massive trunk. In contrast, the arms were very long, the fingertips scraping the ground when the creature allowed them to dangle earthward.

Its jaw was more a muzzle than the lower part of a true face, and a straggle of beard waggled from the point of it. Altogether the thing was a nightmare such as a child would awaken from screaming for comfort.

Now it shuffled forward, planting one wide fist against the barred door, plainly exerting pressure. Sander heard the grind of the wood against the bar. Whether that would hold—?

He dropped hastily from his perch. The creature outside now aimed blows against the door, and the bar might or might not continue to hold, while the snarling of the koyot and the fishers grew into a wild crescendo. It was plain that they had reason to fear the attacker.

"It is—" Sander gave the girl a quick explanation of what he had seen. "Have you heard of such before?"

"Yes, from a Trader," she returned promptly. "He said that these haunt the lands of the north and are eaters of men. You see, smith, here is one of their tales indeed proven true."

The crashing against the door was steady. The bar might hold, but would the pins that supported it prove as stout? For them to be caught within—As far as he had seen, the thing carried no weapons, but with those mighty hands what more would it need?

No wonder the builders of this place had set it above that floor bolt-hole. Sander crossed quickly to that, jerking the wooden latch he had inserted with such care. As he levered up the round top, the whole house began to tremble under the assault from without.

"Get a torch!" he ordered Fanyi. She had warned him of the limited life her own light might have, and he had no wish to be caught in some dark run below.

The girl ran to the fire, snatched up a long piece of wood, and thrust one end into the flames. Silken fur swept past Sander's arm. The fishers were already flowing into the opening. Rhin—could Rhin make it? Stripped of his burdens, Sander hoped so. The koyot trotted to the smith's side, dropped his head to sniff into the opening.

Then he turned his rump to the hole, cautiously backed in. As the outer door cracked down its middle, Rhin disappeared as if he had fallen. A moment later he yelped reassuringly from below. Sander tossed down the bags Fanyi handed to him, held the torch while the girl swung onto that patched ladder.

After she was well down, Sander wriggled the cover back halfway over the hold, leaving but a narrow space to squeeze through. He lowered the torch to her reaching hand, lying belly-flat to accomplish that exchange, then sought the ladder himself.

Partway down, he tugged at the metal cover, making a last great effort at the sound of wood breaking aloft. In the flame of the torch he could see now a metal bar fastened to the underside, a crude piece of work that must have been added long after the Before Days.

With a last frantic lunge he sent that across, locking the lid above his head into place.

They had descended to a large round tunnel, he discovered. There was no sign of the fishers, but Rhin waited. The koyot whined softly, plainly liking none of this place, now and then noisily sniffing the ill-smelling air.

If they were to advance from here, the koyot must drop to his haunches and crawl. Fanyi had stuck the torch upright in a ring set roughly into the wall. Now she was busy knotting their gear into back packs, since it was plain Rhin could not transport it along these confined ways. Sander hoped desperately that the tunnel grew no smaller or the koyot could not force a way through it.

"Look!" Fanyi pointed with her chin as her hands flew to tighten knots.

The piece of wood she had brought from the house was nearly consumed. But, leaning against the wall under the hoop that held it, were a number of better-constructed torches, their heads round balls of fiber soaked in what Sander's nose told him must be fish oil.

It would seem by these preparations that the builders of the house had foreseen emergencies when it would be necessary for them to take to these underground ways. Was the presence of the beast now above the reason why they had left their well-wrought shelter?

Sander lighted one of the torches and divided the rest, giving half to the girl. Then, bending his head a little, he started down the tunnel, hearing the complaining whines of Rhin as the koyot edged along with Fanyi behind him.

There was no way of telling how long that stretch of tunnel was nor even in what direction it ran. Part of it had collapsed, been redug, and shored up. Finally they came to a hole hacked in one side and struggled through it into a much larger way, one in which Rhin could stand upright. The floor of this was banded by two long rails of metal that came out of the dark on one side and vanished into it again on the other. The fugitives paused, Sander unsure whether to turn right or left.

"Aeeeeheee!" Fanyi gave her summoning call to the fishers, and she was straightway answered from their left.

"That way." It was plain she had full confidence in her companions. "They have ranged on and now believe they are heading out—"

The smith could only hope her confidence was well placed. Torch in hand and held at the best angle to show them the uneven footing, he turned left.

There seemed to be no end to this way under the Before City. Though Sander was almost sure that the thing that had besieged the house could never squeeze its bulk through the opening in the floor, even if it could tear loose the lock on the lid, he kept listening intently for any hint they were being pursued.

His torch picked out trickles of slimy moisture down the walls of the larger tunnel. Yet it seemed quite intact otherwise, with no fall of roof or sides to threaten them. Then the light picked up a mass that nearly choked it.

As Sander drew nearer, he saw that this was not composed of any slippage of the wall, rather it was rusting metal that filled the opening top to bottom, leaving only narrow passages on either side. Those the fishers had undoubtedly been able to venture through. And he and Fanyi could undoubtedly do so also, but he doubted if Rhin could force a way.

Handing the torch to the girl, Sander shrugged out

of his pack and brought from that his tool bag. He chose the heaviest of his hammers and went to face the rusty mass.

Under the first of his blows the metal crumpled, some of it merely crumbs of rust. Whether it could be treated so, to open a passage, he could not be sure, but he would try. In spite of the chill damp his exertions brought the sweat running so heavily that he had to stop and strip off his shirt as well as his hide jacket. And his back and arms, having foregone the discipline of daily work for too long, ached.

Still, he swung and smashed with a rhythm that speedily returned since he was so used to it. Foot by foot, he cleared a wider passage to the left. Luckily not too much of the obstruction needed to be beaten away. Rhin pushed carefully along behind Fanyi, who held the torch high. Midway through, that brand was exhausted, so she lit a second from the supply she carried.

The metal was very brittle. Sander guessed that constant damp had fed the consuming rust. He studied the wreckage when he paused for breath, trying to guess what it had been. It had, he decided, probably transported men or supplies beneath the surface of the city.

They coughed as the dust from his hammering arose, until Fanyi tore strips from her clothing and tied them over their mouths and around Rhin's muzzle, wetting them from the water supply in their bottle.

The crashing blows of the hammer made Sander's head ring. If the monster had followed them down, it would be in no confusion over which direction it must take to follow them.

There was a final subsidence of a last metal plate and once more they faced the open way. Sander was hungry as well as dry-mouthed with thirst. But any remedy for that state still lay before them. All they could do was to struggle along as quickly as they could.

Not far ahead was a branching of the way. Once more Fanyi sounded her call to the fishers. But this time there came no answer. And though they pushed the torch close to the surface of the ground, they could detect no tracks. Sander turned to Rhin. For the first time the koyot moved out with more assurance than he had shown since they had taken to this underground way.

He lowered his head to sniff along the edge of those rusted shells of rails and to search the ground between them. Then he gave a sharp yelp of command and trotted along the inner of the two ways. Luckily they came to no more of those plugs of metal. But the passage sloped downward, and there were spreading patches of wet upon the walls, signs also that at one time water had risen to a point within a hand's-breadth of the roof.

Sander watched those walls. It could well be that they had been loosened with the passing of the years, that even the small disturbance made by the passing of their own party could bring about a fall, entrapping or killing them all. Under his urging, they made the swiftest passage that they could. Yet that seemed to him to be agonizingly slow, and he listened tensely, not now for the monster that had attacked the house, but rather for any sound of shifting over their heads.

Fanyi called out and pointed ahead. There was a pile of the same rubble as he had seen in the mounds above. And this choked the whole of the way. But over it was a jagged hole in the roof, under which the debris made an unsteady platform.

A head hung in the open, eyes staring down at them. It was plain that the fishers had not hesitated to try that escape route, as dubious as it looked. Kai's head disappeared as Rhin moved forward.

With caution, the koyot placed his forepaws, one after the other, part way up the mound of crumbling stuff, which sent a trickle of gravel and small stones thudding down as he so moved. He stood still, nosing ahead at the next portion of the rise, as if scent could assure him whether or not it would bear his weight.

Sander and Fanyi edged away as Rhin made a slow climb. The koyot panted as he went, his tongue lolling out of his half-open jaws, drool dripping from its tip. He planted each paw with delicate precision.

Up again, and another cascade of finer rubble. Only one more length and his head would be out of that hole. Sander crept to the edge of the mound, held the torch as high as he could to give Rhin all possible help.

Once more gravel rolled, bringing with it that same coarse sand that had slipped under their feet when they crossed the sea-desert. Now Rhin's head and shoulders were out into the opening. His muscles bunched as he lunged up, scrabbling furiously on the edge of the opening with his forepaws.

Sander jumped back to escape the slide the koyot's efforts caused. Now Rhin showed his head once more in the hole, looking downward and uttering a series of barks as if urging the humans to duplicate his feat as soon as possible.

The smith lit a second torch and then a third. These he planted butt down in the pile so they threw full light over that treacherous shifting surface. He shed his pack once more and pulled forth his coil of braided hide rope before he spoke to Fanyi.

"I am going up. When I make it, lash our packs, then stand well clear until I pull those up. After that I will drop the rope. Make it fast to your waist, and take all the time you need for the climb."

With the rope's end tied about his middle, he faced the slope. That last slide of gravel and small stones had luckily uncovered the edges of a few larger rocks that promised more stable footing. He tested the lowest of them as best he could and then cautiously scrambled up on it.

The space was narrow, hardly wide enough to afford room for his toes as he felt above, his hands slipping through loose material twice, before, under the moving stuff, he could locate a firm block. Wriggling carefully along, he managed to reach the second perch. Rhin gazed down, his yelps increased in volume. It was plain he was offering his full encouragement.

This last bit was even more tricky. Rhin's emergence had broken the edge. In order to reach the crumbling remains, Sander must squirm forward over what looked in the limited light to be a very uncertain bit of surface. He remained where he was for a long moment, trying to breathe evenly, to steady his nerves before he moved out. Though he had never admitted this weakness, Sander had never taken joyfully to any scramble up a height, even when the surface he sought to climb was more hospitable. He did know enough not to look back, to concentrate only on what lay immediately ahead. He could not remain forever where he now was; there was nothing left to do but trust to fortune and his own strength and make this last attempt.

Now he dug both hands into the mass, seeking some better support. His nails tore, and he felt sharp pain in his fingers, ground between moving stones. But at last, he tightened his hold on something that did not shift as he slowly exerted more and more weight.

Sander pulled himself up as the whole surface under him appeared to crack. Somehow he got a firm brace under one knee, used that to push out farther ahead.

He was still inches away from the edge, and he feared more than ever to trust any hold.

Rhin's head had swung. Without warning the koyot snapped, his jaws closing on the hide jacket that strained tightly over Sander's shoulders. The fangs in those jaws grazed skin as well as covering, and Sander gave a startled yell.

Rhin's unexpected move brought him up, and he surged, much as the koyot had before him, out, skidding free across the self-encrusted ground under the full light of a large and glowing moon.

After that it was easy enough to jerk up their gear, find a convenient small rock to weight the rope, and drop it once more to Fanyi. With a line lashed about her, and Sander's strength added to hers, her ascent was far easier and speedier than his struggle had been.

Once both were aloft, they had a chance to look about them. To the west rose the lines of a sloping beach. To the east was the plateau that once must have been an island, holding the near vanished city. The tunnel they had followed plainly had once run under the arm of the sea to connect the island with the main continent.

But where they were was certainly too open. That monster had perhaps not followed them into the lower ways. But if it or perhaps its fellows were denned in the city, one such could sight their small party here in the open and be on their trail again.

Sander found his body trembling as he stopped for his pack. His exertions in the tunnel, his hunger, and the tension of that last climb were taking their toll. To reach the one-time shore—to somehow find a shelter there—that he must force his body to do.

At least they could give the packs to Rhin here in the open. Sander fumbled with the rope, packing and lashing the gear. They had the rest of the torches still, but it was better not to light them and so mark themselves to any hostile eyes. They must make the moonlight do.

Stumbling often, Sander walked beside Rhin, Fanyi on the other side of the koyot. The fishers had again vanished. The smith supposed they had headed toward the beach.

He wavered as he walked, trying to control the shaking of his hands, ashamed to display his fatigue to Fanyi.

Luckily the terrain sloped upward gradually. There was no cliff to climb. Once up on the shore, they were ankle-deep in beach sand, faced by a wilderness of rocks, with grass growing among them. Sander lifted his head enough to look for the wood that had masked this same shore to the south where they had left it what seemed a very long time ago.

However, there was no dark line of trees. This land was far more open, though here and there were the same mounds of rubble that had marked the island. It was plain that this city had been a place of great extent, its buildings spreading also to the mainland.

"Let us find some shelter quickly." Fanyi's voice held a note of strain. "I cannot say how far I can now go or how long I can keep my feet."

He was grateful to her at that moment, he did not know how much longer he could keep going either. Yet some inner pride kept him from making the same confession.

In the end they both hooked a hand in the ropes that held Rhin's burden, so that the koyot was more than half supporting them as they reeled into a fairly open space, a hollow where some bushes had rooted.

Snow had fallen here and still lay in small patches, reflecting the moonlight. But the punishing wind had died, and the night was very still. Sander shivered. His fingers were stiff and numb as he fumbled with the knots that fastened their gear, letting it thud to earth. Out from behind one of the hillocks that marked the ruins flashed the fishers. Kai carried a limp body in his mouth, dropping his burden at Fanyi's feet. He had brought in a very large hare.

Rhin, now bare of back, sniffed once at the game, made a low sound in his throat, and trotted off purposefully, intent, Sander knew, on providing his own food. The smith studied this hollow they had chanced upon. At least two of the rubble hills stood between them and the arm of the sea-desert. They could not spend the night without warmth and food.

He knelt to hack at a wiry bush. The dry and sapless growth broke easily under his touch. Moments later he had a small fire ablaze and was able to turn his full attention to skinning and gutting the hare.

For two days they kept to the campsite. There was no threat here of any of the dangers they had met elsewhere, no sign that the monstrosity from the old island had its kin here. Sander went hunting, using his sling to knock over hares and a stunted-looking kind of deer that was smaller than even Kayi. These animals were so bold that Sander believed they had never been hunted—a further proof this land was safe for the wayfarers.

The days grew colder, their nights were spent between fitful dozing and care of their fire. Snow fell again, not heavily, but enough to cover the ground. Sander disliked the fact that their tracks to and away from their camp were so well marked across that white expanse. He tried every dodge known to disguise these, only to admit that he was unsuccessful.

There was no way of adequately curing the hare skins. But they scraped them as clean as they could, then lashed the pelts together in a bundle. Sander already knew that their clothing was not heavy enough for this climate, so they might soon be reduced to using those hides, smelly and unworked as the pelts were, for additional warmth.

Fanyi sat for long spaces of time, the pendant clasped tight in her hands, so entranced that she was little aware of what was going on about her. Twice she reported that she had again encountered what she persisted in calling the "seeking mind." Neither time, she was sure, had that thought carried awareness of her. Nor was there, to her infinite disappointment, any way of her tracing it to the source. Which was just as well as far as Sander was concerned. He mistrusted her accounts of what he still could not accept as possible.

During his hunting he also prospected for metal. But if anything useful had remained here after the Dark Time, it must have been mined long ago by Traders. He did come upon holes recent enough to suggest that they had not been made during the catastrophe which had changed the world, but were due to burrowings since that time.

The sheer size of this expanse of debris-strewn wilderness was amazing. How many Before Men had lived here? Far greater numbers surely than any Mob could count. Sander had followed Rhin to the bank of another river, this one half-choked with fallen stone, which must wind to the now distant sea on the other side of the raised island.

Man and animal were both wary of the water. Rhin stood guard while Sander filled the water bag. So far, however, Sander had neither heard nor seen any evidence of amphibians. There were some fish—he took one with an improvised pole and line—a long narrow creature that startled him with its likeness to a snake and that he quickly loosed again, knowing he could not stomach its clammy flesh.

It was near the river that he found the head. Not the head or skull of any creature that had lived, rather one wrought in stone. Big as his two fists balled together, it was clearly very old, the neck being broken raggedly across. And it was the head of a bird, with a fierce proud look about it that somehow attracted him.

He brought it back to show to Fanyi. She turned the carving around in her hands, examining it closely.

"This," she pronounced firmly, "was an emblem of

power or chieftainship. It is a good omen that you have found it."

Sander half laughed. "I do not deal in omens, Shaman. That is not the way of my people. But this is a thing that was well made. If it had a special meaning for him who wrought it, then I can understand why he dealt so well in its fashioning—"

She might not have heard him; that withdrawn look had returned.

"There was a great building," she said. "Very tall—very, very tall. And this was part of a whole bird with outspread wings. Above the door was that bird set—and—" Fanyi let the lump of stone fall to the ground, rubbed the back of her hand across her eyes as if to push something away. "It had a meaning," she repeated. "It was the totem of a great people and a far stretching land."

"This land?" Sander glanced around the heaped mounds. "Well, if it were such a totem, then its power failed them in the end."

Slowly Fanyi reached forth a hand once more and touched the broken-off head. "All totems failed in the Dark Time, smith. For the land and sea, wind and fire turned against man. And what can totems do to stand against the death of a whole world?"

She took up the head once again and set it on a stone, wedging it upright with smaller pebbles. After she had made it secure Fanyi bowed her head.

"Totem of the dead," she said softly, "we pay you honor again. If there lingers any of your power to summon, may you lend us that. For we are the blood of men, and men fashioned you as a symbol to abide in protection above their strong places." Her hands moved in gestures Sander did not understand.

Let Fanyi deal with unseen powers and totems; he was much more interested in the here and now.

Yet looking upon his find, Sander thought that he would like to wrap it in clay and bake from it a mold into which he could run easily worked copper, to fashion a symbol tied with the past. But the head was too heavy to carry with them now. It was far better he cling to the scraps of metal he had found in the wreckage of the ship.

He grew impatient. They had rested here long enough and gained their needed supplies, for he had dried some of the meat in the smoke of the fire. To remain longer brought them nothing.

"Your guide—that thing you wear," he said to the girl. "Where does it point now?"

Again she turned her head to northwest. But to go in that direction meant trailing through more remains of the city. He would have felt freer and more at ease had they headed straight west where he guessed these graveplaces of Before Men's holdings might dwindle away.

Sander, in spite of his impatience, allowed two more days to add to their supplies. The weather was clear but colder each morning. However, there were no more such storms as had struck at them earlier. Finally, on the fifth morning after their winning to what had been the old shore line, they started off. Above, the sun was bright as it climbed, giving a welcome warmth.

As usual the two fishers slipped away and were soon hidden from view by the mounds and walls of rubble, leaving here or there a pawprint to mark their going. But Rhin was content to accompany Sander and the girl.

Fanyi had the pendant ever in her hand. Now and then she pointed out a direction with such certainty that Sander accepted her guidance. He wished that he could examine for himself that oval with its winks of what he took to be shining stones. That the Before

Men could have fashioned a true direction finder he did not doubt, but neither did he believe he could fathom its secret now.

At last, however, at last he asked: "How does that thing speak to you, saying we must go right or left?"

"That I do not know; I know only a little of how to read what it has to say. See?" She beckoned him closer. "Look, but do not touch. I do not know how another's spirit might influence this."

The pendant was oval, but not flat, having a thickness of about the length from the tip of his little finger to the first knuckle, while the metal from which it had been fashioned was bright and untarnished, probably one of those mysterious alloys whose secrets baffled all those of his calling. Set in a circle stood the stones, round and faceted. These were of different colors and there were twelve of them. But, bright as they were, Sander's full attention was caught by something else. In the metal moved a visible line of light, which was not steady.

"Watch," Fanyi bade him. She swung her body abruptly to the left. On the pendant the line moved also, so it still pointed in the same direction that it had previously, save that now it touched a different one of the stones.

"My father," she said softly, turning again so that the short bar of light touched the same stone it had formerly, "knew many things. Some he was able to teach my mother and later she taught me. But he died before I entered this world. This was his great treasure. He swore by some magic of the Before Men it could guide the one who wore it to the place from which it came. The closer one approaches that place, the brighter will grow this pointing line. And that is the truth, for I have seen it do so each day we have traveled. I know that which we seek is a place of great knowledge. Perhaps the Before Men had some warning of the destruction of their world and were able to prepare a storehouse that even the great upheaval of the Dark Time could not destroy."

Sander was impressed by that band of light. It was true that it did swing when Fanyi moved. And he could believe it was meant for a guide. What manner of man had her father been? A Trader who had hunted through the ruins and chanced upon such a cache as he had not believed existed? Or some other, whose tribe perhaps possessed a Rememberer with a greater store of Before Learning than any the Mob knew?

"Your father—was he a Trader?"

"Not so. Though he traveled with the Traders to Padford. He was a searcher, not for metals, but for other men. Not to enslave them as do the Sea Sharks, rather to learn what they had kept from the Before Time. He had recorded much, but"—she looked unhappy—"when they made his grave barrow, my mother placed within his hands that book he had used to set down what he had learned. A book is of writing—much writing marked on pieces of smoothed bark or cured skin. My mother knew that was his greatest treasure; therefore it was meet that it be laid in the earth with him so in the Afterward he would have it as another would have his tools and weapons. For my father said that words so marked down were the greatest tools of all—"

Sander shook his head at that. The saying was foolish. How could marks such as she had made in the dust with a bit of twig be more to a man than the tools with which he wrought something or the arms with which he could defend his very life?

"So my father believed!" Fanyi raised her head proudly, as if she might have caught Sander's thought.

"But if his records lie with him, I have this." Her fingers closed tightly about the pendant. "And I think it is only a small part of other wonders."

During their journey that day Sander took a chance now and then to glance over Fanyi's shoulder at the pendant. They had to detour, sometimes even to backtrack, around piles of ruins. Each time the line of light changed course, so that it ever pointed in the same general direction, no matter which way they went.

It seemed to Sander that there was no end to this city. Whence had come so many people; how long and hard had they worked to bring hither this stone to raise buildings? His wonder intensified.

During the ranging of the Mob, they had at times found remains of old cities. Mostly they had avoided the piles of debris, for there was a taboo because such were sometimes the source of a sickness-to-death. The younger men had once or twice prospected a little for metal. However, what they found was so rust-eaten as to be of little account. It was better to depend upon the Traders, who apparently were ever ready to risk any danger to secure the lumps they brought to the mobs.

No city Sander had seen went on forever! Or near to that. But if there had been any metal worth the plundering here it had been taken long ago. Birds nested among the bushes that cloaked the sides of the more stable piles of rubble, left white smears of droppings down weather-worn blocks. At this season the nests were deserted, but they could be seen because the leaves were stripped from the branches by the wind.

Twice Sander used his small sling. And once was lucky, bringing down another of the giant hares. This they roasted at nooning, saving their dried meat for later. They had seen nothing of the fishers. Rhin sniffed at some of the stones and now and then growled low in his throat, as if he caught some faint scent there he did not like. Each time Sander tensed, searched the ground nearby for any track. He feared most a monster like that on the one-time island.

Still, whatever traces the koyot picked up must have been old, or perhaps not of the lumbering creature. And there were no trees about to attract the forest people.

In his searching for wood at their night's camp Sander stumbled on a discovery that shook him. A huddle of bones lay in a small hollow, and not the bones of man. The leering skull, its jaw supported by a rock, was twice the size of his own. And he saw, driven into one of the eye holes, a dart.

Cautiously, he freed the missile. In pattern it was not too different from his own. The metal had been well worked, the handicraft of a trained smith. But it carried no marking Sander recognized. He squatted down to examine the skeleton more closely.

This must certainly be the remains of a monster. However, he believed the kill more than one season old. He wondered why the slayer had not retrieved his dart. Such were not to be wasted and each hunter thought first, after bringing down his prey, of reclaiming his weapon. Perhaps the monster had been shot at a distance, then still living, but wounded to the death, had reached here before it collapsed.

Sander made a careful circuit of the surrounding territory, to come upon a second find, a gaping hole in the side of one of the mounds. A later landslip had nearly refilled it, but the original opening was not so obscured that it could not be distinguished. Perhaps Traders, intent upon uncovering some treasure here, had been attacked by one of the half-beasts. He could almost reconstruct what had happened.

Perhaps the men had suffered so grievously from the monster's onslaught that they had fled, taking their dead and wounded with them. This evidence of a battle, old though it might be, was alarming.

He pried loose the dart. The point showed a small film of rust, but that he could scour away with sand. And any addition to his own supply was useful.

Sander was not yet satisfied. With a whistle he summoned Rhin. The koyot, once he sniffed the skeleton, growled fiercely, showing his fangs. But when Sander urged him past the collection of bones to the hole, he showed no great interest. Whatever scent had hung there must have long since disappeared. Now Sander sighted something new, beyond a ragged pile of rubble—deep lines rutted in the earth.

There was only one interpretation for those. A cart had been brought here, a slightly smaller one, Sander estimated, than those the Mob used for their plains travel. And it had been loaded heavily, enough to impress this signature of the wheels deeply into the soil. So the diggers had not been entirely routed, they had taken away whatever they had found.

But if this land was the hunting ground for a band of Traders, his own party could be in danger. Even though they had not the outward appearance of seekers for metal, the Traders were jealous of their sources. They might attack any intruders in what they considered their own territory, without waiting for any explanation of the trespassers' business there.

This site was old, judging by the condition of the landslip and of the monster bones. However, that did not mean that the explorers who had left that excavation were gone from the ruins. A city as large as this would prove too rich a ground to be forsaken quickly.

So now they had a new element to guard against. Sander knew that Rhin would not accept any stranger unless he himself vouched for such a one. Even Fanyi might have been attacked at sight had it not been that the fury of the fishers had won her protection until Sander had accepted her in peace. Therefore, they must depend upon the koyot to give them both protection and warning. The smith had no wish to trade darts with any Trader. He needed the knowledge and the supplies those could uncover too much. The ones he had met were amiable men, though shrewd in bargaining. They were not like the Sea Sharks with whom all men had a quarrel from the moment of sighting. He hoped that if any exploring party did cross their path, Rhin would give warning early enough so that they themselves could make plain their lack of threat.

When he reported his findings to Fanyi, she did not seem disturbed.

"It could even be the men of Gavah's kin. It is he who comes down coast in the spring—did come down coast"—she corrected herself bleakly—"to deal in Padford. Our Smith, Ewold, swore his metal was very good."

"What did you trade in return?" The Mob had offered dressed leather and woven wool from the herds, both of which the Traders appeared pleased to accept. He wondered what Fanyi's kin had produced that had moved the Traders to carry their metal hither. To his mind the village had not seemed productive of much that would lure any speculators to their doors.

"Salt fish and salt itself," she returned promptly. "Our men went out to the sea-desert for that. And we had sometimes a surplus of grain and always dried fruit. My mother offered herbs that their healers did not have. We were not so poor a people as you believe, smith!"

"Did I say that?" he countered. "To each people their own way of life."

"Perhaps you did not speak it, but it lay in your mind," Fanyi replied with conviction. "The Sea Sharks took more than kin out of Padford in their raid. I wonder why do they so prey, snatching those of their own species to bear away captive on their ships?" She asked that question as if she did not expect an answer. "We have heard of them, not only from the Traders, but from our elders. In the south they preyed upon us also. We were once a more numerous people, but we lost youths and maids to the Sharks. That is part of *our* memory, smith, though we have none of your Rememberers to call it forth at will."

"I have heard of the Sharks only from Traders," Sander confessed. "At least they keep to the coast, and we have not seen them inland. Unless the White Ones were of their breed—"

"The White Ones?"

"When I was very young, they came. They were a strange people, charging to instant battle as if their lives depended upon our deaths. We were not able to parlay with them to establish the boundaries of grazing lands as we do with other Mobs. No, they killed all—child, woman, man, koyot even—for they had a peculiar dread of them. Out of the north they traveled with their wagons. To draw those, they had not koyots but creatures like deer, save they were very large and carried on their heads huge spreads of branching horns. They acted as if they wanted all the world for theirs alone, to clear out all the Mobs of the plains. When my people learned of their blood-swollen madness, Mob linked with Mob, together we met them on a field where they and their beasts died. For when they saw that we would triumph, the women slew their own children and themselves. They put edge even to the throats and hearts of their beasts. It was such a slaying no one of the plains shall ever forget.

"We found strange things among their wagons. But it was decided that all they carried must be accursed because they acted as madmen. Thus their possessions were piled in great heaps. On those we laid their bodies and the bodies of their beasts. They were fired until at last there remained only ashes. Then did all the Mobs who had gathered to defend their land decide in council that a Forbidding was to be laid upon that place, one set in all our Rememberers' minds. Thus, none of any clan-kin gathered there would ever visit that field again.

"Our own dead we buried in hero barrows along the way to the place of blood, so that the earth-spirit part of them might watch for us. Though some men believe," he added, "that men have no earth-spirit part, that just the body, like wornout clothing, remains of a man when breath is gone from him. But there were enough of those holding otherwise that this was done. Now when any of the Mobs range to the north with their herds, the new-sworn warriors and the maids near to the time that they will choose a tent mate, all ride with a Rememberer to the line of the barrows. There he chants the tale of the White Ones and their madness."

"Why were they called White Ones?"

"Their hair, even among the young, grew very pale, and their skins, though they rode under the sun, were also bleached. But it was their eyes that betrayed the greatest strangeness, for those were of one color, having no pupil—being only like balls of polished silver. Unlike those we have seen in the forest or that thing that battered into the house, they wore the forms of men so that we could call them kin. But for the rest—no, they were not of our kind."

"Whereas the Sea Sharks are," Fanyi said firmly. "They wear the forms of men like ourselves, but they have the inner spirits of devils spawned from the dark."

She was anchoring the sticks holding their meat at just the right distance from the fire to broil. Twilight was already drawing in. Rhin had vanished. But Sander could not deny the koyot that chance to fill his stomach, even with so many possible menaces ranging in the dark. The smith gave a start, his hand instantly on his dart thrower, as there was movement in the shadows. Fanyi's fingers closed about his wrist.

"It is Kai and Kayi," she said. "Though one may mistrust all shadows here, yet there are still some we hold as friends." She crooned softly to welcome the fishers.

Fanyi caught the head, first of Kai, and then Kayi, holding them between her palms as she gazed into the eyes of each fisher in turn. Then she spoke:

"They have found no sign of others here. In this much, fortune continues to favor us."

Perhaps fortune favored them, Sander decided somewhat grimly, yet he was still uneasily aware that in this broken land a whole Mob might move silently and unseen. There was no reason to relax their watch.

Again they shared out sentry duty for the night. He sat in the early morning hours, feeding the fire now and then. Rhin watched beside him as he listened to the sound of the river below and to noises out of the dark.

The attack came suddenly—between one breath and the next—not springing from the shadows, but somehow within his own mind. Sander could not even cry out against that invasion, and he had no defense to raise. Instead he felt as if he stood in another place, the features of which were veiled from him, even as he could not see the one—or thing—that had summoned him, overbearing his will as easily as a man might overbear in strength a child.

This was a sensation he could not find words out of past experience to describe. His very thoughts were seized upon ruthlessly, to be sifted and drained of what the other wished to learn. Sander had confused mental impressions of scenes—broken buildings, movement in and among those. Yet when he fought to see clearly any part of that, all faded, dissolved, changed.

Then there was only the fire with the night beyond. Yet Rhin's head was up, the koyot's eyes blazing with reflection from the flames. Beside him the fishers had reared, all turned to face Sander. Alone of their party, the girl still lay quietly asleep.

Sander heard Rhin growl softly, deep in his throat. A light hiss came from at least one of the fishers. The smith raised his hands feebly to rub his forehead, feeling weak and frightened. No hint that such could happen to any man had ever come to his people, been hinted at by a Rememberer. He had been in two minds over Fanyi's claim of unseen, intangible power—was this what she had meant by "seeking thought?" Who had so sought *him* and for what purpose? Sander felt violated by that invasion of his mind.

Kai hissed, baring teeth in Sander's direction. The smith flinched from the beast's open enmity. Rhin— Sander glanced quickly to the koyot. There still came that low growl from the animal. Yet, when Sander's eyes met Rhin's squarely, the sound died. The smith, who had never tried to communicate with the koyot after the same fashion Fanyi used with her fishers, had now an impression that Rhin had detected the mental invasion but now accepted that Sander was again himself.

The smith longed to shake Fanyi awake, to demand of her what could have caused this attack that was certainly of some Shaman's brewing and not of normal man. As his first fright and dismay faded, he knew a rising anger. No one must know that he had been so used. He sensed there had been contempt in that exploration of his thoughts, that he was deemed to count for little in the estimation of whoever had netted him for a moment or two with that invisible mind control. No, he would not ask her.

Instead, Sander began to rummage in his smith's bag.

As he did so, he repeated mentally one of the secret working chants. Dimly he recalled something his father had once commented upon. There were supposed to be places from the Before Time where strange influences could seize upon a man, bend him to an unknown service. But there was an answer to such, a defense that was part of a smith's own secrets.

Sander's fingers closed upon some of those lengths of wire he had ripped loose in the old ship. Measuring them, he began to wind the strips into a braid as tight as he could pull them. Then he fitted the loop around his own head, so that a portion of it crossed his forehead directly above his eyes. That done he pulled it free once more to weave the ends and make it firm.

Iron—cold iron—had a meaning reaching from the Before Times. It could be a defense when worked in certain ways. He had never had reason to test that belief, though many of the Mob wore amulets of cold iron. Some he had fashioned himself according to their desires. Then he had secretly thought it a baseless superstition, only in favor because having such toys about them gave men a feeling of security within their own minds.

Now—now he could accept the idea that there were enemies—or an enemy—here who were in some way to be more greatly feared than monster, White One, or jealous Trader.

Having finished his crude diadem of rusty metal, Sander set about weaving some smaller bits into a complicated knot that he strung on the thong of hide. This for Rhin. He did not know whether the koyot might be influenced by the same invasion that had shaken him, but what precaution he could take, he would.

There remained Fanyi and the fishers. The animals,

Sander believed, might not let him near them. They were an aloof pair, tolerating man and koyot only because of the urging of Fanyi. While the girl—she had seemed excited, even pleased when she had caught a suggestion of that "seeking thought," making it clear she welcomed contact with any who could use it. He supposed that was the result of her Shaman training. But if such contacts were accepted as normal and right by the Shamans—! If he had his way, he would leave her at this moment, strike out into the dark.

Outrage and fear pulled him strongly. However, such emotions he would not yield to. No, they would continue to travel together until—until Fanyi might give him reason to believe that she was far more akin to that—that seeker—than she was to him and his kind.

The metal pressed harshly against the skin of his forehead. Sander still repeated mentally the words of power that must be said at the fashioning of any tool or weapon. Now he fed the fire again. The fishers settled quietly once more beside Fanyi. Whatever influence had invaded their camp to strike at him must have withdrawn.

Sander lashed shut his smith's bag, stowed it with his gear. He could see the dawn light slowly creeping up the sky across the cliffs that banded the river, and he hoped this day's journey would bring them to the end of the city, or, if not that, to the goal Fanyi sought. He had begun to dislike heartily this maze of mounds and wreckage. If earth-bound spirits did exist, then surely uncounted dead walked here. And since it was unlikely that any man had done them honor at their burial, they would be answerable to no restraints.

Sander shied away from such thoughts. He did not believe in any earth-bound part of the dead. And he would not now be reduced to a child who fears the dark because his imagination peoples it with monsters. No—no—and no!

Fanyi stirred, opened her eyes slowly. Her expression, Sander noted with a return of uneasiness, was much like that she wore when she fondled the pendant at intervals and seemed to retreat from the outer world.

"It is there—he is there—" Her voice trailed away. She blinked as if throwing off the last remnants of a vivid dream. Then, as she sat up, her face was alight with an eagerness he had never seen before. The excitement she had shown when she had caught the "seeking thought" was but a pale illusion compared to this.

"Sander—*it* is there! Do you hear me?" She caught at his arm, shook him with a fierce energy. "I have had a foreseeing!" Her face was still alight with excitement and joy. "We shall come to it soon—the secret place. And there will be someone there, someone important."

"Who?" he asked flatly.

A small shadow of bewilderment crossed her face, driving out the joy.

"I—do—not—remember. But—this was a true foreseeing. We shall find what we seek!"

Her enthusiasm daunted him. Had she had reservations all these days behind the confidence she seemed to draw from her pendant? Was it that she truly had not been sure that it *would* lead her—them— anywhere? He guessed so, but said nothing. It was plain that she now was very sure indeed of success.

"What," she asked, "is that you are wearing?" Her gaze was fastened on the band he had braided. "It is made of metal wire. Why did you make it? Why do you wear it?"

"That is my own secret," Sander answered stolidly. He had no intention of letting her know what had happened. "A smith's secret."

She accepted that. Nor did she question it when he fastened about Rhin's throat the other bit of twisted metal, though he knew she was watching him closely.

The fishers flowed away with their usual speed. And after eating, Sander reloaded the koyot, making fast the back burden in such a way that not more than two jerks of a single cord could loosen it. If they were to face danger, Rhin was not to be handicapped at the onset of any fight.

Fanyi led out, her eyes ever seeking the pendant. The mounds of rubble were thinning, with more space between them to give room to a stronger growth of first brush and then trees, the latter thickening in girth the farther they went. They continued to parallel the river bank and gradually the land sank, so that the cliffs which hung above the water were no longer so high.

Not long after leaving camp they came into a wide, open stretch rutted with the marks of carts. Rhin lowered his nose to sniff, but he did not growl. To Sander's trail-wise eyes, these all looked old, made some time ago. But there were so many of them, crossing and recrossing, that it was plain in the past there had been a great deal of traffic in and out of the city. Also the deep impression of most ruts hinted at heavy loads.

He caught no sign of any koyot pad tracks mixed up with the cut of cart wheels. Rather there were others— those of the famous greathounds of the Traders. For the first time since they had left their night camp, Sander broke the silence, though he believed Fanyi had been so intent on her own thoughts, perhaps mulling over the dream she termed a "foreseeing," that she had hardly been aware he and Rhin were with her.

"If your sign points us in this way," he observed, "we may not be the only ones to find your storage place. The Traders, or whoever has combed this city, seem to have passed here in force."

The girl shook her head. "I do not believe that any Trader knows of what we seek. It is not metal, the work of Before Men's hands, rather it is work of their minds. I know of no Trader who would concern himself with such."

"Do you know of all the Trader clans?" he countered. "We, on the plains, have contact with four bands who come regularly, nearly thirty men in all. We have never seen their women. How many came to Padford?"

"I can remember twenty," she answered promptly. "And my father—but he was no Trader. There may be others like him, seekers of knowledge."

"Yet he traveled with the Traders," Sander pressed. "And it is known that that is not their way, to allow any not of their kin to follow their trails."

"My mother said that those who brought him treated him oddly, almost as if they feared him in some manner. Yet he was not a man who carried his weapons loosed or who quarreled easily. She said she was sure that the Trader chief was pleased when they left and my father chose to remain behind for the winter. Yet he said he would go with them when they came again, for he thought to travel even further to the south to learn what lay there. And they did not refuse him when he spoke."

Sander grew a little tired of this mysterious father who had been laid in his grave place before even Fanyi was born. He seemed to have made such an impression on the Shaman mother who had taken him to her house that she treated him with a reverence and awe that was not usual among her sex.

The women of the Mob chose their mates. Yes, and discarded them if they were not satisfied with their bargains. His father had been chosen twice. But the latter time he had declined the proposal, for he already had a son to learn his mysteries. And no smith wanted to divide his power when the days came that his own arm was no longer strong enough to swing the greatest hammer. Sander had been raised mainly in a household of men: his father, his uncle, who had so sharp a tongue and narrow a mind that no woman had ever looked upon him with favor, himself who was apprentice.

Any tenthold was eager to supply a smith with well-worked clothing, a portion of baked meal cakes, blankets woven from the wool of the herds, in exchange for what his father could fashion in return. Those of their own tent had never gone empty of belly or cold of body, even though no woman's loom or cooking pots rode in their travel wagon.

But for the most part a man owned only his weapon and his tools, all else belonged to a woman. It was she who fitted out her daughter, when the maid came to choose, and count led her to choose wisely and with an eye for the future, mainly among the older men and not the youths whose skills were yet unproven.

Was this custom also held among Fanyi's people? If that were true, and Sander expected it was, then the women of Padford could well have drawn aside from a stranger such as her father, seeing no security in such a union that was bound to be a short one. However, their Shaman had welcomed him, spoke of him with unusual respect, nursed him until his death. The unknown traveler must indeed have had some force of character to win such a response.

"It is not usual," Fanyi continued, "for a Shaman to wed. Her powers should not be limited by showing favor to any one man. Yet it is also necessary that she breed a daughter to follow her in her craft. Therefore, when my mother chose a far traveler, the village was content.

Only she found him to be much more than she supposed. And when he died, her mourning was not of ceremony only but from the heart."

"You say"—Sander felt a little uncomfortable at that note in his companion's voice, as if he had walked into the private portion of a tent without being so urged by its owner—"that a Shaman must bear a daughter. But what if there comes a son—?"

Fanyi laughed. "That will never happen, smith. We have our own secrets and in some things we can even outwill the ways of nature. The first of my clan, she who survived the Dark Times, had a learning new even then. And this she gave to her daughter, and from daughter to daughter that was passed. *We* do not breed sons, only daughters—and only one to each generation. For that is our will—though it can be altered if we are minded, only we are not. For there is no place for a boy-child in a Shaman's house."

As they were journeying, the land had opened out before them. The outline of an abrupt rise ahead showed such sharp pinnacles, such knife-edged clefts as Sander had never sighted before. Here the river rushed faster, with a roar. They rounded a point to see before them a mighty falls, a mist half-veiling the falling water, spinning out in filmy threads to hide the full length of that downpour.

On the other side of the river the land lay more level, those nodules of saw-edged rock less discernible. Sander halted in some dismay as he sighted plainly what lay ahead. Some great force had twisted and rent this land. Flows of lava had caught blocks of stone, tangles of warped metal, now rusted and eroded. The landscape was such a gigantic mixture of things made by man held captive by nature, frozen into what seemed an impenetrable barrier, that it daunted them.

Yet the ruts of the cart tracks headed directly

forward into a country they would have sworn no wheel could cross. Fanyi stared at that jumbled barrier across the land.

"A wave—a wave that swept in from the sea," she murmured. "A wave as high as a mountain. A wave that carried with it most of the city—a wave that broke here and so lost its hold upon that which was heaviest. Such a wave as it is said carried the ship of my people inland. Now I marvel that they survived—unless their wave was smaller."

"It does not matter how this was made." Sander came directly to the point. "We are concerned with finding a way through, if your guide still tells us that must be done."

She studied the pendant and then nodded. "The indicated path still lies straight before us. But these"— she pointed to the wagon ruts—"say that others must have found a road, one large enough to take their carts."

Sander did not point out that traveling such a well-marked path might well be inviting ambush. For the moment he could see no other chance of penetrating that unbelievable mass ahead.

"Look!" Fanyi pointed. "A building!"

For a moment he was startled by what she pointed out. Then he saw the wreckage was not a complete building, merely blocks still perhaps connected by the metal sinews the Before People used to tie together their masses of stone; but enough of those blocks were intact to make a shell of sorts hard-rammed against a pinnacle.

The hugeness of the disaster that had left its own monument here was overpowering. He had accepted all his life the tales of the Dark Times, of the titanic forces that had overpowered the Before World; he had seen the rubble of tumbled cities, the sea-desert. But not until he stood before this breath-taking crumbled mass that been thrown by the force of a raging sea upon tormented and shaken earth, there to be rooted after the water's retreat, had it even been directly brought home to him what fury had been loose upon his kind and their world. As Fanyi had said, it was hard to believe that any man could have escaped what had struck in the Dark Time. Even the chants of the Rememberers did not reveal the deep despair of those who must have fled, only to be licked away by water or engulfed when quakes opened the very land under their feet.

Fanyi had covered her face with her hands.

"It is—" She could not find words, he realized. Any more than he could summon them at this moment.

He put his arm about her shaking shoulders, drew her against him, two small humans standing before the death sign of a world.

At length Sander, with difficulty, wrenched his gaze away from that incredible wall.

"Do not look at it," he told her. "Watch the ruts; maybe you are right and those will guide us through."

Resolutely, he stared down at the rough marks on the ground. Here and there were bared lumps of stone over which the wheels must have grated. The way turned farther from the cliff edge, away from the falls. Those, too, Sander would not look upon. There was a kind of horrible fascination about the down-dash of that water, as if a man observing it too closely might be led to leap, following the flow. The thunderous sound beat louder and louder in their ears as they half stumbled, half fled along the path.

Sander noted that Rhin was now running, nose to the ground, as if on a hunting trail. The koyot did not even appear to notice the horrible mountain range of debris. Of course, the smith understood, to Rhin's mind, intelligent as the animal was, it would have no meaning. Only to man who had lost so much would the sight deliver a hard blow out of the past.

Now the wagon track narrowed. They drew opposite the falls, and the sound was such they could not have heard each other, even if they had tried to exchange some form of encouragement. There was a single set of tracks and those ran perilously close to the drop. Sander edged his back to the wall of the heights, facing out, drawing Fanyi with him. Their clothing, hair and faces, were wet with spray as they moved along crabwise, as far back from the edge as they could push. Rhin had bounded ahead, but they moved by slow degrees. Sander felt giddy, he fought a desire to leave that mass of stone and tangled debris behind him, to advance to the water side. If he did that, he believed, he would be lost.

Fanyi with the fingers of one hand gripped his furred overjacket so tightly her knuckles were bleached pale. In her other hand she had palmed the pendant, and her lips moved as if she recited some Shaman's words of power.

Their journey seemed to last forever. Twice they dropped to their bellies and crawled in order to continue to hug the side wall, for masses of stone or rusty, broken metal projected outward. Yet the wagon ruts continued, and Sander knew a vast respect for those who had dared to drive along this way, or else the others had done this so often that the first surge of terror in the face of the overwhelming disaster of mankind had been long since forgotten.

To the right, now that they were at last past the falls, there spread a lake, dotted with islands of rock and a reef or two of long-cooled lava. On the far side of the lake, which they could only just sight, was an opening that must lead to another river, as if the lake had two outlets.

A second wall of debris began to rise, this time between them and the lake. Here Sander saw evidence that the road had been opened partly by man's labor, using tools that had left marks on stone blocks, or cut away masses of metal. The space so cleared was hardly wider than a wagon, a small wagon, while the labor it must have cost could only make Sander believe there must lie at the end of this trail some rich reward equal to such effort. Having passed the falls, Sander began to trot, Fanyi running lightly on beside him. He sweated as he went, his heart pounding as he refused to look any higher than the surface of the very rough way before them. It began to slope downward.

They had passed beyond that portion where the road had been cut by man. The way opened out again. Ahead they could see that this slope continued down nearly to the level of the lake's water.

On their side of the lake there was no sign of vegetation. This grim and deadly mass supported not even the most stunted bush. But across the lake the yellow and red of trees in fall leaf showed, and a green line along the shore where reeds might be growing.

It was as they dropped down into this lower way that they met Rhin and the fishers. All three animals stood barring their path as if in warning.

Rhin gave a summoning yelp, and Sander began to run, though he watched his footing that he might not crash by catching a foot in one of the deeply worn ruts. The koyot's stance suggested excitement, also a certain wariness. Now Rhin's pointed muzzle swung to the heights where the gigantic flood had deposited what it had carried inland.

When the fishers saw that the two humans were coming, they humped away to be lost among the crannies and pit holes of the distorted range. Rhin gave a last warning yelp, scrambled off in the same direction.

Among these fantastic heapings of stone, twisted and broken spikes of metal, some caught in congealed lava pools, there were plenty of places one could take refuge. The boom of the falls was loud behind them. Though he strained his ears, Sander could catch no sound which arose above that, since Rhin had given tongue. The smith climbed a spur of wreckage, testing each step above before he put his full weight upon it, then turned to reach down a hand to Fanyi.

Together they reached a place where a jagged pinnacle had split off from the mass of parent rock. Jammed into the cleft between the two was a mass of debris that looked none too steady. There were far too many sharp-ended bits to afford them any but a precarious perch. Yet here the fishers had flattened out, clinging to their choice of support with their claws. Rhin crouched, his belly tight against the uneven rock and metal, frozen into immobility. So well did his gray-brown coat fade into the background that Sander knew the koyot was practicing one of his hunting tricks. He could thus lie for patient hours intent upon the burrow of a hare or a deer trail that led to water.

There was barely room enough left for Sander and the girl to crowd in beside the koyot. Once there Sander made ready his dart throwers. Rhin gazed back down trail, the way they had come. His ears pricked forward, and Sander could feel the vibrations of a growl the animal did not voice aloud.

Sander leaned closer to the girl so his lips nearly brushed the now unkempt hair above her ear.

"Do your fishers know what danger comes?" Not for the first time he wished that he and Rhin had a more complete form of communication. He believed that Fanyi could read the thoughts of her two furred ones, or at least guess more accurately what their action indicated.

She wriggled about to gaze steadily up at Kai. The fisher's fangs showed in wicked promise.

"Something comes," she made answer, "and from more than one way. See how Kayi faces forward, while Kai faces back? We are between two sources of trouble."

Sander grimaced. This was all he needed. He had perhaps ten bolts, and there was his sword knife, also the sling with which he hunted. A pebble propelled by that might be useful and dangerous in its own way, but it would be necessary to aim with great accuracy. He laid his darts ready to hand, then jerked loose Rhin's burden, leaving the koyot free if there was to be a fight.

For a long space it seemed that the alarm had been false. However, Sander knew the range of the animals' hearing far exceeded his own. They might even have scented what prowled along that narrow road. Then—

The sound that filled the air whirled him back in time to his childhood. With it came a stab of fear as sharp as a sword point thrust into his flesh. Such a clamor had long ago tortured the ears of the Mob so much that they had stuffed in bits of grass to deaden their hearing.

It was the battle horn of the White Ones! No one who had ever heard could forget it. Now that bray pierced the roar of the falls as easily as if the clamor of unleashed water did not exist.

In turn the horn was answered by a croaking, a booming series of cries, which were even more startling. For they did not proceed from any human throat.

Up the trail from the lake they came in great hops, those weird amphibians who were like the river dwellers in the desert. Their bodies were encased in the same shell-fashioned armor, while each held a wickedly barbed spear. The huge shells from which they had made their helmets so overhung their countenances that, from the perch where Sander's party hid, they could see nothing but the shells themselves.

As the amphibians came into sight, they broke ranks, climbing into hollows and crevices, squatting there on their haunches. Like Rhin, they carried with them an inborn camouflage that made them nigh invisible as they burrowed into their chosen nooks, preparing an ambush, Sander was sure.

Once more came the sound of the battle horn. One of those huge antlered beasts, such as had served the White Ones who had died on the plains, came into view. This time the creatures did not pull a trail wagon; rather, it carried a rider, his boot toes tucked within a band lashed about its middle. The White One who so rode advanced with caution, his mount picking a slow way. Only two or three steps did the antlered one take into the open. Then it shied back, grunting deeply.

There was bared metal, a sword twice the length of the knife Sander wore, in the hand of the rider. His head, covered by a peaked hood of hide, swung slowly right to left and back again. Only when the battle horn boomed again, delivering an order, did he urge his mount on. Fanyi reached up, laid one hand on each of the fishers' muzzles, to quiet them. Once more Sander felt the vibration in Rhin's body. But they all froze without a sound.

A second of the huge deer (if deer those were) advanced into the range of their vision, with more behind. However, the riders moved with such caution Sander was sure they expected trouble. Not one of the amphibians had moved. In fact, when Sander glanced in their direction, even though he had seen them settle in, he could distinguish only one or two of them, and these only because he recognized the crevices they had chosen.

The White Ones' eyes searched the ragged walls. As the last one pushed out into the descending trail, Sander saw the long sweep of the war horn now slung across his back. Their party was small, only a half-dozen. They could well be scouts for just such an invasion as the Mob had defeated when Sander was a child.

Their outer coats were made of long and shaggy fur, matted and filthy. Binding the coats tightly to their bodies were wide sashes of stained and dirty cloth. They did not appear to speak to one another as they drew to a halt, but their hands were upheld, the fingers moving in quick jerks, which perhaps conveyed meaning.

It was apparent that they disliked what they saw or sensed ahead, yet some strong need pressed them forward. The leader urged his mount on, his hand ready on his sword. However, the spears of the hidden

amphibians were twice—three times the length of that
weapon. Any of the water creatures could bring down
such a rider before he would be in range to retaliate.

Sander, now watching the enemy, saw a movement
of one of those shafts, a readying for battle. At that
moment an impulse arose in him to cry out—to warn
the White Ones. Only his knowledge of what had
happened on the plains more than ten years ago kept
him dumb. Then the White Ones had been like
demons, slaying without any mercy, finally killing themselves lest they have any contact with his own people.
Their utter ruthlessness was so much a part of his clan
tradition that normally he would have had no wish to
raise a single finger in their behalf. But they still wore
the guise of men of his own species, while those waiting
to spear them down had no part of any world he knew.

Fanyi's hands fell on the smith's shoulders. She
exerted force to pin him in place, cramping his arms
so that he could not have launched a dart without a
struggle, which would betray them to both parties.

Her lips formed a distinct "no." He had a flash of
dislike and fear. If Fanyi could read his brain, as she
might be doing, he did not like it.

The leader of the White Ones paced warily on. Then
a spear whirled out of nowhere. Only a swift swerve
of his mount kept the man from impalement. The
amphibians boiled out of hiding, hopping forward,
spears forming a wall of points. It was apparent the
White Ones could not hope to attack, having only the
weapons Sander saw in their hands.

The man bearing the horn, riding several lengths
behind the swordsmen, now made the first move. He
swung the horn around, setting the rounded mouth-
piece to his lips, steadying the length of dull metal
against the neck of his mount. His cheeks puffed and
he blew mightily.

The shock of sound sent Sander's hands to his ears. He felt Rhin quiver, as if the high notes were a lash laid across the koyot's muscular body. Fanyi loosed her hold on the smith. Instead, she pressed a hand again on each fisher's head, though those animals twisted and writhed.

As much as that blast had affected their own party, it had an even greater effect on the amphibians. Two dropped their spears and fell to the ground, where they lashed out with arms and legs, as if in torment. Their fellows retreated, a retreat that became a rout when they reached what seemed a safe distance from the swordsmen. The White Ones booted their mounts into a trot and rode after the fleeing water creatures. Now the leader of the riders leaned over to strike at the necks of the two amphibians on the ground, stilling their writhing bodies. Both parties vanished in a whirlwind of dust, rounding the turn in the trail up which the amphibians had come earlier.

Sander made no move to lead his own party out of hiding. He still suspected that the White Ones were a scout squad and behind them toiled such a tribe as had come down on the plains.

However, Rhin relaxed and the fishers squirmed from Fanyi's hold, uttering cries as if to urge their companions on. Thus Sander was forced to accept the idea that these White Ones were not being followed, at least not closely. If that were true, the sooner he and the others were away from this debatable land the better.

He paused by one of the fallen amphibians, though he did not look, or want to look, closely, under that mottled brown shell helmet, at the thing's face, now slack in death. But he picked up the spear and trailed it with him.

The shaft was far too long, but he believed it could

be cut to a shorter length. The barbs that crowned it were so cleverly wrought that, against his inclination, he paid tribute to the smith who had fashioned them. The material was not metal, rather bone, skillfully carved. He shuddered at the thought of how such a head would tear into flesh. The barbs were slender. Undoubtedly they would break were the spear to be withdrawn, leaving fragments to fester within the wound.

Released by the lifting of Fanyi's will and hand, the fishers humped around the curve of the trail and disappeared, following both the White Ones and the retreating water creatures. Sander remained in two minds about the wisdom of continuing. If there *was* another company of White Ones somewhere behind them, they could well be caught in a pincers between two deadly teams of fighters. But for the same reason he could not suggest retreat.

If they could be as fortunate the second time to find a hiding place among the chaos of the rocks, they might have a chance to escape. But a man should not risk his life easily on the turn of fortune alone.

The mass of storm wrack still towered over them. As they went, no more shattering blasts from the battle horn sounded. However, when they turned a curve, to see before them the shore of the lake, they witnessed the last of that engagement.

The White Ones rode up and down along the shore. Plainly they were not tempted to follow their enemies into the lake where those swam with the ease of creatures in their natural element. The escaping amphibians left tell-tale vees of ripples, showing very little even of their heads above the surface.

The land, which was level here, widened out. Sander made a quick decision to leave the road and turn left to skirt the edge of the heights. A quick climb aloft there might be their own salvation if the White Ones sighted them.

In this manner they crept along, sometimes traveling on their hands and knees; Rhin also crouched. Stone cut through their garments, bruised their hands; yet that hardship was nothing if they could pass unseen as far as riders and swimmers were concerned.

To the north the White Ones seemingly gave up their hopes of attacking those in the lake. The riders drew together, and Sander caught the flutter of their hands as they conferred in soundless language.

Finally the party of mounted men broke apart. Two booted their antlered beasts back the way they had come, sending Sander, Fanyi, and Rhin flat against earth behind the nearest outcrop of the heights. The smith lifted his head cautiously. In so much his fears had been proven right. Those riders heading east must be going either to report or gather reinforcements. His own party's salvation was to make their way as quickly as possible past the other riders settling down on the lake shore.

Keeping to the broken foothills was the best answer. The enemy mounts, larger and much heavier than Rhin, needed room in which to maneuver. They could not crawl along the ground as the koyot now prudently moved.

Still, to hug the side of the heights made for a very slow advance. The one advantage was the many hiding places the rough exterior of the slopes offered.

Luckily, the White Ones appeared to have no thought of immediate exploration here. Perhaps they feared other opponents beside the water things they had so easily routed. This land was made for ambushes. A handful of the Mob, had they darts enough, might tumble the whole of the White Ones' tribe into swift death. Sander was certain he had not sighted any dart throwers among that band. Surely, if the riders had had such weapons they would have loosed them at the amphibians.

Their creeping carried them well past the riders at last. Now Sander waved Fanyi and Rhin to their feet. A screen of debris, studded with outthrust masses of stone and eroded metal, stood as if it had been intended as a barricade. Behind that, although they could not hurry, at least they made much better time.

Twice Sander climbed the crest of the barricade. It was really a vast layer of completely fused material, which must have broken from the heights behind it, to form a jagged foothill. From cover there he could survey the back trail.

He marked the ruts of the road, which still ran along the bank of the lake. The riders were now following it at a slow walk. Plainly, the White Ones were not pushing their pace.

Finally, the leading rider slipped from his beast, with the others following suit. Their mounts strode out into the shallows of the lake where some green of water plants not yet stricken by frost showed. Dipping their heads, the animals wrenched off great mouthfuls of the vegetation, champing lustily. The men had taken up their position beside a large jutting rock and were opening their saddle bags.

Sander realized that he, too, was hungry. But they could not linger here. The more distance they put between themselves and those scouts, the better pleased he would be.

His party worked their way on, discarding no caution, through great masses of refuse crushed by the ancient waves and left by the draining sea. Sander longed now and then to test some bit of metal he saw embedded in that debris. With this at hand—why had the Traders ever sought the more eroded and destroyed city? Or had that trail been meant to lead here in order to plunder this huge chaos?

Yet there were no signs of any delving about. In fact, Sander believed, it would be very chancy to try it. Now and again, just as the mounds in the city had been trimmed by a brisk wind, these masses broke loose and came crashing down. So he kept one eye overhead, to avoid passing near any height that looked unstable.

They halted at last because they were too tired to keep going. Sharing out their meat and water, Fanyi gave a great sigh. Rhin lay panting heavily after he had gulped his portion. The humans' boots had suffered from the broken ways over which they had come. Sander cut loose the bundle of uncured hare skins and tied them around their feet, fur side in, hoping to provide a little cushion and protect what was left of their boots.

Fanyi rubbed the calves of her slim brown legs. "Never have I traveled such a trail as this," she commented. "Those ruts were bad enough, but this scrambling up and down is far worse. And how long will it last?"

He knew no more than she. The crumbled stones, the lava-engulfed wrack of the ancient sea, was everywhere. Some peaks of rock rose mountain-high, plainly up-thrust from the earth's crust at nearly the same time the sea had swirled in. It was a nightmare land, and Sander gave thanks to fortune that they had traveled it so far with no more than scraped skin or a bruised and battered hand, to show. It was plain that they must hole up before the coming of night. Even Fanyi's precious Before light could not guide them over such rough ground.

The lake was so large that even with all their traveling they had not yet reached the western end.

It tantalized Sander every time he climbed to view a path before them. But he had been warned by the adventures of the White Ones. To go near that occupied water would be an act of folly. They must keep to these harsh, broken lands for safety.

Some time before sundown they chanced upon such a place as Sander thought would serve. Two massive slides from the heights had spread into the lower land, now forming walls of fused fragments. Between these lay a stretch of relatively smooth ground. They dared not light a fire, even if they could have found wood. Fanyi had recalled the fishers, and she curled down between their furred bodies, perhaps warmer so than she might have been by a fire. Sander had Rhin.

The animals rested quietly, displaying no unease. They ate quickly, with evident relish, the chunks of dried meat Sander doled out, though the fishers were so easily satisfied the smith suspected that even in this desolate land they had found game during their earlier roaming. However, none of the three showed any interest in vanishing again as the night closed in. When the dark was really thick, Sander borrowed Fanyi's Before light. Shading that with one hand, he made his way down to the edge of the slip that formed the western wall of their refuge.

There he snapped the light off and stared intently eastward. If the White Ones still followed the wagon trail, they might not be adverse to setting up a camp with a fire. But he caught no sight of any flame.

It was only when he turned again west, ready to grope his way back to their own hollow, that he sighted a spark of what could only be firelight. He was sure that the White Ones had not ridden past them during the afternoon. Therefore those scouts had not lit this beacon. For beacon it appeared to him, so high was it set. As he watched, it began to blink, slowly, in a pattern of off-and-on.

In the same fashion the Mob sent warnings across country when there was danger to the herds. But these blinks bore no resemblance to the code in which he had been trained. Sander whirled around, facing east again.

Yes, he had been right with that guess! There was another high-placed spark of light that blinked in answer. White Ones? Somehow he doubted it. The men who had scattered the amphibians this morning appeared to be riding a new, unknown trail. But who else would signal among these tormented hills?

Traders? That seemed far more of a possibility. All that Sander knew concerning the strictly kept secrets of their own places arose in his mind. They could well have posted sentries in the heights, sentries who had marked both the coming of the White Ones and Sander's own party. Were the White Ones as much enemies of the Traders as they had proven to be for the Mob on the plains?

At this moment he fervently hoped so. That fact would make his own position and that of Fanyi much the stronger. A mutual enemy could draw together even unfriends in a time of peril.

The light to the east gave a last wink and vanished. As he turned his head, he saw that that to the west was also gone. He crept carefully back to their camp and settled down beside the koyot. He could hear Fanyi's breathing through the dark, even and peaceful. He guessed that she was already asleep.

But Sander did not follow her swiftly. There was something that seemed to loom over him, spreading outward from the congealed storm wrack. This had been a place of death, not only of men, but also of their ambitions, their dreams, all that they had fashioned. If any earth-tied spirits existed, where better could one hear their broken whispering, their pleas for life, their fear of a death so terrifying that their minds could not imagine the blotting out of their world?

Some of that horror that had gripped him in the morning, when he and Fanyi had looked for the first time upon this place, stirred in him now. He was cold with more than the chill of the night. Almost, he could hear screams, shouts of those lost and long gone.

Sternly, Sander set himself to the regaining of good sense. His lips moved as he recited the power words of the smith. A man made tools and weapons with his hands—after a pattern his mind sketched for him. Those who used them in time died and were laid there in their barrows. This was the natural way of life. The dead who might have perished here in the Dark Times—they were long gone. And the things they fashioned were not the things Sander understood. He might be of their distant kin, but he was not of their clan; they had no hold on him.

He fought imagination, put out of his mind as best he could that memory of the fragment of a building he had seen still partly intact and plastered against the cliff. The Before Men had had great knowledge to serve them, but it had not helped them escape the Dark Time. What good then was all their special learning when the earth and sea turned against them?

Slowly, he considered the quest that had drawn him here. Very far in the past now lay the taunting words of his uncle. They no longer awoke a flame of anger within him. Below these tormented mountains, his own life seemed very small, nearly meaningless. Yet it was *his* life. And if there lay ahead what Fanyi had promised, the wisdom of the Before Men that he could take for himself, then he would not be as small either.

His fingers flexed as he lay, thinking of patterns he had long carried in his head, things he would do if he could work the unknown metals—

It would not even matter much whether he returned to face down those elders of the Mob who had decided that he was too untried and young to take his father's place. No, what would matter most was the fact that he would *know*—know and use skills he had dreamed of but never found.

He pillowed his head against Rhin's haunch, resolutely shutting out the terror of the heights, intent upon what lay here and now.

With morning they circled down to the lake where Sander filled their water bottle while Fanyi and the fishers kept watch. Here the water had an odd, metallic taste. But Fanyi pronounced it harmless, saying that the minerals in it might well be beneficial, for she brewed such for healing. There was no sign of the amphibians. However, Sander noticed on one of the rocky islands, well out from the shore, a mound of set stones in which a dark entrance hole opened directly on the lake. He believed that this might mark a home of the creatures.

They turned away again from the easier surface of the wagon road, to scramble along at the edges of the hills. The open space was slowly narrowing again, sooner or later they would be forced back closer to that rutted track. Sander kept listening. Their own feet, muffled by the hare pelts, and the pads of the animals woke little or no sound. But even the slip of a stone seemed to echo far too loudly!

Once more the road began to climb. Here some of the ruts had been filled with stones, and the debris had once more been cut back on either side. They must now return to that cut, for to climb jagged rocks on either side offered a risk Sander did not want to contemplate. There was too much danger of a fall.

He forced the pace, wanting to be quickly out of this gap where they were so clearly visible. Somewhere in the battered heights above, that light he had sighted in the night must mark a sentinel's post. He had no doubt that they had already been noted and spied upon. Yet the challenge Sander continued to expect did not come.

Beyond this second narrowing of the level land, the heights sloped once again. And from the peak the road cut, they caught a good view of what lay ahead. There were some rises, but none as tall as those behind, and far less of the battered wrack of the waves had been planted here.

Instead, below was a growth of grass, scattered trees wearing scarlet and gold, some stands of pines showing dark green. And—Sander paused, in startlement.

It looked like a cross between the village of Padford, with its wooden and stone walls, and the mobile tents-on-wheels used by the Mob. A deep ditch had been dug, into which some water from a river feeding the lake had been diverted. Beyond that ditch, earthen walls mounted high, crowned with a wall of tree trunks. The tops of these were hewn into points like a defensive stake barrier, save these trunks were larger and more firmly set than any such wall he had ever seen before.

Clustered within were tents-on-wagons—much larger than those the Mob hauled to form their own temporary clan-towns up and down the plains. The tents-on-wagons circled an open space wherein stone had been used to construct a rough tower, standing perhaps twice the height of the tents about it. From cooking places before each tent rose trails of smoke. People stirred about, coming and going. A band of loose animals, herded by one mounted man, trotted out of the enclosure, across a bridge which could be lowered or raised to span the ditch.

Hounds! Then this must be a Trader stronghold. Unlike the people of the Mobs, the Traders bred different animals. The hounds, as they were called, were akin to Rhin, yet different, in that their ears did not stand erect, but flopped on either side of their heads. And instead of uniform coloring, they were splotched, spotted, marked with white and red-brown patches or feet. No two ever looked alike. The Traders seldom rode on their long treks, but used these beasts to carry their stock. But Sander had never seen them in such number before.

Surrounded by the trotting hounds was an inner core of deer-like creatures, larger than those Sander had long hunted. Having left the village, the hounds were spreading out, still guarding the deer, their noses close to the ground, coursing off in different directions much as a koyot would do when released to hunt. Their herder kept on, riding alone straight after the deer in the general direction of the gap.

The fishers, reared on either side of Fanyi, began to sound their hissing battle cry. But she instantly had a hand on each. It was plainly her will, not her light hold that restrained them. Rhin watched with interest but did not growl. He knew Traders of old and had fraternized with the hound pack-hounds they had brought with them.

The hound that bore the rider suddenly gave tongue and began to run. And behind Sander came a voice, sharp and clear:

"Stand! Or do you want your throats torn out, fools?"

That question was asked in such a tone that Sander did not doubt the questioner was quite ready to enforce his command. He allowed his hands to drop into full sight, his weapons still in belt and shoulder strap. Inwardly, he was deeply ashamed to be thus easily taken by a hidden sentry.

The rider arrived swiftly, for the hound ran at top speed, while the fishers snarled in open rage. Still Fanyi kept them under control. Rhin yelped, the hound answered with a deep bay.

Sander longed to turn and see who kept watch behind, but he knew the folly of making any move, which might bring instant hostile reprisal.

The rider pulled to a halt before them. He wore the leather breeches and furred overjacket of a plainsman. But his face was half-hidden by a black beard trimmed to a point, and his ear length hair was mostly covered by a cap of yellow-white fur. His hands held a thrower ready, dart in the slot, and there was no welcome to be read in his expression.

"Who are you?" His demand was abrupt, as he eyed first Fanyi and then Sander, though, Sander noted, he kept shooting wary glances at the fishers.

"I am Sander, smith. And this is Fanyi, Shaman of Padford—" Sander answered with an outward show of confidence, which he hoped he could continue to assume.

"A smith and a shaman," returned the rider. "And why do you wander? Or are you outriders of some Mob?" His two questions were frankly hostile.

"You are Jon of the Red Cloak," Fanyi spoke up in return. "I have seen you in Padford. That was five seasons ago."

"I was there. But a Trader goes many places during his travels. And what does the Shaman of Padford do here? You are tied to your people by the Great Will you obey. Do the men of Padford wander, then?"

"Not so. Most lie dead, Trader Jon. How many the Sea Sharks might have taken, I cannot number."

Though he still held the dart thrower steady, now the man gazed intently at the girl.

"Sea Sharks, eh? You say they raided Padford?"

"They killed, they burned, they took," she repeated with emphasis.

"But he—" The thrower moved a fraction to indicate Sander. "This smith is not of your people. How came he, and why, to this land? No Mob favors leaving their plains, except for good reason."

"I had good reason," Sander returned. "No Mob has two smiths. Therefore I come to seek knowledge— more knowledge of metals."

The man's gaze grew fiercer. "You are bold, smith, to say thus you come to steal our secrets!"

"I care not," Sander answered, "where the metals are found. It is the working of them that means much to me."

"So," commented the Trader, "any man might say, were he found where he has no right to be."

"Do you then," Fanyi asked, "claim all this?" She indicated the land about them.

"What it contains is ours by right of discovery. You," he snapped at Sander, as if by any prolonged conversation he weakened his case, "loose your gear"— he pointed to the bundles on Rhin—"and let me see what you have stolen—"

Though he had no idea of the strength of the force that might stand behind him, Sander refused to play meek any longer. He knew enough of Trader ways to realize that if one did not stand up to them and bargain, one was completely lost. He folded his arms across his chest.

"Are you then chief here?" he asked. "You are not head of *my* Mob, nor even a Man of First Council, unless you so declare yourself. I do not take orders— I am a smith, one with the magic of metals. Such are not to be ordered about by any man without reason. Nor," he continued, "does one so address a Shaman."

The man made a sound that might have signified scornful amusement.

"If she was Shaman of Padford, and Padford is no more because of the Sharks, then is her claim of Power false. As for you, smith," he made a taunt of that title, "more than words have to prove your worth."

The fishers growled, Rhin echoed them, while the hound bristled and showed his fangs in turn.

"Control those beasts of yours," ordered the Trader, "or else look to see them dead. Move on, carefully. We shall see what the Planners make of you."

Fanyi glared at Sander. He read warning in her look. The fishers were still growling, but they had gone to four feet again and she walked between them, her hands resting on their backs as they moved, flanking her, down toward the town.

Sander followed. There was little else he could do. He heard a scrabbling behind him and realized that his caution had been right as three riders on hounds moved forward to box him in as he went.

Some of the loose hounds came bounding closer as the party followed the rutted road toward the ditch bridge. They bayed and growled. Rhin and the fishers, their fangs showing, made ready answer to the challenges the other beasts offered. But there was no attack, for the riders sent the hounds off with a series of cries not unlike barks.

Men issued from the village to await them. It was one of these who called to their captor:

"Ha, Jon, what have you gathered in? These are no Horde stragglers."

"They are invaders no matter what they look like," the rider returned. "But if you want to trade blows with the Horde, those also come. The signals have been seen."

Fanyi stopped short of the bridge. "Trader, my companions will not enter here. Bring out your Planners."

"Dead animals can be easily transported—"

The girl raised her hands and brought them together in a loud clap. Her eyes caught and held the eyes of the threatener. He looked as if he were struggling vainly to make some further statement or give an order, but something had locked his lips.

"I have spoken, and the Power is mine, Jon of the Red Cloak—know I not your true name? Thus, I can command you to do this thing. Get hither one of authority that we may speak together."

Sander believed the rider struggled between his own will and that of the girl. He looked furious, yet he slid down from the back of the hound and tramped heavily over the bridge, those gathered there making way for him.

Fanyi's face bore that look of concentration that Sander had seen her wear when she had sat with the pendant in her hand. Though he found it hard to believe in her reputed "power," it was plain at this moment a man, who was not even conditioned to accept her decisions as her own people had doubtless always been, was obeying her orders against his own will.

There was a closed look about the men who surrounded them. Though this was obviously a well-established town, no women or children showed in that silent crowd. Sander did not like the inferences one could draw from their quiet and from their set expressions. The jovial, open friendliness the Traders displayed when visiting the Mob was gone. All those warnings concerning their jealous guardianship of their own territory were now, to Sander's thinking, made manifest by this lack of welcome.

In a world where strangers, unless they were openly hostile like the White Ones and the Sharks, were made guests and asked for stories concerning their travels and lands farther away, this suggestion of hostility shocked Sander. However, he was a smith, no one could

deny that. And in any civilization a man of such skill
must be truly welcome. He glanced from face to face
among that assembly, striving to see a forehead tattoo
matching his own. Was there no smith here at all? As
fellow members of a craft that had its own secrets, he
could claim acceptance from that one man at least in
this village.

But he could not sight on anyone's skin the blue
hammer brand. Still he rehearsed in his mind the work-
words by which he could prove his claim to the metal
mysteries.

There came another parting of the crowd and
Sander saw Jon again. With him was a much older man.
The newcomer walked haltingly, using sticks which he
dug into the ground to support his forward-leaning
body on each side. He held his head at a stiff and
surely painful angle. For all his crookedness of body
his gait was swifter than Sander would have thought
possible. He nearly matched Jon's strides in spite of
his own more limited steps.

Alone among the Traders the newcomer bore a
forehead marking. For a moment Sander thought that
here must be the smith he had sought. Then he
realized that no man so frail of body could carry out
any but the easiest metal work. And his tattoo was not
of a hammer, although it had a strange familiarity. At
first, Sander could not remember where he had seen
before the profile of that fierce-eyed bird head. Then
he recalled the broken bit of stone he had found along
the river, the symbol Fanyi said had once stood for a
great and proud country.

The bird-marked man stopped before Sander and
his group. For a long moment he studied each in turn,
both people and animals. At last he spoke in a voice
so deep and rich it seemed almost too powerful for
his thin body.

"You"—he singled out Fanyi from the first—"are of Power. You"—now he swung his head around a little to look at Sander—"are a smith of the plains people. Yet you travel together with these who are your companions. What matter brings so strange and diverse a band together?"

"I am of Padford," Fanyi replied. "But Padford no longer is. The Sea Sharks came and—" She made a gesture of negation.

"I have heard it said," the other said, "that the Power of a true Shaman can walk in those people who believe."

"It was the time of the Great Moon," Fanyi answered steadily, though her face was bleak. "I answered the call of my need. It was at that time they struck."

The old man's lips and jaw moved a trifle as if he chewed upon words in some manner that he might thus test truth by the taste of them. He made no comment, only swung a second time to Sander.

"And you, smith, as you name yourself, what brought you out of the plains, away from your Mob and kin?"

"My father died." Sander gave him the truth, seeing no reason to disguise it. "I was young, too young, my uncle claimed, to be full smith, though my father had named me so. There is no place in any Mob for two smiths—therefore I claimed out-right."

"The impatience of the young, was that it, smith? You could not bend your pride, but rather chose to live kinless?" There was, Sander believed, a note of derision in that query. He held his temper manfully.

"There was also the wish for knowledge."

"Knowledge!" That sharp word cut him short. "Knowledge of what, smith? Of some treasure trove you could plunder to buy your way back to your kin? Was that it? Hunt metal for yourself so that Traders cannot make their living!"

A growl akin to Rhin's rose from the crowd about them. Before Sander could answer, the other continued:

"And what treasure have you looted, smith? Turn out your gear."

Sander wanted to balk, but he knew that he would thus only provoke a struggle that would do no good. Sullenly he went to Rhin, unknotted the bag holding his work tools and the small bits of metal he had pried and broken loose in the ship. As he unrolled the covering, Jon pounced on one of those lengths of battered wire.

"See, he has—" the Trader began with a kind of triumph, then he held the wire closer to his eyes. Dropping that length, he pawed over the rest of Sander's small store. "Look you, Planman!"

The Trader held a fistful of the ship's stuff closer to the old man.

"Whence had you this?" the latter demanded.

"There was a ship, one caught in the sea-desert. This came from the inside of that," Sander explained. The Planner must be half-smith, himself, or have an eye smith-trained, else he would not have seen that it was any different from what they might find in a ruined city.

"And this ship was of metal?" demanded the Planman.

"All of metal. There were dead men within its belly, and they were not bones."

To his surprise the Planman nodded. "It is then like unto the one Gaffred uncovered in the mountains last year, one made to travel under the surface of the water."

That, to Sander's incomprehension, appeared to convert the Planman from suspicion to at least the first stage of offering hospitality. Fanyi repeated that her animals would not enter the town, which for a short period raised again a chorus of doubts from the Traders. But at length it was agreed that Sander take housing with their smith (who had suffered an injury, which had left them for a time without a worker), while Fanyi would be allowed to stay without, camping in one of their trail wagons now parked for the season.

Sander did not like being separated from the girl. She had let these people assume that they had been drifting along together, two lost ones without kin, saying nothing of the strange storage place she sought. He had followed her lead, as after all hers was the claim on the site to which that finder of the Before Time served as a guide. But he thought that the Traders believed there was some deeper tie between them than just expediency and so considered him hostage to warrant Fanyi's presence.

Sander knew that to be untrue. There was nothing to prevent the girl from going off by night. And if she did so disappear, his lot among the Traders was going to be anything but easy. There was also the knowledge of the White Ones heading this way. But when he mentioned them, he discovered the Traders were confident of their own means of defense.

Kaboss, the smith, greeted Sander's arrival with a hardly enthusiastic grunt. He surveyed the plainsman's kit of tools, not quite with a sniff of disparagement, but with the air of a man who had in the past discarded as unworthy very similar pieces. The bits of ship wiring, however, intrigued him. And he put Sander through a most exhaustive examination concerning everything he had observed about that stranded hulk.

One of Kaboss's own heavy hands was wrapped in bandages, and once or twice when he flexed his fingers without thought, he gave an exclamation of pain. He allowed Sander to eat—such a bowl of well-seasoned

stew as the plainsman had not tasted since he left the
Mob—and then bore him to the smithy where he
pointed out a pile of repair work that had stacked up
there because of his injury. Like any Trader he haggled
over terms, but at last Sander struck a bargain that was
satisfactory enough and went to work with a will.

Rhin had been quartered in a stable and given a
gorge-feed of dried meat. Now after licking his paws,
sore from the travel in the mountains, the koyot had
gone to sleep.

Sander paid close attention to his work, though
the time for it was short, since the day had been
well advanced before they had reached the Traders'
town. Yet also he tried to think what might come
next. That Fanyi would calmly settle down as a part
of this clan, even if she were granted full kin-right,
he did not believe. And neither would he stay if she
went.

Kaboss was full smith and would take over again
entirely once his hand healed. Sander had left his
own people rather than be counted apprentice for
more years. He had no intention of playing that role
among strangers. And in spite of what he continued
to tell himself was reasonable common sense, he did
believe that the Shaman knew something when she
talked of a storage place of knowledge. The pendant
had more than half converted him to her point of
view. He had never heard or seen anything like that
before.

Kaboss's household was small. His housemate was
a silent woman, looking older than her chosen man,
her hair streaked with gray, though she was dressed
in a manner to show the importance of their household, wearing a thick necklace of much burnished
copper, four silver rings, and a belt of silver links
about her dull green robe. She did not speak often

and then only to the serving maid, who scuttled about, an anxious frown on her face as if this were a mistress no one could hope to please.

There was no sign of an apprentice. Then Kaboss mentioned that he had such, a younger son of his brother, but he had been gone for some days now on an expedition scouting for metal to the north.

Under questioning, Sander told something of their trip, their meeting with the amphibians, and the attack of the monster upon the house on the one-time island. Kaboss was much interested in that portion of his tale.

"Such are still to be found then!" he commented. "They were once so great a danger that we could not hunt lest they corner us. Then we had a great roundup, calling in the clan of Meanings and the clan of Hart, and that day we killed full twelve of them. Since, they have troubled us no more, so we thought them all gone. Now come these you call the White Ones, also to cause danger. The stream people—they are of little account. One can handle them easily enough on land."

The woman suddenly leaned a little forward in her cushioned chair. She stared intently at Sander, as if she heard nothing Kaboss had said, or if she did, it meant but little. Now she pointed to their visitor.

"Tell me, stranger, why do you wear iron in that fashion about your head?"

He had forgotten the twisted wire he had set there in hope of not repeating that experience with what Fanyi termed the "seeking thought." Now his hand went up to touch the band in half-surprise.

The woman did not wait for his answer but continued:

"You seek the protection of the 'cold iron,' is that not the truth, stranger? There has come to you something you cannot understand, something no man seeks, is that not so?"

Kaboss stared from questioner to Sander and back again. Now he edged a little away from the younger man.

"Spirit-touched!"

The woman smiled, not pleasantly. "I wonder that you did not see it for yourself, Kaboss. Yes, he is spirit-touched. And such I will not have under this roof. For it can be he might open a door for what we cannot see or feel. Take him forth and leave him with that other, who frankly says she speaks with that which is not. Do this for the safety of not only this house, but all our clan."

"Planman Allbert sent him here," Kaboss began.

"This house is mine, not that of Planman Allbert. And I think if any discover you have sheltered such a one, you will find we have more unfriends than friends."

Reluctantly, Kaboss arose and beckoned to Sander. "The house is hers," he said heavily. "So any choice is hers. Come, stranger smith."

Thus did Sander find himself again in exile, a whispered explanation to the gate guards enough to send him and Rhin packing out into the night.

Still bemused by the rapidity of what had chanced, he started for the tent-wagon that had been assigned Fanyi. He was not in the least surprised to find it empty, even her pack gone. Slinging his own burden up on Rhin, he impressed upon the koyot a need for trailing. And mounted, his koyot's nose sniffing the trail, he rode out once more.

That Kaboss had expelled him so easily from the village without referring to the Planman made Sander uneasy. As he rode on, he pondered what appeared too quick a change of attitude. The woman had certainly made clear her own feelings—which suggested that perhaps the Traders themselves had encountered just such a brain-touching invasion as Sander had met. They knew the meaning of "cold iron," which had been for a long time a legend. Sander had never known it to be invoked among his own people. Perhaps this circlet would have awakened questions had he worn it while with the Mob, but here the trader-woman had instantly named it for what it was—a protection against the unseen.

But the Planman had been so emphatic that he remain with Kaboss.

Had the old Trader been slightly too emphatic on that point? Sander's thoughts coasted away in another direction. Suppose the Traders suspected that it was not chance wandering that headed Sander and Fanyi in this direction. Being constituted as they were to think first of the discovery of hidden treasure, they would readily accept a suggestion that these trespassers had some such search in view. But, rather than try to force a secret from them, the easier way to discovery would be to loose both on some pretext and then trail them.

Sander did not doubt in the least that the Trader hounds could scent with the same efficiency and expediency as Rhin. Already men might be mounting, to skulk behind.

There was, however, the matter of the White Ones. Would their invasion be feared enough so that the Planman dare not detach any of their fighting force to hunt down Sander and the girl? The smith had nothing but guesses to add together, but he thought that the sum of them was enough.

For himself, he saw no need for secrecy. If there was any knowledge to be had, why should it not be open to all comers? He would not deny the Traders their share. But what if it were the White Ones who came after them? Sander shook his head firmly as he rode, though there was no one to witness. No, he wanted no enemy to benefit by anything Fanyi might uncover.

Rhin was plainly following a trail that was open and fresh-set. For the first time Sander considered Fanyi's attitude. She had made no attempt to wait for him. Did she value his possible aid in her quest so little that she had shrugged him off? He felt a pulse of anger at that. It was as if he were inferior, one who was of no use to her now. Perhaps the pendant had given her some secret sign that she was close enough to her goal to make his company no longer necessary. He resented the idea he might have been used and then so easily discarded.

Half believing this, he did not urge Rhin on, hot as the trail was. The fishers were too-formidable opponents. And if he had been only a temporary convenience as far as Fanyi was concerned, there was no reason to think the girl would not use the animals against him. They had no kin ties—she and he.

Now and then he glanced back at the dark blot of the Trader village. There was certainly no stir there yet. However, that did not mean that he was not under observation. They might want him well ahead before they began their hound-mounted pursuit.

There was no cover in this part of the valley. The village was situated closer to the heights on one side, while to the north curled the river. Rhin trotted toward the water, sniffing now and again at the ground. The night was frosty-clear. Sander huddled into his fur over-jacket, drawing the hood, which usually lay between his shoulders, up over his head, pulling tight its drawstring.

He was tired, and his arms and shoulders ached dully from the unaccustomed labor of the afternoon when he had exerted his best efforts to impress Kaboss with his skill. Before that had been the tension and fatigue of their struggle through the heights with the alarms along the way.

Sander knew that he could not fight off sleep too long. Even as he rode his head nodded until he would snap fully awake again. How could Fanyi have gone so steadily, though of course *she* had not labored at a forge for part of the day past.

Rhin reached the river bank and paused, nosing the ground a few paces right and then left. Finally the koyot barked, and Sander realized that those he followed must have taken to the water here, though he wondered at Fanyi's recklessness since she knew that this flood in the lower regions was occupied by the amphibians.

Did the trail here go west or north? Sander tried to push aside the heavy weariness of his body and mind to decide. Ever since they had reached the land from the sea-desert, the pendant had pointed continually west. He could not believe that the direction had now changed so abruptly.

Therefore, Fanyi and the fishers had taken to the water in a simple move to confuse any hounds set behind them. If he prospected up stream, he might come across the trail where they had issued forth again.

Only the point of emergence could be on the other side of the stream; if so, he would have only half a chance to find it.

With knee pressure he urged Rhin west, paralleling the river. There was a moon tonight. But it was on the wane and its light was limited.

As he rode in and out among a growth of brush, Sander suddenly jerked entirely awake. That band he had set about his head—it was warm! No, hot! And getting hotter! His hands went up to jerk it off, and then he hesitated. That was what the unknown wanted. Cold iron. No, hot iron, iron that could blister and sear. The pain was to force him to rid himself of his defense.

It was iron heated in a strong blast of air-fed flames. Impossible for it to be this way in the chill of the night. It could not be! Sander began the chant of the smith's work-words. The band about his head burned like a white-hot brand, only that was what the other wanted him to think! Somehow Sander realized that. So the heat was only an illusion—a dream—that was sent to rob him of his first protection.

If this torment was only a dream—then that heat did not really exist. Determinedly, he kept his hands down, fought against the agony of the branding. This—was—not—*real!*

Now Sander singsonged aloud the smith's chant. He had not believed in Fanyi's boasted powers. But he had to believe that *this* existed, or he would not feel it. Yet he stubbornly told his shrinking, hurting body, it is *not* true! There was no fire, no forge, therefore there was no heat in the thing he wore. Cold iron—*cold* iron—

Those two words became mixed with the others he spoke. *Cold* iron!

He was not quite sure when the heat began to ebb. For by that time he was only half-conscious, clinging to one thought alone, that the iron was truly *cold.*

Within his overjacket, his coarse wool shift was plastered to his body by the sweat of pain. He wobbled so that he could not have stayed on Rhin had he not seized with both hands upon the koyot's hide where it lay in loose rolls about the animal's neck. The iron was cold!

Rhin stopped—or had the koyot been halted for long moments while Sander fought his battle for survival? The smith did not know. Only, he realized, he was slipping from the saddle pad. On hands and knees, he dragged himself under the down-looping branches of a pine, sinking deep into a drift of ancient needles. There he huddled, passing quickly into exhausted sleep from that unimaginable battle.

Sander's sleep was dreamless, and when he awoke, a shaft of sunlight flashed on the stretch of river he glimpsed between two bushes. His first memory was of the strange attack. Quickly he slipped off the band, his fingers searching his skin for the tenderness of a burn. But there was no mark there. Soberly, he once more put on the band of wire. Perhaps, if he had allowed belief to settle in his mind, he *would* have been scarred. It was still hard for him to accept the fact that such things could happen.

Yet who knew what marvels the Before People had controlled? Fanyi's pendant was more than Sander had ever imagined could exist. There was Fanyi's father—that stranger she had never seen—the man who was not a Trader, but one who, of his own will, traveled to seek out new knowledge of the world. Sander knew of no other man who was so moved. A Mob crossed plains lands because of the needs of the herds on which their wealth was based. The Traders made their long treks for gain. But a man who roved merely to see what lay on the other side of a hill or beyond a valley, such Sander could not yet understand.

Rhin! Sander stared around. The koyot was not sharing his sleeping place as they always did when on the trail together. There were no paw prints in the needle carpet. And Rhin must still be burdened with all of Sander's gear. Cautiously, the smith edged down the river bank, onto a stretch of coarse gravel. He knelt, threw back his hood to splash chill water over his face. The shock of it brought him completely awake.

Because he had no other choice, Sander loosed the whistle the koyot would answer if within voice range. But, though he listened, there was no yelp, no matter how distant. Only one thing remained, lying on the pine needles—the knot of iron he had made for the koyot. Caught in it was a tuft of yellowish fur, as if Rhin, in some agony like to his own, had pawed it free.

Had Rhin run before the hounds of the Traders? One hound the koyot could have met fang to fang. However, if those of the village had loosed their pack in full, it could well be that the koyot had fled before a collection of enemies he dare not face by himself.

If so, why had Sander not been captured by the Traders? His hiding place under the pine was certainly not so secure a one as to be overlooked by any of their hounds.

Had Rhin gone on a hunt of his own? Perhaps, but deep inside, Sander doubted that. The smith drew up his hood once more and lashed it tight. He had his dart thrower, his belt long-knife—and little else save the clothes he wore, which by now, his nose told him, should be discarded for fresher ones. His gear, tools, food—all else had vanished with the koyot.

Sander had no intention of returning to the Trader village. He might lack the koyot's nose for a guide, but he had a strong feeling that westward lay the answer. Also such a trail carried him away from that haunted land where both the amphibians—he warily glanced at the river, striving to sight any suspicious disturbance of the water—and the White Ones could lay ambush.

Sander drank deep, striving so to somewhat satisfy the hunger he felt by filling his empty stomach with water, then climbed the low bank. There was no sign of any trail, so he strove to keep the river in sight in order to make sure he was not wandering heedlessly. Now and again he gave his summoning whistle, hoping against hope that the koyot would either return or answer.

As the sun grew warmer, Sander unlaced his hood. Being a plainsborn man, he did not like this wooded country, thinly set though these trees were. He remembered, with shame for his own heedlessness, how back by Padford he had thought that the forest could provide shelter. Now he knew what the tree-shadowed land really held.

So he strode along, thrower in hand, dart set in the groove ready for firing, his hearing strained to catch the least sound. A light wind shifted leaves from the trees, and once or twice Sander caught the call of a bird. But he might have been the only man crossing a deserted country—until he sighted a streak of mud where a clump of sod had been pushed aside.

There, in the clay, was half of a handprint—a small one. Once his eyes were so alerted, he discovered other indications that here Fanyi must have emerged from the water, slipped on the clay, and thrown out a hand to support herself. That she had made no attempt to hide such traces argued to Sander that for some reason the girl had not feared any pursuit this far from the village. Or else she was now in such a hurry that haste meant more than concealment.

Realizing that she could not be too far ahead, he searched for other signs of her passing and found a few—a broken branch tip, a twisted stem, a smear of leaves scuffed up from last year's carpet. The trail angled away from the verge of the stream, heading more to the south where trees grew thicker on upward-sloping ground.

Sander passed through young woods onto the surface of an ancient road. There was no trace here of the wreckage that stretched behind. Perhaps in this small pocket of the earth there had been less havoc wrought during the Dark Time. The road, to be sure, had breaks in its surface and was drifted over by soil in which grass and weeds, now fall-dried, rooted. But it was an easy path. In that soil Sander read not only of the passing of Fanyi and her fishers, but imposed over those in two places was an unmistakable paw print which could only belong to Rhin! That the koyot had deserted him to follow the others shook Sander.

He knew that Fanyi exerted a greater measure of control over the fishers, or perhaps one might say she was able to communicate more fully with them, than he did with Rhin. But he would never have believed that the Shaman could have such influence with the koyot as to deliberately draw the animal away from Sander himself. Unless, he corrected himself, she saw in this action one way of defeating pursuit.

To discover that Rhin must have been tolled away only made stronger his own determination to hunt Fanyi down. He plodded ahead, not with speed, but grimly, not now to be turned from the way.

Those he followed had kept to the old road, going openly, as far as he could judge from their tracks, as if they had no reason to expect pursuit. The road began to climb more steeply on a grade that nearly equaled the stark heights behind.

Sander was hungry, but that no longer mattered. Though once, when he came across a place where nuts were being gathered avidly by bustling squirrels, he picked enough of the tough-shelled harvest to nearly fill his hood. He paused to crack a few nuts and munched as he went. Although they tasted good, they were hardly as satisfying as the stew he had eaten in Kaboss's house, a meal that seemed now like some long-past dream.

Reaching the crest of the slope, the smith could look ahead down a long descent. A light haze hung in the air, yet he did not sniff smoke, only saw that tendrils were clouding the distance. However, there was no mistaking what did lie directly ahead and to which the old road ran. Here once more were ruins, yet these had not been reduced to mere mounds of rubble lacking any sign that said they had once housed men. Nor were these battered fragments flattened by a storm like the ones he had viewed yesterday. No, there was enough form left here and there to reveal distinct structures. It seemed to Sander that, even as he studied the ruins, an odd haze began to descend upon them, ever thickening to hide more and more of the structures.

That this must be the place Fanyi had sought, of that he was convinced. He lengthened his stride, trotted down the broken road with a desire to reach the ruins as soon as possible. His aching legs, his empty middle, as well as the westward-reaching sun told him that the day was fast waning.

As soon as he approached the ruins closely, he could see that the road was choked in places by barriers of fallen stone, and no attempt had been made to clear them. In fact, he spotted several large chunks of metal undisturbed, and wonder grew in him. This certainly was within easy range of the Trader village. Why had they not come mining here?

The very fact that such treasure lay in the open

roused his caution. Sander hesitated, searching the
ground for tracks of those he had followed. When
he saw nothing, he retraced his own steps until the
claw marks of one of the fishers—Kai's by the size
of it—drew him to the right. There a second road
opened, narrower than the other, which turned north
sharply, heading away from the main mass of the
ruins.

Trees and bushes narrowed in, reducing the
surface to perhaps a quarter of its original expanse,
so the way was hardly wider than a foot path. But
pressed into the leaf mold and soil there were
tracks, clear and deep, openly left to be traced.
Fanyi, the fishers, and Rhin. Sander could not tell
whether the koyot had already joined the girl or was
still simply following her.

The roadway curved twice, then ended in an
expanse of pavement that reminded Sander of that
on which the Trader house had been built back in
the lost island city. There were three buildings, or
the remains of them, bounding three sides of the
square, the road having led into the fourth. Their
windows watched him with hollow eyes that opened
on emptiness.

Sander took one step out onto that surface and
swayed, falling forward to his knees. The pain in his
head, shooting inward from the iron band, was so
excruciating that he could feel nothing but its agony,
he could not think at all. Instinct alone made him throw
himself backward. Then he lay gasping from the shock
of the pain, though it was now gone as suddenly as it
had struck.

Some time later he squatted on his heels at the
mouth of the road to study the scene before him,
thoroughly baffled. He had fought through tough brush
and around trees, making an outer circuit of the place,

only to discover that it was surrounded by an invisible barrier that could react to his "cold iron" viciously and instantly, dared he attempt to approach past a certain point.

No legend from the Rememberer's vast store, no tale of any Trader, mentioned such an experience as this. There was, as far as he could see, no movement, within that protected area. Yet Fanyi, the fishers, and Rhin had certainly come this way.

After intent study he had noted several tracks across the disputed space where he dared not venture without being literally swept from his feet by a force generating sheer agony in his head. So he had proof that they were here. But why he could not follow—?

Sander believed he need only remove his self-wrought protection and step out. But an inner core of caution argued against any such act. To surrender to the unknown so completely was not in his nature.

Though he had tried the same trick he had used on the trail, striving to make his mind dismiss the onslaught of the pain attack, that did not work here. This force was infinitely greater, and perhaps his own power to withstand it had been sapped somewhat during the first bout.

Go—he had to go on, that he knew. But he could not, wearing the band. His choice was as simple as that. Nevertheless, his dogged desire to find out what lay behind all this would not let him retreat. Slowly, with a feeling that he was surrendering to an enemy, Sander worked the wire circlet loose, stowing it in the front of his outer fur jacket beside the knot he had made for Rhin.

Rising to his feet, he approached the open, moving with the caution of a scout in unknown territory, his weapon ready to hand. Still, he was convinced that what he might find here could not be brought down by any dart, no matter how well aimed.

Out he went, stopping where he had been struck down before. For a moment there was nothing—nothing at all. And then—

Sander stiffened, set his teeth. That thought—the thought that was not his! Now he had no escape, for it held him enmeshed as securely as had the web of the forest men. Against his will, his most fervent desire, he marched forward, straight toward the middle of the three buildings.

Was this the answer to Rhin's desertion, to the open trail he had followed? Had Fanyi and all three of the animals been so compulsively drawn in the same fashion?

Sander wavered as he went, his will battling against his body in a way he would never have believed possible. Was this a taste of the "power" Fanyi had so often spoken of? But he could not believe that the girl he knew generated *this*.

He was not being compelled toward the tottering walls of the building after all. Rather, he was being pointed directly at an opening in the pavement on one side. He could see that this was not part of the original building, for the edging of the cut, though fashioned from blocks of stone, was very rough and crudely made in comparison to the rest of the structures.

The thought of going underground gave him an additional spurt of strength to battle the will controlling him, but not enough to break its hold. Nor could he raise his hand to the iron circlet he had so recklessly put aside.

Sander reached the crude-faced opening. He could see the end of a ladder, and his body, enslaved by that other's will, swung over and began to descend. This must have been a tight fit for Rhin. But undoubtedly the koyot had come this way, for Sander caught the acrid scent of the animal's body in the enclosed space.

This burrow was not dark, so there was no need for torches, as Sander saw when he reached the bottom of the ladder and looked down a corridor. There were cracks across the plain white walls, but none had split open. Set at intervals along those walls were rods giving forth a glow of light. Not all of them were burning; several were twisted and befogged. But enough were in action to give full sight.

Save for those bars of light, there was nothing else along the hall, not the break of a single door, while the way appeared to stretch on and on. Only, part way down its length, that same haze that had half veiled and distorted his view of the city hung again, so he could not be sure what lay behind it.

He was given no time to pause, for again his feet moved him forward, passing between the first two bars of light, heading forward. When he screwed his head around as far as he could to look back some moments later, Sander discovered that the distorting haze had closed in behind him even more thickly, so he could no longer see the ladder at all.

The corridor was wide enough for half a dozen men at least to march abreast and high enough so that Rhin would not have had to crawl on his belly to traverse it. The walls had a slick coating that looked shiny in the subdued light. But the floor, made of small, closely fitted red blocks, was not slippery.

Sander breathed in air that was fresh, carrying no such taint as had that of the tunnel under the city. Now and then he was sure he could detect a faint current against his cheek.

Then the way ended in a cross hall, wide and well lighted in the same fashion. This ran both right and left, its sources hidden by the haze in either direction.

No decision was allowed to Sander here either. His path was already decided for him. Mechanically, he swung left and walked steadily ahead.

Though side openings showed here both right and left, Sander was held to the main passageway. Eventually he reached the head of a stairway, one again leading down. There was evidence that some of the ceiling had fallen. Props of metal had been rammed in place against the walls; beams of the same crossed overhead, supporting cracked masonry.

Once more Sander descended. Had some of the Before People waited out the Dark Time in underground burrows? The stories he had heard of the rending of the earth itself by quakes could not have made any such plan a safe one. Here in this broken portion most of the wall lights were dark, leaving only an eerie glow at intervals. There was no change, except for the cracking in the walls themselves.

He counted the steps as he went down—twenty of them. And he could only guess at how deep this way now lay below the surface of the outer world. The props, rough as they looked against the remnants of the smooth wall, had been well set and braced. There had been a great deal of work down here to insure that these passages would continue to be usable.

By whom? Traders? All the metal-hunting Sander had seen evidence of had been carried on aboveground. The fact that so many of these reinforcing beams and braces were made of solid metal—strong, unblemished metal—made him wonder. To waste such a highly marketable product was not the way of the Traders.

The mist that had floated the upper ways was missing here. Instead, where the lights still existed, the monotony of the corridor showed clearly. The will that was not his continued to force the smith ahead.

He passed a small wagon—if wagon it was without a means of harnessing any sort of draft beast. The object against the wall did have two seats in the front with a smaller fifth wheel mounted on a post before one of those seats. The thing was completely wrought of metal.

In his excitement at the profuse use of a material rarely found in an unbattered, much less uneroded condition, Sander could almost forget for an instant that he was as much a prisoner as if his arms had been lashed to his sides and he was being jerked along by a rope.

The first horror of his predicament had dulled a little. He no longer struggled uselessly against the compulsion, rather yielded, conserving his strength, his mind busy with questions that perhaps never could be answered, but among which might just lie some suggestion that would serve him later.

No Rememberer's tale had ever hinted at an unbelievable situation where the will of another could take over the rule of a man's body, compel him to action. But the knowledge that a Rememberer carried from the Before Days was admittedly only fragmentary.

Sander's people had not even been natives of this part of the world in that legendary time. Therefore, they might not have known what was being accomplished elsewhere. That someone could activate very old machines, such as the wagon he had just passed—yes, that he could accept without question. For the work of one man's hands might be repaired with patience and the proper tools. It was that very hope of accomplishment that had brought him north.

But the tampering with another's thoughts—that was another matter. To him such an invasion by mind was as alien as the monster on the ancient island. He decided now he had but one possible chance—to allow whatever force was summoning him now to believe that he was wholly docile, until he could learn what lay behind his capture.

The wall braces were no longer in evidence. Sander had passed beyond the section of corridor that had been threatened. Here the walls showed no cracks at all under the lights, none of which were dark here, all glowing equally. By their light Sander saw a doorway at the end of the hall, with further radiance beyond it.

Then he heard something—Rhin's sharp bark! The sound was the same the koyot always gave when greeting Sander after any absence. In this much he had been right—the koyot was waiting for him. He stepped through the door and blinked, for the light within was far greater than that which had lined the corridor.

He found himself in a room of medium size, but an odd room, for the side walls ended just above the level of his head, sprouting pillars to rise farther, ending against the ceiling far above. The room was empty and without any break in the walls at all, save that door through which he had just entered. Yet he was sure that it was only part of a much larger space.

At that moment the compulsion that had led him here vanished with the swiftness of one snap of a dry stick. Yet Sander was sure that, should he try to retrace his way, he would not be allowed to do so.

He had heard Rhin's bark, and it had come from this direction. Therefore, there must be a way out of this room, leading beyond. Methodically, Sander turned to the nearest wall. Though his eyes could detect not the faintest line of any opening, he began running his fingertips over the slick surface. Squatting down, he began a search upward from floor level, rising up to stretch his arms near to the wall top in a careful sweep of touch.

The construction was not of any stone that he had ever known, for this surface was smoother than any rock could be worked. And it was chill to the touch. Yet in some places he chanced upon a slight radiated warmth. Some of those spots were hardly larger than the fingertips exploring them; he could span others with a flattened palm.

And they occurred only on the wall directly facing the door, he discovered, after he had made a complete circuit of the small chamber. Since these were all he had found, Sander returned to them, tracing their positions carefully.

Hands—they were set in hand patterns! If one laid one's palm so, fitting into the larger space, then one's finger tips just touched the small spots if the fingers were spread as wide apart as possible. One hand was directly right and one left, but to fit them properly one had to stand with one's body pressed to the wall, arms extended to the farthest limit. Sander took that position and pressed his flesh into the warmth of those invisible holds.

Heat flared. He had wit enough not to snatch away his hands. In a second he knew that this radiation was not as hot as it first seemed. But he was equally startled when a disembodied voice spoke out of the air overhead, as if some invisible presence now stood directly behind him.

What it said was gibberish for the most part. But to his vast amazement Sander grasped words out of the smith's chant, words that were the deep secret of his own trade. There was an interval of silence, and once more the same stream of sounds was uttered.

Sander moistened his lips with his tongue. A—*smith*—? One of his own calling? Well, he could only try. With his hands still on those hot areas, he raised his own voice, to send, echoing hollowly through the space, the work chant, that which contained those words he was sure he had heard.

And the wall—the wall turned! The section of flooring on which his boots were planted swung with it, completely around, carrying him to the other side. This was so far different from all his past experiences that he could not move for a long moment or take his hands away from the wall that had behaved in so improbable fashion, to look about and see where it had transported him.

Shivering a little, the smith forced himself to face around. He stood in another room, perhaps slightly larger than the first. However this one was not bare. There was a table with a top clear as glass, only he had never seen any fragment of glass so large. Its legs were fashioned of metal tubes. There were two stools fashioned of the same material, clear-topped, metal-legged.

In the corner of the table rested a box about the length of his full arm, the width of his forearm. While on the top of that a number of small knobs were raised, each of a different coloring or shading of coloring. Again there was no door. And when he ran his hands over the wall that had so unceremoniously delivered him here, he could no longer locate those warm places for his hands.

Baffled, he approached the table cautiously. On the small surface of each box knob there was a marking, akin, Sander was sure, to that "writing" Fanyi boasted she knew. But the purpose of the box he could not guess. Gingerly he bent over it to study those knobs. Perhaps this controlled another door; anything was possible here. He no longer doubted that Fanyi had discovered the end of her quest. There were certainly marvels gathered in this place unlike any found in the outer world.

One line of knobs was red, shading from a very dark crimson to near pink. The second rank displayed shades of green, the third yellow, the last brown, which ended in one near white. Sander touched each line very lightly. No heat here. But that this had an important purpose he did not in the least doubt. And he wondered gloomily how many combinations of the various colors could be worked out.

Since the compulsion had released him, he felt very tired, and he was hungry enough to ache with the emptiness. Unless he could somehow force this box to yield its secret, he might well be a prisoner here indefinitely. How long did it take a man to starve to death?

Stubbornly, he refused to be beaten now. If the way through another wall lay with this machine, then he was going to find it!

Begin with the first row—then the second, then combine—pushing the buttons on those two in every pattern he could think of. After that try the third and the fourth rows. Sander did not allow himself to be shaken by the thought that what he would try might take hours of effort.

He seated himself on one of the stools and leaned forward, exerting strong pressure with his forefinger on the first button in the red row. He was halfway down the line when there was a response. But it was not the one he hoped for. No wall slid aside, rose or sank into the flooring. Instead the button, upon pressure, snapped down level with the surface of the machine and did not rise again.

Sander looked hopefully at the walls hemming him

in, no longer intent upon the box itself. Therefore, it was only at the sound of a click that drew his eyes back to it. An opening appeared in one end, from which slid a brown square, and then another, both about the length of his little finger. Now the button flashed up again into line with its fellows while Sander stared questioningly at the two objects lying on the table.

It was the odor arising from them that startled him the most. Meat, roasted to a turn over a fire under the care of a most attentive cook. But why—what—how?

Warily he picked up the nearest square. It was warm—having the texture of perfectly browned crust. He could no longer resist the odor and recklessly bit into the biscuit-like offering.

As it crunched between his teeth, he could not have truly named it. Was it a kind of bread? No, for the taste was like its scent—that of well-done meat. Yet it was plainly *not* the roast both smell and taste proclaimed it.

And though it might be loaded with some drug or fatal herb, Sander could not have refused to finish it after that first taste, any more than he could have, in his present state of dire hunger, thrown a grilled fish from him. He finished the biscuit in two bites and eagerly bit into the second.

Oddly enough, though the morsels were small, two of them gave him a feeling of repletion, though they added to his thirst. Now he eyed the remaining untried buttons, wondering if this box also had an answer for that need.

He went at the matter methodically. Another red button gave him a bar, darker brown, but of somewhat the same consistency of the square, which smelled like baked fish. The green line produced three different wafers, unlike in shades. These he put aside with the fish bar. The yellow had only one button in working order. But after pressing it, the box offered him a small cup of some thin, shiny material that was filled to the brim with a semi-soft, pale cream substance. A touch of his tongue informed him that this was sweet. The last row—at the next to the last button—slid out to his hand a slightly larger shiny cup, a lid of the same substance creased tightly over it. When he had worked that off, Sander held a measure, not of water, but of a liquid with an aromatic odor he had never smelled before. He gulped it down though it was hot. Like the cream stuff, it was sweet to the taste but it slaked his thirst.

Carefully, he put the fish bar and the wafers inside his coat. The cream substance, for want of any spoon, he licked clean of its container.

Would the same knobs work again, providing him with extra provisions? Once more he tried the same combination of pressed knobs, but no more supplies appeared. Did it only then work once? Had there in the beginning been food delivered from each of those buttons—but now that abundance had failed through the long seasons, so only these were left—and perhaps he had exhausted the last of what the box had to offer?

The thing was a machine of some kind, of course, but how it worked he could not guess. It was certainly too small to hide, within its interior, supplies to be cooked and offered. Sander got down on the floor, looking up through the transparent surface of the table at the box's underside. But it was entirely solid.

He was no longer hungry or thirsty, but he was still a prisoner. The stool on which he sat—if it were moved against the wall, would it give him extra height so he might reach the top of the partition?

When he tried to shove it, he found that it could

only be drawn back from the vicinity of the table far enough for some one to be seated, no farther.

Sander shrugged. He suspected there were no short cuts here. It would require patience and all the wit he possessed to learn the secrets of these rooms. Rhin— if he could win an answer from the koyot, he would at least know in which direction he must advance, which of the three walls was the barrier to be crossed.

He whistled, and the sound seemed doubly loud and strong. Listening, he could hear nothing but his own faster breathing. Then—from afar—came the yelp. However, it was so echoed within the area, he could not pinpoint the direction.

Once more he began a patient and exhaustive search of the wall surface. He knew what to look for now. Only this combing of the walls was fruitless. No warm spots were to be found, even though he made that sweep twice.

Finally Sander returned to the table, flung himself on the stool and rested his elbows on the surface, which supported the box, holding his head in his hands as he tried systematically to think the problem through. There were none of those mysterious handholds on the walls, that he would swear to. He had leaped several times, trying to catch at the top of the same barriers. But so slick was the coating there, his hands slipped from any grip he tried to exert. Then—how did he get out?

For Sander was very certain that there was a way out of this room, doubtless one as cleverly hidden as those handholds had been. What was the purpose of this place? It seemed that whoever had constructed it— unless that mind was either entirely alien or warped— had intended to make it difficult for any one to travel through. The situation, Sander decided, looked like some kind of testing.

Testing—he considered that idea and concluded that such an answer fitted what small facts he knew. The purpose of the testing, unless it was to gauge the imagination or intelligence of the captive, he could not now know. But its former purpose was immaterial, it was how he might confront the problems offered him now that mattered.

So far, by trial and error and the use of what he considered good sense, he had solved two problems. He had found the first door and he had supplied himself with food and drink. Both of those answers had merely required persistence and patience. Now he was faced with that one that demanded more in the way of experimentation.

The walls were sealed, and he believed any attempt to scale them would be useless. So—what did that leave? The floor!

Again he thought that he could be better served by his sense of touch than his sight. Sander slipped from the stool to his hands and knees, and selecting the nearest corner, he searched that carefully before he started out, sweeping inch by inch across the pavement which, though not quite as smooth as the walls, was uniformly level. First he made a circuit around the base of the four walls, hoping to find at one of them the release he was convinced lay somewhere.

Failing any such discovery, he launched farther into the middle of the room. It was only when he realized that he had entirely swept the whole of that surface that he sat down, with his back to that impenetrable wall, to again consider what he termed the facts of his case.

He had entered through that wall, the one now directly opposite to him. But the hidden latch there was plainly unresponsive to any return. He had searched the three other barriers, and the floor. Nothing.

Dully he leaned his head back against the wall at his back and forced himself once more to consider that room. There were four walls, a floor, high above his head a ceiling that the walls did not reach. There was the table, the box that had fed him, two stools that could not be moved far enough to aid in any climbing.

Table—stools—box— He had explored everything else. Did the secret lie in the center of the chamber after all? Excited by hope, he got up. Neither stool could be shifted any more than his first try had proven. And the knobs—surely they were meant for food delivery, not as he first conceived, for operating some device of the walls. Now—the table.

Despite his strongest efforts, he could not shift it even a fraction of an inch. The metal legs, though they appeared to rest on the surface of the floor, might well be embedded in it for all the good his pushing and pulling did.

Table, stools, box—

Once more Sander subsided on the stool to think. The patterned colors of the knobs were before him— red, green, yellow, brown—Red, since the beginning of time had registered with his species as a signal of power—of danger. It was the red of a fire that destroyed if it could not be curbed, of the flush that anger brought to a man's face.

Green soothed the eyes. That was the color of growing things—of life. Yellow—yellow was gold, treasure, sunshine, also a kind of power, but less destructive than red. Brown—brown was earth—a thing to be worked with, not that would work of itself.

Why was he wasting his time considering the meaning of colors? He had to find the way out—he had to!

Still, he could not break his intent stare at the

rows—red, green, yellow, brown. They provided food; they were useless for his other need.

Brown—yellow of the gold hidden in the earth—green of the things that grew on it—red—of fire that could lick earth bare of life. Somehow a pattern began to weave in his mind, though he tried to drive such foolishness out, to think constructively of what he must do. But were such thoughts foolish? Fanyi would say no, he supposed, her belief in her Shaman powers being such she was able to accept without doubt strange vagaries of the mind. Sander had never believed—really believed—in anything he could not see, touch, taste, hear for himself.

Still, on this journey he had already met with that which could not be measured by the senses. As a smith he labored with his hands, but what he so wrought was first a picture in his mind, so that he followed a pattern no other man might see. Thus he, too, in a way dealt with the intangible.

Should he after all his experiences of these past hours now refuse to use imagination when that might be the one key to defeat the walls? That voice from the air that had addressed him earlier had used a smith's words. True, they had been intermingled with others Sander could not understand, but he was certain of those few. He must take that as an omen of sorts and now trust his guesses, no matter how wild they might seem.

"Brown," he spoke aloud, and thumbed the darkest of the buttons on that row. "Gold." He sought out the brightest there, one that reminded him most of molten metal as it ran, fiery swift, into a mold. "Green." Not the dark top one there, but one halfway down the row, which was most akin to the fresh growth of early spring. "Red." And this one was that shade a dancing flame might own.

A grating noise sounded. One wall broke apart as a panel pulled upward, leaving a narrow space open. Somehow Sander was not even surprised. He had had the feeling as he pressed the buttons in his chosen order that he had indeed solved another small segment of a mystery.

Now he walked forward with some confidence, passing through the opening to face once more the unknown.

T his was not another room as he had expected, rather a narrow corridor boxed in by blank walls. Sander strode along with that new confidence his solving of the door code had given him. Nor was he surprised when, as he approached the far end of the way, a section of the blank expanse facing him rolled aside without any effort on his part.

Sound filtered from beyond. There was a hum, a clicking, other noises. Once more he slowed, trying to judge what he might have to face. Sander had an idea that whoever used this strange maze was not one to be easily bested or even menaced by either weapon he carried. The dart thrower and his long knife were as far removed from the things he had seen as those weapons in turn were from some unworked stone snatched up by a primitive being to do battle.

Making his decision, he fitted the thrower back into its shoulder case to step through that second portal empty-handed. An increased glare of light made him blink. Nor could he begin to understand what he saw— webbings of metal, of glass, squat bases from which those webs grew, the flashing of small lights.

Among all this there was one familiar sight. Rhin bounded toward him, giving voice to yelps that meant welcome in such a crescendo of sudden sound that spoke the koyot's vast relief at Sander's arrival.

The animal's rough tongue rasped across Sander's cheek. He himself clutched the loose hide across Rhin's shoulders. In all this strangeness the koyot was a tie with a world Sander knew well.

At that moment, once more he heard the voice out of the air. This time he could not understand even a few words of its gabble. The machines, if these rods sprouting webbing were machines, stood about the walls, leaving the center of the area free. Sander advanced into that, one hand still resting on Rhin's back. There was nothing in this place that was in the least familiar though he was forced to marvel at the workmanship of the installations.

What was their purpose? Now that he could see those lines in their entirety, he was also aware that not all of them glowed. In fact, on a few of the the heavy bases the remains of webbing lay in broken fragments. From others issued a pitch of sound that made him flinch and the koyot yelp in protest as they passed them.

But there was no sign of any living creature. Sander raised his voice to call Fanyi's name. There was no answer, save the clatter and drone of the machines.

"Who are you?" For the first time then he dared the Voice to answer. It did not reply.

With Rhin beside him, glancing quickly from right to left, half expecting a challenger to arise from behind an installation, Sander crossed the room. There was a second archway, beyond which he found quite a different scene. Here, the center of a large chamber was occupied by an oval space surrounded by two similarly curved lines of cushioned chairs. The oval itself was sunk below the surface of the floor and filled with what Sander, at first glance, thought was a remarkably still pool of water. Then he realized that this was also glass or some equally transparent material.

Leaving Rhin, the smith pushed between two of the chairs which he found to be firmly fastened in position. He stood gazing down at that dull glassy surface, dark blue in color. Sander was sure that, like the food box, it had some highly significant use. The whole arrangement of this room suggested that people had once gathered here to sit in these chairs, to look down onto that surface.

It was not a mirror, for, though he stood at its very edge, it did not reflect his image. Nor were there any of those knobs along it, which the food box had displayed. Slowly, he went from chair to chair, until he reached the one at the left-hand curve of the oval. There, for the first time, he noted a difference. This chair had very broad arms studded with buttons, each bearing some of those symbols Fanyi had called letters.

Slowly, Sander lowered himself into that seat. It was very comfortable, almost as if the chair instantly adjusted itself to his form. He studied the knobs. They had something to do with the glass surface just beyond the toes of his worn boots, he was sure. But what?

There were two rows of them on each of the wide arms, arranged for the ease of anyone resting his elbows on those supports and stretching out his hands naturally. There was only one way to learn—and that was by action. He brought the forefinger of his right hand down on the nearest button.

There came no response, to his disappointment. But it was only only one button—perhaps like so much else, it had ceased to function over the long years. He could hope that enough remained active to give him some idea of why men had gathered here to watch a dull-surfaced and non-reflective mirror.

Methodically, he pressed the next button in line with no better response. But a third gave him an amazing answer. Points of light appeared on the mirror, lines glowing like quickly running fire came to life, outlining large patches, irregular in size and shape. Sander leaned forward eagerly, tried to make some meaning of the display.

There were four—no five—large outlined shapes there. Two were united by a narrow, curved string, the other two larger shapes had a firmer junction. There were also smaller ones here and there, some near to the larger, others scattered farther away. The brilliant points of light were, in turn, strewn by no orderly method over the outlined patches.

Regretfully, though he studied it hungrily, Sander could deduce no possible meaning. He pressed the next button and the pattern flashed off. New lines moved, assembled in another quite different form. Only the bright points of light now totally vanished, and many of the outlines of the patches were blurred and weak.

"Our world—"

Sander swung around, his hand already reaching for the hilt of his long knife. He did not need Rhin's growls to alert him, though for a moment he wondered why the koyot had not given earlier warning. This voice had not come, disembodied, out of the air. Those two words had been spoken by a man, a man who hobbled forward, watching Sander as warily as the smith eyed him.

The stranger was not an attractive sight. Once tall, he was now stoop-shouldered and bow-backed. His overthin arms and legs were emphasized, as was his swollen belly, by the fact that he wore a gray garment made to cling tightly. His head was covered with stiff, whitish bristle, as if the dome of his skull had been first shaven and then allowed to sprout hair again for an inch or so. A long upper lip carried a thin thatch of the same wiry growth, but his seamed face was otherwise free of beard. What skin showed—only his face and knobby-fingered hands—was so pale a color as to resemble that of the White Ones, yet it also had a grayish cast.

In one hand he held a tube that Sander believed was a weapon. He kept it carefully pointed at the smith in spite of trembling in his hands so severe that at times he had to strengthen one hand's grip with the aid of the other. And for any armament that might match the surroundings of this place, the smith already had a hearty respect.

"Our world," the apparition in gray said for the second time, and then coughed rackingly.

Sander heard a whine from Rhin and glanced in the direction of the koyot. The animal, whom he had seen charge even a herd bull and keep that formidable beast busy until the riders of the Mob could rope it, was crouching to the floor as if he had been beaten. And at the sight of that Sander's temper flared.

"What have you done to Rhin!"

The stranger grinned. "The animal has learned a lesson. I am Maxim—no beast shall show teeth to me. Be warned, boy, be warned! I have"—he made a gesture to embrace perhaps more than the room they were now in—"such powers at my command as you poor barbarians outside cannot even dream of! I am Maxim, of the Chosen Ones. There were those who foresaw, who prepared—We, we alone saved all that was known to man! We alone!" His voice scaled up thinly with a note in it that brought another whine out of Rhin and disturbed Sander. The smith thought that the line between sanity and madness already had been crossed by this twisted man.

"Yes, yes!" the other continued. "We preserved, we endured, we are the only intelligence, the only civilization left. Barbarian—look well at me—I am Maxim! There is here"—with one knotty finger he tapped the front of his head—"more knowledge than you could hope to gain in two of your limited life times. You think to steal that now? There is no way—it is locked here." Again finger thumped forehead. "You cannot even understand what you lack—so reduced is your species. You are not human as were the Before Men—!"

His babble grew more and more strident. Sander had only to look at Rhin to realize that this madman had formidable weapons, and he did not doubt that the other was equally ready to turn them on anyone or thing he might encounter. What had happened to Fanyi and the fishers? This must be the storage place she had sought, of that Sander was sure. But had she met this Maxim and paid for it? As his anger had been aroused by the sight of Rhin cowed by this mockery of a true man, so it was heightened by a mental picture of Fanyi perhaps meeting death at his hands.

"What want you?" Maxim demanded now. "What have you come to ask of Maxim? Ways of killing? I can show you such as will melt your mind with horror. We knew them, yes, we knew them all! There are diseases one can sow among the unknowing, so that they die like poisoned insects. We can keep alive a man's body to serve us, but destroy his will, even his thinking mind. We can blast a city from the earth by pressing a single button. We are masters. This place, it is of our planning, for we knew that some must be saved, that our civilization must live. And it was preserved, and we did live—"

His voice trailed into silence, the animation faded from his unhealthy face. For a moment he looked lost and empty as if he himself had been the victim of one of the mind-destroying weapons he had described.

"We live," he repeated. "We live longer than any man has done before. And after us our children live—How old do you think I am, barbarian?" he demanded.

Sander refused to make a guess that might be wrong, one that would arouse the ill will of this mad creature.

"Each people," he chose his words cautiously, "has its own norm of life span. I cannot tell yours."

"Of course not!" The man's head wobbled in a nod. "I am one of the Children. I have lived near two hundred of the years by which men used to reckon."

Which might even be true, Sander decided. How many more of these inheritors of what seemed the worst of the Before Men's knowledge still existed?

"Near two hundred years," Maxim repeated. "I was wise, you see. I knew better than to risk my life going out into the dead world, mixing with the barbarians. I told them they were doing wrong. Lang, I told Lang what would happen." He laughed. "And I was right. Barbarian, do you know how Lang died? Of a pain in his belly—of something that a minor operation would have cured. She told me that—she who said she was Lang's daughter. Of course she lied. No one of us would mate with a barbarian. She lied, but I could not deal with her for her lies because she had Lang's own transmitter.

"We were programmed from the first so there would be no quarrels among us. We were such a small number then—and it might be that we would be sealed here in this complex for generations. So there must be no quarrels, no misunderstandings. All of us had the transmitters for our own protection. You see, barbarian, how everything was arranged? How there could be no trouble we were not equipped to handle?

"And the children. Like Lang, they had their transmitters from birth. It was all so carefully thought out. The Big Brain in the sealed chamber—it knew everything. It knows everything. It has not made any contact for a time now. There is no need, of course. I, Maxim, I know all that is necessary."

"This girl who told you of Lang's death"—Sander had no doubt there was a reference to Fanyi—"where is she now?"

Maxim laughed. "She lied to me, you know. No one must lie to Maxim. I can see a man's thoughts if I wish. I can see your thoughts, barbarian! When she came, I knew there would be others. I used the—" He stopped again and eyed Sander warily. "I brought you here, barbarian. It was amusing, very amusing. There were the old testing rooms, and it was of interest to see you working your way through. She did not have to do that—not with Lang's transmitter. But you showed a certain cunning, not human, but amusing, you know. I had to have you here. The rest of your kind—they want my treasures—but they can be stopped. Since you came through my barriers, I knew I must get you all the way to be safe."

"I am here," Sander pointed out. "But the girl—what did you do with her?"

"Do with her?" The laugh degenerated into a giggle. "Why, I did nothing, nothing at all. There was no need to. The Big Brain has its own defenses. I listened to her, pointed her in the right direction, and let her go. There was no need at all for me to concern myself farther. She was even grateful to me. I—" That same tinge of bewilderment crossed his pouched and flabby face. "There was something about her. But, no, no barbarian can have any trait that Maxim cannot master! To control beasts—that I can do too. See how this mangy creature of yours fears me. Now the problem is—how to make you useful. You have no transmitter, so, of course, you can be mastered."

"But I have!" Why he claimed that, Sander did not know. But he was certain that he must make some move of his own to face up to this caricature of a man.

"You cannot!" The man's tone was petulant as that of a stubborn child. "Lang was the last to go forth. He left me, in spite of what I told him over and over, he left me! He was stupid, really. Being the youngest of the children, the breeding must have worn thin in his generation. And Lang had only one transmitter. They do not last long—not more than fifty years or so. Then they have to be recharged. So yours, if you do have one, is inoperable. It would be that of Robar perhaps. And he went longer ago than Lang. Do not try to trick me, barbarian! Remember, I am Maxim and the knowledge of the Before Time is all mine!"

"I will show you." Carefully Sander reached for the front of his outer coat. He saw that tube in the other's hand center on him, but he had to take this chance. He brought out the band of woven wire.

Maxim cackled. "That is no transmitter, barbarian! You are indeed no more intelligent than this beast. A transmitter! You do not even know what the word means. *She* did not know. She thought it magic— magic such as the superstitious savage plays with! And now you show me a mass of wire and call it a transmitter!"

Daring to provoke some action from Maxim, Sander again fitted the band around his head. Perhaps it would serve his purpose now if this survivor of the Before Men judged him as he had judged Fanyi—childlike and superstitious.

"It is cold iron," he said solemnly. "And I am one of those who fashion iron, so that it obeys me." He began the smith's chant.

A flicker of faint interest answered him. "That— that is a formula," Maxim observed. "But it is not right, you know. This is the way it should be." His voice took on something of a Rememberer's twang as he recited words. "Now that is the right of it. So you hoard scraps of the old learning after all, do you, barbarian? But what is cold iron? That expression has no meaning whatsoever! And—I have wasted enough time. Come, you!"

He pressed one of the spots along the side of his tube. Instantly Sander swung partly forward, pulled by the same compulsion that had brought him here. But his hands tightened on the arms of the chair.

Iron—cold iron. His smith's belief in the Old Knowledge—belittled as it had been by Maxim—that was the only weapon he had left.

He concentrated on holding to the chair, setting his teeth against the pain of the iron heating about his forehead. No—no—and NO!

Maxim's face contracted, flushed. His mouth fell open, showing his pale tongue and teeth that were worn and yellow.

"You *will* come!" he screeched.

Sander clung to the chair arms. The misery of that struggle within him was fast approaching a level where he could no longer bear it, he would have to surrender. And if he did, then he would be lost. He did not know why he was sure of that, only that he was.

The air between him and Maxim was aglow. Sander held on to the chair so fiercely his grip deadened all feeling in his fingers. His head was afire. He must—

A tawny shape arched through the air, paws thudding home on Maxim's hunched shoulders. The thin man was slammed down and back against the pavement to lie still with Rhin's forepaws planted on him and the koyot's muzzle aiming for the old man's throat.

As the tube spiraled out of Maxim's grip, the intolerable pressure on Sander winked out. He managed to croak out an order to Rhin not to kill.

He could not allow the koyot to savage the other in cold blood. After all the man was mad and he was old. And what was most important now was to find Fanyi and warn her. Into what kind of trap Maxim had sent the girl, Sander could not guess. But he suspected that the end of it was death in one form or other.

He used part of his rope to bind Maxim. Then he raised the skinny body to put it into one of the chairs, again making fast more binding.

Finished, Sander turned to Rhin:

"Find Fanyi!" he ordered.

The koyot still faced the unconscious Maxim, growls rippling from his throat as if he had no other wish than to make an end to him. Sander came over, slapped the animal's shoulder and reached up to tug at an ear.

"Fanyi!" he repeated.

Even in this place the girl's scent must lie some-where, and Rhin was the best tracker he had ever known. With a last threatening growl, the koyot looked from Maxim to Sander. He whined and nudged at the smith's shoulder. The animal's puzzlement was clear to read. Rhin saw no reason to leave Maxim alive; his reasoning was sensible. But at the same time Sander could not bring himself to kill the now helpless man or to let Rhin do it for him.

One might kill in defense of his own life or to protect those he had some kinship with. He would confront the amphibians, as he had, or the White Ones and feel no qualms as he watched his darts go home. That abomination they had faced in the forest glade, or the monster on the once-island—those were such horrors as aroused Sander's deepest fear. But it was not in him to put an end to this flaccid being roped into the chair, held in place only by the bonds Sander himself had set.

Sander stooped and picked up the rod Maxim had dropped. There were five dots along its side. But he had no idea what forces it controlled nor any desire to experiment with it. What was important now was time, to find Fanyi before she blundered into full disaster.

"Fanyi!" For the third time Sander repeated her name, waving Rhin away from their captive.

The koyot barked once and came. He rounded the oval and seats and kept straight ahead, Sander trotting at a brisk pace to match his guide's. Rhin moved with such purpose Sander believed the koyot knew exactly which way they must go. Perhaps the animal had even witnessed the girl being set on her way by the malicious, ancient guardian of this place.

Sander could not accept that Maxim was the only inhabitant of this hideaway. Though the other had mentioned only two names, both of the men now dead, that did not mean that all the colony meant to outlast the Dark Times had entirely vanished. Nor was the smith sure, after witnessing the confrontation between Rhin and Maxim at their first meeting, that the koyot would give him any alarm. It was only because Maxim had been so intent on taking Sander that Rhin had had a chance to rebel.

They threaded a way through rooms and halls opening one into another. Some were filled with installations, some were plainly meant for living, with divans and various pieces of oddly shaped and massive furniture.

Sander paused once when he came to another chamber where a food machine sat. This was larger than the one that had occupied the room to the forepart of this maze, with more numerous rows of buttons. Sander used his fingertips confidently and produced more rounds, wafers, and cups of water, not only to feed Rhin and himself, but to carry as extra rations in his food bag and water bottle. How a machine could produce food apparently from nothing was a mystery, but the results were tasty, not only for man but for koyot also. And Sander was more satisfied in results and less interested in means at the moment.

Rhin pattered on until they passed from a last grouping of rooms into another long hall, one with the same smooth walling and bars of dim light, though here all those were lit. The air remained fresh, with a faint current now and then. Sander continued to marvel at all the knowledge that must have lain behind the building and equipping of this refuge.

Sometime he would like to return once more to that room with the pool of glass and see the strange outlines that could be summoned to appear there. If Maxim had been right that the second series of pictures showed their world as it now was, then the earlier series must have been the world of the Before Days.

Sander carried with him a memory of the vast changes in those lines. But if the alteration had been so great, then how had this particular series of burrows managed to survive practically intact. He could understand that the inhabitants, once they had survived the worst of the world-wide changes, had their own methods of protecting themselves against the looting of any wandering band that approached their outer gate. But he could not conceive of a protection strong enough to stand against the fury of earthquakes, volcanoes, and disrupted seas.

This hall seemed to continue forever. Now and again Rhin dropped nose to the floor, followed by one of his small yelps. They were on their way, the right way— to where?

At the end of the passage, a ramp led downward again. The bars of light were fewer here; thick patches of shadow lay between each. At first the slope was gradual and then it grew steeper. It would seem that whatever the Before Men wished to hide here they had buried deeply to insure that it would not be disturbed by any upheaval of the earth.

Nor was the air as good. This supply had an acrid smell leading Sander to cough now and then. He remembered Maxim's threat—that what Fanyi had come this way to seek had it own defenses, an idea that made him proceed with added caution. What had Maxim called it— the Great Brain? Could a machine *think*? Sander wished he had paid stricter attention to the Rememberers. Had any of their tales ever hinted at such?

Just as Sander thought that they would continue to descend forever, deeper and deeper into the heart of the world, the ramp straightened out. Here the glow of the wall lights was dimmed by films of long-deposited dust. Underfoot, he shuffled over a velvety carpet of the same. However, it was disturbed by prints. Even in this subdued light Sander caught sight of the fishers' claw-tipped tracks and boot impressions only Fanyi could have left.

It was colder here. He drew up his hood, tightened its string. He could see his breath in small frosty puffs on that too-still air. Rhin fell back, his muzzle on a line now with Sander's shoulder, no longer ranging ahead. Now and then the koyot uttered faint whines of uneasiness.

There was movement in the shadows ahead. Sander came to a halt, freeing his dart thrower, having thrust the weapon he took from Maxim into his belt. Rhin growled, then gave an excited warning yelp. The answer was a clanging sound that had no kinship to anything Sander had ever heard, unless it was the ring of a light hammer against metal.

The thing that trundled forward, weaving in and out of those patches of wall light, was not a living creature. It could not be. It reminded Sander of a round kettle such as the Mob used for a fall feasting. The thing moved on rollers, set beneath its surface, at a steady, though slow, pace. But what erupted from the kettle made Sander wary. For it sprouted a series of waving, jointed arms, all of seemingly different lengths, and they ended in huge claws with formidable teeth. These arms were in constant motion, sweeping the floor, or scraping along the walls, while the claws clashed open and shut. The thing was an opponent no dart could bring down, no matter how skillful the aim might be.

Rhin uttered a series of heavy growls, pushed past Sander to snap at the trundling metal thing. But the koyot kept well beyond the reach of the arms that now swung toward him. The clatter of the claws grew louder as they opened and shut faster and faster.

The koyot danced just beyond the extreme limit of the arms, snapping in return, but always retreating. Sander reached for the rod he had taken from Maxim. If this weapon had any power, it could be their only chance against a moving machine.

Still holding the more familiar dart thrower in his left hand, the smith sighted along the tube, which he now cradled in his right, then he brought his thumb hard against the side. But not before he whistled Rhin back out of range, for he could not be sure what was going to happen in that attack.

A beam of light shot out past the koyot, to catch the kettle shape dead center. For a moment there seemed to be no effect. Sander began to stumble backwards, Rhin once more beside him, for those flailing arms with their trap claws clattered in a snapping whirlwind toward them.

Then, where the beam was touching that swell of metal, there appeared a spot that grew deeper and deeper red. The ray appeared to be burning into the thing's body. But the moving machine showed no discomfort; if anything, its rush toward them speeded up. One of those clutching set of claws caught on a dusty light pillar, tightened, and crushed it with the ease of a knife slicing through a meal cake.

Sander whistled again to the koyot, signaling retreat. He wanted to turn and run, but if this Before Weapon was to be stopped, he must go slowly and keep the rod steady, eating in upon the same glowing spot.

A darker heart grew in that circle now. The force of the focused light must have eaten through the outer casing of the creature. Sander held the beam steady, backing away, trying to match his retreat to the pace of the thing's forward roll.

Then—there came a flash of light so intense and searing that he was blinded. Crying out, he grasped for Rhin. He could see nothing, but his hold upon the koyot pulled him back until his heels hit the end of the ramp that had brought them here. Only then was he aware that the rumble, the clashing sound, which the thing had made, was stilled. It must at least have been stopped by the ray.

Still Sander retreated farther, partway up the ramp, blinking his eyes, striving to regain his sight. The fear that the explosion of light might have indeed blinded him was a terror that he flinched from facing.

Rhin pulled free from the smith's hold, padded away

in spite of Sander's voice commands. He heard a clatter and the growling of the koyot. Then Rhin bounded back, nudged Sander with his shoulder.

Warm metal brushed the smith's hand. He put his weapon away, groped outward until his hands closed upon a jointed rod. He felt it with his fingers and found on the end of it a claw frozen well apart.

He *had* put the thing out of action! But his elation at that fact was tempered by his blindness. What if— if he was never to see again!

Sander put the thought firmly out of his mind. The crawling thing had been stopped. And there was no need to retreat again. He had Rhin—the koyot would give him warning if any more such disputed their road. Better go forward than skulk back into the intricate complex where he had left Maxim. Let the madman discover that Sander was in any way helpless and he would have no defenses.

Taking a tight grip on the lashings of Rhin's harness, he moved forward. His confidence was heightened as he began to capture, if dimly, a small suggestion of light to one side. He must be sighting one of the wall lamps.

Rhin paced slowly, then stopped with a whine. Sander, still keeping his grasp on the koyot's lashings, used the detached arm Rhin had brought him to sweep the floor before him. Metal rang against metal with a clatter. They must have reached another destroyed thing.

Sander knelt and felt about with both hands. Broken metal, hot to the touch, lay in a mass. Slowly and carefully he pushed and piled the pieces to one side. His eyes were watering now, moisture trailing down his dust-powdered cheeks. He could see a little, enough to clear their way.

Then, once more with Rhin for his guide, he started on, tapping before him with the iron claw to be sure nothing lay there to stumble over. His eyes smarted, but he was careful not to rub them with his dusty hands. Was the machine just destroyed the only one roaming these ways? At least, unless the weapon had exhausted itself in that attack, he had a counter for such. But he remembered what Fanyi had warned about her light; that these tools and weapons of the Before People had limited lives, and he might have expended the full force of Maxim's tube in that single action.

Sander sneezed and coughed. Fumes, which must have come from the destruction of the clawed sentinel, made his throat hurt, attacked his nose. Rhin wheezed in answer. But at least the smith could pick out of the general fog ahead new gleams of wall lights. And the sight of those heartened him. Maxim had said that whatever Fanyi sought was well protected. Could this machine have been one of those protections?

The smith fingered the arm, touched gingerly the teeth in the claw. It was a vicious thing, like enough to those weapons Maxim had boasted were controlled by those who had built this place—disease and all the rest. What kind of people had they been? The White Ones, the Sea Sharks killed. But not at a distance, and not without risking their own lives in return. There had been that female thing that the forest men had given them to, the monster on the island. Again, those were flesh and blood. And so, in a manner, to be understood. But this metal crawler, those other weapons Maxim had listed with such mad satisfaction—

More than the dust and the fumes struck at Sander. His own revulsion against those who had fashioned this lair made him sick. Had they all been mad from the beginning? Was Maxim merely tainted with a legacy that was his from birth?

The corridor took an abrupt turn. Herein the air was

slightly better, though the lights were still befogged when Sander looked at them. He swept the arm back and forth, stirring the dust, his hearing alert to any sound that might come from their own passing. It was thus that he became conscious of a kind of beat or vibration that might have been carried by the stale air itself. Where had he felt this before? The sensation was dimly familiar. In the forest! When they had been snared by the tree men!

But there were no trees here, nothing overhead except the walled roof of the corridor.

"Rhin?" He spoke the koyot's name aloud because that familiar syllable somehow linked him with another living thing.

The koyot was silent, save that his nose touched Sander's cheek for an instant. There was the feeling of awareness, of danger to come, flowing from Rhin to him more strongly than the man had ever felt such a warning before. Still the koyot was quiet. Not even the near soundless growl he sometimes used could be felt through Sander's hold on him. The smith searched within his jacket, brought out the thong with its knot of wire, and put it once again about Rhin's throat.

They moved on, aware of what was akin to the beating of a giant heart not quite in rhythm with the pump of Sander's own blood, but near enough to it. The smith blinked his dust-assaulted eyes. Finally he stopped, freed the water bottle from its lashing, wet part of a spare shirt, and held the damp, cool compress on his closed lids. Three such applications and his sight cleared, showing him details of the dusty hall.

With the disappearance of the haze, he could also see a door ahead. It was shut fast, and there was no sign of a latch or knob or any way of opening it. All that was visible on the smooth surface fronting them was a hollow at about eye level. Reaching the barrier, Sander strove to insert his fingers into that hollow, to so exert pressure that the surface would either slide to one side or lift up. But it remained stubbornly immovable.

Would the cutting power of Maxim's rod clear a path for them here?

Sander fingered the Before Weapon. There was a risk in what it might do. Use of the beam might trigger some retaliation. Yet he could not just give up and walk away.

Fanyi must have gone through here—what method had she used? Was it that gift from her father that had perhaps brought her safely past the guardian he had beamed down? He ran his fingers about the depression in the door. Though he was only guessing, Sander believed it was just of a size that Fanyi's pendant might fit into.

Being not so equipped with any answer to the barrier, he held the rod closer to one of the two wall lamps that flanked the door and studied it. This was the spot he had pressed on the rod to bring about the destruction of the sentry. But there were four other such markings on the part of the rod that formed the hand grip.

There was only one way to make sure—that was to try. Waving Rhin back so that the koyot might not be engulfed in any sudden disaster born from the smith's recklessness, Sander set the firing end of the tube directly into the edge of the door's depression.

He pressed the first button.

There was nothing at all! Nothing until Rhin gave a howl and lowered his head to the floor and pawed at his ears. Quickly Sander released that button. Was this what Maxim had used to bring the animal to submission?

Rhin shook his head vigorously; his growls were deep-chested. Now he looked at Sander, baring his teeth.

The smith was almost argued out of trying the next of the marks. He had no wish to unleash upon himself Rhin's full anger. And he did not see how he could make the koyot understand that he had applied such torment, not by wish but through ignorance alone.

To go at once to the full power of the rod—yes. But first make sure he was not temporarily blinded a second time. Sander draped his head in the dampened shirt, tucking its folds into the edge of his hood. He sent Rhin back down the corridor, then set the rod firmly into the depression again. Bearing down hard, he applied the full force of whatever power it held.

Even through the improvised shield across his eyes, he caught a flash of white fire. There was a clank of tortured metal. Then carrying acrid fumes, a blast of damp heated air hit him full in the face.

He also heard something else. There was no mistaking that savage hissing. The fishers! And by the sharpness of the sounds they now faced him.

Sander pawed the shirt away from his face. The door had split into two, providing a space wide enough perhaps for both him and Rhin to squeeze through, but still not clearing the whole of the archway. Light, stronger than that of the corridor, streamed out, showing very clearly both Kai and Kayi, one on either side, humped and ready to spring into battle. Beyond them was a confusion of objects, brilliantly lighted, that he could see clearly.

To harm the fishers was unthinkable. He raised his voice and called, over the dryness of his throat:

"Fanyi!"

The vibration grew stronger, beat with greater power, while the hostile sounds made by the fishers became louder. But the girl did not answer.

Had she been injured—trapped by one of the protective devices Maxim had hinted at—thus arousing her companions to battle anger? Or had she purposefully set them here on guard to ward off any interference with what she would do? Either answer could serve, but it would not remove Kai and Kayi.

They must know his scent and that he had been accepted by Fanyi and had traveled with her. Would that small familiarity aid him now? Behind him he heard the pad of Rhin's feet. There must be no fighting between the animals.

Sander retreated a few steps, eyeing the fishers narrowly. They made no move to advance from the other side of the door he had forced open. He searched in his food bag, brought out some of those small cakes that tasted so much like fresh meat, the ones Rhin had gobbled with a visible relish. To each of the fishers he tossed three of these.

Kayi sniffed first at her offering. She tongued one of the biscuits and then gulped it whole. A second one was crunched between her jaws before her mate consented to try his share. They still watched Sander as they ate, and their hissing continued. But they licked up each crumb avidly as if they had been long hungry.

Sander could not touch them as the girl did, that he was wise enough to know. But he squatted down, bringing out two more cakes, tossing one to each. As they snapped them up, he spoke in a voice he made purposefully level.

"Fanyi?"

Perhaps he was as stupid as Maxim thought him to be, to try to communicate with the fishers by voice. How could his repeating a name mean anything to animals still watching him so intently that their stare was daunting? But patiently he repeated that name the second time.

"Fanyi?"

Kai reared on his haunches, his head now well above that of the squatting smith. From this position the fisher need only make one pounce to carry Sander down under rending jaws and claws. Kayi stared, but she did not assume the same upright position.

"Fanyi—Kai—Kayi—" This time Sander tried the three names in linkage. What might be passing through the fishers' alien thinking processes he could not even guess.

Kayi stopped hissing. She bent her head to lick her right paw. But the bigger male had not changed what seemed to Sander his challenging posture.

"Fanyi—Kai—" Now the smith only used two of the names, aiming his voice at the big male, with a slight turn of his head that cost a special effort of will, because to let Kayi out of his full sight was a risk.

Kai dropped to four feet. Though Sander could not read any expression on the fisher's face, somehow he sensed that the beast was puzzled. And beneath that puzzlement was something else. Fear? The man could not be sure.

Taking a last risk, Sander got slowly to his feet and made a movement forward. "Fanyi!" he repeated for the fourth time with a firmness he was not sure he could continue.

Kayi backed away. Her eyes swung to the looming back of her mate and returned to the man. She uttered a sound that was not a warning. Kai hissed, showed his fangs. But Sander, taking heart from the attitude of the female, moved a step closer.

The male fisher subsided to four feet, backing away, still hissing, but yet retreating. Kayi had turned around and was padding off. Finally the big male surrendered, though he still eyed Sander suspiciously.

Rhin followed at the smith's shoulder, crouching a little and making a struggle to win through that door slit. But the fishers did not threaten now. Together they had turned their backs on Sander, seemingly satisfied, and were on their way, threading among incomprehensible masses of glass and metal that seemed to fill this chamber.

Here the lighting was brilliant, a glare enough to cause Sander trouble with his impaired sight. And the room was alive. Not alive as he knew life, but with a different form of energy, one that caused colors, some strident, some richly vivid, to flow along through tubes and otherwise bathe some of the installations. The warm and humid heat of the place made him unlace his hood, unfasten his jacket.

He had no desire to pause to look about him. The play of the colors, the wholly alien atmosphere of this place, repelled him. Once he found Fanyi they must get out of here! His flesh tingled and crawled as if some invisible power streamed over him.

Sparks shot from the band of metal he wore. It was warming up. Still, he would not take it off. Cold iron had saved him twice, and he clung to what he had learned might work for him, the more so when he now was surrounded by what he could not understand, dare not even examine too closely.

The fishers guided him directly to a very small room on the other side of the place. It was hardly larger than a good-sized cabinet. Its walls were clear, so that one could look through them. Seated within, her hands clenched about the pendant still lying on her breast, was Fanyi.

Though her eyes were wide open, seemingly staring straight at him, Sander realized she did not see him.

What did she see? He grew chill for a moment in spite of the heat of the outer room. Expressions passed fleetingly one after the other across her face. There was fear, a kind of horror, revulsion—

Her bush of hair stood erect, as if each strand were charged with energy from root to tip. Small beads of sweat gathered on her upper lip and forehead and rolled down her cheeks as if she wept without ending. There was a terrible stiffness about her whole body, which betrayed some tension beyond the ordinary.

Kayi pawed at the front of the cabinet, but there was no shadow of recognition on Fanyi's distorted face. She was like one sealed into a nightmare with no means of escape.

Now her body began to jerk spasmodically. Sander saw her mouth open as if she were screaming. But he could hear nothing. He ran forward and caught at the bar at waist level on the door, hoping it was the latch. Against it he exerted all his strength. It did not budge.

It was as if she were locked in past any hope of escape. He could see her eyes rolling from side to side, her head moving back and forth. He grabbed one of the darts from his case, inserted it between the bar and the door and tried to pry it up.

Now Fanyi's whole body was jerking steadily as if she had no control over her own muscles. There was no longer any sign of intelligence in her face, her mouth fell slackly open, while from her lower lip drooled a thread of spittle.

Sander fought the door. The dart snapped in his hands, but not before he had forced a small amount of movement. He snatched a second shaft and this time dug with all his might at the line of cleavage just beyond the bar. The dart point caught and held; he pounded it deeper.

There was a splitting crack as he gave a mighty heave upon the bar, stumbling back nearly off balance as the whole front of the cabinet yielded at last. Fanyi slumped with it. Sander was just in time to catch her totally inert body and lower her gently to the floor.

For one moment of such fear as he had never before known, he thought her dead. Then he felt the pulse in one thin brown wrist, saw the rise and fall of her breasts in fast, shallow breathing. Her eyes were rolled up, so he could see little but white between the half-closed lids.

Not even getting to his feet, he crawled and dragged her with him, away from the prison in which he had found her, seeking temporary shelter in a corner of the room as far from that cabinet and the rest of these devilish installations as he could get her. There he settled her head on his folded coat. Her hands were still so fixed about the pendant that he had to work slowly and with all the gentle force he could exert to loosen them finger by finger. He was sure that the pendant itself was part of the danger that had struck at her.

She still breathed with those quick and shallow breaths, as if she had been running, while her skin felt cold and damp in spite of the heat that filled the room. The fishers came to her, Kayi crowding in on the far side, stretching her length beside that of the girl as if, with the additional warmth of her fur-clad body, she could give some comfort.

Fanyi muttered and began to turn her head back and forth on the pillow Sander had provided. Clearly, unslurred, she began to speak, but he could not understand the words that came out, save that now and again he thought he caught an echo of the voice that had addressed him out of the air.

He drew off his second jerkin and put it over her, then caught her head in a sure grip while he dribbled a little water between her lips. She choked, coughed, and suddenly opened her eyes.

"**D**ead!" her voice shrilled. "Dead!"

Though she gazed straight at him, Sander realized that Fanyi saw something else—not his face, perhaps not even this room.

"I—will—*not!*"

Fanyi struggled to sit up until Sander caught her shoulders, pushed her gently down again. He was afraid. The eyes the girl turned upon him held no recognition. Had her experience in that prison box made her as mad as Maxim?

"You do not need to do anything"—he strove to keep his voice under even control—"which you do not want to—"

Her mouth worked as if it were nearly past her power to get out word sounds.

"I—will—not—" and then she added, "Who are *you?* One of the machines—the machines—?" Again her tension was rising, her body grew rigid under his touch. "I will *not!* You cannot force me—you cannot!"

"Fanyi—" As he had when greeting the fishers, Sander repeated her name with authority, with the need to win awareness from her. "I am Sander, you are Fanyi—Fanyi!"

"Fanyi?" She made a question of that. And the import of such an inquiry chilled Sander even more. If she could not remember her own name—! What had this devilish place done to her? He was filled with a rage so powerful that he wanted to flail out about him, smash into bits everything in this chamber.

"You are Fanyi." He spoke as if to a small child, schooling the anger out of his voice. "I am Sander."

She lay still, looking up at him. Then, to his relief, a measure of focus came back to her eyes. She might have been peering through a curtain to seek him out. Her tongue tip moved across her lips.

"I—am—Fanyi—" She said slowly, and gave a great sigh. He watched her relax, her head turn on the pillow he had improvised, her eyes close. She was asleep.

But they must get out of here! Perhaps if he could lift her up on Rhin—That tingling, skin-crawling sensation he had felt ever since he had entered this place was growing worse. There was something else—a kind of—nibbling was the only word Sander could find to describe the feeling—a nibbling at his mind! He brought both hands up to the wire circlet. It was warm—hot— he should take it off—much better—better.

The smith snatched his fingers away. Take that off! That was what this—this presence here wanted! He looked over his shoulder quickly. So sure was he at that moment that there was another personality here that he expected to see Maxim, or one like him, coming down the aisle between the installations.

Cold iron—

Swiftly Sander beckoned to Rhin, and when the koyot crowded beside him, he lifted Fanyi and fastened her on the animal's back. Kayi snarled at his first move to disturb the girl, then apparently saw that Sander meant her no harm. The smith made her slumped body fast, so she lay with arms dangling on either side of Rhin's neck.

When he was sure she was secure, Sander started back through this nightmare chamber that was haunted by the will plucking strongly at him. Could the unknown take over the animals, turn Rhin and the fishers against him?

That a sensation which they disliked and feared had reached the animals he knew by their incessant snarling and the way the fishers swung their heads back and forth as if seeking an enemy they could identify. Rhin growled, but he did not hang back as Sander urged him forward.

They passed the broken-open block in which he had found the girl. With that behind them, Sander drew a breath of relief. He did not know what he had expected might reach out of it—he had begun to believe that he could not really trust his own senses or impulses here.

The outer door was before them, and the fishers flashed through the crack. However, the opening was too narrow for Rhin carrying Fanyi. Sander unstrapped his tool bag and, as he had done in the tunnel out of the city, took up the largest of his hammers.

With all his might he swung it first against one side of that slit and then the other, dividing his energy, until, at last, the leaves of the opening yielded with a harsh grating and Rhin could wedge through successfully. Sander did not return the hammer to his bag, rather carried it in one hand as they went. Like the iron band he wore, the feel of its familiar heft in his hand gave him more confidence than he gained in handling either the dart thrower or the rod weapon from Before. This was part of his own particular calling, and as a smith he was secure. At this moment he needed such assurance.

The fishers did not range well ahead as they were wont to do outside. Rather they paced along, one on either side of Sander and Rhin. Now and again they uttered soft hisses, not of anger and warning, but simply communicating with each other.

There had been no sign of consciousness from Fanyi since she had said her name, claiming her own identity.

That she now lay in an unnatural sleep Sander was certain. He wanted to get her as far away from the place he had found her as he could.

They passed the scrap heap of the machine sentry. At another time Sander would have liked to study the remains of the thing, perhaps appropriate other bits of its arms. Now he had a feeling that the less he allied himself with anything belonging to this maze, the more sensible he would be.

Rhin climbed the ramp, Sander steadying Fanyi with one hand and carrying the hammer in the other. That climb seemed twice as long as the descent had been. But it was good to emerge into fresher air, fill his lungs again with that which was not tainted with the acrid odors so strong below.

In the upper hall Sander decided to head back to the room where he had found the larger food machine. Though the fishers had wolfed down all the biscuits he had fed them, he guessed that they were not yet satisfied. Also perhaps he could coax from that strange supplier of nourishment something to revive Fanyi.

Rhin went forward confidently and Sander did not doubt that the koyot was retracing their journey. The feeling of pressure, of nibbling, was growing less, the further he withdrew from the chamber below. If the seat of that disturbance lay there, perhaps there was a limit to its influence, though it had reached out before to draw him here. He had no intention of taking off his iron protection to test its strength.

They reached the room he sought. There he loosed Fanyi and lowered her from the riding pad, once more stretching her on the floor with his coat under her head, and though she did not open her eyes or seem conscious, she shivered.

Recklessly, he thumbed the buttons on the machine, tossing to the three animals the meat-tasting biscuits that they snapped up eagerly. But at length, one lucky choice provided him with a capped container that was nearly filled with a hot liquid having the smell and consistency of a thick soup.

Cradling Fanyi's head against his shoulder, Sander called her name, roused her so she murmured fretfully and feebly tried to escape his hold. But he got the container to her lips, and finally she sipped.

As she drank at his soft-voiced urging, she appeared to welcome the liquid and finally opened her eyes as if to look for more. He speedily got a second helping from the machine and supported her until she finished that also to the last drop.

"Good—" she whispered. "So good. I—am—cold."

Fanyi still shook, visible shudders running through her whole body. Sander managed to get his coat on her, rather than merely laid over her. Then he turned to Rhin, stripping the koyot of all their gear and pulling over the girl the thick riding pad, strong-smelling though it was.

Having covered her as best he could, he called the fishers and they obediently settled down on either side of her, lending their body heat. Only then did he go to the machine and feed himself.

He was tired; he could hardly remember now when he had slept last. And that ordeal in the lower ways had sapped his strength. Dared they remain here for a space? If Rhin and Fanyi's fishers would play guard—

In all his journeying through the rooms of the complex, Sander had come across signs of no other inhabitants. The rooms that he guessed had been intended for living quarters seemed empty of any presence save their own as they passed through. Still Sander could hardly believe that Maxim was the sole remaining inhabitant of the place. And any such would have weapons and resources past his own knowledge.

The sooner they themselves were out of this underworld, the better. But even as Sander thought that, his head slumped forward on his chest and he had to fight to keep his eyes open. There were too many chances of facing disaster still to come, and he could not meet them worn as he was now. Rest was essential.

He made a further effort and gave hand signals to Rhin. The koyot trotted to the far door and lay down across the entrance, head on paws. He would doze, Sander knew, but he would also rouse at the first stir beyond.

Sander stretched out, the haft of his hammer lying under his hand, on the other side of Kayi. The strong smell of the fishers was somehow comforting and normal, part of the world he knew and trusted, not of these burrows.

"Sander—"

He turned his head. There was an urgency in the call that woke him out of a dream he could not remember even as he opened his eyes. Fanyi was sitting up, his coat slipping from her shoulders, her face drawn and worn as if she had not yet thrown off the effects of some daunting and debilitating illness.

"Sander!" Now she stretched forth a hand to shake his shoulder, for Kayi no longer lay between them.

He sat up groggily and shook his head.

"What—" he began.

"We must get out!" There was a wild look in her eyes. "We must warn them—"

"Them?" Sander repeated. But her excitement reached him, and he got to his feet.

"The Traders—the rest—all the rest, Sander. Your people—everyone!" Her words came with such a rush that he had trouble understanding them. Now it was his turn to lay hands upon her, steady her so he could look straight into her wide eyes.

"Fanyi—warn them against what?"

"The—thinker!" she burst out. "I was wrong—oh, how wrong!" Her hands clutched his wrists with a grip tight enough to be painful. "The Thinker—he—it—will take over the world—make it what it wants. We shall all be *things*, just things to do *its* bidding. It has summoned the White Ones—is pulling them here to learn—learn monstrous things. How to kill, destroy—"

Once more she was shaking. "It was made by the Before Men, set to store up all their learning because they foresaw the end of their world. And it did—by the Power, it did! Then, when it was ready, something twisted it—maybe the Dark Times altered what the Before Men set it to do. They—they could not have all been so evil! They could not! If I thought so—" she shook her head. "Sander, if I thought that in my mind lay such inheritance from them, then I would put a knife to my own throat and willingly. That—that *thing*, it remembers the worst. It wanted me to serve it. And it was taking me—making me into something like it when you came. We must get out of here! I know that it controls this place and—"

She paused, looked to Sander. "But it did not hold you. Was that because you did not have one like this?" She pointed to the pendant Sander had not taken from her, not knowing whether if he did he would remove some protection she needed, as Maxim had suggested.

"It can take over one's mind, one's will. It—it promised me"—her lips quivered—"all I wanted, all I sought. I was only to go into its direct communication chamber, open my mind. But what it poured into me—hate—Sander, I thought that I hated the Sea Sharks, but I did not know the depths, the black foulness of true hate, until that taught me. And it wants everything, all of us, to serve it. Some people it can rule quickly. The Shamans of the White Ones, it has already made its own servants. Do you understand, it summons them now—to learn.

"There are things stored here, other things that can be made, easily made with *that* to teach. And it shall then loose death. Because in the end it wants no life left—none at all!"

"You say 'it' and 'that,'" Sander said. "What is 'it' in truth?"

"I think"—she answered slowly, again shivering, her hands loosing their hold on him to half cover her mouth as if she hardly dared speak her belief aloud—"that part of it was once a man—or men. It has a kind of half-life. And through the years it has grown more and more alien to man, more and more monstrous. Those who stayed here—while they tended it, it kept to a little of the purpose for which it was made. But as those grew fewer, feebler, it grew stronger and finally cut all ties with those who were left. Some—like my father—went out to see what had happened to the world because they were not influenced by *that* so much.

"But the ones who stayed—Have you seen the one who calls himself Maxim?"

Sander nodded.

"He is a thing, though he knows it not. For a while yet he will serve as eyes and ears for *that*. It still needs humans if it would contact the uncorrupted outside, bring in fresh minds—Sander, it feeds upon men's minds! It strips from them all their knowledge, all their spirit; then it fills them with what it wants—hate and the need for dealing death!"

"As it tried to do to you. And how were you saved?" Sander demanded.

"I am Shaman born, Shaman trained. Not as the Shamans of the White Ones, who use men's blood and terror to summon up their power, but working with life and not against it. It could not reach that part of me it wanted most, the source of my Power. Though it might have blasted through, had you not come. And you, Sander, why did it not seek you?"

"Cold iron—it is smith's power." He was not sure that the band about his forehead had saved him, but he thought that it had.

"Cold iron?" she repeated wonderingly. "I do not understand—" Then once more her fear flared. "Out—Sander—we must get out! It will not let us go willingly, and I do not know what Power it can command."

He had summoned Rhin with a snap of his fingers and was repacking the burdens. Then he lifted Fanyi once more to the riding pad.

"Can this thing of yours control the animals?" He wondered if their companions might now prove to be the weak lines in their small company.

"No." She shook her head. "Their minds are too alien, lie beneath the range of *it*. Kai, Kayi tried to stop me from going. I—I used my power to hold them off." Her face was stricken as she glanced at the fishers.

"Maxim used this on Rhin." Sander held out the rod. "Press this and Rhin is in agony." He indicated the stud on the side.

"How did you get it?"

"From Maxim," Sander said with satisfaction. "I left him tied up. He gave me all his attention, so Rhin brought him down." The smith paid credit where it was due. "And it was Rhin who traced you."

"Let us get out—quickly!"

Sander agreed with her urging. He did not know how much to accept of the crazy story she had gabbled. This business of draining a man's mind and refilling it— But the suspicion, which had long been his, that the Before Men had far more than the Rememberers knew, was enough to make him agree they would be much better out of this place. He had no longer any desire to learn anything connected with this complex. Fanyi's descent into hysteria, her fear, brought grim warning that there might be far too high a price to pay for learning what lay on the other side of the Dark Time. He was willing enough to head out and away with all the speed they could muster.

The smith was not sure of the way they had come, but he depended on the koyot to nose out the back trail for them. As they went, Fanyi appeared to regain her control somewhat. Sander caught glimpses of things in the rooms through which they passed that intrigued him a little, that under other circumstances he would have paused to examine more closely.

But Fanyi looked neither right nor left. She stared straight ahead as if the very fervor of her desire to be free was forceful enough to speed their retreat.

"How many people still live here?" Sander asked, after they had gone some way in silence, during which he had found himself listening for some hint that they were not going to escape so easily, that there would be someone or something in ambush.

"I do not know. Certainly very few. It needs more to serve it. I think there is some service it cannot itself perform that keeps it alive. Therefore, it wants more empty minds to control. For the rest—it will kill. It hates—" Tears spilled from her eyes and she did not try to wipe them away. "It is sick with hate, swelled with it as a corrupted wound swells with evil matter. It is foul beyond belief!"

Sander had kept a careful lookout as they traversed the rooms. Again he was sure he saw nothing to suggest that any had been recently occupied. Was Maxim perhaps the last remaining servant the thing had? But Maxim had not considered himself so—he had spoken of a "Great Brain" that had withdrawn from communication with man.

Now the smith had a new cause for worry—this departure was far too easy. He had expected to meet some opposition before now. Fanyi claimed vast power for the thing she had met; surely if it controlled the installations here, it must be working to capture them again.

When nothing moved, illogically his wariness increased. Fanyi still rode, looking only ahead. Sander stole glances at the koyot, the fishers. They padded along at what had increased to a trot, though Sander had not urged that. The animals were alert; he saw as well as sensed that they were using their own methods of testing what lay about them. But they gave no warning of any ambush or attack.

Their party came at last to the chamber where the chairs were lined around the oval, which was not a pool. Sander pushed ahead here, ready to handle Maxim. But the chair in which he had tied the madman was now empty; not even cut or broken bonds remained. Sander swung his hammer, weighing its strength in his hand.

"He's gone. I left him here."

For the first time since they had started, Fanyi turned her head a little, her gaze shifting to Sander.

"We must find the way out," she told him, and there was a new note in her voice, as if some of the hysteria was again rising in her. "The way—it can be hidden."

Her hand moved toward the pendant and then away. "This thing—I can use it perhaps. But also—it is of this place. Through it one can be controlled."

"Then do not try it!" he answered her. "Leave our passage to Rhin, to Kai and Kayi. I will depend upon their senses before I will on mine."

The animals pattered on out of the room of the

chairs into that which held the webs. Those that were intact blazed high with light. Rhin threw up his head to howl with a note Sander had heard out of him only once before—that time he had touched the wrong button on the shaft of the rod. To his outburst were added cries from the fishers. The animals pawed at their ears, slobbered, and foamed. Sander felt a strange pain in his own head. Fanyi held both ears, her face twisted in agony.

To this, Sander could see only one answer. Though his body was suddenly awkward and his coordination faulty, he tottered to the nearest of those flaming filaments. Raising the hammer despite an involuntary twitching of muscles he had to fight to control, he brought it down to smash the webbing.

Sparks burst; there was a throat- and nose-rasping odor in the air, but Sander staggered on to the next web and demolished it with a blow, then the next and the next.

He moved through a world that had narrowed to hold just those alien creations, his only thought that they must be destroyed. Sometimes his aim was faulty, and he did not bring the object he fronted into fragments with one blow or two, but had to stand wavering and pounding for three or four misdirected and weakened swings until he had shattered it. He had cleared one row; he was aiming now for the first installation of the second. Around his head the band was a searing brand of fire that dimmed his thoughts. Only instinct kept him going. Three—another—

Then, as it had come, so was the outside pressure gone. Sander sank to his knees, panting heavily. His head felt light; he was dazed. But the light that had hurt his eyes had ebbed.

"Sander!"

That shriek aroused his half-conscious mind, jerked him around.

Maxim was there, raising a rod. His face was contracted; there was nothing human remaining in his bulging eyes. He was going to—

Sander made the greatest effort of his life, lifting the hammer—Maxim was too far away to pound. There was no time to try for a dart or even the rod tucked in the smith's belt. He whirled the hammer once around his head and threw it, despairingly, sure that he was already Maxim's victim.

A furred fury burst past Sander, Kai's shoulder striking his as the animal leaped. That touch, light as it was, knocked the smith off balance. He fell against the base of one of the machines, but not before he saw the hammer strike, not with the head but with the edge of the shaft against Maxim's chest.

The man staggered. Sander felt a searing heat lick his own upper arm. Then Kai made a final leap, carrying Maxim down, the rod whirling out of his grasp. Maxim screamed, a sound that was cut off with shocking suddenness as Sander clawed his way once more erect, drawing himself up by pulling on the base of a shattered installation.

Sander groped for words to make clear to himself the nature of what filled the air and weighed so heavily upon him he could hardly move. It throbbed in waves of raging hate as if the very walls were the living tissue of some vast creature. The fisher drew back, his muzzle foully stained. He reared, snarling, hissing, striking out in the air with extended claws, though there was nothing visible to threaten him.

Sander swayed back and forth. Only his grip upon the base of the shattered installation kept him upright, for that mighty rage sent impulses of force through the chamber to beat at him like physical blows. The wire around his head was hot agony, but Sander fought back. His teeth were bared like the animals'. He voiced, hoarsely and defiantly, the smith's chant.

He was not a *thing*, he was a man! And a man he would remain. Step by wavering step, he clawed his way along the base that was his support. His attention was fixed on the hammer, which lay a little distance from the body he willed himself not to look at. Kai might have brought Maxim down, but his own blow had opened the way for the fisher.

Sander stooped, his hand closed upon the haft of the heavy tool. And once his fingers were around that familiar grip, he felt a small sense of victory.

He was a *man!*

With care he turned around to see the fishers drawn close to Fanyi and Rhin. Their fangs were visible. The koyot snapped at the air, white bits of froth gathering at the corners of his lips. The fishers were battle-ready, yet saw no foe to attack.

Fanyi sat erect on the riding pad. Her face was drawn, haggard with strain and pain. With head thrown back, she too mouthed words, words he could not understand. As he tottered toward them, seeming to breast some hostile current as he moved, she met his gaze.

"*It* will not let us go," she said simply.

"I know the doors—"

"There will be no doors now, not unless it wishes."

He did not want to accept her certainty. But before he could speak again, she grasped the pendant.

"*It* will let me come to it—with this I can reach *it*—"

It seemed that when she spoke there was a lessening of the pressure about them, that the rage, which was almost a tangible cloud to wall them in, ebbed a fraction.

"No!" Sander raised the hammer.

"If I go, I can perhaps make terms—"

He could read the truth in her eyes. She knew that if she went she would be lost—as lost as that husk of a man Kai had killed to save them all.

"I am half of the blood of those who have always been its servants. It will listen—"

"To no one," Sander returned. "The thing is mad, you have read that for yourself in its thoughts. You will save nothing, you will accomplish nothing."

"To get me it will bargain." She refused to accept his refusal. "I can get it to let you go forth, you and these—" With a gesture she indicated the animals. "If you are free, you can carry a warning. The White Ones must not be allowed to reach here, the Traders must be prepared."

"If this thing is all-seeing, all-knowing," Sander replied stubbornly, "then it will never let anyone free to carry such a warning. Why should it?"

"There is a difference," Fanyi said slowly. "If I go to it willingly and without any barriers raised, it will gain more of what it wishes than if it must wrest my strength from me. It wants me whole, not maimed. To it you are of no value, save that you have disturbed it by violence. It would be willing to let you go— thinking that would be only for a short space of time until it can muster into its forces those others whom it has summoned. Do you not see—I can buy you time!"

Sander shook his head. "There is no way you can trust any bargain. Listen—" His mind was working faster now, like a runner who has gained his second wind. "Can you find where this thing is?"

She must have had an instant flash of his intentions. "You cannot! Its defenses are complete, there is no way to reach it save by its will."

"But you can go—"

"Yes, if I surrender my will. It will have gained a victory—and you can profit by that."

"Yes, in my way." Sander swung the hammer a fraction. "Can it overhear us?" He glanced from one line of the shattered machines to the other.

"I do not think so. Or else it does not care what we say. It can strive to control us through its own will, and it deems itself invulnerable." A little color had returned to her wan cheeks.

Sander once more swung the hammer. With it in hand he felt himself, somehow apart from the fear of things he could not touch. This "thing" thought itself invulnerable, yet it had not been able to defend the outer part of its own domain without Maxim. And Maxim had died as perhaps none of his kind had done for generations, by the fighting fury of an animal.

The smith had no plans, only a determination. Fanyi's offer to surrender to the thing—that could even be dictated by a residue of its attack upon her when she was imprisoned in the box. Sander was sure of one thing—no trust could be put in any bargain with this enemy. To even try to bargain was a defeat, for the Presence that ruled this complex would consider that to be an admission of weakness. It could promise anything and break the oath as it pleased.

But he did believe that Fanyi might be the key to reach it. He raised a hand, ran a thumb along the band on his forehead. There was no "reason" in the working of the old superstition, yet work it did. If he could take the force of the pain that had struck at him before, they would have a bare chance—a small one, but still it was there.

"You have a plan." Fanyi did not ask a question, she made a statement. Leaning forward on the riding pad, she gazed at him intently.

"No plan," Sander shook his head. "We do not know enough to plan. We can only go—and hope to find a chance—"

"We? But you cannot! It will not let you!"

Once more Sander touched that band. "We cannot be sure of that until we try. You say it cannot deal with the animals?"

"It could not with the fishers. They tried to keep me from it before. Though what it can send against us when aroused—that I do not know."

He remembered the many-armed metal creature. But he now knew how to handle one of them. And he would have two rods, the one he had taken earlier from Maxim and the new one the man had wielded here. Sander went to the crumpled body to reclaim it.

When he returned, he pushed the first of his trophies into Fanyi's hands. With a few words he made plain how it was used.

"You will do this, you are determined?" the girl asked, when he had done.

"Is there any other way? A man holds to life while he can. I believe that we are dead unless we can best this Power."

"I tell you—I think it would let you go if I went to it willingly."

"You will go to it willing, if you agree," he told her. "But I shall go with you. Perhaps it will know that I am with you—but this we shall do—if you go ahead it may believe that you have eluded me, that I once more am hunting. Not too far apart—we must be close enough so that it cannot take you and perhaps shut me out."

Fanyi sat silent for a moment. Then she slipped from Rhin's back.

"This is an action that will bring you to your death, smith. But be sure of one thing. Though I seem willing, it shall not use me for its purposes. I have this." She weighed the rod in her hand. "It can be turned one way as well as the other. And *that* cannot use a body blasted beyond repair. What of our companions?"

"They, too, can play a part," Sander said. He pulled the gear from Rhin's back. "This we shall leave." He did not add that they might well never need any of those supplies again. On top of the pile he placed his dart thrower, though he kept his long knife, principally because he had worn it so long he was hardly aware that it still hung at his belt.

The smith's hammer that was his heritage, from which he now drew inner strength, that stood for all that was normal and right in the world he knew and the rod that was a part of this—those were his weapons. No, rather his tools, for he did not altogether look upon what faced them as a battle, but rather a need to deal with something that was badly flawed.

"This is your free will?" Fanyi looked now as might a chief about to bind someone by blood oath.

"My will," Sander agreed.

She turned from him to the animals. The fishers came to her and she rested a hand on each head. They stood so for a moment, then they rose to lick at her cheeks. Rhin had watched them. Now the koyot also moved, but he came to Sander, nudging the smith's shoulder with his nose—their old signal that it was well they move on.

"Their will also," Fanyi said.

As Sander had suggested, she took the lead. He allowed her and the fishers perhaps the length of an aisle, then he and Rhin followed. Fanyi once more clasped her pendant in her hands. She had not retraced her path to the doorway through which they had come. She went to the right, down another short way between the stumps of the installations Sander had smashed.

Within moments she fronted what looked like a blank stone wall. But, reaching up, she held the pendant between her flattened palm and one block of that barrier. A section pivoted to give them a door.

The way was narrow. Rhin could barely scrape through. And there were no lights. The door shut with an intimidating snap when they were all inside. Sander could only trace those ahead by the faint sounds of their passing.

There were curves and corners, some of which he struck with bruising force as he moved blindly. But there was only one passage and no choice of side ways, so he advanced with what confidence he could maintain, sure that Fanyi was ahead.

Finally, there came a burst of light, and he believed she had opened a second door. He hurried forward, lest that close and leave him and Rhin caught in the dark. The room they came into was unlike any he had seen elsewhere.

Fronting him was a wall with a glassy surface, much like that on the oval in the floor, the one Maxim said had shown the outlines of the world—the Before World and theirs. But here was only one chair and that was placed with its back directly to the slick surface. Fanyi sat in that chair, the fishers crouched before her, growling.

Her hands rested on the arms of the chair, but there were no buttons to be touched. As Sander came to face her, she raised one hand and pulled the loop of chain supporting the pendant from about her neck, throwing it from her as if she so removed all that might keep her from the domination of the thing holding rule here.

Sander caught it in the air by the chain. He could not wear the device himself, but there was a hope that it somehow might still provide a weapon. Now the girl drew the rod from her belt and tossed that away as well. In the chair she sat defenseless and alone. And then—it was not Fanyi who sat there.

Her features seemed to writhe, to grimace, twist, to partly assume the countenance of someone else.

"Come to me!"

There was nothing enticing in that command, for it was a command, baldly uttered, with the arrogance of one who expected no refusal. And such was the power of that order that Sander took one stride toward Fanyi-who-was-no-longer-Fanyi.

Rhin was beside him in an instant, the koyot's mouth closed upon the man's shoulder with force enough to awaken pain. That pain in turn broke the spell.

Fanyi smiled, but the smile was none that Sander had ever seen on any human face.

"Barbarian—" Now she laughed. "Your straggle of people—you—" Now her tone changed, became cold and remote. "You pollute the earth. You are nothing, unfit to walk where true men once walked."

Sander heard the words, let the thing that had possessed Fanyi talk without dispute. The clue to its hiding place must be here somewhere—he needed that. But would he be able to gain it in time?

"Give me your weapons, barbarian," Fanyi said with icy contempt. "Do you think any such can be used against *me?* Fool, I have the means to blast you into nothingness a thousand times over. I let you live only because you can be of some small service to me—for a while. Even as this female serves me—"

Rhin swung a little before Sander, edging him away from Fanyi. But the koyot's head was pointed toward the wall behind the chair. The smith saw that slight prick of ear. Though Rhin appeared to be facing Fanyi, herding Sander away from the girl, the animal's attention was rather on the wall behind the chair.

Sander gripped the haft of the hammer more tightly.

"You are mine, barbarian—"

There was a timbre in that voice which rang in Sander's ears. Was a mist curling up about the chair on which Fanyi was seated, or were his own eyes in some manner failing him? The metal on his forehead was heating, too. He found it hard to breathe.

He was no one's property! He was himself. By cold iron, which only a smith could fashion—he was himself!

"Barbarian, I can suck the life from you by will alone. Thus—"

Sander fought for breath. This was the time he must move—he had no longer any choice.

Cold iron. He fought against the pressure the other had set upon him, seeking to batter him to the ground, to make him crawl as no man should ever humble himself.

"Cold iron," he cried aloud.

There was a slight change in the pressure, as if the thing he confronted was surprised.

Sander moved—not toward Fanyi, where the thing that ruled here had meant him to grovel, but rather to the wall. Exerting all his strength, with an effort even mightier than that which he had used against Maxim, he brought the hammer crashing against the smooth surface.

There was a splintering, a radiation of cracks running out from where the hammer head had met the wall.

In his mind, gathering about him—such a force, a pressure meant to crush him.

No! He denied that will bent now to stop him. His body swayed. Rhin and the fishers, he could feel them close, supporting him. For the second time he struck, and the blow fell true on the same spot.

There was a crackling, a tinkling as of falling glass. A hole slightly smaller than his fist opened. In return Sander was slammed nearly to his knees by a wave of force that he could never afterwards describe.

But he crawled closer, fighting that pressure with all his will, with his belief that if he surrendered, all that made him what he was would be lost, he reached the wall.

He inched his hand up and up, having dropped the hammer. Now he hooked fingers into the hole, though the jagged edges cut into his flesh. When he was sure his hold was complete, he swung the weight of his whole body on that hand.

For a moment of agony and fear, he was afraid his effort was not enough. Then the glass, or what was like glass, broke, to shower his head and shoulders with splinters. A gust of air blew over him that had the same taint as had been in the lower reaches when he had shattered the cabinet holding Fanyi.

Sander groped for the hammer. His right hand was

slippery with his own blood. He was afraid that he could not keep his grip upon the tool. But with his left hand—yes!

He brought up his hand, holding the hammer awkwardly and ill-balanced. Even so a blow fell again, to break the edge farther. This was the door to the thing, even though he could pass through it only on his hands and knees, near crushed with the pressure.

Sander pulled himself over the high threshold formed by the frame. He fell forward into another chamber. There was no one here. He blinked in dull surprise. Though Fanyi had referred to the ruler of these ways as "it" or "the thing" or "that," he had somehow pictured it with at least some kind of a body—maybe like the metal traveler with the claws. But what he saw were only tall cases, rows of them. On the faces of some, lights flashed or rippled.

There was one relief. As he had fallen through the aperture beyond the feeling of pressure had vanished. If this was the lair of Fanyi's enemy, then here its defenses were singularly lacking—maybe it never expected to be found.

"Unregistered and unlawful entrance—"

That was not the voice that had issued from Fanyi's lips. It sounded more like the one that had gabbled at him earlier during his journey through these burrows. Where *was* what he sought? Hidden in one of these cases—?

"Mark one protection—"

He did not know the meaning of all those words. It was enough that they must be a threat. Not attempting to get to his feet, Sander took from the front of his belt the rod that had armed Maxim. He thumbed the highest button on its length and aimed it at the tall box that showed the most lights. The beam struck full, ate into the metal. At the same time Sander was aware of a trundling noise. Coming toward him out of the shadow was a mobile metal thing.

"Seize for interrogation—" yammered the voice, as the metal creature scuttled toward Sander.

He was backed tight to the broken wall. Dare he turn the rod on that thing moving toward him? If it were controlled elsewhere, what—

There was a flare of light. The box he had attacked spurted small tongues of flame. He did not wait, but swung the beam to the next one that showed activity. Something closed about his ankle. A line had snaked forth from the running machine, had locked about his flesh. Another was whipping toward his body. Then a furred form flashed between. There was a growl as the line wrapped around Kai, imprisoning the fisher.

Sander continued to play the beam on target. The second panel blew. Kayi had joined her mate, only to be caught, yet keeping the lines spun by the sentry away from Sander.

Pulling away as far as his trapped ankle allowed, the smith sprayed the beam down the line. Four, five, six— suddenly the line that held him uncurled, fell limp to the floor. Sander scrambled up, moved to destroy more of the panels. When he reached them, the beam no longer responded. But then neither did any more lights show. The burnt odor was stifling. He attempted to close his cut hand. If that would serve him, he would try to finish off the rest by hammer. Was this the lair of the Presence? If it was not—

Sander choked and coughed, his eyes smarted, his throat was painfully dry. The air here hurt deep into his nose and throat as he breathed. He must get back— out, even if he had not completed the job—

Through a haze, Sander pulled his way back, holding onto one half-melted panel and then the next, seeking the entrance hole. When he pulled through, he saw

Fanyi—not sitting now, but lying in a small heap on the floor, as if she had slid helplessly from the chair. He lurched to her, but the fishers were ahead of him, Kayi licking the girl's face, pawing at her body, uttering small whimpers.

Sander went cold. Had—had he killed Fanyi? Was she— He stumbled to her. Kayi growled warningly, but let him lay hands on the girl, his cut one leaving bloody prints on her shoulders and her arms.

Her eyes were closed, her face empty of expression—but she was alive!

He rested there, her head resting in his lap, his wounded hand stretched along the seat of the chair. Then he remembered the pendant he had tucked into his belt. One-handedly he drew it forth and laid it on her breast where she had always worn it.

Fanyi's eyelids moved. She gazed up at him in an unfocused way that again awoke his fears. Then her gaze cleared. It was plain she knew him.

"*It* is—crippled!" she said.

He gave a sigh. So he had not won completely after all.

"How badly?" he asked.

There was a long moment before she replied. "It— it is part gone—those who know how might still use some of it."

"No!" He remembered what had brought him here. The thing he had destroyed might make any man master of this riven world. But there was no man strong enough, wise enough, no man left to use such knowledge.

"No," she echoed him.

"Your weapons to save your people—" he said.

"Your smith's knowledge—" She matched him.

"*It* is of another world," she said slowly. "Even though that which made *it* our enemy has gone out of it, let it be. It is not ours."

He thought of the Traders, of the White Ones whom this thing had summoned.

"It must be no one's."

She nodded, pulling herself up. Then with a cry of concern she caught his hand.

Later they sat on the floor by their worn trail gear. He had dragged Maxim's body out of sight. Fanyi treated his hand with her salves, but it would be days before he could use his hammer again.

There was a coldness in this place, a sense of life gone, that was akin to the terror they had felt earlier on those storm-battered heights. The girl fingered Maxim's first rod, which she had thrown away in the chamber of the Presence.

"*It* cannot repair itself. And I do not think it has anyone to serve it here now. Maxim must have been the last, but there might be those who would try."

"There is still some power in that," Sander nodded at the rod. "Perhaps enough to seal the outer entrance."

Fanyi touched the pendant that still hung around her neck. "I do not think there is another one of these. If we can do that—seal the entrance—no one will find it. The White Ones, they do not know exactly what they seek. Their Shamans are dreamers—of dreams sent by that thing."

"Machine—or man?" Sander wondered.

Fanyi shivered. "Both. But how the Before Men could do that—! It may still live, though you have destroyed that which gave it power. If so—what a horror faces it—life locked into a prison without end."

"What of your people?" he asked.

"What of yours?" she countered.

Sander answered first. "Mine do well enough. They have a smith, not as good as my father, but one they trust. I—they are kin. Still I find it hard now to remember any face among them that I long greatly to see again."

"I am yet bound." Fanyi held the pendant. "We may be able to seal one danger in the earth. There are others without. What I can do to aid my clan, that I shall, though I bring no greater strength with me. I failed Padford, therefore the debt is mine."

"And how will you repay?"

"There are ways to travel south. If any of my people live captive there, then they still have claim on me."

Sander stirred, his hand hurt when he moved it, in spite of the dressing she had put on the cuts. Traveling one-handed for a while would be awkward.

"South it is then. Once we have made secure what lies here."

She frowned. "This is no duty of yours, smith!"

He smiled. "Perhaps so. But I have chosen the out trail. Does it matter where one wanders when one is kinless by will? There is this thought in mind, Shaman. We came here seeking knowledge. We have found it, though not as we expected."

"What's your meaning, smith?"

"Just this: we have tried long to live upon the remnants of the Before Time, ever looking backward. But why should we? There is no night without stars, and the blackness of our night can be lighted by our own efforts. We are ourselves, not the Before Ones. Therefore, we must learn for ourselves, not try to revive what was known by those we might not even want to call kin were we to meet them. I am no kin of Maxim!"

"No kin—" she repeated. "Yes, that rings true, smith! Neither am I kin to those who stored such knowledge as that thing strove to make me use. We begin again, light our night stars, and hope to do better."

"We begin again," Sander agreed and then added, "to the south, Fanyi, since you are duty-bound. Let us see if the Sea Sharks can be defied by our own means. After all, have we not bested here something far worse than any peril we knew?"

"Smith, you are a man who believes in his own worth."

Sander, nursing his torn hand, rose to his feet. He put out his sound one to rest on Rhin's shoulder.

"It never harms a man to value himself," he returned mildly. "And if he has good companions and a trade, what more does he want?"

Fanyi laughed now. "Well, perhaps one or two things more, Sander. But those shall doubtless also come in their own season. No night lasts forever."

When it comes to the best
in science fiction and fantasy,
Baen Books has something for *everyone!*

IF YOU LIKE ...
YOU SHOULD ALSO TRY...

Marion Zimmer Bradley .... Mercedes Lackey,
Holly Lisle

Anne McCaffrey .... Elizabeth Moon,
Mercedes Lackey

Mercedes Lackey .... Holly Lisle, Josepha Sherman,
Ellen Guon, Mark Shepherd

Andre Norton .... Mary Brown,
James H. Schmitz

David Drake .... David Weber, John Ringo,
Eric Flint

Larry Niven .... James P. Hogan,
Charles Sheffield

Robert A. Heinlein .... Jerry Pournelle,
Lois McMaster Bujold

Heinlein's "Juveniles" .... Eric Flint & Dave Freer,
Rats, Bats & Vats

Horatio Hornblower .... David Weber's
"Honor Harrington" series,
David Drake's, "RCN" series

The Lord of the Rings .... Elizabeth Moon,
The Deed of Paksenarrion

IF YOU LIKE ...
YOU SHOULD ALSO TRY...

Lackey's "SERRAted Edge" series .... Rick Cook, *Mall Purchase Night*

Dungeons & Dragons™ .... "Bard's Tale"™ Novels

Star Trek .... James Doohan & S.M. Stirling, "Flight Engineer" series

Star Wars .... Larry Niven, David Weber

Jurassic Park .... Brett Davis, *Bone Wars* and *Two Tiny Claws*

Casablanca .... Larry Niven, *Man-Kzin Wars II*

Elves .... Ball, Lackey, Sherman, Moon, Cook, Guon

Puns .... Rick Cook, Spider Robinson Harry Turtledove, *The Case of the Toxic Spell Dump*

Alternate History .... Gingrich and Forstchen, *1945* James P. Hogan, *The Proteus Operation* Harry Turtledove (ed.), *Alternate Generals* S.M. Stirling, Draka series Eric Flint & David Drake, Belisarius series Eric Flint, *1632*

SF Conventions .... Niven, Pournelle & Flynn, *Fallen Angels* Margaret Ball, *Mathemagics* Jerry & Sharon Ahern, *The Golden Shield of IBF*

Quests .... Mary Brown, Elizabeth Moon, Piers Anthony

Greek Mythology .... Roberta Gellis, *Bull God* and *Thrice Bound* Eric Flint & Dave Freer, *Pyramid Scheme*

IF YOU LIKE ...
YOU SHOULD ALSO TRY...

Norse Mythology ...... David Drake, *Northworld Trilogy*
Lars Walker

Arthurian Legend .... Steve White's Legacy series
David Drake, *The Dragon Lord*

Computers .... Rick Cook's "Wiz" series
Spider Robinson, *User Friendly*
Tom Cool, *Infectress*
Chris Atack, *Project Maldon*
James P. Hogan, *Realtime Interrupt*
and *Two Faces of Tomorrow*

Science Fact .... Robert L. Forward,
Indistinguishable From Magic
James P. Hogan, *Rockets, Redheads, and Revolution*
and *Minds, Machines, and Evolution*
Charles Sheffield, *Borderlands of Science*

Cats .... Larry Niven's Man-Kzin Wars series

Horses .... Elizabeth Moon's Heris Serrano series
Doranna Durgin

Vampires .... Cox & Weisskopf (eds.), *Tomorrow Sucks*
Wm. Mark Simmons, *One Foot in the Grave*
Nigel Bennett & P.N. Elrod, *Keeper of the King*
and *HIs Father's Son*
P.N. Elrod, *Quincey Morris, Vampire*

Werewolves . Cox & Weisskopf (eds.), *Tomorrow Bites*
Wm. Mark Simmons, *One Foot in the Grave*
Brett Davis, *Hair of the Dog*